Praise for *The Ways We Hide*

"Resourceful Fenna Vos is a magician's assistant, channeling her claustrophobic fear of confined spaces into a career designing ingenious outs for Houdini-esque stage stunts. Recruited by British intelligence to invent escape gadgets for Allied POWS, Fenna must ultimately design an escape of her own when a mission goes awry. I love this book!"

—Kate Quinn, *New York Times* bestselling author
of *The Rose Code* and *The Diamond Eye*

"A riveting tale... While using her remarkable skills to help captured soldiers, Fenna finds herself face-to-face with what she loves most and what she fears most, trapped in a place where each decision she makes could unlock the paths to freedom and a future...or death."

—Lisa Wingate, #1 *New York Times* bestselling
author of *Before We Were Yours*

"Set to a beautifully drawn backdrop of terror, grief, and overwhelming love and chock-full of meticulously researched history, including the fascinating use of seemingly innocuous Monopoly boards to smuggle escape aids to Allied POWs, *The Ways We Hide* is a one-of-a-kind adventure suffused with magic and hope."

—Kristin Harmel, *New York Times* bestselling
author of *The Forest of Vanishing Stars*

Praise for *Sold on a Monday*

A *New York Times* Bestseller • A *USA Today* Bestseller

A *Wall Street Journal* Bestseller • A National IndieBound Bestseller

"A tender love story enriches a complex plot, giving readers a story with grit, substance, and rich historical detail."

——*Publishers Weekly*

"Poignant and compulsively readable... Based upon a haunting historical photograph, this story will linger long after the pages have all been turned."

—Stephanie Dray, *New York Times* bestselling
author of *The Women of Chateau Lafayette*

Also by Kristina McMorris

Sold on a Monday

The Edge of Lost

The Pieces We Keep

Bridge of Scarlet Leaves

Letters from Home

the
ways we
hide

a novel

KRISTINA McMORRIS

Published by Sourcebooks Landmark, an imprint of Sourcebooks
P.O. Box 4410, Naperville, Illinois 60567-4410
(630) 961-3900
sourcebooks.com

Library of Congress Cataloging-in-Publication Data

Names: McMorris, Kristina, author.
Title: The ways we hide : a novel / Kristina McMorris.
Description: Naperville, Illinois : Sourcebooks Landmark, [2022]
Identifiers: LCCN 2022011076 (print) | LCCN 2022011077 (ebook) |
   (trade paperback) | (epub)
Subjects: LCGFT: Novels.
Classification: LCC PS3613.C585453 W39 2022 (print) | LCC PS3613.C585453
   (ebook) | DDC 813/.6--dc23
LC record available at https://lccn.loc.gov/2022011076
LC ebook record available at https://lccn.loc.gov/2022011077

Printed and bound in the United States of America.
MA 10 9 8 7 6 5 4 3 2

For those in the shadows

1942

CHAPTER 1

September 1942
Brooklyn, New York

Deep within me, a sense of dread buzzes and crackles, an electrical wire threatening to short. I'm trapped by the stage lights, the performance well in motion. I assure myself that Charles's behavior, subtle oddities throughout tonight's tricks, falls within reason. It was at his prodding, after all, that a top New York critic agreed to attend. As a faceless judge in the shadows, the lone man can render a verdict that could pack future shows—or trigger a decline.

Even so, what I detect from Charles differs from nerves.

Only with disciplined effort do I resist rushing through the grand finale. I distribute a padlock to each of the volunteers: two airmen, a banker type, and a trio of sprightly ladies. With all the poise and undulating cadence of a showman's assistant, I encourage their inspection. My narration flows out, as programmed as a song on a player piano. On this stage alone, it's my fourth performance in two days.

Stewing in a haze of cigarette smoke, aftershave, and floral perfume, the medium-sized theater could be any one of a hundred. The attendance is respectable at two-thirds full. Largely from the "cheap seats" of the balcony, periodic catcalls remain standard fare, with no help from my galling if customary outfit. Astoundingly, the sequined halter and midthigh skirt are rather modest for my role.

Displayed on the prop table are two pairs of handcuffs and a set of minuscule keys. I'm retrieving them all when Charles reappears in the right wing of the stage to await my cue. He's traded his top hat and tails for a black bathing costume that hugs his lean build from shoulders to thighs. All in line with our usual act, save for the object in his grip.

An ax.

I bristle, less from startle than confusion. A stagehand was supposed to brandish the tool, not Charles. And certainly not yet.

For a show that blends illusion and danger—from the magical mending and vanishing of items to mind reading and death-defying feats—there's purpose to every step, glance, and gesture. To timing above all. At the climax of the act, as fears arise over the escape artist's ability to elude his bonds, a harried display of the ax implies need for its imminent use, amplifying suspense.

It's hardly to be used as—what? A parading of bravado?

Still, we've performed together with such frequency over three years of touring that my speech hitches only slightly. "Now…that our 'committee' of volunteers from the audience has keenly inspected the padlocks for authenticity"—I pause, prompting nods from the lock-bearing group—"death-defying escapologist Charles Bouchard shall be sealed into the galvanized-iron milk can, airtight and filled with water to its very brim." Grandly I gesture toward the barrel-size container, just as Charles interjects.

"Een fact!" He reemerges prematurely with his faux French accent, turning the sea of heads. "So superior are my abilities to those of Harry Houdini himself, I balk at even zee most basic safeguards."

The affront to my late idol, a legend for this very trick, irks me but briefly. More pressingly, I struggle to decipher Charles's intentions as he strides past the volunteers to reach center stage, his slicked ebony hair tousled from his costume change. "Observe, for instance, zis emergency tool, which I have primed with a hacksaw. For what, you ask? Why, to do…*zis*." Against an edge of the milk can, he slams the ax handle—once, twice—and breaks the handle in two.

My chest tightens, despite murmurs of surprise and delight. Charles slings the pieces aside with a hearty "voilà," barely missing my T-strap heels. Even the four-piece band, routinely dispassionate in the pit, gawks with interest.

"What is more," he proclaims, swooping toward me barefoot,

"one with supernatural gifts has no need for caution. Is it not so, Mademoiselle Vos?" I'm still eyeing the can—finding no damage, gratefully—when he snatches from me the tiny ring of keys. He jangles them high, pinkie in the air, as if ringing a bell for tea service, before tossing them into his mouth and swallowing them whole.

A ripple of gasps. A mix of groans.

Another maddening, bewildering detour.

Unless vitally called for, never stray from the act. Of the many rules I've taught him, this was the first. The most crucial.

I dredge up a smile nonetheless, bright with Victory Red lips, ever accustomed to wearing a mask as much onstage as off. And besides, I'm well aware the keys are unnecessary, the padlocks a ruse. The neck of the can is, after all, rigged with an outer and inner wall. Telescoped upward, the lid detaches with secured locks intact. It's a deceit based on presumption, a twist on a story viewers convince themselves to be true. Just as experience tells them a book holds full-sheeted pages and a shoe heel is built solidly through, to their minds, a milk can opens only one way.

Mind you, Charles's ingesting of the keys is real. For escapologists, a trained resistance to gagging is required to handily swallow an item, then reproduce it on cue. Compliments of a sword swallower, I learned the rather unsavory skill while on breaks from my old sleight-of-hand acts. It was at the very dime museum where I first met Charles, back when his unruly black hair wasn't yet slicked with tonic, his average if pleasing face still free of smugness; when labeled a "curiosity," he drew the upper crust of society to point and cringe.

Who could have guessed he'd become my greatest illusion?

"*Alors*, zee final touches!" Charles holds out his wrists and regards me with a jerk of his chin, a sign to administer the handcuffs and resume my patter. His granting of permission.

Annoyance curls my fingers, interrupted by a heckling sailor.

"Hey, honey, I could think of some better ways to use those handcuffs!"

"Yeah, Kazlowski, like to lock up your ugly ass," calls another.

"Pipe down, all you! We got ladies here!"

The exchange is typical nowadays, with an abundance of enlisted boys high on hormones and sips from their flasks, antsy for glory half a world away. For people like me, the war could as easily be set in another universe.

Ordinarily I'd toss out a clever comeback, but distracted, I simply reassume control with a clearing of my throat. Somewhere in the room, a critic looks on.

"As you will see," I declare in a voice that, based on a rare press mention, *outsizes my graceful ladylike frame*, "both pairs of handcuffs, also diligently inspected by our committee, will be fastened to Monsieur Bouchard's wrists."

More nods from the group.

Back on script.

I apply the cuffs, tempted to attach them overly tight. Evading my glare, Charles makes a display of being firmly bound. After I remove the milk-can lid, he wriggles into the container with more sloshing than usual. The theater's stagehands—one burly, one bearded—join us with prefilled buckets and quickly remedy the water displacement.

I discovered long ago, for help with shows and rehearsals in any theater, advance gratuity ensures a job done right. Or done at all.

"Once sealed," I continue, "the milk can will be enclosed by a three-walled cabinet. Its triangular shape allows no room for trickery and, most notably, can be unlatched only from the inside." The stagehands are now fetching the roofless structure from just offstage. "Upon a countdown of five, I challenge each of you fine ladies and gentlemen to hold your breath along with Monsieur Bouchard, who shall be submerged in five...four..."

The audience joins in. Charles inhales and exhales in exaggerated preparation. On the collective utterance of "one," he plunges below the surface. My internal timer begins as I affix the cover, catching a whiff of his breath. Under the faint sweetness from his usual cherry Luden's drops comes a citric-juniper scent, one I know well from my past.

Gin.

God in heaven...

The root of his behavior is finally clear.

But the volunteers have descended on the can. They're securing padlocks to the latches as I've instructed. The band launches into a peppy tune—"Praise the Lord and Pass the Ammunition"—as the stagehands heft the wooden cabinet into place. Swiftly assembled, the tall but sturdy barrier obscures Charles from everyone's view.

Including mine.

A surge of fear shoots through my veins. I manage to point the volunteers back to their seats, where the audience has gone silent, breaths held. In the front row, a pigtailed girl puffs her cheeks with all the verve of Dizzy Gillespie.

Thirty seconds.

Beside the cabinet, I wait on my mark, hand on hip. Calm and confident. Already Charles should be free of his cuffs. They're merely trick pairs, the norm for underwater acts. I deftly swapped out the real ones after the volunteers examined them. Though certain of this, I furtively confirm their distinctive weighted feel in the lower pockets of my skirt, among the many hidden compartments I've designed for our acts.

Forty-five seconds.

A good portion of the crowd yields to their lungs. A smattering of ladies giggle at their own folly. Fellows tend to hold out longer, surely sneaking air through their noses while attempting to impress their dates or protect their pride, likely both.

All the while, through the strategically blaring music I listen for hints of the outer neck sliding from the can. That simple step is all the escape requires. A person could finagle it deaf or blind. Drunk, even—not that Charles is. Yes, he's become one to indulge, at times heavily these days, but after the show, never before.

Until now.

One minute.

Heat pours from the stage lights in compounding waves. Sweat prickles my scalp, my updo tightening against its pins. The last few holdouts in the auditorium are gasping for air. At any moment, a stagehand should emerge with an ax to boost anticipation, as if ready to bust through the cabinet and break off the padlocks. But that ax now lies in pieces.

At least destroying the handle didn't damage the can, so far as I could tell.

Oh, why didn't I stall for a closer look?

One minute thirty.

Thoughts of another escape artist barge into my mind: Genesta. His is a cautionary tale to promote double- and triple-checking. The famed performer failed to notice a critical dent in his milk can from being dropped during setup, preventing the lid's upward slide. His fatal, final act.

It's for this reason I demanded Charles practice for months, stretching his lungs in baths—up to three minutes, three seconds by my pocket watch—and why we use only a lid that reserves air at the very top.

Granted, tonight his compromised state could make all those precautions worthless.

Two minutes.

"Hey, toots!" The same heckling sailor. "So much for your pal's superpowers, huh?"

His jeering this time is largely lost to others' worries, evident in faces and fidgets and murmurs. The reactions, which I normally relish, feel like viruses invading the room.

I train my gaze on the cabinet hinges. Only recently did I agree to remove the outer latch—Charles's idea, for heightened drama—but with one provision: an inch-wide gap at the corner would allow me a peek if needed.

My yearning to do so swells, bridled by his own stipulation: even if concerned, I wasn't to look until the three-minute mark. We're not there yet, I know this, with every second an impossibly slow tick. Charles's reasoning is technically sound; he's never once faltered escaping the can, and an overt gauging of progress would dilute the act. Particularly in the mind of a critic.

But then, so would a drowning.

The decision is my call, and I'm making it.

I move with a purposeful stride to the far corner of the cabinet, as if following a choreographed routine. With a few sharp tugs, I form a narrow opening and glimpse inside. The lid appears in place, same for the padlocks, a sign of all going right. Or horrendously wrong.

My eyes strain for a fuller view, for any sight of Charles. But there's nothing...

Scenarios skitter through my head, of his fainting underwater—as even Houdini's skillful brother once did—or passing out from the booze, or having the keys lodged in his throat. Whichever the case, the trick is over.

"Charles! Can you hear me?" The musicians trample my voice, their notes like bootheels squashing each syllable. I snap toward the pit. "Stop!"

The song ends raggedly, giving way to dull thunks. Not from the musicians but from Charles. Muffled by water, handcuffs are striking the can. The lid must be stuck!

Suddenly there's quiet, an audible ceasing of metal against metal. The absence of sound is smothering. I stave off panic, remembering the ax—what's left of it.

"Hold on, I'm coming!" Heart hammering my ribs, I scramble to retrieve the head of the ax from the stage floor. I clutch its handle, a jagged stump, and thrust the blade through the cabinet gap, trying, trying to break the latch. Failing. Pain shoots through my palm. Splintered wood tears at my skin.

At the vision of him inside, trapped in darkness and starved for air, ancient memories creep from the caverns of my mind, of tangled limbs and muffled cries, an endless procession of caskets in the snow.

I block them out, seeking a solution.

Whatever am I doing? The cabinet can be toppled. This is the means of backup that Charles claimed would never be required. Like the ax he destroyed, the keys he swallowed.

I drop the blade and start shoving the cabinet with both hands. The triangular structure slides and clunks against the can, refusing to tip. I scan the wings for the stagehands. Why aren't they there? *Where did they go?*

I've forgotten the crowd. Patrons stare with hands over mouths, perplexed, questioning. Many are half-risen from their seats, clutching the arm of a neighbor. Unblinking eyes stare down from the balcony.

"Please, help," I yell. "Anyone!"

Comprehension flashes. Frightful cries erupt. I push at the cabinet again, fruitlessly, as a blur of uniforms and suits scurry for the aisles. I search for a military nurse or medic's insignia, anticipating Charles's next need, but the strangers freeze. All of them. Turned to statues.

Are they still deliberating, doubting if this is real? A fierce command gathers in my throat, ready to burst, when a noise sweeps through the room. A pattering, like drizzle growing to a downpour.

Clapping. People are applauding.

No—stop! I think as their grimaces morph into smiles, gasps reversing into sighs.

And then I see it. A metallic glint swings me around. Two sets of handcuffs hang from the crook of a finger. Charles—he made it out, alive and safe! Panting with a look of exhaustion, he stands sopping wet at the opened cabinet. The milk can looms in the background, sealed with all six locks.

Zealous hollers and whistles bloom. Many in the crowd pat their chests, calming their hearts, laughing from the thrill. Charles absorbs it all with grandeur, bidding "*Merci.*" His grin widens with his every bow.

Still overcome, I command myself to breathe, to repel the memories stacked on my chest.

Nudged by Charles, I stiffly join his side and catch sight of the child in front. Her face bears the light-headed shock of a near plummet from a cliff. Though equally dizzy, I seek to uphold the facade that nothing actually went astray. My sense of relief gains purchase until a pointed wink from Charles. Appreciative, it seems.

But not for me. Not even for some bombshell in the audience as I've come to expect.

This wink is for the right wing of the stage. More aptly, for the pair of stagehands who have conveniently reappeared. From their boastful smirks of those in the know, every obstacle of the act floats back through my mind. They join like patches of clouds, snips of a riddle, conjuring a whole: the ax and keys, the newly added latch, Charles's urgent pounding that halted at my calls…

My attention cuts back to his face.

There's arrogance in his eyes, underscored by his stance. No authentic trace of fear, nor true relief from a tragedy averted.

Why would there be? All had gone according to plan, *his* plan, including my role as an unwitting pawn.

CHAPTER 2

Two knocks on my dressing room door precede the turn of the knob. The caller doesn't wait for an invite.

This is how I suspect it isn't some fellow from the audience bearing a bouquet and sheepish smile, touting my resemblance to sensuous starlet Hedy Lamarr—which incidentally is a right stretch in my view. Not to say the remark is why, after my gracious bidding of thanks, I always send them on their way.

I verge on doing the same now, albeit *ungraciously* as Charles steps into the room. But first I'll see what's left of his decency, if any.

Seated at my mirror, I close the gap in my satiny stage robe—indeed to cover my brassiere but also the residual quake in my hands—and eye his reflection. Already he's switched into his trousers and undershirt, quick changes being a necessity of the trade. When the fall of the curtain launched me seething from the stage, I left him and his cohorts to corral our supplies.

He has nerve, approaching me so soon. I'll grant him that much.

Then again, it's a trait I personally helped cultivate.

"Swell space ya got," he says, easing in, glancing around. His practiced stage diction is replaced by his casual Louisianan speech. "I reckon we could do a whole lot shabbier."

The remarks would once have been laced with playful irony, given the pitiful accommodations we've endured, specifically while traveling with variety shows before breaking out on our own. Surrounding me here are theatrical posters neatly hung, a proper costume rack, and a pair of cushioned chairs accented by a table—each incredibly with all four legs. Most comforting of all, I have a window large enough for an emergency exit.

So yes, the room is rather nice, if smaller and mustier than the one assigned to Charles. I'm certain of this without having to check; he's a man and the star. And long gone are the days when he at least offered to trade.

"What do you want, Charles?"

"Just, uh, making sure you're okay."

"Oh?" I say, since we're apparently playing games. "Why wouldn't I be?"

He goes to speak but resorts to a shrug, both shoulders draped with a towel. "I…guess ya put two and two together."

"If by that, you mean your reckless, pompous, devious—"

"C'mon, Fenna. Don't be sour."

"Sour? You think I'm being petty?"

The quirk of his thin lips says everything before he drops into one of the chairs. Even without the shadows from my vanity lights, he appears a decade beyond our common age of twenty-four. Escapology can wear on a body, it's true. But his accumulating vices have by no means helped. Only his drying natural curls provide fleeting evidence of the friend I used to know.

"Look, I'm sorry it shook you up. I swear it."

"Is that so? Because you didn't appear to regret a thing. And frankly you still don't."

He hesitates, unable to argue. "Ah, geez. You heard 'em out there. We were a smash!"

Typical misdirection. Another lesson I passed along.

I clutch my robe harder, triggering a throbbing in my palm, a gouge of which Charles isn't aware. If he was, he would inquire about it, hands in our profession being as vital as those to a concert pianist. Fortunately the wound required only iodine and a small bandage, giving me no cause to divulge the depth of my foolishness as he rattles on.

"Tell me you at least got a load of those dogfaces. Even the big beefy ones came charging for the stage. When I busted out of the cabinet, saw it myself, them dopes were scared outta their wits."

"I agree. They were *dopes* to ever worry."

The barb soars right on by. Charles is too busy savoring the coup against his favorite targets. To him, with flat feet barring him from the draft, all enlisted men have become macho buffoons hoodwinked into fighting someone else's war. *Battling Japan, I can see,* he'd say—in light of Pearl Harbor, obviously—*but why Germany and Italy and all those others?* Admittedly skeptical of printed propaganda since my childhood, I had no answer.

"Oh hey, did ya hear the news flash?" he goes on. "House manager says the critic definitely caught the show. His ticket was picked up at the window. Just think of the write-up we're bound to get. In the *New York Herald Tribune* of all things."

"I can imagine." Easily so. Featured will be the lone achievements of Monsieur Charles Bouchard, an exotic title based less on his ancestry and basic French speaking skills than my foresight to gain us prestige. But that's not the issue. "And if you ask me? None of it matters a whit."

His eyes go wide. "None of—? How can you say that? I thought this was about ticket sales. About building our reputation, top bookings…"

I swivel to face him. "What matters is you should have warned me."

He shakes his head, flabbergasted, as if dealing with an obstinate child. "Fenna, for Pete's sake. Me not letting on, that's the reason it worked. Your honest-to-goodness fear is what got 'em believing. All those surprises you didn't count on—"

"You should have *warned* me," I start again, "so I'd have known when to shout for help." My failure to calculate the clues, to anticipate his plot, is a point I'll begrudge myself for some time; it's my main cause now for not exploding. "What if those people had made it to the cabinet seconds earlier? They could have pushed it over while you were in the milk can. Or even in the midst of climbing your way out."

He ponders this, then exhales and shows his palms. "Okay, fine. I did cut it a li'l close."

A little? I abandon refuting this, diverted by the drop and drag of his syllables, even heavier than usual. And I remember.

"Alternately, I suppose, we could just blame the gin."

14

His expression stalls. With an element of surprise reversing our roles, I press on. "At least tell me it was the first time you've been dim-witted enough to drink before a show."

The plea is real. I need to believe I haven't missed previous signs.

Gathering himself, he insists, "It was the first, all right? But it was nothin'."

I nearly laugh. "You cannot possibly be serious."

"Only a few nips with the stagehands while ironing out details."

I clench my teeth, unsure which bothers me more: his cavalier take on risking our livelihoods—with more than a "few nips" no doubt, and perhaps even between our acts—or that I had been ganged up on, in a show of my own creation.

Fuming, I shift back to the vanity. I'm tempted to hurl my wooden brush his way, but I resist. A lump to his skull, though much deserved, could interfere with the conclusion of our three-day run tomorrow, and I'm in no mood for another debacle. Including at our next stop, a promising venue in Boston. For now, my hairpins will have to take the brunt.

I yank each one free, tossing them aside. My twist unravels in a light-bronze mess as I steer toward matters of business. "We'll need a replacement ax. And a new latch if it's damaged." I meet Charles's gaze in the mirror. "Naturally, they'll come out of your share of the wages."

"Yeah. Sure. Why not?" His indifference to any drain on his "hard-earned dough" suggests a touch of guilt. Or maybe it's the imbibe-ment. "I'll grab them at a hardware store in the mornin'."

I'm about to reinforce that he'll do just that when I envision, a mere day from now, revisiting that dratted cabinet. Although a kiddie show is taking our last matinee slot, leaving us just an evening performance, I still think better of it.

A change is in order.

"I'll get them myself."

"Ah, c'mon," he groans. "There's no need."

He thinks I'm being dramatic.

I'm being practical.

"I have to buy new pieces of wood anyway. For the time being…" Reluctant, I finish: "We're shelving the Milk Can Escape."

His forehead scrunches. But then he sits up, comprehending. "You mean we're swapping it for the Goblet?" The hope in his voice makes me wince. I detest that the switch seems a reward for tonight, yet my desire to resume control, at least behind the scenes, wins out.

And so I nod.

He celebrates with a clap. "Hot dog. Finally!"

Despite his harping—about our timing and maneuvering being fine-tuned for almost two months—I'd refrained from incorporating the flashy finale, even at theaters with workable layouts like the one offered here. Though I've had my reasons.

"You just wait till the big finish," he murmurs. "The audience'll go batty." He's already visualizing the adulation heaped upon him, among his few priorities as of late.

I cut short the vision. "I presume I *won't* need a fresh set of keys?"

"Huh? Yeah, yeah. Already handled." It's a civil way to address the topic of regurgitation. "And *yes*, Fenna, they'll be washed up good as new."

His thwarting of my next question, fingering me as predictable, is just fine by me, as little good in my life has come from surprises. But it's the bother in his tone, an edge he's become so quick to employ, that grates on my ears. As if I'm a wife nagging over a chore as trivial as wiping his shoes at the door. Still, I refuse to give him the satisfaction of vexing me—more than he already has.

"Dandy. Now, if you don't mind, I'd like to finish dressing up."

He obliges by rising, only to stop, bemused. "You sayin'…you got some fancy plans?"

I realize I misspoke. My senses remain frazzled, all by his doing. "No—I meant, to finish getting dressed."

He lifts a brow, probing like a nosy brother.

"I'm simply going home," I insist.

Home. It sounds lovelier than the reality of my latest boardinghouse in a ceaseless string of rented rooms. On the rosy side, it's several city blocks from Charles's motel, a sizable distance presently welcome.

At my unflinching gaze, he looks convinced, then inspired. "Ya know; if you're game, we could paint the town. We got a half day off tomorrow, remember?"

"Oh, I remember." And that break is just as welcome.

"I've found a great jazz joint—the Tin Kettle. It's a real gasser. Or we could hit a supper club if you're hungry. This is New York, after all. Lots of pretty swell things to do."

Sure, and for a pretty penny.

"I'll pass. You enjoy though."

His shoulders sag and his smile goes weary. "Yeah, well. Can't fault me for tryin'." My answer isn't a shock to either of us. "Want company for the walk back?"

"Thanks," I say, "but I'm fine on my own."

After a beat, he nods. "You always are." He might have intended the comment as lighthearted, maybe even snide. What emerged, paired with his deep-set amber eyes, reflects more of a sense of hurt.

I stiffen as he heads for the door. The rift between us, ever growing these days, feels wide and ragged as a canyon. Partnership aside, we used to share a friendly comfort, often trading advice and opinions—his generally on food and politics, mine on his fashion picks and potential dates. Of course, that was before the girls more closely resembled conquests, and certainly before his bloated ego made him averse to any insight I'm inclined to give.

Through it all, nonetheless, it does seem strange. He has no inkling of the history I've buried, of what I've survived, the wonder of how I survived at all. If he did, he might understand my dire need for self-reliance, why I hoard every cent I earn. Why the walls around me serve to protect not only me but those I yearn not to hurt.

"Charles…" As I angle toward him, he turns back, expectant. I prepare to share, the words stringing together like colored kerchiefs from a conjurer's mouth.

But at the shimmer of his hair and skin—still wet from his rogue stunt—logic intervenes. While minor in the grand scheme of things, his actions were a betrayal, an exploitation of trust. And beyond that, gratuitously dangerous.

I voice only what's relevant. "Drink again before the final curtain, and I'll call off the show."

His jaw sets at the ultimatum. He grabs both ends of his draped towel and half bows. "You're the boss." He shuts the door hard behind him. As if he's the one with a right to be incensed.

How is that even remotely reasonable?

I twist back to the mirror, thankful I confided nothing. Relieved! And yet, I appear as worn and agitated as I suddenly feel. I long for a bath, to scrub the rouge from my face and the kohl from my eyes, along with every memory of this night. Including Charles and his parting sneer.

Although, he does…have a point.

From the get-go, I've been the person in charge. The one teaching, envisioning, solving. Both the composer and conductor, virtually unseen at center stage.

Perhaps someone—other than Charles—ought to be privy to that fact.

CHAPTER 3

This time, as the final act approaches, more than dread churns within me; it's the stifling apprehension, I'd imagine, of releasing one's child into the world. The worries, the hopes, the last-minute doubts over whether you've done enough. If you could ever truly be ready.

While purchasing fellow magicians' tricks is a lesser-known yet common-enough practice, my personal forte has always derived from analyzing, deconstructing, and re-creating others' works, dependably with improvement. True, for the Milk Can Escape, I altered nothing, but deliberately so, as a tribute to the Handcuff King and Master of Magic. For it was Harry Houdini who saved my life in more ways than I could measure.

The Goblet Escape, on the other hand, is mine alone. It's a valid reason in and of itself to be wary of a public debut, let alone for such a crowd. Few seats tonight are vacant, due in part—I presume grudgingly—to our review in today's *Herald Tribune*. One would think the brief yet complimentary write-up would leave Charles satisfied.

Prior to the show, I braced for an onslaught of his gloating, but he was too busy complaining. The top critic he'd pursued had sent a cub reporter instead, leading to "four lousy sentences inked by some nobody writer." It was these petty quibbles that firmed my choice: tonight's finale would gain a dose of humbling twists.

With the moment here, however, I'm seized by the reality of my plan.

Cued by my introduction of the trick, the theater's usual pair of stagehands carry out the lidless crate. Measuring three feet per side, the box smells of cedar from fresh veneers over multiple nail holes. I'm reminded of my and Charles's exhaustive rehearsals—for an escape I'm about to upend, with a version we've yet to attempt. The chances of failure are raised exponentially.

Shoving away doubts, I watch to ensure the proper setup.

At center stage waits a planked table, which I designed to be sturdy yet handily disassembled for travel. Like a capital H on its side, the square tabletop and base are connected at the center by a two-foot-tall stand posing as a solid block. In actuality, it's hollow through the middle and painted black to exaggerate its slimness.

Curiosity in the room mounts perceptibly as the stagehands place the crate on the table, creating the silhouette of a goblet. Hence the trick's name.

"Now," I say, "that our committee from the audience has keenly inspected the padlocks for authenticity"—the six volunteers on my left concur, each with a lock in hand—"the astute naval officer to my right will examine the crate for manipulations of any kind."

Never resorting to the use of planted "confederates," I handpicked the silver-haired gentleman for good reason. The more stripes on a sleeve, the less accustomed one becomes, ironically, to performing close inspections, specifically with aging eyes.

At least that's what I'm counting on.

The stagehands tilt the box forward for a view of the interior. I knock on one sidewall at a time to convey solid construction and, more than that, to dictate the focal points. The officer nods along. I allow him several taps of his own until he reaches farther in.

"Goodness me!" I expel a remorseful sigh. "I nearly forgot. The lid too needs verified." Aware to move on, the stagehands fetch the wooden top, plus a small stepladder and hammer from the wings. There, Charles is stripping to his underclothes for maximum mobility.

The navy man assesses the lid as I announce, "While Monsieur Bouchard rids the last of his formal garments that could potentially harbor an escape tool, I will ask the officer to lend a close eye to one additional restraint." From my prop trunk, I hold up a strait-jacket. Whispers swim among the audience; things are getting more interesting.

The officer complies by testing the sleeves, straps, and buckles. To reduce the awkward quiet, as well as my chance to reconsider, I muse, "I'd wager such a coat could be useful with a troublesome sailor or two."

He smiles lightly in agreement.

"Or," I add, "even a feisty admiral." That one causes him to chuckle just as Charles returns to the stage. A passing of the baton.

"*Merci, mademoiselle. Alors*, before continuing, may I have zah keys to all six locks?"

"Why, of course." Preplanned this time—to his seeming credit and delight—I hand over the requested ring from my visible skirt pocket. He turns to the audience and boasts of bravery and supernatural gifts and having no need for safeguards before he ingests the tiny keys, inciting gasps and groans.

The bearded stagehand reappears, forearms draped in steel chains. I picture what he's agreed to do, what *I'm* about to do, and my newly purchased scarf tightens around my neck.

"Monsieur," Charles says to the officer, extending both arms forward, "if you will be so kind."

Per the routine, I guide the seaman in applying the backward-facing jacket with buckles running down the gap. Charles expands his chest stealthily before crisscrossing his arms, layered in a way to provide undetectable slack. As the officer and I fasten the straps, the volunteers remain engrossed and Charles provides narration.

"Once zee crate is nailed shut, plunging me into darkness, six chains will be wrapped and locked to seal my fate, lest I escape before your eyes—as no curtain or cabinet shall impede your view!"

Murmurs ramp through the crowd. Necks crane for a better look when he ascends the stepladder and carefully, without use of his arms, climbs into the crate. The musicians prepare by lifting their instruments. Charles keeps standing to make a show of worried concentration, then nods in my direction.

He's ready.

Am I?

"Ladies," I say, "and gentlemen…please join me…in a countdown."

Charles's eyes light on me. In them sits a glimmer, an offer of assurance, a presumption of trust.

And I realize...

It's not too late.

I can whisper to the stagehands, quashing our arrangement. The extra dollars I slipped them are hardly refundable, but that alone isn't cause to go forward, to put myself on vulnerable display, to compound the risks. In an industry fraught with competition for bookings and crowds, rumors of a flop can spread faster than a wired message.

"Ten!" An impatient patron initiates the count. "Nine..." As the rest of the room follows, my admonishment of Charles circles back. On the verge now of a similarly secretive plot, I note my hypocrisy.

"Seven...six..."

But this isn't the same, I counter. Comparatively my changes are minor. Plus, there's no booze involved, no lives jeopardized.

"Four..."

Choice teetering, my hands ball into fists, reigniting the pain in my palm. Each pulsing throb carries a memory from the night before: of my standing on this very stage, bleeding and panicked, clambering to save Charles—who, all the while, was manipulating my emotions, pulling my strings like a puppeteer.

For a published rave that only made him scoff.

"Two...one!"

My resolve hardens to bedrock.

The instant Charles folds into the crate, the stagehands proceed in haste. They nail down the lid and wrap the box in chains, which the volunteers padlock toward the crowd. "Take the A Train" blasts from the pit as I usher the officer and committee down toward their seats. The box creaks and shakes from Charles's unseen efforts.

His contortionist skills—once deemed "freakish" by onlookers— were among the initial reasons for our partnership. Thanks to years of more practice, he can shed a straitjacket with relative ease, even in dark and limited quarters, like now. Next, he'll pry free a portion of the crate's base, via camouflaged hinges and spring bolts, to reach the tabletop's removable center.

It's not by accident that the rectangular table leg is positioned with the narrow width facing the crowd. This gives little hint that a lean contorting body could pass through and descend a ladder under the stage. That is, if the floor's trapdoor has been unlocked…

Slow and deliberate, I tug each padlock to illustrate they're secure and, subtly, to set their placements. The quaking of the box is growing. Charles does this for effect, even when already out of his restraints.

The audience is amply baited. Blinks are turning sparse. Civilians and uniformed patrons alike are peering at the nails and locks, as if the bindings will somehow release themselves. How else could Charles reappear in plain sight? Vanishing from steamer trunks isn't uncommon, but this is a sealed crate with no draping to shield his escape.

Through the blare of a trumpet, I hear it: a discreet thud from center stage, followed by another, sending vibrations through my heels. Charles's controlled knocks are meant for a stagehand, a demand to open the trapdoor.

My heart is thumping.

At his third alert, I circle the crate with practiced grace until another knock reaches my ears. This one from inside the box. Charles has reversed route to signal to me that something is wrong.

I give no tap in return.

I have other plans.

Channeling distress into my expression, I tip off the crowd that there's a problem. The showman is taking too long.

Ignoring a heckle or two, I wring my hands and wait for a harder knock from Charles, which comes soon enough. Then a shake. His confusion is rising, frustration brewing. I lean closer and whisper-yell, "Everything all right in there?"

As though unable to hear the answer, I hush the band and plead through the box, "Please, if you need help, knock to say yes."

The room's focus is on the crate, listening for Charles. His silence infuses the air with tension.

"Monsieur?" I urge.

Folks are sitting forward in their seats.

At last comes a pound. An aggravated fist. Charles understands: this isn't an error.

"Don't fret. We'll get you out." I motion to the stagehand, the sole one nearby, but abruptly cease. "Wait…the locks. Monsieur Bouchard swallowed the keys!"

The audience is whispering, ruminating on the reminder. In my periphery, intrigue rides their faces, mouths falling agape. Public failure, you see, can summon even more attention than success, merely from the unexpected.

I pivot toward the crowd. Solemn with embarrassment, I draw on their sympathies. "Ladies and gentlemen, as you have witnessed, not every act goes precisely as intended. All escape attempts require some level of risk."

Whereas Charles used me to capitalize on fear, I'll shoot for fascination. And not with the shortcut of a death-defying element but with a skill they have likely never seen.

"It is therefore vital to remember," I add while untying my scarf, "as the Great Houdini would say, there's more than a single solution to any given problem. Finding the right one is simply a matter of belief, perseverance, and imagination."

The cherished theorem helps steady my hands. Keeping my back to the crate, I move toward center stage. Interest clearly escalates as the burly stagehand prepares to blindfold me with my scarf. I stiffen from the darkened view yet continue, faintly aware of the suspenseful score being played by the band.

Dramatically I pull from my updo two small picks that at a distance could pass as hairpins. Feeling the stagehand's forearm across my spine, I take a deep breath before leaning backward, arms overhead. My legs cross at the ankles, an act of modesty with my skirt toward the crowd. He lifts me with little effort and steps toward the crate. Straight as a board, I reach the first padlock.

And that's when I begin.

Well rooted in old training, I race with my tools to navigate the lock. Through my mind's eye, I see the mechanisms shifting and turning, until a click. The lock swings loose and clanks to the floor, dropping with the chain.

"*Next*." At my order, I'm delivered to the neighboring padlock. I go to work, adrenaline and confidence accelerating my pace. Another lock and chain drop. "Done!"

On to the third.

The box suddenly shakes, pulling the lock from my hand. I recover, despite more knocks from Charles. He thinks I'm making him look the fool—he's wrong, but I can't worry about that now.

"Next!" Fingers working robotically, I sprint through the fourth, the fifth. In the wake of the sixth, applause breaks out.

Joyful relief courses through me as the stagehand sets me on my feet and the musicians end their song. I toss away the blindfold, pride stretching my smile. Cheers from the audience, the ladies noticeably louder, almost cause me to forget there's more. I take two heavy steps forward, subtle stomps amid the noise, cueing the stagehand below to open the trapdoor.

My internal clock is ticking, timing Charles's movements. I take a pair of curtsies before inviting the burly stagehand to unnail the lid. The audience goes quiet and music builds as my helper opens the box. Riveted gazes watch me climb the stepladder and lean over the top for a good, private look. What I find, of course, is even better than an empty space.

I reach inside to produce the unfastened straitjacket for all to view. After pausing for gasps, I resume my original script: "Ever so kindly, please welcome back"—I gesture with a flourish to the rear of the room—"Monsieur Charles Bouchard!"

Heads swoop his way with the unified movement of a flock. The crowd locates Charles at the far-left corner, behind the last row of seats. Arms raised in triumph, he's materialized out of nowhere!

Folks rise, pointing and chattering in awe. Applause reaches a crescendo. Charles grins and bows. He hides his panting fairly well, having just dashed up the spiral staircase from below, then out a staff door camouflaged between the auditorium and lobby.

Enthusiasm appears shared by all—save for one. Amid khakis and olive drab, a balding man in a suit stands in the second row, not clapping. Through spectacles, he stares with such scrutiny I feel pinned by crosshairs.

Just then, Charles directs the crowd's focus back to the stage for me to share in the glory, causing a boomerang of whistles and hoots.

The gracious move jars me.

He hasn't fully fathomed the situation. Perhaps he blames the stage-hand and presumes I improvised to fill the time, that I even rescued the act.

The thought washes me in a startling wave of shame.

Then his gaze meets mine. With the audience's attention briefly diverted, his eyes burn with an icy fury. Sharp as a dart, it shoots clear across the room. A shiver prickles my skin as he reapplies his smile, accepting praise from the masses, pretending all went exactly as he planned.

Only he and I know a fallout awaits.

CHAPTER 4

At the drop of the curtain, I steel myself for the unknown. Charles has never been the tantrum-throwing sort, though these days I wouldn't stake a wager on his behavior.

In his notable absence from gathering supplies with the stagehands, I envision varied possibilities of our confrontation. To allay my simmering guilt, I remind myself who instigated this tug-of-war, one that has assuredly run its course. By the time the stage is cleared, I'm prepared to mitigate an eruption or endure a scolding. I'm hoping for a meager lecture.

Still in costume, I enter Charles's dressing room and try for a light tack. "And with that, I hereby declare a truce."

Charles doesn't so much as pause while buttoning his white collared shirt, standing before the illuminated mirror. "A truce..." He repeats the phrase as if sampling a foreign flavor. Suspenders hang loose down the sides of his slacks. His unfastened necktie lines his collar. "Funny. Didn't know we were at war." His tone is pure nonchalance, a scenario I find oddly unsettling.

"Listen, Charles. We've both had our fun. After tonight, well, I figure we're square."

He moves on to the ends of his sleeves, applying his cuff links.

"Charles?"

"Hmm?"

His room, indeed more spacious than mine, lacks a window, compelling me to leave the door open a crack. I advance inside for privacy's sake and address his reflection. "Did you hear what I said?"

A brief glance upward. "Sure. I heard ya."

"And?"

"Haven't caught a question."

"I'm...trying to say..."

It dawns on me that his impassivity is but a facade, a demonstration of my inability to affect him. I brush aside a needling of resentment and continue. "My trick with the locks, I just thought it would add some pizzazz. As you saw, or must've heard at least, the crowd really responded."

"Ah. So *that's* why you did it." His tone, though revelatory, makes it clear he's not fooled.

The repercussions of our respective schemes don't strike me as equal. Yet I suppose I can muster the gumption to come clean for my part. "All right, I confess. It *was* a small act of revenge, and...for that I'm sorry." And I genuinely mean that.

Even if I did enjoy showcasing my own special skills.

Charles begins fastening his necktie without looking my way. Without even a courtesy of acknowledgment. Good grief, he expects me to grovel. How convenient of him to forget all about last night's finale.

Refusing to lose my composure, I merely pivot and start for the door.

"I don't think so."

The remark stops me cold. Plausible meanings riffle through my head: a command not to leave, a rejection of my apology. Against my better judgment, I turn with arms crossed, a silent demand that he elaborate.

"Way I see it," he says, still facing the mirror, "it wasn't so much revenge. It was jealousy."

I suppress a laugh, barely. "Of?"

"The rave review. My feature in a major paper."

How absurd. I'm about to remind him of his own gripes over his paltry write-up when he adds, "Course, it's all fine 'n' good. In the end, the longest and loudest applause tonight was still for me." He adjusts his knotted tie. "But then, that's what makes me the showman and you the assistant."

I'm as stung as I am dumbfounded. "That...that's what you think?

That I'm just your assistant now?" Sure, it's always been my title to those on the outside, but never in reality.

Not between us.

"Actually, you got a point." He pauses from preening, and through the mirror's reflection, he narrows his eyes at me. "Even *basic* assistants would climb into the crate themselves. They get sawed in half, vanish from one container to another. In fact, they do dozens of other tricks that happen to be off-limits for our show. Because, obviously, that'd be beneath you."

I strive to be incensed but the core of the matter sends me reeling. "That is entirely untrue."

"Yeah? Then why?" He snaps to face me, his intensity returning from the show's end. "If I'm really your partner—your friend, least of all—how 'bout you explain it to me?"

"Explain…what?" I'm stalling now, scrambling.

"The *truth*," he stresses, as if nothing could be more obvious. "You come up with all our fancy tricks. Figure out every maneuver and mechanic. Hell, you even build the props. So why? What the devil could be the issue if it's not about being high and mighty?"

Whether sincere or rhetorical, the questions border on interrogation, hammering, chipping. Prying up my past. Once more, I hear them from the depths of my mind: a baby's hoarse wails, hands clawing plaster, notes plunked on a piano by a child unaware.

I break from Charles's eyes. My attention darts, seeking an escape, and snags on a glint of metal. A flask. Lid unscrewed, it sits on the vanity amid his grooming supplies.

"You've been drinking." As though this alone is the cause of everything.

His brow crumples before he traces my sight line, then huffs, exasperated. "Yeah. *After* the show. Making it none of your business."

"While in a theater, it's entirely my business." Desperate, I add, "Unless you want to find yourself a new *assistant*."

He flinches at the threat and his expression deflates. Yet a moment later, his mouth becomes a hard line. "Ya know what? I might just go and do that."

"Splendid," I say. "And maybe I'll snatch up some clown off the street and simply create another you."

As soon as the words leave my mouth, shame tries to pull them back in. But it's too late. They hang between us, turning the air brittle.

"You're welcome to try." No sign of bluffing, no backing down.

We've come to a standoff after all.

A tap on the door interjects. "Mr. Bouchard?" It's the tentative voice of the theater's assistant manager. "You, um, have admirers waiting?"

Charles and I have more to say, much more, but not in our current state. Not if we want any chance of containing the damage.

Before he can dismiss me, I salvage my dignity by replying on his behalf. "Send them in. We're done." The double meaning isn't intentional—or maybe it is. I exit and jostle past the small cluster of faceless fans in the hall.

In my dressing room, I lean back against the closed door. We've had disagreements before, but nothing like this. Anger and sadness spiral through me.

I bypass my change of clothes and grab only my brimmed hat and overcoat, my pocketbook. I'll be returning tomorrow anyhow to pack for our next stop…

Or, perhaps, just to pack.

Moisture wells in my eyes as I bolt from the theater. I stride down the dark streets of Brooklyn, headed for my room at the boardinghouse. My vision adjusts to the night haze, aided by a three-quarter moon elbowing its way through the overcast sky. Cool sprinkles of autumn rain dot my legs, bare but for foundation mimicking stockings in an era of rationing, the seam line forged by a cosmetic pencil and a steady hand.

Steady… By morning, that's how Charles and I will be. After our emotions dissipate, along with his booze, we'll straighten out the snarls and swap apologies, meet in the middle. I block out the alternative.

Between the clacking of my heels, I catch a rhythmic sound. Faint footsteps behind me.

Glancing back, I spot a figure in the shadows a full block away. Charles immediately comes to mind—hopefully to set things right, rather than to unload another rebuke—but the man's frame appears unfamiliar.

I quicken my pace.

The stranger seems to do the same.

The rumbling of a motorcar fades in the darkness. I clutch my pocketbook to the front of my coat, starkly aware of my scanty costume beneath and, even more so, of the unusually deserted route. No servicemen with their sweethearts. No locals walking their dogs. The rain, increasing now, has made people scarce.

"*Liss!*" A deep holler.

Or was it… "Miss"?

I brave another glance, only partially slowing. A fedora shields half the man's face, leaving the rest a sketchy silhouette.

Unlike the copper-mining town of my childhood, New York teems with as many shady characters as dingy back alleys. I've skimmed enough big-city papers to know how unspeakably this could end.

The voice calls out again, muddled by my footfalls and a groan of thunder. I veer around a shuttered store at the corner.

A bark then a howl pierce the air, made more ominous by distant clanks of a can. My heeled shoes, given the wet, uneven pavement— and yes, caution over being foolish—restrain me from a sprint. He could simply be hurrying due to the weather and addressing someone I failed to see. Or maybe he's a drunkard speaking with nobody in particular.

The latter brings minimal comfort.

On both sides of the street, blackout shades and drapes obscure views from apartments. If I were to scream, would anyone rush to help?

Three long blocks remain until my boardinghouse. No other soul in view. Save for the man who just rounded the corner. Once more in my wake. Closing the distance.

CHAPTER 5

"Miss, wait," the man calls from behind. Then more insistent: "Miss Vos!"

I startle at my name before relief seeps in, slowing my steps. He knows me.

But then I recall my name printed on posters at the theater, making it less likely that he's an acquaintance than a zealous fan. Flattering, if he wasn't following me home—and home, thank goodness, is quite nearly where I am.

"Please, I mean you no harm!" His breathless voice holds urgent sincerity. Moreover, it's softened by a British accent that, warranted or not, lowers my perception of danger. Enough anyhow to draw me to a stop, though with caution.

"My apologies if I caused you a fright." He allows a buffer of space and raises a gloved hand. "A moment, if you will…" Mildly panting, he blows out a breath. His spectacles, perched on a sturdy nose and flecked with rain, obscure his eyes. "Sadly, I am no longer the spry lad I once was."

Indeed, he looks to be in his fifties, with a tweed suit and checkered bow tie peeking from his overcoat. At this proximity, his face is familiar but unplaceable.

As his breathing settles, I press, "Sir, have we met before?"

"We have not, I regret to say." He extends a hand. "Christopher Clayton Hutton."

I retract out of instinct, which he appears to understand. "How may I help you?"

"My hope," he says, "is that we might help each other. First, may I ask, is there somewhere dry you would prefer to speak?"

Raindrops slide down my legs, rousing goose bumps. But it's after nine, thus any cafés within a block are closed for the night. And my boardinghouse is decidedly not an option.

I fold my arms snug to my chest. "Right here will do just fine, thank you."

He gives a nod. "Quite."

Then he removes his glasses, revealing steeply arched brows, and glances swiftly about before continuing. His affirmation of our privacy only adds to my discomfort.

"Miss Vos, I have a prospect that I believe will pique your interest. It's of my firm opinion, you see, that your unique and innovative skills should be utilized for a grander purpose than amusement on a stage."

So there it is. A pitch I know well. Every so often, a crafty charmer will come around, flaunting Tinseltown connections, seeking much more than a screen test.

And yet, something about this man doesn't fit the mold. "You're not a Hollywood scout...are you?"

"Me? No, no." He chuckles. "Although I *was* in the employ of the film industry at one time. As a director of publicity, as it were."

I smile courteously. But just then, from the tilt of his shadowed face, recognition hits. He's the man from the audience. The one who stood without clapping, his stare penetrating, unreadable.

My feet angle slightly away.

"Mind you, that is neither here nor there, in view of the matter at hand."

"Which is?"

"Why, a tremendous opportunity to do your bit."

I blink at him, thrown off. "My bit?"

"For the war effort."

"Yes, I...understand the reference, but..."

"Allow me to explain." His manner is proper but amiable, as if we were chatting over tea, not standing in the middle of a dark, rainy street discussing—what? Performing at rallies? Promoting war bonds?

"It is strictly official business, for my work in the War Office in London, that has brought me here this week—to America, that is.

Nevertheless, having learned of Monsieur Bouchard's performance, I had planned to attend for leisure. I daresay I have long been an admirer of escapology and, like you, of Houdini in particular."

In the show, my "mind-reading" act with Charles relies heavily on observation to gather clues and people's tells. Although this man presents as genuine, I remain skeptical. "And what, sir, now brings you to me?"

"If I am to be candid? Intuition," he replies without irony. "Furthermore, you are the mastermind behind the scenes, are you not?"

His knowledge of this is surprising.

Then again, he could be probing.

"What ever would lead you to think that?"

He shrugs a shoulder. "Your stagehands were kindly informative."

Ah, yes. For a couple bucks, no doubt.

"At any rate, there is an assisting role I have been keen to fill for some weeks. By luck, or fate perchance, it seems I have found an unlikely candidate." He tips his head toward me for emphasis, sending drips from his hat, then warns, "For form's sake, the War Office would require your completing some paperwork, a bit tedious—pettifogging bureaucrats—but there is a war on, and the Hun spies could get in anywhere, you know."

My thoughts jumble at the rush of it all. I attempt to wrangle the pieces.

"So this…is a job offer."

A corner of his mouth perks. "Indeed."

"In London."

"Thereabouts."

"For the position of…?"

"A temporary civil servant."

"Meaning, what exactly?"

"Your work would be, shall we say, extremely specialized and, above all, devoted to saving Allied lives." His eyes shine with enthusiasm, an expectation of invoking intrigue.

I must admit, everything about this meeting seems straight out of the silent films I grew up watching, all the spy and detective adventures that provided escape from the clutches of my tragedies.

But then, I can think of nothing more tragic than war. It's a veritable reason to steer clear of such turmoil. Sure, plenty of entertainers do their bit, through USO shows and propaganda reels. Yet by that reasoning, it could be said I already contribute by boosting morale on the home front, performing to American troops on their breaks from training. What's more, the suggestion of my jaunting off to Europe, plumb into the thick of things, is altogether ludicrous.

Just now, another groan of thunder sends a timely message: When a hurricane makes landfall, who in their right mind races toward the storm?

"Mr. Hutton, it's a fascinating opportunity, and I'm terribly honored. But I already have a good many obligations. By this time tomorrow, Monsieur Bouchard and I will be on a train headed for our next series of performances."

The fellow's brows dip, forming a pleat between them. It's a look of perplexity that quickly gains a layer of abashed reluctance. "I hope you'll forgive the intrusion. Backstage at the theater, I happened to overhear a discussion. It left me with a strong impression that you might...be in want of a fresh pursuit."

The reference takes me a moment to dissect. He must have been among the admirers waiting in the hall and caught my quarrel with Charles. Another way he learned of my role behind the curtain.

My crossed arms tighten. Even if at no fault of his, I prefer my private affairs to stay private. "Charles and I have a long-standing partnership. These sorts of professional squabbles are minor and meaningless." This much is a lie; I taste its bitterness even as the words tumble out. "Therefore, I will have to pass on your offer, generous as it is."

He opens his mouth, clearly to persist, but refrains. "I am very sorry to hear that." The pattering of shallow puddles fills the silence. "Well. It was a pleasure nonetheless."

This time, I accept his handshake, genial if brief. While he replaces his glasses, I proceed to leave.

"Miss Vos."

I twist back only partially.

"Should you change your mind, I shall be at the Waldorf Astoria until my evening flight tomorrow. If you so desire, I would be obliged to save you a seat."

Before I can decline, fixed in my stance, he starts away and fades into the darkness.

CHAPTER 6

Though muffled, the noise upstairs is utterly maddening.

Parked on my bed in my old cotton robe, I strain to focus on a borrowed book. The task is near impossible thanks to tenants on the floor above, whose bursts of laughter compete with tunes from their RCA. I have half a mind to climb onto the room's wooden desk and make my case by pounding on the ceiling.

Rather, I proceed to wait my turn for the house's lone tub. The group's gaiety, anyway, isn't the true problem. It's the clashing of my thoughts.

Starting with Charles.

His accusation of jealousy is spiteful and enraging. But is it wrong? From the birth of our endeavor, I swore I didn't need public credit; I just hadn't banked on feeling invisible. And, worse, disposable.

Now my options are glaring: plod forward together or split off with respective partners.

Or, perhaps, let Charles take the act completely while I embark on a daring new adventure.

To say I haven't dreamt of one day seeing London's glorious gardens and palaces firsthand would be a lie. In all fairness, England is a far distance from the front lines, and through the Battle of Britain, its Royal Air Force has proven a formidable defender.

But still—me, recruited for specialized wartime service. What lunacy. That's to say nothing of being transported in an aircraft, wholly encased while shooting like a cannonball through the sky.

Unless, that is, ship passage could be arranged...

If only my initial fear of being stalked tonight had held. Instead, ultimately nothing about the man rang false. This includes his assertion that, rather than amusing Allied troops, my skills could help save their lives.

Utilized for a greater purpose, he said, echoing an indelible message from my past.

It's this bit that itches at me most, deep and insatiable, along with thoughts of the sole person able to relate—now in yet another way. The very person I've been tempted to contact time and again.

Arie.

Three years ago, well before the nation's day of infamy spurred fellows to enlist in droves, he joined the U.S. Army Corps of Engineers, according to my updates from back in Michigan. Since then, his reassignment to military intelligence, an apt fit for a keen observer with a skill for languages, has stationed him safely in DC. That knowledge has provided me immeasurable relief, especially given the likelihood that my actions were to blame for his unexpected enlistment. One more reason I avoid bookings in his area. Not that this stops me from occasionally mistaking soldiers for him in any number of audiences.

Thank goodness it's not him, I always tell myself when my instinctual joy dissolves. For what would I say? Casual comments about the weather, the army, our past? Nothing is that simple. Not after what I did.

Tonight, however, I've been handed a gift. The job offer, regardless of my tenuous interest, might be just the excuse I've needed to reach out to hear how he's been faring.

If nothing else, it could provide a chance to—

"Bath's all yours!" The unseen boarder gives me a courtesy knock from the hall, then her steps shuffle away.

My rejuvenating soak is waiting.

As is the telephone downstairs.

I release a breath and rise to my feet. Surrendering the seclusion of my room, I head toward the door.

In the study, a lamp's glass mosaic shade casts ghostly streaks over the ceiling-high shelves. From a painted portrait on the wall, the black eyes of a mustached dignitary stare down, accusing.

The instant the operator connects the call, launching a series of strident rings, my throat goes dry. Seated at the telephone table, I yearn for a cup of water, a pitcher. Scents of lemon oil and aged books further strangle the air.

There's still time to hang up and leave well enough alone. My two-handed grasp on the handset alternately tightens and loosens from a mental skirmish that halts when the call to his apartment is answered.

"Jansen here."

Despite my sprinting pulse, Arie's velvety rasp eases something inside me. Even as a young boy, he possessed that ability, the soothing timbre.

"Anyone there?"

I realize I haven't spoken.

"Hello…" My greeting barely surpasses a whisper. I try again. "Arie, hi. It's—"

"I know." His voice thins, hollow with shock. After four years with no word from me, the reaction is natural.

Then comes a noise—is it a click? The operator switching off? I'm gripped by fear that Arie has hung up. Only traces of his breathing assure me that he hasn't.

Yet.

"I hope I didn't wake you. I know it's rather late." I'd considered the hour briefly but was certain from experience my resolve wouldn't last the night.

"I was up."

"Oh…right. Silly me. Of course you were."

Ever a restless sleeper, he'd often receive chidings from his mother over his morning grumpiness. From the next room, I'd hear her liken him to a bear, her accent labeling him an "angry berry."

My smile at the memory withers in the silence, as does the speech I mentally rehearsed before daring to make the call. *Say something, Fenna! Talk.*

"Tell me, how have you been?"

A pause. "I'm fine."

"That's marvelous. And your parents? They're well?"

"Yeah," he says. Nothing more.

I wonder if he knows I send them funds when I'm able, against his father's insistence. It's hardly a fortune but the least I can do.

I mention only, "I ring them to check in. From the road. When I can."

"I've heard."

He's cold. Resentful. I can imagine the slate blue of his eyes turned glacial. I picture him on the other end of the line, with his ash-blond hair likely buzzed for the service, his broad build in an army-issue undershirt, dog tags looping his neck—perhaps the source of the click I heard. Or was it a tap, a knock?

Suddenly it all rushes back: our years of signaling through bedroom walls, of messages passed in secret, the shared losses and laughs. Two interwoven worlds abruptly severed.

My heart twists in my chest, wringing out words long overdue.

"Arie, I have to tell you... I need you to hear how sorry, how incredibly sorry I am. The last thing I ever wanted to do was to hurt you." I'm fighting back tears, painfully conscious of how trite I sound and that no words could possibly suffice.

He inhales, exhales. "I regret all of it too."

It takes me a second to register: his reply isn't reciprocal but a dig, made clear by the density of his tone. He regrets that he trusted me, that he gave so much for so little. Surely that he met me at all.

I deserve worse.

"Arie—"

"I've got an early meeting. So if that's what you called for..."

The unspoken coils between us, sharp and tangled as barbed wire. I want to explain my reasons. To prove I made the wisest decision for us both, regardless of how deeply I care. To clarify how those feelings are precisely what drove my actions. But really, what would saying any of that change? All the same, I'm not ready to end the conversation, aware it could be our last, that in fairness to him, it should be.

"There's more," I hasten to say.

He waits, and I recall the initial prompt for my call, the excuse of it. "You see, I–I need your help."

"My help," he repeats, assuredly astounded.

"Just your opinion. Since you're assigned to intelligence now. Already a first lieutenant from what I hear." I pause for confirmation, or any response.

"That's right."

"My, that's grand." I worry that I sounded surprised. "No doubt you've earned it. You've always worked so hard—at school and the factory, with the house and helping others. At everything you ever do."

"Thanks…" He's softening, only a fraction, but enough to give me hope that he doesn't entirely despise me. "What's the question, Fen?"

His old name for me causes a glitch in my thoughts. I push through. "I met a gentleman, here in New York. He claimed to be from the War Office in London. Said his name is Christopher…something Hutton. Clarence, or Claude—"

"Clayton," Arie corrects, plainly taken off guard.

"Oh, yes, that's it! You know him?"

"I know *of* him."

A stroke of luck, giving me reason to press on. "In that case, I'd… really appreciate your insight."

"About?"

"I guess, if there's something unseemly I should be aware of, with his work. Or his character. Anything about him really."

Another quiet spell. Though now I envision Arie pondering, in spite of his puzzlement. "The man's pretty eccentric but resourceful. An inventor," he says and tacks on, "back in civilian life, if I remember right."

An inventor? Interesting.

"Why do you ask?"

I have to scrounge for an answer, the topic being secondary. Wishing I could simply listen to Arie speak, I recall how his voice and stories would lull me through the gloom of sleepless nights.

"The fellow approached me tonight after the show. It made me jumpy at first, to be frank, what with him following me home. But then we started talking, and he mentioned his admiration of Houdini." Arie would obviously recognize the pertinence. "He also knew quite a lot about my show partner—the challenges we've been having, I mean. Not that you need to hear any of that."

Gracious, listen to me spouting off. I ought to get to the point.

"Look," Arie cuts in, "that's all I can tell you. The rest is none of my concern. Not anymore." The shift in his voice startles me, the ire in it.

Heavens to Betsy, he thinks I want courtship advice. I could laugh over the misunderstanding, almost. "Please. Arie, if you'll just listen."

"Goodbye, Fenna." The words carry such finality that I fail to reply. Then the line goes dead.

A jolt of panic shoots through me. Mortified, I reach for the base of the phone. I need to summon the operator, to call again, to explain—

For what?

It's over.

He's gone.

Once more, reality closes in, a merciless fist. Tears at last break free and roll hot down my face. From the portrait on the wall, the figure isn't just peering but gloating.

It was a mistake to go backward. Moving forward is the way I've survived, eluding traps of all kinds, charging toward the unknown.

In light of this truth, I recall my options for the road ahead.

And I see that, really, there's no choice to make.

CHAPTER 7

"Lady, ya gettin' out or not?" The cabbie addresses me from the driver's seat without looking over his shoulder. He reeks of pickles and pipe tobacco and wears a flat cap low over his pockmarked face.

The prospect of a return ride with this man is actually more daunting than my impending mission. I hand off change from my pocketbook, and in my hastily donned wraparound dress, having skipped the bath altogether, I step out onto the sidewalk. Compared to the gals funneling past me into the Tin Kettle, dolled up with their sweetheart necklines and hair in perfect victory rolls, I resemble a matted stray.

But then, I haven't come here to impress.

I enter the teeming club, where swirls of cigarette smoke mingle with the bluesy notes of a jazz quartet. The musicians on the small stage pour their souls into their horns, strings, and keys as couples on the dance floor engage in a moody Lindy Hop.

The melancholy tune well befits my purpose for coming. It's true I could apologize, as could Charles, and the bruises we inflicted would gradually fade. But beneath the surface, our long-held resentments will fester unless one of us changes course. Perhaps a break is all we need. In the meanwhile, it only makes sense for him to continue the show. And thanks to Christopher Clayton Hutton, there's no need to divvy up supplies, bookings, and the rights to each of our tricks. Like the branches of a grafted tree, how would we ever begin to unravel them?

All that's left for me to hear is that Charles will be fine on his own—despite my suspecting as much.

While I indeed mentored his showman skills and designed our flashiest acts, he's the one who performs them. Plus, even back in our days of bit shows and small-time, he shrewdly knew to charm house managers and publicity folks. As I scribbled away backstage, consumed by new ideas and improvements, he was planting seeds for future bookings that would otherwise have taken us years, even decades, to secure.

Part of me aches in admitting it, but the fact is: he'll be more than fine.

My gaze roams the dimly lit space. Suits are fairly easy to spot in rooms dominated by servicemen.

"Eh, sweetheart!" a GI calls to me, slurring. He can't be more than seventeen. "How 'bout a special send-off?"

Slipping past him, I ignore more leering eyes. I was confident Charles would be here to wind down. He could have come and gone by now or simply chosen another place. I can wait at his motel, but who's to say when he'll return after a night of gallivanting?

Again I scan the room, more thoroughly. That's when I spy his profile. At a far corner table, he sits with glass in hand and eyes downcast. He's alone, lost in thought. A surprise. A relief.

Our spat could actually be taking a toll…

Nevertheless, I plod toward him with proposal ready. He could agree resentfully. Or eagerly. Perhaps he'll at least suggest I reconsider. He could attempt to drill reason into me over fighting "some other countries' war," point out the sheer insanity of what I'm contemplating. He could challenge me to compromise and to hash out our issues.

Or with sincerity, he could just ask me to stay.

The notion slows my steps. A flittering of hope unexpectedly prompts second thoughts, supported by sensibility. I don't even know specifics of the job with Hutton nor have I officially agreed. There's nothing yet to be undone.

Charles lifts his gaze as if to turn my way when a gal approaches him from behind. Clad in a snug dress, she pulls a plum-colored scarf from her ample bosom and lays it over his eyes. He smiles before she swings around and engages him deeply in a kiss.

The act, while audaciously intimate, isn't alone what grinds me to a halt; it's my recognition of that scarf, a silk kerchief I'd gifted him the day of our first performance. For me, in many ways, it became a symbol of our journey. The gambles and successes. Our friendship.

Now, as he bursts into laughter with the woman, showing no worries over where we stand nor over replacing me with a "basic assistant," I realize that outside of creating a contentiously awkward scene, there's nothing left for me to say.

Not in person, anyhow.

Spurning doubts, I wheel toward the exit and hail a cab. In my room, I'll scribe a letter, unhindered by emotion. I'll explain my decision as best I can and outline details for proceeding without me. Come morning, while taxiing to the Waldorf Astoria to accept Hutton's offer, I'll drop it by the theater to await Charles's arrival.

He'll be better off in the end. As will I.

On the winding path of my life, through all I've endured, I've had few certainties as great as this.

1928

CHAPTER 8

December 24, 1928
Eden Springs, Michigan

The sweet smell of saffron cake infused the air, but treats that day were ancillary. Beside a Christmas tree adorned in crepe paper and tinsel, two heaping barrels of toys, candy, and a variety of other gifts awaited onstage like glorious beacons, captivating every youngster's attention, including mine.

In my aisle seat two-thirds back, I absently mumbled through the Latin hymn "Adeste Fideles" with the rest of the packed assembly hall, located on the upper floor of the two-story brick building in the heart of town. I was just shy of eleven, yet I can still recall the anticipation vibrating through my bones.

Of course, if I had known how the day would end, I'd have recognized the sensation as foreboding.

Maybe I should have regardless. The place was viewed as unlucky by some. The original building had blown down in a storm, and the replacement had burned to ashes. But wasn't the third time a charm? And besides, I figured, what could sour such a gleeful day?

As children numbering four hundred or more, we were antsier than chickens in a coop. Most parents in the room sat alongside us or stood toward the rear. Other men like my father had slipped away to the café downstairs, converted from a saloon thanks to the Eighteenth Amendment, and were still known there to sneak nips from their flasks and gripe over their employer.

For miners in the "Copper Country," up in Michigan's Keweenaw

Peninsula, there was no shortage of grievances when it came to C&H, or Calumet & Hecla. Slashes to wages, benefits, and safety had pushed the men to strike. Back during the Great War, higher demand for copper drew thousands of workers to the area, until the market's eventual decline sent many off to auto factories in big cities like Detroit. My father was among those who stayed and held out for what was fair.

If a house want electricity, it is needing copper, Papa would say, insisting that lower demand was still demand. Then he'd mutter in Dutch about the higher-ups living fancifully in their mansions while seeking shortcuts to bolster their stocks.

My mother, whose fine nose and cheekbones I'd apparently inherited, passed away from scarlet fever in my toddler years, leaving me virtually no memories of her. No photograph even. Nonetheless, I presume she'd have been the one to gently warn me against expecting gifts during these trying times. As it was, I didn't have to be told. Funds were scarce enough prior to the walkout. After four subsequent months, most of our meals were possible only with union support.

Hence a Christmas Eve party for the union members' children, hosted by the Women's Auxiliary, seemed a miraculous thrill—minus the infinite string of carols. Several were sung in Finnish, unsurprisingly; the Finns formed a hefty sum of the guests. Reflective of Eden Springs, there were also Croatians and Germans, Italians and Irish; Swedes, Hungarians, and Cornish. The majority of the rest, including us Dutch, were like *salt in the dough,* according to Papa: though amounting to a pinch, we were essential to the whole.

In truth, despite many of us kids being born in the States, "essential" never described my place with the other girls, certainly including at social to-dos. But on this particular afternoon, it was the least of my concerns.

When the ninth song ended—indeed, I was counting—"Big Vera" stepped in front of the tree to speak. President of the Women's Auxiliary, she was a woman of Slavic descent whose six-foot-some height presumably aided her collection of eighty whole dollars from businesses to buy presents for the affair. Who with any scruples would refuse her?

"Boys and girls," she projected in a booming voice, "now that we've concluded the singing portion of our program…"

Elation over what this could mean rippled through the crowd. So much so, a boy launched himself from the front row and with him a swarm of followers.

"No, no! Not yet!" Big Vera motioned as if fending off piglets from a trough.

Volunteers jumped in to reverse the stage rush. With relative order restored, they huddled to confer with Big Vera, who readdressed the room.

"Children, we can see you're all very excited about the goodies waiting for you. We've therefore decided to bypass the play for the time being. If you'll kindly line up at the stairs to my left—*in a mannerly fashion*—you may approach to receive…"

The rest fell away. Like the pop of a pistol, the announcement unleashed a massive dash for the queue. I too joined in, determined not to be left empty-handed. Squeals and grunts arose as competitors jockeyed for a spot. Bony elbows and shoulders pegged me from all sides. Though I kept from tumbling, I wound up toward the rear of the endlessly snaking line.

When a man dressed as Santa Claus settled on a chair by the barrels, a pack of kids clambered straight onto the stage. A volunteer looked displeased. She gave them no turns with St. Nicholas but dispensed their presents with haste. Then she shooed them past the piano toward the steps designated for descent.

I frowned at their unjust reward but continued to inch my way forward. One child after the other chatted briefly with Santa before leaving with items from the barrels. Observing the interactions, as was my usual pastime, I fidgeted with my dress and the buttons of my coat. Two years earlier, a kindhearted Bulgarian woman gave me the outfit, which her daughters had outgrown. Soon widowed by the mine, she packed up her family and moved away. The dress—with embroidered pink petals, a Peter Pan collar, and a tie at the waist—was the sole one

I owned and obviously fancier than my usual overalls. As for the fit, it had grown a bit short and tight around the ribs, but that wasn't the current core of my unease.

While I progressed steadily toward the stage, the first barrel was emptied. Much too fast, the final mound was depleting. The deeper the volunteers reached, the more my nerves jangled. A trio of brazen boys slid into the line a second time. Quickly thwarted by vigilant parents, they half smirked through their punishments—ear tugs for the smaller two, a cuff to the head for the eldest—as if the gamble was still worthy.

On the main floor and up in the balcony, where columns and arches added flair, parents yakked away in ethnic clusters. Mothers soothed infants by rocking and bouncing. Laughter and languages clamored, growing loud enough to require near yelling. Framed by windows spanning a single wall, the cloud-laden sky began to dim.

The line lasted so long that Santa had to excuse himself "for a break to feed the reindeer." Since the remaining kids were all older like me, aware of the truth and caring most about the gifts, Big Vera stepped in to keep the queue moving.

At last my turn came and I scuttled into place.

"Hello, my dear," she said from a mile overhead. "How about a little doll? Would you like that?"

I nodded vigorously, too excited to speak. The closest thing to a real doll I'd ever possessed—not the paper kind that I'd wrinkled and ripped over years of play—had been sewn from a sock and became so tattered it resembled a one-winged penguin.

But as Big Vera rummaged through the barrel, her smile wavering, my heart plummeted even before the news.

"I'm ever so sorry, honey. I could have sworn I saw another one down in there." She brightened. "I know! How about a special choo-choo train? Would that be all right?"

Girls traded mutterings behind me. Though expressed in Russian, their impatience needed no translation.

I replied to Big Vera with another nod, this time hiding disappointment as Papa would insist I be grateful. Politely I accepted a small wooden train and a handful of penny candy—butterscotch and taffies, which I stuffed into my coat pocket. I thanked her with the toothiest grin I could muster, perhaps not the most convincing, and was shuffling away when she tapped my shoulder. Leaning down, she slipped me an additional gift: a pair of thick mittens, dark green and fuzzy.

"A match to your lovely eyes." She winked, and my cheeks warmed from being seen.

Recalling she was unmarried, I tried to envision her and Papa engaged in a courtship. Whereas some called me a "Dutch runt," my father was the standard kind of tall. But Big Vera was even taller, and to my dismay, I suspected that wouldn't work.

"Merry Christmas," she said.

I bid her the same before being guided offstage and funneled through a lengthy hallway. The path hooked me into the back of the main room. By then, piano notes drifted from the stage. As a young girl with a big red hair bow played "Away in a Manger," I reviewed my loot off in a corner.

The mittens were a tad big. This only meant they'd last longer, I realized. I relished their softness on my cheek before storing them in my pocket. The locomotive, hand-carved though unpainted, could never top a doll, but at least the wheels spun. As did the smokestack—or was that a flaw? Maybe it needed glue.

To find out, I raised the cylindrical piece. When it stopped from an internal block, the conductor's cab fell off in my hand, exposing a hollow middle. I cringed. Had I broken the train in two? I scrambled to put it back together, but the cab wouldn't fit, not until I fully lifted then lowered the chimney. Sure enough, the toy was whole again. Like a secret key, the smokestack locked the cab into place.

I wanted to run back and show Big Vera, then wondered if she already knew.

"I told you it's mine!" The outburst turned my head.

Along the wall, just yards away stood a boy I almost didn't recognize. Shined up like a new penny, Arie Jansen wore a sweater vest over a collared shirt with cuffed gray pants, hair slicked and combed. Add to that his jutted chin and puffed chest, and he didn't appear at all the solemn kid from the apartment next door.

"Yer really that daft, are ya?" The freckled boy dominated in height and mass, yet neither deterred Arie, who answered through gritted teeth.

"I warned you. Now give it back."

The bully studied the small wooden plane he held, surely a gift from the barrel, as if contemplating the threat. "Eh...I don't think so."

Arie's glare narrowed as the other boy continued to goad him.

"Course, if it's that bloody important to ya, you can go and get—"

Arie hauled off and lunged for the airplane. The two fiercely grappled until the larger boy wrenched his arm free. I gaped when he pushed Arie against the wall, but Arie retaliated by slamming the kid's chest, causing the bully to jerk in surprise.

"Fergus!" a man barked, and the boy grimaced. "It's time we were off. Give the lad what's his."

Fergus apparently knew not to argue. With a huff, he held the plane out for Arie. "Fine, have it, ya *amadán*," he said—clearly not an endearment—as his father started away. Before Arie could accept, Fergus dropped the toy and stomped it with his boot. Arie flinched, I gasped, and a snickering Fergus took off after his father.

Slowly Arie bent and scooped up the pieces. After more than a year of our living in proximity, with Arie just one grade higher at school, we'd yet to exchange even a single word. His only sibling, a sister with a honey-blond ponytail and sapphire eyes, would offer smiles in passing. But already eighteen, she was rarely seen for all her activities.

The mine administrators had assumed they did Papa and me a service, placing the Jansens in the neighboring apartment. Really, how dissimilar could Dutch people be? They didn't understand that the Netherlands was like a bunch of tiny countries squished into one, its shape as orderly as a splotch of ink. While my father spoke standard Dutch, Arie's parents used a dialect from the Groningen province. More than that, with their family being Protestant and mine Catholic, we mixed about as well as oil and water.

Right then, however, from the doleful way Arie stared at what was left of his plane, he didn't seem so foreign. No doubt it was the only present he expected to receive.

I ventured closer, wanting to help. "Maybe you can fix it." Even as I said this, I knew it was unlikely. The wings and propeller had been reduced to little more than splinters.

Through hair now mussed, he looked at me with a tinge of defiance. "Doesn't matter. It was just a dumb toy anyway." His voice had an older quality, the natural huskiness in it. Sadness might have contributed, certainly; if tears filled his eyes, I couldn't have blamed him. But he appeared intent on upholding his pride.

I angled away to leave him be, then remembered the object in my hand. It was a gift I never would have asked for. One of two I'd been given, not even counting the candies.

Father Lawrence's homily echoed back from last Sunday's mass: *Christmas is not about receiving but giving however we're able, especially to those less fortunate.* Already I sensed the looming guilt.

I gave the locomotive a final glance. Allaying my conscience, I turned back. "Here. You can have it."

Confused, then comprehending, he shook his head. "That's yours."

"It's okay. I got two things. And I've never even liked trains that much." Historically that was true, though it did pain me the tiniest amount to say so right then.

I straightened my arm to press the offer. Temptation stirred on his face.

Good grief, he was making this tough. "It's even got a hiding spot inside. Watch."

At my demonstration, his expression perked. He set the aircraft remnants on the floor and accepted the train halves. After examining the compartment, he reassembled the pieces, studying how they worked. With the toy nestled on his palm, the curled tip of his pinkie holding it in place, he examined the features from different angles in the style of a shrewd judge at a science fair, and a glimmer entered his eyes, the lifting of a fog.

He seemed to be wrestling with how to say thank you when a shout sliced through the din.

"Fire!"

I snapped toward the voice. In the doorway of the nearby vestibule, a man was waving his arms. He wore his coat collar high and hat pulled low. "There's a fire!" he hollered, and someone shrieked in response.

Startled, I watched the fellow race out. Fear gripped faces around me, marking those who understood him. Others puzzled over the language they didn't speak.

I strained for a whiff of smoke. Where was the danger? The kitchen, the café?

Warnings spread in scores of languages, overtaking the event hall, stopping the music. Folks in the balcony leaned out from between columns for a look. On the main floor, parents were swooping up their children and rushing into the man's wake. The narrow staircase past the vestibule would lead straight down to the street. Down to Papa.

I caught Arie's eyes mirroring my panic a second before a throng of people shoved past, dividing us and pushing me into a wall. Beyond the blur of movement, Big Vera fluttered her hands from the stage, either urging calm or reinforcing the alert. Adults climbed on chairs in a furious search, scanning faces, calling out names.

All at once, I was traveling without will, swept off in a flood of bodies. My feet scrambled to keep up on a floor I couldn't see, could scarcely touch. The mob pressed in, enclosing me head to toe, shortening my breaths.

"Papa...help..." I wheezed out, unthinking and desperate.

We crossed the threshold of the vestibule, where something seized my collar. It was a hand reaching through a web of arms. Arie's. I latched onto his grip, a lifeline, as we were carried toward the stairwell. Like a log at a waterfall's edge, I braced for a plunge.

The drop was indeed a fluid slope, the steps wobbly and slippery and moving. But how? I sought traction over dips and bumps. A glimpse revealed fabric and hair. People—we were walking on people! They must have stumbled on the way down. Unseen hands were pulling at the bottom of my coat, my dress. Terror whisked through me. Bile rose to my throat.

There was pounding at the base of the stairs. Strangers' cries collided with bellows: "Open the doors! God, please, open the doors!" Foreign words shrieked past my ears. No more than a yard away, a baby wailed, hovering above the crush. A woman with bright-yellow sleeves was holding the red-faced infant high overhead.

Suddenly I was hurled onto my side. Shoe heels stepped on my hip and ribs and neck. I screamed from the pain, protecting my head as much as I could without surrendering Arie's grasp. I had to hang on—it was my only coherent thought. Then a weight collapsed on me. It felt like sandbags, uneven and stifling. Fallen bodies. They wriggled and struggled, darkening my vision. My lungs battled for air, shallow bursts in and out.

The stairwell was a grave. We were being buried alive. I screamed again.

Pressure cinched my hand, a sharp squeeze. "Don't yell." The directive was Arie's. Slivers of light through tangled limbs shifted across his face, his frightened gaze locked on mine. "Breathe. Just breathe," he urged, as if commanding us both.

Calm. We needed to be calm.

I attempted to nod, constrained by the snarl of arms and legs. The encompassing heat intensified. I heard nails scraping walls, clawing to escape. The weight upon me grew. More whimpers below. More bodies above, binding me from all movement—except for my heart. It thundered in my chest, unyielding as a fist, while I fought to level my breaths.

Inhale, two-three-four. Exhale, two-three-four.

Through the sounds of gasping and howling and crying, chords from a piano faintly played. Not imagined but real. The girl onstage— how could she not know what was happening?

Plinking notes ricocheted in my head with snapshots of colors. I blinked hard, and the kaleidoscope narrowed to floating specks, like dots left from staring at the sun. Like snowflakes drifting at night.

My mittens? What happened to my mittens?

Inhale, two-three-four. Exhale, two-three-four. The bodies around us were waves, fluctuating, deepening. The tide threatened to drown us all. My fingers quaked around Arie's. I found his eyes once again and recalled what brought us to this.

A fire. At any moment, smoke and flames were sure to come. My solitary comfort: I wasn't alone.

As the minutes stretched and thinned, the sea eerily quieted. Gales of the storm were passing, at least in my mind. Moans were dwindling and screams muffling. Still the infant bawled. It paused only to choke on tears, and I lost myself in the rhythm. *Waaaaaail, sputter, sputter. Waaaaaail, sputter, sputter.* I could taste the tang of sweat, smell the stench of despair.

Finally, from somewhere above, came a deep shout: "Hold on, everyone! We're getting you out!"

Arie pumped my hand, a signal of hope. *We're going to be okay.* The assurance looped within me, round and round, as rescuers peeled away the layers of lifeless debris from a senseless squall.

Quite literally and horridly senseless.

For as we'd all learn in the hours and days to follow, there was more than one way to exit the building.

More maddening yet, there had never been a fire.

CHAPTER 9

Clearing the stairwell took close to two hours. This was the account I later heard. A genuine surprise, as I would have estimated double. I suppose when you're on the brink of being smothered, trapped by a hundred bodies stacked the height of a grown man, your sense of time can expand in remarkable ways.

With the fire hall but a block away, volunteer firemen had raced over to help. To pull me free, one began prying my fingers from Arie's. The fireman's coaxing wasn't enough. I let go only when Arie told me to do so. In the span of an afternoon, he'd become my singular source of reason.

Carried back into the main hall, I was set on a chair. The rows were disheveled, random portions toppled. In the middle of what had been an aisle stood a girl's buckled shoe. Perfectly upright, polished to a shine. As if waiting for a salesman to offer it for a fit.

Did the girl walk home with one foot bare?

"Sweetheart, is any of your family here?" a woman asked, dimly to my ears.

Papa, I remembered. *He's just downstairs*. I meant to relay this but couldn't be sure what came out. My observations had gained a hazy distance. I was told to stay put. I think.

Motionless figures were being laid out in the room. Small ones on tables, large ones on the floor. Some by the tree. Rescuers worked tirelessly at reviving many. A fortunate few prevailed.

Across the aisle from me, Arie too had been guided to a seat. An aproned helper was attending to a wound on his arm.

The baby was still crying, impressively, though the sound had turned hoarse. An older woman was holding the child, patting its back, shushing it with gentle words. Tears cracked her voice. At her feet, a limp form in a yellow dress stared at the ceiling. If not for the blankness of her gaze, I might have looked up to discover which sight had so intrigued her. Perhaps her own soul, ascending, untethered.

A priest appeared to affirm this by kneeling to lower her eyelids. It was Father Lawrence, with his silvering hair and gentle paunch. Bible in hand, he prayed over the woman, touting her final act on this earth as saving her child.

I noticed a baby buggy then, vacant in the corner. Did it belong to the same mother? A teacher once told me that instruments, violins in particular, forever carry with them a piece of their owners, that musicians imprint themselves in grains of the wood, store their tales in the strings.

If only infant carriages held similar power, a mother's love might be felt in the grooves of the handle, her voice heard in the rattle of the wheels.

I was imagining this when a worried little boy passed by. A lady was helping him hunt for his parents, weaving him through the shocked and grieving crowd—a grieving that took on various forms. Some came in silent weeping, others in anguished sobs. Big Vera openly raged.

She cursed at the deputies who dared enter the hall, most of them nonstriking miners. It was no secret that pro-management forces made for a ruthless enemy. She accused the men of having blocked the exit at the base of the stairs, even of plotting the false alarm. A heinous prank, or worse.

Father Lawrence tried to calm and restrain her. But she pummeled his arms and blasted him for initially preaching against the strike. When the deputies threatened to lock her in the courthouse, her tirade soared until they forcibly escorted her out.

A couple auxiliary members huddling by my row spoke with sympathy of Big Vera and her evident sense of guilt. The idea of the party, they said, had been hers.

All the while, people were still scouring and calling for family, searches that led to surveying the dead. There were wails of sorrow or bursts of relief depending on the find.

A thought arose in me: Was it possible Papa returned to fetch me earlier? Maybe he too was pulled down the stairs. He might still be in the stairwell...

"*Živ si!*" A portly woman rushed over. Beaming, she bent down to my level. "Mirta! Mirta! *Živ si!*" She took my cheeks in her roughened hands, jarring me fully back into myself.

Then a twenty-something fellow arrived and touched her shoulder. "*Ne, Mama. Nije ti kći.*"

She shook her head, resolute, and angled my face toward him as if to prove her assertion.

He didn't bother to look. "*Tamo leži* Mirta." He gestured gravely toward one of the tables, where a dozen or more children lay in their Sunday best. Round, sweet faces with nary a mark, small hands resting at their sides, eyes closed so peacefully they could have been asleep.

"*Ne, ne!*" she argued, holding my face firmer. The man pulled her hands to his suited chest. He repeated himself emphatically, and her expression contorted. Despite her reluctance, he ushered her away, his arm a protective shawl.

She wasn't ready for the truth.

"Fenna..."

The name floated above the collective crying, past the muddled voices. I turned to trace the caller, seeing more strangers, fearing I'd misheard.

"Fenna!" Papa was threading through the crowd. "*Fenna!*"

"Papa?" My voice was strange in my ears. Coarse as sandpaper, it appeared to soften his hard features. I scrambled to stand on legs that suddenly trembled. The instant he reached me, I crumpled into his arms and my tears poured. The smell of pipe smoke on his coat, even the alcohol on his breath, was as comforting as a winter quilt.

"It is okay, *schatje*. It is okay." The endearment, sounding wispily like *shaht-cha*, named me his little treasure. His full, dark beard felt scratchy on my forehead, but I only clung tighter. He patted my back tenderly, a rare act of physical affection.

From years spent drilling underground, Papa was an ashen boulder of a man. He was the sort gossipy ladies whispered about. *On account of his being a widower,* they'd say of his draw to the bottle, his aloof demeanor.

To me, he was a quiet yet kind provider. And though we didn't constitute a "real family" in the traditional sense, it was all I ever knew.

He gently broke away when a woman approached. She informed him that drivers outside were taking survivors to be checked over at a local hospital. Only then did I note a soreness in my muscles, an ache in my joints. My fingers were tired and stiffening, as if having scaled a rope to the sky. Arie must have felt just as worn.

I glanced over to gauge his condition, but he had vanished.

"We go now," Papa said to me.

At the memory of the exit, a sense of panic resurged. "But I can't... I won't... The stairs—"

"*Maak je geen zorgen,*" he assured me in Dutch, saying not to worry, that we'd leave the way he came in.

Relaxing a little, I hiccuped a sigh. Then I clutched his arm and followed him to a fire escape on the side of the building, where we joined others in line for the ladder.

I should have realized the stairwell wasn't an option, no doubt still blocked by those inside. At the thought of the final layers being exhumed, I recalled Arie's toy plane, lying on the floor, crushed.

How quickly something so cherished and whole could be damaged beyond repair.

CHAPTER 10

On the morning of the funerals, snow blanketed the town. The fresh layer of powdery flakes normally encouraged laughter and frolicking, snowball battles and snow-fort building. Not on that day. Instead, the colorless landscape served as mere contrast to supporters in black, flanking the road for a full two miles.

They had come from neighboring counties, states even, to pay their respects. Awaiting the procession, the thick lines of mourners stretched to a cemetery just past Eden Springs, on land not owned by the mine.

Papa and I stood on the road's edge, a quarter mile or so down. When we'd arrived for the services, the churches were overflowing. I was glad for it, having dreaded the promise of open caskets. I had seen enough death to haunt me.

Finally bells tolled from the steeples. Bundled in my coat, green mittens, and winter stockings, my body went rigid from more than the cold. With the services over, fleets of hearses would merge on the main road and roll this way.

Faces all around me were creased with sadness, if underpinned by anger. The propaganda war between company-leaning papers and pro-labor bulletins, trading blame and claims of exploitation, had further ratcheted tensions. Even here on this day, hushed word spread that the man who yelled "fire" was a strikebreaker whose Citizens' Alliance pin, as spotted on his lapel, proved his malice.

The group's members, after all, were seen as anti-union thugs. Same went for local lawmen, allegedly prompting the sheriff to have secreted the murderer out of Michigan. Thus, charity from any of their pockets wasn't exactly welcomed.

We no want your blood money, I'd recently overheard a mother seethe. At her apartment door, down the hall from mine and Papa's, a suited Alliance leader looked flustered with envelope in hand. *We bury our own,* she'd told the man and slammed the door.

Two days after Christmas, the families were doing precisely as she claimed. Flatbed motorcars and horse-drawn carts served as their hearses. Crunching past me in the snow, each held long, black caskets, fifteen for the adults who'd perished. Many had been kin. A few had been married.

Escorting them on foot, surviving relatives used handkerchiefs to wipe streams of tears. They clutched rosaries for strength, photos for meaning. Others gripped their chests, as if to keep what remained of their hearts from crumbling.

Past the observers across the road, a local woman caught my eye. She stood back a bit with her young daughter held tight to her chest and a guilty gaze fixed on the ground, a testament to the rumors. People said that after the stampede, in a frenzy of despair, the mother carried a deceased child believed to be hers all the way home, where she found her youngster alive and well, having snuck out of the party early.

What relief the woman must have felt, only to be struck by the gravity of her error. The trek back to the assembly hall had to have been unbearable as she delivered that lifeless child to a frantic-yet-hopeful mother, shattering another's world.

Suddenly glimpsing the parade to come, I clung to Papa's arm.

Traveling in clusters, pallbearers carried pure-white caskets low at their sides. The dimensions of each befitted a child, the weight miniscule compared to the burden.

I squeezed my eyes shut, but briefly. Darkness brought the memory of heels trampling my body while curled on my side, defenseless as a newborn. The position, a nurse surmised, had ironically helped. For it kept my mouth uncovered and lungs inflated, as did my location somewhat high in the pile. My breathing too had likely saved me, calmly hoarding air versus squandering it in screams.

Whatever the case, I was out here. And they were in there.

Every county in the region had supplied what funerary boxes they could. No solitary town could have been prepared for seventy-three concurrent deaths, the majority of them kids.

Fifty-eight to be precise.

The enormity of the number had been hard to comprehend until that moment, as one small casket after another and another and another crept down the road. Gasps and soft cries seeped through the crowd. Mothers and grandmothers treaded in pairs, arms hooked to sustain the interminable walk.

Dozens of caskets had just gone by when, a few feet away, a pallbearer of mountainous build stumbled onto his knees. The rest of the carriers scrambled to keep the casket from hitting the ground. Immediately the man tried to stand but faltered, like a marionette gone limp from slackened strings. Or, in this case, a father who had lost all three of his children.

I'd seen him outside the assembly hall while Papa searched for a driver to the hospital. Bodies that had been laid out on the sidewalk were being carried across the street; the local theater had become a temporary morgue. But this man had pled for them to stop, to not take his son, his daughters. A swarm of onlookers had watched as he stroked his children's faces, choking on his tears, broken.

Papa, now relinquishing my hold, moved to the casket. Wordlessly he grasped the abandoned handle and leveled the case. Another pallbearer gave a nod and the group continued on, leaving the grief-racked father to the supporting arms of his wife.

I might have stayed put for etiquette's sake, but on that day, I refused to be left behind. Chin lowered, I trailed the group while avoiding the expanse of eyes. Among the tens of thousands of attendees were hundreds of iron miners who'd arrived by train. They had come as protectors should any trouble arise from pro-management brutes.

As I ambled through the center of it all, vulnerable again, I focused on my breaths, misty puffs of white; on my nose, chilled from frost; on my bruises, throbbing with every step. A backward glance affirmed that the scores of people lining the road had melded into a herd that tacked onto the procession.

In the cemetery awaited the rectangular communal graves. Two long ones for the Protestants, three slightly smaller for the Catholics. All had been dug by miners, a team of a hundred, I'd heard. They were strong men for certain, skilled at hammering through rock, but still. How many hours must that have taken? How many hands wrecked and backs strained to move that frozen dirt?

The ponderings slipped away as I followed Papa, still pallbearing, over to the Catholic trench. One by one, caskets were passed down into the earth to be aligned and neatly spaced. A choir in the background sang "Nearer, My God, to Thee." Somberness hovered like the thickest of smoke as the congregation amassed, the white ground eclipsed by the color of grief.

The day ahead wouldn't be short.

Upon placement of the tenth casket, I noted a feeling of being watched. I twisted to scan the area and traced the gaze to the Protestant side. Like others who'd climbed the trees to view the ceremonies, Arie was perched on a branch, but off on his own. Peering from under his cap, his eyes held mine for only an instant before shifting away.

No surprise.

Since our time at the event hall, we had seen each other around yet always with our parents near. Aside from subtle looks, we'd reverted to our usual distance. Any closer might mean talking. And what ever would we say? Revel over how fortunate we were when so many, literally around us, weren't?

Among the children in the stairwell, just two others survived, making us subjects of whispers and awe. Of bitter jealousy for some. To those like Father Lawrence: divine inspiration.

He soon paid a call to each of our homes, the Protestants included, to offer comfort. When he visited mine, he contended that the Lord had a reason for sparing my life, that it was up to me to uncover that purpose.

What I didn't have the heart to confess—to him or anyone else, back then and to this day—was that, in the deepest parts of my being, my survival didn't seem a product of God's will.

It felt lucky at best.

At worst, a mistake.

CHAPTER 11

Standing before the trench, I noted the jagged silence, a break in the eulogies. My attention had drifted. I surveyed the caskets below. All had been placed in the ground. Grouped by families, their black and white cases resembled piano keys in a curious order.

I glanced up and found myself alone. Attendees had receded as if fearing I was contagious, their gazes set in my direction, waiting. Alarm and bewilderment whirled my thoughts. What did they want? Had I forgotten? Where was my father?

"Papa…" I called out, a strangled voice, searching.

Then I saw it.

The crowd's withdrawal exposed a solitary white casket. Its lid lay askew, revealing the emptiness of the box—save for two etched words inside. Wary though anxious to make them out, I trudged closer. The rough letters looked carved by fingernails, a name darkened by blood.

FENNA VOS

The casket was mine.

I jolted and felt something binding my legs. Panting, scrambling, I worked to break free—

It was a blanket and quilt. Over my mattress. On the floor.

I shot upright, heart thrashing and lungs pumping. A half-moon cast muted light through the window and over the main room of the apartment, my home. Shedding the dream, I sought the familiar: the swooped line of laundry and a washtub for a sink, the cast-iron skillet amid a shelf of scant food, the square supper table, two wobbly chairs.

Beneath my flannel nightgown, sweat trickled down my sides.

Inhale, two-three-four. Exhale, two...three...four.

I lay back down. My pillow, damp from perspiration, felt cool despite the heated potbelly stove within reach.

Nine days had passed since the stairwell rush, and each night left me the same: awakened by terror, drenched in fear. Sometimes I was trapped in a casket, shoveled dirt drumming the lid as I futilely clawed and screamed. Other times I was back on those steps, either submerged in bodies—occasionally just limbs—or clambering on my own, unable to find a door as the space shrank around me.

As usual, it would take time to fall back asleep. Likely hours, if at all.

You're home, I insisted. *You're safe.*

Still, nighttime had become an enemy, as much for its smothering darkness as its amplification of sounds. There were noises from tenants through wafer-thin walls; creaks from the building, like aging bones; hail and icy snowflakes whipping at the window. I'd listen to them all while lying in the main room, where I had dragged my mattress into a corner to sleep.

In winters past, I'd moved here merely for the stove's warmth. But as of late, the small bedroom I shared with Papa felt too confined with a lone door for escape. A door under which now emitted a flicker, along with gravelly snoring.

Papa was back from the café—a grand relief! I'd come to dread his absence, after dusk most of all. *You are big girl,* he'd reminded me when I asked him to stay. He wasn't wrong.

I'd always been one to busy myself and wander about on my own. Papa claimed it ran in our blood. *Vos* meaning *fox,* my surname said I was fated to be inquisitive and friendly yet sly and elusive, a solitary creature not meant for a pack. And like the Arctic fox, whose fur changes color with the seasons, I was adept at fading into the background.

In town, I would read borrowed books or observe passersby, fascinated by the stories they divulged without even knowing. At parks or the shore or places like Torch Lake, existing in my own bubble, I'd create rubbings of leaves, petals, and shells, capturing the shapes and veins that made them unique.

These days, I preferred the safe predictability of home, ideally sharing Papa's company, like now.

His bedside candle, I thought. If aware, he'd want it snuffed out.

Clutching onto the excuse, I stood and cocooned myself in my quilt. Double layers of threadbare socks would fend off some of the cold but not all. On tiptoes, I padded across the worn floorboards, as Papa hated to be woken abruptly.

"Papa? *Bent u wakker?*" I whispered at his door, asking if he was awake. He tended to respond better to Dutch when partially asleep. Receiving no answer, I entered to find him sprawled over his covers, still dressed for the day with even his chook, what the locals called a knit cap. His presence was a veritable comfort.

Past my bare metal bed frame, atop our shared night table sat the candle. It had been reduced to a puddle of wax, but its flame's orange glow smoothed Papa's face, erasing years and hardships in a way that made me both happy and sad.

Of course, the scent of his pipe smoke lingered. As did liquor fumes out of his pores from another late-night visit to the café. There, strikers' talks had reportedly shifted to demands for an investigation into the stampede. Called a "tragedy" by some, a "massacre" by others.

Given Papa's manner since the funerals—his quiet turning morose, his drinking turned heavier and daily—I'd say he viewed the event as both. Perhaps nearly losing me had shaken his core. That or the onslaught of deaths had revived despair over the wife he'd lost.

Either way, I knew not to ask. Probes about my mother rarely produced answers, most cut short by a dimming in his eyes and the excuse of a pressing chore.

I remember at age six mulling how to broach the subject of his choosing another wife. At the time, we still lived in Little Chute, a Dutch-Catholic community in eastern Wisconsin; it was where my newlywed parents had settled after my mother swayed her groom into the overseas adventure, lured by rumors of a prosperous new world— and one particular river. Since the village sits along the Fox River, it promised a fairy-tale ending, before life there took a turn.

In truth, when I'd finally plied Papa with the question, I was hankering for him to propose to a certain woman in our boarding-house. For years after my mother's passing, Miss Roosa assisted with my care and cooked our meals, eventually allowing me to help. She was kind and commonly pretty, if a smidge bothersome with lessons in posture and speech, both in Dutch and English, and often smelled of the vanilla she added to her *boterkoek*. Like her bubbly giggles, the sweet, buttery cake even pried smiles out of Papa. I was sure I'd soon be calling her "*Moeder*" and we'd become a real family, maybe with a set of siblings—fun ones, not the annoying sort.

But Papa had replied with a stern shake of his head: *For man and woman, there is only one love in life.*

Within weeks of my suggesting remarriage, Papa quit his factory job and relocated us to Eden Springs. I didn't realize my question had instigated the winter move; being a child, I was concerned solely with the strangeness of a place that wasn't our home. As I'd heard it, the dreary peninsula on Lake Superior was shaped like a demon's thumb, and the closest thing to Dutch folks in Houghton County were mostly Belgians, hence not our kind.

In short, every element struck me as foreign. It was the very reason Papa had selected the area, I eventually came to understand. For a truly fresh start, a person had to move on. Wade into the unknown. And if that didn't work, one could drown out the past.

Or try.

Careful not to rouse him from sleep, I lifted the unlidded flask from his callused hand and went to set the container down. Its swishing sound teased my curiosity.

I took a sniff. Potent and piney with a touch of lemon. The home-brewed gin was known as a close substitute for genever from the old country. What I learned right then was it smelled more appealing straight out of the flask than stale on a drinker's breath.

Papa was a levelheaded man. He must have had good reason for ignoring the homilies that warned against indulgence, to say nothing of his skirting the law.

His snores and weighted breaths plodded on.

He did say I was a big girl…

Tempted, turning away, I raised the flask to my lips. What was intended as a sip flowed out a gulp. It blazed down my throat and lit a fire in my chest. I dropped my quilt, suppressing an eruption of coughs.

Papa twitched and shifted his legs, eyes still closed.

Palm over my mouth, I put the flask on the table and extinguished the candle with a flurry of hand flaps. Darkness set my pulse to a gallop.

Hastening back toward the moonlight of the main room, I snatched my quilt and closed the door behind me. I muffled my release of coughs while retreating to my mattress. Gradually the flames inside me tapered to a smoldering warmth. And at last I understood:

Papa didn't drink to drown his memories; he drank to burn them away.

Thankfully, soon after, I found other ways to forget.

CHAPTER 12

The very next night, I was trapped in a casket, struggling to escape, when something grabbed my arm. I belted out a shriek as the grip shook my body, shook it again, until yanking me free of the box and out of the dream.

Or was I still in it? It was hard for me to know, balled up on my side, quaking with Arie's eyes locked on mine. Were we back in the stairwell, crammed in the pile?

"Hey, it's okay," he whispered. "Just a nightmare."

In a lather, I assessed my surroundings. The stove and clothesline. The tables and chairs. Moonlight through the window. My home... where Arie was kneeling at my mattress.

Startled anew, I sat up and pulled away. "Why...why are you—"

"I was passing in the hall," he volunteered, my question obvious. "Tried knocking when I heard you yell. But didn't want to wake the whole floor."

At his reference to the hour, I recalled my nightclothes. They were modest in flannel, though nightclothes all the same. I cinched my quilt up to my neck and swallowed. The slight soreness of my throat suggested he had saved *me* from waking the whole floor—excluding Papa, that is, whose typical liquored snoring drifted from the bedroom.

I mumbled my thanks, and Arie nodded, not looking at me.

Then he rose. "See you around, I guess." With those words, his husky tone encouraged a sense of calm. It was the same voice that through the din of the stairwell had kept me quiet and breathing. Alive.

He went to leave, yet within a few steps, I blurted out, "Wait."

As he turned, it dawned on me that I had no inkling of what to say. All I knew was I didn't want him to go.

"It was awfully late," I ventured, "for you to be up."

He hedged, fidgeting with the hem of his coat sleeve. "Yeah," he said.

That was when I noted his clothes. I would have presumed he'd made a quick trip to the outhouse if not for his hat and fully buttoned coat, his daytime trousers and laced-up boots. Shiny white specks on his shoulders indicated a jaunt through drifting snowflakes.

"Were you out doing something?"

"Just...on a walk."

"A walk? It's the middle of the night." I didn't intend to sound doubtful. Nor challenging. I only meant: "Where did you go?"

He answered without meeting my eyes. "Around."

I never took him for a mischief-making kid, but he was being rather cagey.

"Were you out meeting someone?" As in maybe some *girl*.

He shook his head in a manner that seemed sincere, and a possibility came to me. "Trouble with sleep?"

He lifted a shoulder, a nonverbal yes.

The commonality surprised me, though honestly it shouldn't have.

"Fresh air helps," he murmured.

I peered beyond the window, taking in the wintry scene, and found perfect sense in it. "Must be sorta freeing," I mused, "under that big night sky. And with all that bright snow, stretched out every which way."

When I looked back at Arie, he regarded me with an eased expression. But then he resumed picking at his sleeve, making his departure seem imminent.

"You...wanna stay a minute? We don't have to talk or anything. I just figure since we're both awake."

He contemplated for a brief, worrisome moment. At his nod, I tendered a smile.

Beside the mattress, he sat with his back against the wall. I resettled on my pillow and gazed toward the ceiling. For a time, we remained like that, absorbing the silence, the darkness. Breathing.

Oddly, nothing about it felt strange. Only…content.

Then a cry rang out and I flinched. A baby's wail. It grew from the apartment below, where the child and its mother had come to visit family. A brief stay, I prayed. For at the strained cries, again a vision flew back of an infant in the stairwell, propped up by its mother suffocating below.

Tears flooded my eyes. Desperate to block out the memories, to not feel alone, I reached across the mattress but caught myself. I started to pull back when Arie's gloved hand covered mine.

Once more, he made me feel safe.

Before long, the rhythm of my breathing matched the tempo of his. Slow and soothing, loosening my muscles from head to toe. Then my blinks lengthened and eyelids drooped. And somehow, as if by magic, it was instantly morning. The sun was breaking through the clouds and reflecting off the snow.

Arie had vanished, just as before, but not from my life.

Not yet.

———————

There were more nights to come when he would save me from the throes of a nightmare. Not hurrying away, he'd distract me by spinning fantastical tales. He'd whisper about brave knights and dragons or pirates pillaging on the high seas. In time, we'd trade stories of our lives and families. Like most immigrants, his parents' ancestral ties were essentially severed when they boarded the boat, ditto for mine. But what brought us to Eden Springs differed.

Skilled in machinery, his father had been recruited by an acquaintance to move from central Michigan to oversee the maintenance of mining equipment. Mr. Jansen's negative stance on unions made him especially appealing to management. Yet after working alongside the miners and encountering the conditions firsthand, he sympathized with their cause and supported the strike fully.

"Don't tell anyone though," Arie inserted. "About why they picked him, okay?" It was a reasonable request. He didn't want his father viewed as a planted informer, which very likely had been the company's intent.

All that mattered to me was where the man stood now.

"Not a soul," I promised.

Arie nodded easily; the extent of our trust went without saying. Then we returned to competing in jacks, embracing the extra challenge of quietly bouncing the ball. Even though, really, it would take more than that to wake Papa.

We enjoyed other pastimes too. On my drawing pad, we'd play the dots-and-boxes game, erasing the lines for additional rounds, as most pages were covered with my tracings and rubbings. After discovering he had learned standard Dutch at his old school—a delightful surprise—I persuaded him to improvise skits in my dialect. We'd pretend we were far off in the exotic cities of Holland. My preference was for the dramatic, his for the silly.

Other nights, if I were awake and heard him coming in from the cold, I would hurry to my front door and raise a hand to say good night, to which he'd respond in kind.

I volunteered once to join his walk, but sensing his reluctance, I withdrew the offer. He didn't need to expound. Those solitary outings were his own means of finding peace.

We told no one of our friendship. At school or elsewhere in passing, catching his eye would bring me hidden joy. Ours was a bond cultivated in secret—for the most part. A knowing wink from his sister, Thea, implied she suspected a crush. If she did, she'd graciously kept it from her parents. The "sinful influence" of my Catholicism on Arie's Protestant soul would have guaranteed their disapproval.

Papa, I suppose, might have been more lenient; it wasn't as if I'd been named traditionally after a saint, and his confessional visits were hardly regular. Still, Arie and I refrained from taking the risk, even to set Thea straight.

In hindsight, I'd say our private meetings, unlike so much in life, were prized as something within our control. They were a conduit for healing.

Just like the thoughtful gift he passed along.

Left beneath my pillow one day was a thick, pocket-size book with a well-worn cover. *Houdini's Big Little Book of Magic & Stunts.* As Arie later explained, upon seeing it discarded at the barbershop where he earned pennies to sweep up hair, he received permission to keep the publication, yet once he'd flipped through the pages, his gut told him it was meant for me.

When I opened the book, I was only vaguely aware of the late showman Harry Houdini. Chapter after chapter, through narrative and diagrams, were various methods behind his tricks, starting with sleights of hand involving coins, cups, and playing cards. Past the halfway point, the schemes progressed in complexity: slipping out of ropes and handcuffs, mailbags and barrels. His most secretive illusions would obviously be omitted, and yet...

The notion that a person could escape the inescapable was beyond inspiring. More than bewitching.

It was life altering in ways I never could have foreseen.

CHAPTER 13

Soon after the stampede, the miners' passions that had buoyed the strike largely deflated. Like a knife to a ship's sail, each loss sliced through the fortitude of the workers' demands. Come March, negotiations with management ended the impasse but left the families questioning the sacrifices made.

In short, the majority of requested benefits were refused, and equipment that would make half the positions obsolete was to be implemented at a daunting rate. Hundreds of miners moved away, seeking new jobs, clean slates. For those who stayed, including Arie's father and my own, wages and safety conditions improved only slightly.

Black Tuesday did anything but help. That fall, the stock-market crash shook cities like New York with the power of an earthquake. In Eden Springs, we endured the aftershocks—delayed, recurrent, and just as damaging.

Drops in copper sales shut down a slew of competitors. To prevent the same fate, C&H managers trimmed in phases, barring their personal billfolds no doubt. Papa and Mr. Jansen survived the workforce cuts, yet security belonged to no one.

Not that Arie and I discussed such things. For Papa often warned me, particularly when silencing my worries over the hazards of his job: *Be careful, schatje. Fear is giving power to the Devil.*

Besides, there was plenty else to speak about, Houdini's stunts most of all.

Through that summer and autumn, from multiple readings of the book, I mastered numerous sleights of hand. While my skills grew, the rate and intensity of my nightmares fell. Even around Christmas Eve.

With Arie's help, of course.

On that much-dreaded holiday, Papa spared me from the candle-light vigils at the graveyard, though not from attending evening mass. During the homily, Father Lawrence blessed the town's anniversary as a step toward rebirth and prayed about losses I yearned to forget.

Needed relief came later that night. With Papa snoring away in the bedroom, Arie sneaked over with a diversionary surprise: a ball of string for a trick. I grabbed my heavily dog-eared book and sat facing him on my mattress, which by then was a year-round fixture near the stove. Much like us.

"Okay, now," I whispered on our fifth attempt. "Put the string over my left hand again. No, wait—my other hand." The strings, crisscrossed and knotted around Arie's wrists and mine, made it impossible to separate us without severing a line unless—and herein lay the trick—we maneu-vered through specially formed loops. "We've got to be getting close."

Arie sighed, as if he knew better. Which he didn't.

I referred back to the splayed pages on my lap, illuminated by a lamp's flame, kerosene being more plentiful post-strike.

"It's all too tangled," he groaned. "I'm telling you, zero chance you're saving this one either."

That was the thing about Arie: while not cruel in his delivery, he never lied to spare my feelings. It was a trait I generally appreciated, though not always at the time.

After another look at the diagrams, which showed little resemblance to our mess, I huffed. I'd been determined not to need the knife again so had slid it over on the floor with the other discarded strings. A pile of my failures.

"Fine, then," I muttered. "We'll start over." I was struggling with our bindings, trying to create enough slack to reach the blade, when Arie's lips curved up.

"Don't laugh," I told him.

"I'm not."

"You're smiling."

"It's funny."

Frustration boosted by embarrassment, I'd have jumped to my feet right then and pointed him to the door if not for the snarled strings. "You're a lunkhead."

"Yeah? And you're a mule."

"Nincompoop."

"Bad magician."

I scrambled to one-up him before registering the jab. At his widening grin, punctuated by a lone dimple, I couldn't ward off my own smile and swiftly devolved into giggles.

Arie shushed me despite the glint in his eyes. Then we returned to the trick—as usual, finding a solution together while keeping the darkness at bay.

———————

Three Saturdays later, Papa and I spent the whole day on tasks and errands—*his* suggestion. My heightened dependency had receded long before, yet the outing sounded nice. We went to the bakery for a day-old loaf, to the company store for coal and other essentials, then to the cobbler shop to tackle his latest side job. When asked, I cheerily supplied the appropriate tools as he replaced rotting floorboards in the owner's apartment above the store. Papa was handy that way.

Once we finished, I wasn't surprised his service was paid for in trade; what I never expected was to be the sole beneficiary.

All the shoes I ever owned had come faded and patched, and my one pair at the time required shoving my feet in to make them fit and a cardboard liner to cover a hole.

"*Schatje,*" Papa said to me, "for your birthday. You liking these, they are yours." He nodded to the silver-haired cobbler, who pridefully presented a pair of black boots.

Just the previous Wednesday, Papa had gifted me with a brand-new drawing pad for Christmas, ideal for sketching tricks. Plus, three weeks before that, in the Dutch tradition of the *Sinterklaas* holiday, I'd found in my shoe a milk-chocolate bar, which I was still savoring in nibbles. I hadn't anticipated a thing for my birthday, still two days away, and definitely nothing like these, with pristine and polished leather, the laces absent a single fray.

They were beautiful.

And perfect.

And nobody's but mine.

I squealed and threw my arms around Papa, nearly knocking him over. He laughed with a heartiness I'd never heard, a reaction so foreign to his body that he rattled like a rusty engine sputtering back to life. To me, of course, the sound was the loveliest in the world. Woefully, it stopped too soon, snuffed out by one of his coughing fits. Standard fair for underground dredgers.

On the lengthy walk home through patches of snow that lightened the night, my pinkie toes and heels combatted the stiffness of the leather. For the last fifty yards, my feet stayed curled to minimize the blisters. Nevertheless, those boots weren't coming off. Even in my worn overalls, I felt far too fancy to go shoeless before morning. Or at least until I showed them off to Arie.

I was envisioning doing just that while I entered our apartment and noticed an object on my pillow. A small wooden train...the one from the party.

I'd assumed it had been lost to the stampede, crushed like Arie's plane and so much more.

Papa had peeled off for the outhouse but could return any minute. I hurried to pick up the train, marveling that Arie had managed to save it. But why give it back, and without explanation?

Then I recalled the hidden compartment. On a hunch, I detached the cab and, to my sheer delight, pulled out a tiny square of folded brown paper. I set aside the toy, beaming over its use as a carrier pigeon of sorts.

Vigilant before reading, I scurried to the door and listened for Papa's heavy footfalls. Hearing none, I unfurled the note.

> My pop got a factory job in Amesboro.
> Starts Monday so we're moving today.
> I'm sorry, Fenna. I'll miss you.
> Will write when I can.
>   −A

My throat tightened as I reread the words.

Amesboro…moving today…will write.

Arie was leaving—but no. He couldn't!

I tore across the room and into the hall. At his family's door, I knocked. Knocked again harder. I called for him, not caring who knew.

Barging inside, I gasped. The main room was empty, just sparse furniture left askew, paper scraps littering the floor. I didn't have to inspect the bedrooms to know they looked the same.

My closest friend, my only friend, was gone.

The realities of what that meant pummeled me all at once.

No more talking or laughing or doing magic together. No more covert smiles or waves in passing. No more simply knowing he was there.

I wrapped myself with my arms, the note still in hand. Tears streamed as I stood there, chest gone hollow, gutted. Ragged words rode my quiet sobs: "Life couldn't ever be worse, not ever…"

Surely dramatic by some standards, but not at that age. Not with everything considered.

Nonetheless, I should have known better.

Voicing my fears might have risked empowering the Devil; in this case, it seemed I'd offered him a dare.

Ten days later, he took it.

CHAPTER 14

Miners died all the time. I'd long understood this. Every shift was a gamble with fickle explosives, slippery rocks, and rickety shafts. Papa survived each of those and more, only to have his coughs prove symptoms of pneumonia. Quick as a blink, he too was stolen from my life, due to what started as a measly cold.

His funeral was simple. No fancy procession or choir or hordes of ironworkers from other towns. Just a few local miners and Father Lawrence, at least according to my memory. For me, it all passed in an emotionless blur, same as my subsequent trip to Grand Rapids.

Obeying the chaperone from the Children's Aid Society, I clutched my valise and followed her on and off buses and a train. I sat where instructed, rose when told, unwrapped the sandwich she had packed.

"Food will keep you strong, my dear," she said, overly chipper in her navy dress suit, while I forced down pastrami on rye. "Help to shake off your blues."

Yet there was no mood to shake off. I was numb. If not, I would have crumpled into a blubbering heap or exploded in rage over the unfairness of it all. Rather, I trailed my escort into a charmless city building, all concrete, windows, and brick. An orphanage for girls.

When she patted my shoulder to bid goodbye, I remained lost within myself, stuck in a well. Even if I'd wanted to climb out, I wouldn't have known how. In this respect, I wasn't alone. Of the hundred or so girls in a home meant for two-thirds that, with ages running the gamut, many bore an insipid air. Particularly among those as old as me.

No longer babies or toddlers even, we weren't considered malleable enough to most couples who strolled through on Saturdays as if perusing a gallery. We were sculptures already formed by some blundering artist's hand. Our flaws and cracks, if not yet evident, were bound to surface over time. Nevertheless, every Friday evening, we were lined up at the washtubs, where we cowered and shivered, dripping with shame. Swift and systematic, the staff ladies scrubbed our thin bodies raw, checked heads for lice, rinsed hair with squirts of lemon. The responsibility was ours to keep the sting from our eyes.

The orphanage director, to her credit, persisted with this rigamarole to push even her second-rate goods. We were in excessive supply thanks to the Depression; meanwhile demand for all ages slumped. This presumably had been the impetus for Mrs. Atwood's inventive showcase—that or she'd been inspired by a livestock exhibition, where swine were never trotted out in mud and grub.

Likewise, while our shabbier weekday wear was being washed, we were lent pastel ribbons for our hair and pressed white dresses that mostly fit. In the playroom, prospective parents observed our "natural" interactions as Mrs. Atwood presented us with a flourish, unimpeded by her crooked bottom teeth and powdered mustache. She had the towering height of Big Vera and smelled of mothballs. Proudly she would cite our housekeeping lessons in sewing, cooking, and laundering. It was clear some visitors came chiefly for such perks, others for free built-in nannies.

Even in my haze, I was aware enough to dodge attention from those seeking the latter. The thought was unfathomable, my being responsible for the lives of tots, much less of infants, who were fragile as fine china and prone to wails of desperation that never failed to prod my angst.

Mrs. Atwood would then segue into the tragedies that had landed us here. Riveted couples would listen and nod, though most managed to avoid our eyes. Of the women who dared look, many would touch a gloved hand to their chests, gripped by sympathy. But inevitable nudging by sensible husbands—*Darling, we came to see the babies, remember?*—would lure the wives to the nursery on the third floor, never to return.

As I lay awake at night, packed in a small room of ten occupied cots, my mind replayed scenes of the like. Not out of disappointment or yearning. I was merely blockading my memories from just two months ago, when by this hour I'd have been snuggled in my quilt...on my own bed...in my own home—

Stop it, you ninny. Just stop!

I pinched my upper arm hard, the inside fleshy part, summoning a pain I could handle. The spot was already tender and bruised, as I often did this to keep from dozing off. Limiting sleep was key.

Although my nightmares remained under relative control, the dreams I'd come to dread most were the good ones: reminders of the normalcy I'd lost, of the life and family I would never have. Because waking from those visions meant reliving once more my newfound devastation.

By this reasoning, I didn't dare peek at the sole photograph I owned. Though stored in my travel bag under my cot, the image haunted me regardless. I could see Papa seated dapperly in a suit and hat, beard neatly trimmed, and me standing beside him, prim as a peacock in my one fancy dress. No smiles of course, as this was a proper studio sitting, a magnificent trade for Papa's handiwork. The palm-size portrait with scalloped border was altogether stately, the lighting so crisp you'd think you could step right in—now a torturous suggestion I didn't need.

And so I listened: to the late-March wind, rattling the tall window above my cot; the rippling of girls' exhales; the soughing of restless limbs. Here, in the smallest bedroom on the second floor, the sounds helped mute cries from the nursery. They also fought the slowing of my blinks. As did the light.

Across the high ceiling, shadows waltzed from a large lit candle. Set in mason jars, one was placed in every bedroom. The soft flames, ironically, were intended to aid our sleep, banishing monsters of the dark, in turn allowing staff down the hall to rest. The solution worked well for my roommates, minus the curly-haired redhead in the corner who wept regularly into her pillow.

And apparently one other girl.

"Yoo-hoo," a voice whispered. "Whatcha got there?"

In the cot next to mine lay Poppy, a pale snip who'd only recently aged out of a different room. Still, it took me a second to grasp that her question was for me. Having exuded no desire to socialize, I'd grown accustomed to being treated like a ghost.

"Is it a toy?" She was gawking at my hand, the wooden train in it, set on my scratchy woolen blanket.

I'd made a habit of absently rolling my thumb over the wheels, as if rubbing luck out of a rabbit's foot. I had all but forgotten it was there.

"Can I see?" She held out her hand. Such hope danced in her big doe eyes, dark as her pixie hair, I found myself passing the train her way.

She propped on her stomach and ran her fingers over the smoke-stack, then the undercarriage and driver's cab.

"That part there," I said, raspy from lack of use, "it can hide things."

"Jeepers, really?" She studied it closer. "How?"

"Just pull on the chimney. The cab comes loose."

Honest to goodness, I don't know why I divulged anything. A means to keep awake, I guess. Reprieve from the monotony.

She gasped lightly at the discovery, and a rustling followed. I recalled the stowed note from Arie an instant before she held it out.

"Will you...read it to me?"

Her need for the help was surprising. Rumor had it she'd been abandoned in an alley at age three—about five years ago, I'd gather—and lived in the orphanage ever since. With the strict schooling here, I'd have thought her well capable of reading.

As if expecting this, she said, "I'm real good with numbers—arithmetic always comes easy. But letters, they get all mixed up."

The old me would have been curious about why and how that looked. Now I just conceded by accepting the note. The girl waited, expectant.

But then I felt the creases made by Arie's hand, the wrinkles like Papa's fingers on mine, and something deep inside me stirred as if being drawn from hibernation. A misery that shouldn't be roused. I shoved the note under my pillow, weighted by my head.

She shrank back, seeming more wounded than disappointed.

It wasn't my intention to cause either. "Listen," I said. "I'll read you something else. During the day, when it's easier to see. Okay?"

She brightened again. "Like a book?"

"Sure."

"You know, there was a girl who used to read stories to some of us, but then she got too old to live here." A pause. "So you have some?"

"What?"

"Books." She laughed softly, as if I was silly not to be following.

My Houdini book was stored in my valise under my cot. It hadn't seen a speck of light since the morning I packed mindlessly, bringing essentials like my comb and clothes, leaving my drawing pad and all other amusements. Aside from the wooden train, which somehow I'd thought to grab.

"I do have *one*. But it's not the kind with a story."

She knit her brow. "What sorta book doesn't have a story?"

"A book on magic."

"Like...for spells?" She sounded worried.

"Just magicians' tricks. For putting on a show."

Her features eased, then promptly tightened with excitement. "Can you show me some? I've always wanted to see magic." She barely contained her whisper.

"Maybe... I don't know."

"How come?"

Because it was hard to care about such things anymore. "I haven't got my supplies."

"Oh. Well, what do you need? Tell me and I'll find a way to get 'em."

Her prattling should have worn on me. Somehow it didn't. Besides, we weren't sleeping anyway. "Have you got a penny? Or a marble? Something small."

She glanced around. "Ooh. I know." She tugged off a quarter-sized button from the neck of her nightgown and shrugged. "It was loose already."

I sat up and made space on my cot as Poppy crept over. Cross-legged, she set aside the train and delivered the wooden button that was just rough enough for a nice grip.

Her brows dipped in anticipation as I baited her gaze to follow the disk in a slow zigzag between us. I appeared to place it in my left hand, made a fist, and—*poof!*—palm splayed, the button was gone. Her mouth formed a small *o*, which tripled in size when the button reappeared in my right hand, and a squeak escaped her throat.

"Do it again," she urged in a hushed voice, and it dawned on me that she was my first real audience. To prevent my debut from being the shortest in history, I obliged by repeating the zigzag, though deviated slightly from the French drop to vanish the button from both hands. Upon my pulling it from her ear, she silent-clapped, only to plead for more.

Alternating my methods to throw her off—sleeving, palming, lapping—I made the button emerge from her hair, then chin, and out of thin air. My skills were rusty, but the low light was forgiving. When the button fell from her nose, she covered her mouth to contain her giggles. I was contemplating another variation when she asked, "Will you teach me? Please, please, will you?" She was effusive with hope, practically vibrating.

Giving away my secrets—granted, not *my* secrets exactly—wouldn't have been my first inclination. But feeling a tingling in my chest, a sense of thawing, I agreed.

CHAPTER 15

In a couple short weeks, I gained a devoted following. Admittedly, becoming a main attraction wasn't all that hard when it was the sole performance around.

The curly-haired redhead, named Agatha, was the first to tiptoe over to my cot and ask to watch with Poppy. By week's end, the only roommates not joining were a remarkably heavy sleeper and a nervous Nellie too afraid to break the rules—though not of craning her neck, evidently, to observe from her cot.

It wasn't long before braver girls sneaked in from down the hall, expanding my nightly audience if gradually. Attendees were selective in the friends they told, cautious of jeopardizing the show. Eleven gongs from the grandfather clock downstairs signaled my act was about to start.

Some tricks I'd perform on my own, others in conjunction with Poppy. A few I allowed her to present by herself—after ample rehearsal and my approval, of course. We practiced daily, even on Saturdays while spiffed up in the playroom. Our nighttime audience kept their distance, knowing better than to ruin the magic by peeking behind the curtain, virtual as it was.

On one particular Saturday, I walked through the string maneuver with Poppy until she mastered it. Around us, children were mostly hopscotching, stacking blocks, and drawing at low tables. With Mrs. Atwood giving her standard pitch to several couples, I was able to slip out on a mission. I needed supplies for additional tricks.

By the time I returned, armed with a clothespin, fork, and cup, my assistant had attracted a pair of volunteers for our act. A handsome man in a snappy suit and a rosy-cheeked woman in a lavender dress were seated on the floor, where Poppy was demonstrating how to break free of the string she'd looped around their wrists. The instant they succeeded, the couple burst into smiles, the woman calling her "cuter than a June bug." And from the traded warmth in all their eyes, no one could deny the three were meant to be a family.

It was every orphan's dream.

Including mine.

A dark emotion rose within me, a plume of jealousy, reminding me of all I had lost. Straightaway, I did my best to tamp it down. Poppy deserved this and more.

Not surprisingly, after the trio delighted in a lengthy lunch, I heard that Poppy was sent upstairs to pack. Her paperwork was being finalized.

I headed to our room, prepared to share in her glee, at least to try. What I found there left me staring.

On her cot, Poppy sat tearful though adamant, clutching a fistful of our string. "I am *not* going with them. They can't make me."

"But...why? What happened?"

She paused, shook her head.

I moved closer. "Did they say something to you? Something bad?"

Another no, without details.

Assessing people was one of my strengths. Wasn't it? The couple had seemed so nice. Maybe too nice. Poppy might have figured out they were phonies, or something else about them was off.

"I'm so sorry, Poppy. If I'd known, I would've found an excuse to pull you away. I thought you really liked them."

"Well, yes, but—" She huffed. "What about our show? You said you'd teach me a bunch more tricks. So you see? I can't go yet. Will you tell Mrs. Atwood? *Please*, will you?" The look in her eyes caused a pricking of moisture in my own, because she wasn't just asking; she was begging. It didn't matter that the director would never agree.

I realized then: for those who couldn't recall life outside a cage, being set free was a terrifying thing. The orphanage was far from ideal, but it was the only home Poppy knew.

She needed a nudge, one more powerful than words.

Before I could think better of it, I knelt to reach under my cot and fished through my travel bag. A gift meant to be passed to someone who needed it more.

My gut, like Arie's had, insisted on it.

I sat next to Poppy and handed over my book. *The* book. In it were plenty of tricks I'd yet to tackle, not to mention escapes, but they weren't presently my priority.

Mouth agape at me, she was asking, *Are you sure?*

I smiled. "It's yours."

She viewed the tattered cover as if it were a hallowed scroll. But after opening the book with string still in hand, she stopped. "I...can't read any of it though."

Oh, bother. I'd forgotten.

"Not yet," I said, "but you'll learn. In some fancy school, I'd bet. And with a teacher who'd even know how to help you see letters the right way." That was one skill she'd unlikely gain here, along with countless others. "In the meantime, the book's got loads of drawings to follow. And just think, as soon as you're settled, you can start your own show if you want."

I expected that final bit to cheer her, sufficient bait for taking the leap. Rather, she slumped and dropped her gaze. "I don't know if I'm ready."

My mind was scouring for points of persuasion when the dark pluming inside me returned, too strong to ignore, and the full source of my feelings registered. It wasn't so much jealousy as grief. I was about to lose Poppy, the one dear person I had left.

Unless...

We devised a plan.

Would that lovely couple be as eager to take home a child who burst into a tantrum? What if Poppy kicked and clawed, screamed and spat, flatly refusing to go? It just might be that easy. Then she and I could grow up here together, even continue as roommates. I could tell her stories of the outside world, nurture her like kin. We could be a family, the two of us, and never again be alone.

I verged on explaining, optimism growing, but then her eyes raised to mine. She was asking for encouragement, affirmation. The kind you rely on from an older sister.

My plan stalled in my throat, snared by my conscience. For I knew in my heart: in the same way she was clinging to that string, for selfish reasons, I'd be doing the same to her.

Poppy wouldn't be alone; she'd have her own family. And they were waiting for her downstairs. Stowing my own wants, I mustered an assured tone. "You're ready. I promise."

Because, in all truth, she was.

Her face became pensive. But then she gave an appreciative nod and wrapped me in a hug that she couldn't have known how much I needed.

Or maybe she did.

As decreed by Mrs. Atwood, Poppy's adoption was not only cause to celebrate but also to bolster each of us with hope. Not everyone saw it that way. A girl named Ingrid least of all.

A week before Poppy's departure, those same parents had first visited the orphanage and chatted pleasantly with Ingrid, a thirteen-year-old with a long single braid, light freckles, and a deceptive dose of charm. Whether or not the couple had returned specifically for *her* remained unknown. The fact she didn't leave with them was attributed to my calculated, devious string trick—and therefore me.

"Just you wait, ya dopey Dutch," she seethed into my ear the morning after Poppy left. During math lesson, we were in line for the blackboard. "You're gonna be sorry you ever came here."

I was tempted to say, *Aren't we all?* But I kept the retort to myself, thinking restraint would help, that if I didn't fight back, she'd quickly lose interest.

I was wrong.

CHAPTER 16

The one-sided war soon escalated.

Ingrid's glares and snickers were quickly accompanied by stealth shoves and jutting feet to make me stumble. And though it was an "anonymous" tip that led to the quashing of my magic show, I could speculate the source.

Then came the breakfast incident. After she sabotaged her own porridge with heaps of salt and reported me as the culprit, the dining-hall supervisor accepted the word of "darling Ingrid" over my protests as the new girl. Hair plastered in a bun, the woman stabbed her thick finger in the air. "Any urchin on the street would be grateful for the hot meal you saw fit to waste. You'd be wise not to forget that."

To suggest I ever could was ludicrous.

But pressed to apologize, I conceded, simply to move on from a battle I wasn't going to win, unaware my punishment would be to eat the entire bowlful myself. Forcing down each salt-laden bite was repulsive in every way, yet the humiliation from what followed was worse.

On the most recent sheet-changing day, during class hours, a housekeeper replaced my linens with parchment paper when she discovered I'd wet my cot—only I hadn't. I tried to say as much, but a room supervisor brushed away my assertions.

"I understand this can be embarrassing," the woman said. "We just need to be more diligent about going tinkle before bedtime."

We, she said, referring to twelve-year-old me.

I was convinced it had been a mix-up until recalling Ingrid's remark in passing, spoken before she could have possibly known: *Uh-oh, I hear somebody's had an accident.* And I realized with unrivaled disgust: as with the porridge, this was all her doing.

Hunting her down, I found the weasel in her room putting on her boots and implored her to stop.

"Stop what?" She smirked.

I had no proof. At least not in my favor.

Likewise, though more incriminating, the following day another bit of "proof" landed me in Mrs. Atwood's office. A case of stolen chalk, thwarting morning lessons, had launched staff members on a building-wide search. White powdery handprints found on my valise left a convenient trail to the chalk planted inside.

"Think very carefully, Miss Vos." Mrs. Atwood picked up her yardstick. "This is your final chance to come clean."

My continued denial of guilt would earn ten lashes. An admission would reduce them by half.

I imagined Papa watching from heaven, how he would feel if, once more, I claimed fault that wasn't mine, and what Father Lawrence would say about doing what's right, most especially when things are hard.

Though dispirited, I girded myself and silently raised my palms.

There was frustration in Mrs. Atwood's features, lined with reluctance as she began to strike. But even then, I held back the tears rimming my eyes. For setting them free would open a dam I suspected might never close.

"Time to get up!" A tug to my nightgown woke me to an exuberant round face. Agatha stood over me, fully dressed. "Remember? Today's Easter." Spaces from missing front teeth transformed the word into *Easther.* "We're having flapjacks and marmalade and everything."

I yawned and stretched, rustling the parchment paper beneath me. A humiliating reminder. Thankfully, Agatha was already scampering away with nervous Nellie, leaving the room vacant but for me.

I must have slept through the morning bell. Recalling the rules, I hurried to rise. Unless provably ill, arrivals past seven didn't eat.

I knelt to retrieve my overalls from under my cot. But discovering a pair of boots in place of mine, I froze. Though appearing my size, these were brown and stained and scuffed. I didn't need to rub the sleep from my eyes to know whose they were.

Ingrid had stolen my boots. My precious black-leather boots!

A flare of anger surged through my body, joined shortly by a torrent of panic.

Without my boots, my memory of receiving them—of Papa's laugh and voice and embrace—was bound to slip away, along with my cherished thoughts of his patience that night. Never one to complain, he'd simply matched my pace walking home, slowed by my blisters born of stubbornness and pride.

Aside from his pocket watch and our single portrait, those boots were all I had left of him. Take any of them away, and my memories of him could swiftly fade. The possibility wasn't unfounded. It had happened before—with my mother.

All at once, the dam burst. Tears poured from my eyes as I stormed from the room in my socks, not bothering to change clothes. I wove around girls straggling on the stairs, intent as a raging current.

At the entry of the dining hall, chest heaving, I spotted Ingrid's signature braid. She was at her usual table, where under the bench, my boots flagrantly hugged her feet.

I charged forward with the focus of a bombsight. One way or another, those shoes were coming off. The heat inside me burned, hot as flames from a gallon of gin. No doubt my face radiated feverish red. Any chattering at tables subsided as I strode past, giving way to inquisitive stares. I was like Arie at the assembly hall before the stampede, facing down a wretched bully. Fearless.

Stopping directly behind Ingrid, I drew the attention of the girls across from her. One gasped, another pointed. Ingrid twisted in her seat, and her expression morphed from curious to alarmed.

Breaths circled through my nose in the style of a bull in a pen. My fists were so tight my nails bit into my palms, still tender from my lashing.

Because of her.

Ingrid assessed our audience with a skittery gaze. Collecting herself, she attempted to scoff. "W-what in blazes are *you* doing?"

Had I been in a judicious state of mind, I might have answered her question. I might have publicized her crime and demanded my shoes. And whether she snidely refused or donned a veneer of innocence, I might have given her fair warning, even voiced a countdown to let her reconsider.

But no. I didn't do any of those things.

I did, though, detect a voice in the background, echoey and faint, as if spoken through a tunnel. My name, I believe, though I couldn't be certain. I was fixated on Ingrid's eyes and the sight of them going impossibly wide, marking the instant I lunged.

What followed was a tornado of flailing arms and legs, grunts and shrieks, a braid in my grasp. All of it ended with a sharp yank to my collar, snug as a noose. I scrambled for traction, dragged by a grip. Pulled upright, I grabbed my collar to loosen it from my throat.

A male kitchen attendant in a white uniform had intervened. Tall and lean, he was keeping me from Ingrid, who cowered on the floor, flushed and bawling. Her crying was the only sound in the room, aside from the blood pumping in my ears.

Of all the girls in the dining hall, most stood in astonishment, though almost as many were whispering with gratified looks.

Mrs. Atwood tramped into the thick of it. At her command, a staff member guided Ingrid to rise and ushered the girl away—still in my boots. The vicious bully.

Or…was I that person now?

The director seemed to think so, peering down her nose at me. "Miss Vos, what in heaven's name has gotten into you?"

She didn't wait for an answer.

"You keep up with these shenanigans, and placement in any home will be out of the question. One day, you'll wind up on the street, destitute and hungry with no option but to—" She broke off, filtering herself.

The mass of spectators seemed to hold a collective breath.

Regrouping, Mrs. Atwood continued. "As for imminent

consequences…I confess, I do hesitate to punish anyone on this special day, one that specifically celebrates hope and new life." Her phrasing suggested leniency. At minimum, an openness at last to hear my side.

Then she turned and projected for everyone to hear. "And yet such a glorious reward is possible only, as Jesus has taught us, after atonement." She sent a nod to the male attendant. A cue.

He took my arm. As he walked me out, a new wave of whispers gained an ominous timber, though they largely slipped past me. With a sense of detachment, I barely processed my guided path, a zigzagging through halls and doorways and down a set of steps. Lit by a single hanging bulb, a long, narrow room held shelves of food in jars, boxes, and cans. Lining the wall were barrels marked *FLOUR*. The air was stale, smelling of a cellar.

Why were we here? Where were we going?

When the man released me, I was standing in a smaller room. From the ceiling, a cord dangled with a socket that lacked a light bulb.

A closet, I thought. But a thin mattress and pillow lay on the floor.

"You behave now, missy."

I swiveled back to him, trying to comprehend, but stepping out, he was swinging the door shut.

He was leaving me. In here alone.

Snapped back to the scene, I lurched forward to stop him. "No—don't! You can't!"

But he clicked the lock, abandoning me to the darkness. A prisoner's solitary. My living nightmare.

I pounded on the door, the space an unseen tomb. "Please, no! Please, please, no! Please, no!" I begged this over and over, my throat turning raw. Panic buzzed, swarming my body, threatening as a hornets' nest. Nightmares flickered back. Of being smothered by bodies, buried alive in a casket, consumed by a shrinking stairwell. I went to scream but couldn't. I was gulping down air, nearly choking on it.

Calm. Be calm!

Desperate for Arie's hand, I clutched my fists to my chest and stumbled back against a wall. A slit of light shone through a gap below the door. I slid downward, woozy and reeling, and sank onto the cold concrete floor. A chill zipped up my spine and my whole body shuddered.

Hearing the raggedness of my breaths, I worked to control them, but they refused to slow. My heart slammed my ribs—*thud-thud, thud-thud*—and my brain spun, round and round, an endless spiral.

My last coherent thought before the world disappeared was: *Out, I need…to get out…*

And by that, I didn't mean the mere trap of the room.

CHAPTER 17

My confinement met an early end. I was balled up on the floor when someone entered the room: Mrs. Atwood with a meal tray, I later learned. Slivers of her words penetrated my daze. "...not fond of... extremes...discipline...own good..."

What came next were more distant calls of my name, then bellows and footsteps, a mix of taut voices, and soon I was floating, my gaze on the passing ceiling, until landing on what seemed a warm cloud. When I gained clarity, I found myself on a real bed and pillow, the lone child in the sickroom.

A woman checked me over, probing with nurse-like questions. My answers appeared to rule out the need for a doctor. From several months' worth of exhaustion, I drifted in and out of sleep for the remainder of the day and woke just once during the night, when a hand on my shoulder released me from another casket, a nightmare more terrifying than ever. For a split second, I expected the rescuer to be Arie. But my fit had summoned the same woman from before, with the addition of curlers and cold cream.

Mercifully, I was able to drift back off. When Mrs. Atwood perched on my bed in the morning, I gradually registered her softened tone, accentuated by the use of my given name.

"Fenna, as I believe I've made clear, your recent conduct has been very disappointing. You seemed like such a good, obedient girl. Change can be difficult, but it does not give one permission to act out with violence."

For the first time since the incident, I recalled Ingrid huddled on the floor, stripped of her armor, openly sobbing as others snickered.

Despite all rationalizations, shame pulsed through me.

"Having said that, I consider the punishment you received sufficient for the purpose of learning. From here on out, during your time under this roof, I expect your behavior to improve substantially. Are we agreed?"

It was a tough thing to guarantee. Should Ingrid turn meaner than ever, my behavior, perceived or otherwise, was bound to worsen. However, the question did limit the scope to my *time under this roof...*

"Yes, Mrs. Atwood."

Pleased, she rose to her feet. "I'll tell you what," she added. "So long as you behave yourself—and there's not another bedtime accident—I'll see to it that you have some nice, cotton sheets by the weekend. Would you like that?"

I'd have cringed at the reminder if not for the surprise of her offer. Perhaps a product of her own pulsing guilt.

"Yes, ma'am. Thank you."

She smiled, flashing a peek of those crooked bottom teeth. "Good. Now, eat up"—she gestured to the bowl on my night table—"then head down for daily lessons. They've only just begun."

I managed an appreciative look, masking my newfound hatred of porridge. Salted or sweet, it was a meal I would never ingest again.

Once she'd left the room, I sneaked to the toilet down the hall and disposed of the god-awful glob. I was hurrying back when a sight sparked a memory, tempering my pace.

Piled in a wheeled cart were beige canvas bags. They were stuffed with dirty sheets for tomorrow's weekly pickup, all to be laundered and returned three days later to swap with our second sets. The mayor, adhering to a campaign promise—cemented by a photo session at the orphanage—had secured the complimentary service. With it came not only the carts but also the rope-tied sacks, which in that moment reminded me quite a lot of a mailbag...the kind Houdini used for escapes...

Alone in the hall, I tilted a sack in the heap, assessing.

The bag could plainly accommodate my size. Though serving as an enclosure, it was relatively flimsy and, if positioned sideways, could remain wide open, allowing plenty of air and light while being transported.

On several past Tuesdays, just after six in the morning, a rumbling engine had drawn me to the window above my cot. I'd peered down at the alley, where the driver dropped a ramp off the rear of his delivery truck and retrieved the laundry from the kitchen. It was an efficient system, not loading and unloading each individual bag, only the carts. Ones that were taken miles from this place.

The scheme was almost too simple to work. In fact, as I pondered it throughout the day's school lessons, that very worry pestered me—notably without any distracting taunts from Ingrid.

The girl remained stoic. Given the purple bruise on her cheek, chances were high she was plotting retaliation. To ensure I wouldn't be around to find out, I conjured Houdini's mentality by exploring every potential method for escape.

Word had it park outings were in store for us once the rainy season subsided. But strict chaperoning would pose a challenge, and besides, I wasn't about to wait that long. As for doors on the main floor, they required a key, even from inside, and fire escapes were accessible from staff quarters only.

The windows downstairs were nailed shut—after teenagers allegedly fled through them years before—and the upper-floor windows were too high for a safe drop. Shimmying down a rope of sheets might have been an option if it didn't mean waking my entire bedroom, where nervous Nellie was liable to sound an alarm. After all, her observing a show past curfew was one thing; enabling a breakout was another.

With every alternative ruled out, I retired onto my cot that night, firm in my choice.

CHAPTER 18

Four gongs rang out from the grandfather clock. A sheer black sky had blotched out the windows, their panes flickering with the candle's yellow glow.

This hour was my best shot. Aside from restless infants upstairs and any staff tending to them, the whole place would be asleep. If I went now, I could hide in place before the cooks and truck rolled in.

Upon my cot, I slowly rose until a crinkling sounded. My parchment liner. I should have removed it in preparation. Moving in smaller increments, I listened for breaks in my roommates' breathing.

Finally on my feet, I covered Poppy's old pillow and my own with a blanket to craft a sleeping body. Then kneeling on the cold tiles, I retrieved my packed valise. With Ingrid's shoes in hand, I mouthed goodbye to my slumbering roommates—though none were as precious as Poppy, most were accepting and kind—and off I crept toward the kitchen, where the laundry carts awaited pickup.

But first I'd reclaim what was mine.

At the last door in the hall, I set down my travel bag. The girls in the low-lit room outnumbered mine by more than double. A savvier escaper might have bypassed the errand, judging it a foolhardy risk despite the boots' connection to my father.

They never knew Papa.

I tiptoed, hunched over—as if a stoop somehow muted my movements. Nearly at the targeted cot, the eighth one in, I noticed a girl missing:

Ingrid.

A frenetic glance around confirmed she was gone.

Was she escaping too? A doubtful coincidence. Probably just off to the bathroom and returning shortly.

In a cautious hurry, I swapped my black boots for her brown ones and padded back out. I could have taken both, but leaving her shoeless might draw her to my cot. And I'd rather the credit for discovering my absence go to anyone other than her.

As it turned out, that hope, for all its pettiness, was decimated by a feathery sound.

A breath.

Bent over my bag, clutching its wooden handles, I raised my head to find Ingrid.

She looked different in the shadows, disarmed in a way, dressed in a nightgown with hair frizzed and unbraided. But I knew better than to trust appearances. She of all people had taught me that.

I thought to spout an excuse, that I'd gotten up to use the toilet, same as her. Yet her eyes tightened at the items I held—my valise and boots—before her gaze slid past me, aimed at the staff's quarters. Here was her chance to exact revenge. Another horrifying day of me locked in the cellar, maybe more, was a surety.

My gut churned. Any plea seemed futile, our history considered, but I had to try. I opened my mouth to speak just as her chin rose, a quick lift. A nod? With no other indication, she walked right by and entered her room.

I remained there, astounded. When she climbed quietly into her bed, it was clear she was letting me go. But why? In an odd way, I suppose through my assault of her, I could have earned her respect. That or she'd come to believe that her life here would be better off without me. Whichever her motive, we'd both be facing a less preferable scenario if I didn't get going.

I continued through the hall and down the stairs, extra leery around corners. In the dimness of the kitchen, I changed into my pink-petaled dress. The fit was now entirely snug, the length well above the knee, but it would have to do. Faded overalls in the city would read like a billboard: POOR ORPHAN ON THE LAM

After tugging on my winter stockings, I added my boots and coat.

My train and watch were already in my pockets, and my stash of funds left after Papa's burial—three dollars and some change—were still secured behind the coat's lining. A clever trick from Papa.

Apparently he'd had some magic skills too.

Parked by the door were four laundry carts. From the one least filled, I pulled out a sack and emptied it. Then I shoved the sheets and my valise deep into the mound. With the cart reconfigured to make space, I climbed inside and stepped into the bag.

I reviewed my reasoning—how the top would stay untied and open, how the sack was just like a blanket sewn at the bottom. Yet as I raised the canvas up around me, I was struck by the reality of being enshrouded. Was there another option?

Think, think!

I could always hide under the bag instead of inside it. Absolutely, that could work.

Lowering in the cart, I pulled the sack over me and curled on my side. For more cover, I wriggled into the sheets and felt a seam of my dress give out. My fingers located the small gap along my ribs. An issue for later. Keeping a partial view of the ceiling, I waited.

What might have been an hour seemed a decade. Sweat seeped from my pores, dampening my dress. I was tempted to remove my coat, but it was too late for that much movement. I simply rolled the wheels of my train tucked in my pocket.

Forward, back. Forward, back.

Through the window, dawn lightened the room so gradually I almost didn't notice. I fought to keep my thoughts blank, clear of the punishment I'd endure if caught, of the possibility that Ingrid could speak up and play the hero—

A noise trampled the rest. Clacking heels entered the room, muffled by the instant thumping of my heart. Keys jangled. A lock clicked and hinges squeaked, a door being opened. There was clinking and scraping. The milkman's crate of large bottles was being dragged in. The door closed with another squeak.

I moved. I must have, as my seam split even more. I didn't just feel the tearing but heard it. Was I the only one? Waiting to find out, I'd never been so aware of every muscle in my body, every involuntary twitch.

Soon came a hiss. The striking of a match. Clanking suggested a burner being lit.

I'd gotten lucky but wasn't about to relax.

There were more clacking steps, more indecipherable shuffling before I heard it. An engine groaned. Its volume rose, then sputtered to a stop.

The door opened again and a woman sang out a greeting. It was the voice of the dining-hall supervisor. I never pegged her as friendly. Save with Ingrid.

Metal slammed—the ramp being dropped into place. The driver and the woman engaged in small talk about the weather and some new radio show.

At last came a different squeaking: a cart being wheeled out before rattling up the ramp. I focused on regulating my breaths, keeping them soundless. Another cart squeaked and rattled, followed shortly by the departure of a third. I willed myself not to retract farther into hiding. Stillness was critical.

Then all at once, I was moving. The driver was so close I smelled the tobacco smoke on his clothes, the coffee on his breath. I squeezed my eyes shut, wishing to be invisible. The pressure made my sockets ache.

Suddenly the bags shifted over me. My eyes flew open. Tipped at an angle, the cart was rolling up the ramp. I leveraged my elbow against the weighted sacks, and the cart stopped. The driver sniffed, lingering. Did he smell me in turn, perhaps the lemon in my hair? Or did he simply sense my presence?

My stomach leapt to my throat.

But then footsteps thudded down the ramp, which he slid back into the truck. I sagged with relief. At the soonest stop, when the area was clear, I'd slip out fast as a wink. Vanish like a button.

I relaxed my neck just enough to view the ceiling, awarding myself more air. The couple's chat resumed, muffled, something about a snack for the road. Then ragged slams filled my ears. He'd shut the doors, turning the world black.

I covered my mouth to suppress a gasp. I should have predicted this. But from my bedroom window, all I'd seen was a transport to freedom, not thinking of its absolute darkness, nor its lock that could seal me in.

Stay calm! You need to stay calm!

The internal voice was commanding, but already I was scrambling out of the cart. Before I could stop myself or even peek out first, I found the doors by feel and flung them open.

Logic told me I'd been caught.

Yet remarkably, there was no one in the alley. The kitchen door was cracked open, but the couple was out of sight.

I glanced up at the series of second-story windows, each mottled from the overcast sky. While uncertain which was mine, I was gripped by the reversal of view—and a desire not to go back.

My chance to flee was waning.

Still clutching my train, I jumped down and took off in a mad dash toward the street. I steered around the corner, down one block, then the next, making turns here and there. I was a mouse in a maze, frantic for an exit.

Though the city was waking, I focused only on my boots slapping pavement, my rhythmic huffing and pounding temples.

I couldn't say how long I kept up that way, just that I didn't stop until reaching a depot of purring buses that emitted pungent fumes. Inside, hatted men perused newspapers and several mothers fussed with their toddlers. An old woman on a bench *tsked* at the couple seated beside her entwined in a kiss.

In line for the clerk, I eyed the depot entrance, dreading a far more consequential judge: Mrs. Atwood on a rampage. Anxiously I went to retrieve money from my coat and noticed something missing.

My valise…I'd left it in the laundry cart.

I had no clothes but the ones I was wearing, almost all outgrown. Barely any of the possessions I had left, not even—oh no. My photo with Papa. The portrait! I'd packed it in my travel bag.

My heart insisted I dash back to recover it, but my brain quickly countered: *Back to where?* The truck would be long gone. I wanted to sob. But I couldn't. It would only draw unwanted attention. I needed to be strong.

The doors swung open.

A brutish policeman strode in with a billy club. My spine bristled and breath caught. He scanned the room, starting with the far wall. The early-morning crowd wasn't large enough to hide me. I cowered into my shoulders, a turtle without a shell.

The officer angled my way and marched forward, surely to return me to the orphanage. Or would I be put in a home for delinquents?

My thoughts thrashed with notions of running. There had to be another set of doors. Hadn't I learned to find the exits in any room straightaway?

Then the policeman paused. At a bench, he used his stick to nudge a sleeping hobo. The grizzled man woke with a snort and staggered to his feet. When the two lumbered out together, I swallowed past the wedge of fear in my throat.

"Help you there, little miss?" The grandfatherly clerk regarded me from the counter.

I inched toward him, my purpose momentarily forgotten, aside from needing to appear at ease. My hand loosened around the wooden train nearly embedded in my palm. From a glimpse at the toy, I recalled the note inside, featuring the lone destination I could fathom. And I hoped, with every ounce of my being, that once there, I wouldn't be turned away.

"One ticket," I replied with a voice almost level. "To Amesboro, please."

CHAPTER 19

If my wait in the laundry cart lasted a decade, the minutes until the bus's arrival spanned a century. Suffice it to say, I was the first to board.

Over the next hour and a half, through the lulling motion of the drive, I shifted often in my seat: to stay alert, to gauge boarding passengers, to not miss my stop. By the time we rolled into Amesboro, I was more than ready to hustle off.

I scanned what appeared the town's central street, with shops and a drugstore and—yes, a post office! Equipped with every address in the area, the place was a perfect resource.

But my challenges didn't end when I walked through the door.

From behind the counter, a towering middle-aged woman with short sandy-brown hair scrutinized my approach. An incoming telegram clacked away in the background.

"I'm sorry, ma'am, for troubling you," I began. "It's just that I've come to town to visit a family, the Jansens, and...I don't have their new address." At her silence, I continued. "See, my father worked with theirs. Up in the Copper Country. So I was hoping you might—"

"And you are?" she asked flatly.

I was reluctant to provide my actual name, aware that a statewide hunt could be underway. But her owlish eyes told me she could detect a lie through the thickest of forests, and what was more, a tentative answer might give her cause to phone the authorities.

"Fenna, ma'am. I'm Fenna Vos."

"*Fenna*, you say?"

I froze at her change of tone. The mix of intrigue and recognition summoned my nerves to the surface.

"Over in Holland," she said, "my baby niece shares your Christian name. Your family, they're from the old country?"

Relief didn't keep me from stammering. "M-my parents are, yes... or *were*." I pushed through the sting of thinking about Papa in the past tense.

She didn't press for details, gratefully. "Well," she said, "as to the matter of your request, I do abide by a standard rule: for propriety's sake, I never personally disclose residents' private information without their say-so."

Disappointment tugged at me. Not defeat, however. Not after what it took to achieve this much. Maybe a phone operator would help, or a chatty customer at a general store—or at a beauty parlor, better yet.

"Be that as it may," she went on, "my son is about to deliver telegrams on his way to school, and that route just *might* take him near the Jansen residence. As a new visitor, perhaps you should ride along, become familiar with the area." Her lips didn't quite form a smile, but a telling warmth emanated from her eyes.

My Dutch descent, it seemed, had created a fast connection. I wasn't accustomed to such a thing.

I had only just thanked her when she called toward a back room. "Hendrik, hurry along or you'll be late!"

A lanky boy in a peacoat and knickers shuffled out, finishing off an apricot. Around my age, he had a blunt nose and caramel-colored hair, mostly covered by his cap. She leaned toward him and whispered by his ear.

He responded by snatching two telegrams from the counter, using his nonsticky hand, and asked me brightly, "You okay riding handlebars?"

I nodded with vigor, thrilled for the help, before fully digesting his question.

———

As we cycled through a neighborhood, jostling over potholes and around corners, I watched through squinted eyes. I would have enjoyed, even reciprocated, the friendly waves of residents who stepped out for work or morning papers. But clutching the handlebar tight as a vise, all I could think about was preventing a ghastly sprawl—until we skidded to a halt.

"Here you are, kid. Front-door service."

My legs, under the canopy of my coat, quivered from pinning my dress between my knees. The ripped seam at my side had become a full-blown hole, near as I could tell.

I climbed down, out of sorts. "Thanks, Erik. For the ride."

He smiled. "Anytime."

It hit me that I'd blundered his name. *Hendrik*—not Erik. But since he was already pedaling away, I focused on the finish line before me.

I could hardly believe it. Arie lived in an actual house. Sure, the single-story bungalow was small and heavily weathered, with peeling white paint and some roof tiles missing, but it had a charming L-shaped porch and plaid curtains tied off in the window. Touches of a home.

I scurried up the steps, avoiding a broken plank, and knocked on the frame of the screen door. At the sound of footsteps, elation fluttered through me. Not like a few pairs of butterfly wings but a hundred.

When the front door opened, there was Arie, dressed in a brown corduroy coat and patched trousers. Despite our four months apart, I couldn't imagine a closer friend.

This truth had never penetrated as fully as it did in that instant—nor receded as swiftly. Through a lock of his tousled hair, he stared with none of the joy I'd expected.

"Arie, it's me?" The statement absurdly came out a question.

I'd assumed that when I was swept off to the orphanage, I had missed any letters he'd promised. It should have crossed my mind that he'd moved on. Making new friends would be easier in an area filled with Dutch. More than that, maybe we weren't as close as I'd wanted to believe.

He glanced past me. "Where'd you... How'd you get..." He seemed to be reconciling me with his surroundings.

"I caught a bus. From Grand Rapids."

If this was another dark turn of fate, I could survive it. I'd learned that much. But to keep from dissolving into a sniveling mess, I needed to know his stance outright. "I can't go back to the orphanage there—I won't. So if you don't want me here, I'll just…"

What? What would I do?

Everything over the past twenty-four hours had happened so quickly, I hadn't contemplated an alternative beyond our reunion. I now realized, heart plummeting, that I should have.

But then, as if stirred from shock or a sleepy haze—maybe both—Arie brightened with the trademark dimple of his smile. He opened the screen door, and only briefly hedging, he welcomed me with a hug. "Thought you'd just up and moved away," he said in that rasp I had so missed.

I considered his words, the relief in them. He had written to me after all.

He let go then, too soon, and stepped back with a creased brow. "Wait. If you'd been at an orphanage, does that mean…that your pa…"

"He died." It was the first time I'd said it aloud.

"Ah, geez…Fen." Arie shook his head and tenderly clasped my hand. The depth of sympathy in his eyes brought a mist of tears to mine. "I'm so sorry."

Though rendered wordless, at least I didn't crumble. For that much, I was proud.

Then a familiar accented voice shot from the house. "Who is there?"

From Arie's expression, it was evident that all the worries that had drained out of me had siphoned into him.

Before he could answer, his mother appeared, drying her hands on a dishcloth. As always, her wheat-colored hair was tightly knotted, further pronouncing her strong cheekbones. Even in her housedress and apron, if compared to her husband—with his tall yet soft, rounded stature—she could almost pass as more suited for work in the mine.

"Mama," he said, "you remember Fenna."

While her gray-blue eyes were a match to Arie's, his hadn't narrowed at the sight of me.

I offered a tentative wave. "Hello, Mrs. Jansen."

"Why you come now? Is time for school."

The Dutch were ruled by schedules, Papa had taught me, referencing himself as an exception. As was I, evidently.

"Yes, ma'am. Well. The thing is…"

Arie interjected. "How about I fill her in?"

Glad for the handoff, I nodded, but then he shut the door between us.

Intermittently their voices swooped up and down. I could discern only snippets. My legs regained a tremble, making it difficult to keep still.

Would she call the police? The orphanage? The Children's Aid Society?

My future again lay in someone else's hands, dictated by the whim of a virtual stranger. Loathing that fact, I swore to myself in that moment:

One day, I alone would be the one in control.

————————

Later, Arie recounted highlights of their discussion, beginning with his mother's inclination to report me.

I couldn't blame her, sincerely. Immigrants above all people had an aversion to trouble; living between worlds, you survived through hard, honest work and keeping your head down. If nothing else, the strike had shown me that.

So he'd appealed to her faith. He drew comparisons to the innkeepers who shunned Mary and Joseph, and he stressed how the right parents' guidance would ensure my virtuous path.

I suspected that last point entailed saving me from the waywardness of Catholicism, though Arie never told me this explicitly. Rather he veered to his more practical assertions, such as the foolishness of wasting a spare bed. Specifically, his sister's—as a few weeks prior, defying her parents' objections, Thea had run off to elope with a beau from Wisconsin, thereby banning her name in the house. At least when his parents were around, he said.

In short, Arie was persuasive enough for his mother to march off to the auto factory, where she'd confer with her husband during his midmorning break. When she returned, in exchange for my vow to not cause any problems, I had the assurance of a place in their home and a seat at their table—and, from Arie, a friendship that once more I believed would never end.

CHAPTER 20

Several weeks trudged by before my fear of being recaptured diminished and the sight of a police officer, or anyone even slightly resembling Mrs. Atwood, wouldn't incite a swell of angst.

It was a foolish thing, logically. As if the director would plead tirelessly for the return of a violent, bed-wetting, chalk-thieving, porridge-sabotaging delinquent.

Even if she'd sent out a cursory alert, the cops would be busy with more pressing issues. A continued rise in unemployment meant more folks out on the streets, living in shantytowns dubbed "Hoovervilles." Even in Amesboro, there were gentlemen with signs around their necks, begging for work or spare change. Others wandered about like shell-shocked infantrymen, stupefied by all they had lost.

Fortunately the local Dutch community, frugal yet fair, tended to look out for their own, enabling Mr. Jansen to keep his job and without a wage cut. His extensive machinery skills supported his worth, as did his concerted efforts to improve his English. After supper, he would sit in his rocking chair with a pencil and the *Amesboro Observer*, reading, rereading, and circling unfamiliar words.

Although I actually preferred his fractured English, reminiscent of Papa's, one night I offered a correction for a phrase he was struggling to pronounce. Immediately I worried it wasn't my place, but his bifocals bobbed with his head as he scribbled a phonetic note in the margin. With Arie on the porch for broom duty and his mother out back pulling laundry, I ventured to kneel by Mr. Jansen to clarify more phrases. Curious in turn, I thought to ask for their translation in Gronings, his native Dutch dialect. Therein our trade began.

We continued nearly every evening, so long as he wasn't exhausted from the factory and I wasn't loaded up with schoolwork, a strict priority in the house. For me, learning his language seemed a practical matter, as Mrs. Jansen preferred it for family conversation. Plus, the way he chuckled when I'd eviscerate his dialect gave me welcomed reason to smile.

Not until weeks later did our interactions give me pause.

On the porch one sunny afternoon, I was babbling away while handing Mr. Jansen tools for the steps in disrepair when I caught my reflection in the window. There I was, going on as cheerfully as I had at the cobbler shop, the role of the father merely replaced.

Understand, of course, since leaving the orphanage, to sustain my memory of Papa, I often ran through a sensory checklist while lying in bed at night: the smell of pipe tobacco on his shirt, his prickly beard grazing my face, the satisfaction in his eyes when he'd savor a juicy bite of pork, the gravelly snore I hadn't foreseen I would miss.

Still in that moment, guilt struck like a sucker punch. As I struggled to conceal its impact, an assurance came to me: *It is okay, schatje. It is okay.*

Papa's words from the assembly hall applied once again. I told myself he'd understand, as my helpfulness to the Jansens was crucial. I had to earn my keep so as not to be banished—like Thea. Their own daughter was seen in nary a photo in the home.

And yes, I admit, part of me savored the semblance of having two parents.

Hence, when Mrs. Jansen took in seamstress work for supplementary income, I jumped in to assist with sewing and mending—lessons from the orphanage actually proving useful—and made my own dresses with the extra fabric. On Saturdays, I'd often join her at a local soup kitchen where, surprisingly given her gruffness, she volunteered to cook. I ladled soup for bedraggled men, many stooped by shame and despair, a reminder of the meal line at the orphanage and just how fast life could change.

Determined to remain in good graces, I went so far as to express enthusiasm over the Jansen family's church. This wasn't entirely an act;

I did find their services less droning than those of weekly mass. And anyway, I figured God wouldn't smite me for a bit of inflated joy over a service held in His honor.

Arie had smiled subtly, comprehending my motivation, knowing me as well as I knew him. A fact that only deepened with time.

On weekday mornings, after one of his fitful sleeps or late-night walks, his mother would have to drag him out of bed, located in the sitting room. He'd insisted on giving me his bedroom, formerly shared with his sister. With Arie no longer an apartment away, quicker than ever he'd stem my nighttime outbursts, preventing me from seeming a nuisance.

We proceeded to chat some nights, but less frequently than before; his parents, nondrinkers, were lighter sleepers than Papa. In contrast as well, our friendship in Amesboro existed in the open. I'd walk to and from school beside him, attached as a shadow, despite boys taunting us with smooching noises and crass suggestions. At times, I'd drop my chin, using my hair to curtain my burning cheeks. Arie would reject their insinuations as plain-old stupid, declaring me "like a kid sister." Naturally I'd back up the claims—minus the "kid" part. I was twelve and a half, and he was just a year older.

Granted, in early June, after two months of our hassled walks, one of his retorts did leave me miffed. Noticeably.

"So what's nagging you?" he asked. With his parents out delivering a gift to welcome a neighbor's newborn, we were clearing the table after supper.

"I don't know what you mean."

"You've been awful quiet."

I kept my attention on gathering dirty plates, which looked practically clean. Never wasting, we'd all eaten every scrap of our meal, from the liverwurst to the *roggebrood*. The rye dough still scented the air. "I'm tired is all."

"Uh-huh."

"I told you, it's nothing."

"Yeah, and I call baloney."

I rolled my eyes, annoyance climbing. "Just go do your homework.

I'll finish this myself." I turned and carried the dishes to the sink, where the hand-crank water pump normally delighted me. Not then. For as I lowered the stack into the sudsy water, I felt the weight of Arie's gaze. He was analyzing me in silence, like he would the family's furnace or radio, or any other appliances he tinkered with until they worked. As if I were something broken to be fixed.

"Knock it off."

"What? I'm not doing anything."

"I know you're staring, and it's creepy."

"All right. I'll close my eyes."

Above the sink, the orange sunset glowed too bright for Arie's reflection to appear in the window. I had to glance over my shoulder to affirm his mockery. He was as unshakable as a leg cramp and just as maddening.

"For crying out loud. Scram, will you?" I twisted back, grabbed a rag, and scrubbed the top plate harder than needed.

Soon he invaded my periphery, making the room impossibly confining. I was ready to tell him to go suck on a lemon until he said, "Really, Fen. What is it?"

His ribbing was over. Tempered by his genuine concern, I relaxed my hold on the plate, surrendering it to the suds.

"If some kid's done anything to hurt you, just you say so and I'll take care of that sap."

No doubt he meant it. The problem was, in this case, Arie was that sap.

"Fine, if you honestly want to know." I angled toward him. "Today, when we were walking home from school, those obnoxious boys were teasing us, and..."

He tilted his head as if taking stock of their comments.

"You told them I was disgusting."

Arie blinked. He wasn't expecting to be the villain. But then comprehension rolled over his face with a hint of a smile. "Fen, I didn't say *you* were disgusting. Just us. You know, together."

He was trying to make me feel better but only caused me to feel awkward. Why couldn't I have let the issue lie?

"Come on," he said. "You know we're nothing like that." He sounded so certain I'd agree, before a beat stretched between us. "Right?"

Now he was concerned for a different reason. I sensed his instinct to back away, to slink out of our standard radius of comfort. At the same time, my thoughts flashed on a vision: the couple kissing at the bus depot—except it was me and Arie, his arms around me, his mouth on mine. The idea made me squirmy.

He was right. Together, that wasn't who we were.

"Of course," I agreed. "We're *friends*." My tone was adamant enough to drain the tension from his shoulders, if not fully from the air. So I did the first thing that popped to mind: I flailed the dishrag toward him, spraying soapy dishwater across his button-down shirt.

At his jaw going lax, I burst into giggles that broke off when he lunged for the sink and threw suds at my face. I stood there, chin dripping. He snickered and clapped as if victory was his. It wasn't.

I came back with a full scoop of water, and through our laughter, the battle raged. We drenched our hair and clothes, the worn floorboards and floral wallpaper, until a pair of voices swung us toward the doorway.

Whether his mother, beneath her scowl, shared any of her husband's betrayed amusement, I couldn't say. What I did know was that Arie and I were solely responsible for cleaning up, which we did in a hurry with stifled smiles.

I knew this as well: more than anyone in my life, Arie had a knack for saving me from a foul mood. Not just over some nettling comment but over the darkest of causes. Like that of the coming winter.

Mid-December, more precisely.

It was the tail end of 1930, and our schoolmates were merrily counting down the weeks until Christmas. For me, the approaching holiday marked the second anniversary of a dark event and my first Christmas without Papa.

Carols, gifts, holiday sweets—they were all cruel reminders that only intensified my nightmares and revived my sense of solitude. On our walks and at home, Arie too became increasingly reserved. There was no reason to state why; words couldn't reinvent the past. Rather, he found us another way to brave the present.

A few days before Christmas, he dragged me out on an errand, which I took to be a task for his parents. Bundled up in the middle of town, we hopped off the streetcar.

"Cover your eyes," he told me.

"My eyes?"

"It's a surprise where we're going."

"I thought…you said—"

"Never spilled the details. Now go on. You can watch the ground if you want."

"Arie, this is silly. Just tell me what you're up to."

"What, you don't trust me?"

A nonsensical question.

I grumbled, wary of the unpredictable yet admittedly tickled by his efforts. Once I'd tented my gloved hands around my eyes, he led me by the elbow over pavement strewn with snow. A motorcar passed, rattling and slushing down the street. Strangers shuffled by, possibly gawking; my view of them was limited to their shopping bags and shoes.

"Why can't I look?" I groaned.

"Don't be a mule."

"I hardly think I'm being—"

He tugged my arm, pausing my steps. "Two, please."

"Two of *what?*"

"Not you." Then elsewhere: "Thanks." And off we continued, entering a building with the warm whoosh of a door. A buttery smell intensified as we moved over carpet. In a second room, we sloped downward, then he guided me to scuttle sideways and sit on a cushioned chair.

"Ta-da," he said from an adjacent seat. "Merry early Christmas." As I lowered my hands, he beamed above his scarf, cheeks pinkish from the cold, anticipating my reaction.

A picture show. Not a cheap nickelodeon, but the Monarch. I'd seen photos of the place—the nicest cinema in town. Other kids had boasted about sneaking in through an alley door and up to the balcony to catch Charlie Chaplin flicks. And even a real talkie. Sometimes they goaded Arie to join, but he never agreed, saying it was no different from stealing.

"But, Arie...won't your folks mind?" I didn't mean to be a square; I just couldn't afford to jeopardize my standing.

"Pops said it was okay if I saved up. Special occasion and all that."

I knew he'd been picking up jobs around town, more odds and ends than usual, yet not the driving reason why. "I had no inkling..."

"Don't worry." He smiled a bit. "Only had to rob a couple banks."

In all seriousness, earning extra funds was a challenge even before the Depression. I should have told him how impressed I'd been, let alone for getting his parents' permission on the splurge. But I was too distracted by the enormous screen, its decor of burgundy curtains, the rows and rows of velvety chairs—the exit doors in front and back.

Then the wall sconces dimmed. I reached for Arie's hand on the armrest, a reflex, just as a white beam shot through the air. From a clicking projector high in the back, an introduction flickered across the screen. A background tune played.

HOUDINI
IN
'THE GRIM GAME'

I gasped and pointed. "Arie, look."

He gave me a knowing smirk.

My mind swirled with questions—wondering how he'd heard about the show, and what it was about, and did he already know if it was marvelous—but they never left my mouth. From the first reel to the next, every scene featuring the great Harry Houdini held me captive. The man was debonair in his suit, with slicked dark hair parted down the middle, identical to the photograph from his book—except a photo come to life. There were no voices, only typed words for dialogue, but it didn't matter. I was riveted, literally on the edge of my seat.

Working as a newspaper reporter, his character was jailed for a murder he didn't commit. When he broke out of his cell, it was to track down the true killers. Finishing the job required a series of astonishing escapes from chains, handcuffs, and a straitjacket, culminating with a spectacular aircraft collision.

I'd long been aware Houdini died years ago—from appendicitis, people said, spurred by a punch to the stomach—yet here he was, still eluding every trap possible. Including the grave.

By the film's end, the art of escape became more than a tool to rein in my fears and reduce my nightmares.

It was an all-out obsession.

CHAPTER 21

Although viewed as an oddity by the other schoolgirls, my career aspirations flourished. Throughout the rest of junior high, I studied countless piles of Houdini's publications, along with illusions from legends Howard Thurston and Maurice Raymond and loads of others. And naturally, I attended every pertinent show in the area I could afford: carnival acts, vaudeville shows, small-time varieties.

Then based on my notes and drawings, I'd create pseudo-reenactments at home, where Arie served as a—mostly willing—volunteer from my imaginary audience. Doubling as my assistant, on my cues of "Presto!" he'd slip in and out of my makeshift enclosures. This included vanishing inside them, as such tasks remained impossible for me. Meanwhile, my sleights with rings, ropes, and kerchiefs became an absolute breeze.

"The Fabulously Fantastical Fenna," I called myself, sometimes swapping in "Fanciful" or "Fabled" depending on my mood. If not for its corniness, I'd have opted for "Fairylike" solely as a tribute. At a performance of *The Nutcracker* hosted by our local church, while Arie fought off yawns and Mrs. Jansen issued pinches to interrupt her husband's snores, I became rapt with the Sugar Plum Fairy—her hand movements in particular. As if swaying underwater, they were practically hypnotic with a graceful calm I'd thereafter channel into my gestures in magic and illusion.

Still, not until the summer following my freshman year did I dare a public debut. The local junkyard wasn't the most glamorous of settings, but it offered a mishmash of seats and a passable stage made of pallets. I advertised with flyers, which Hendrik Smit—the first boy I met in Amesboro—sweetly agreed to post in shop windows during his telegram rounds. Tickets were three cents each, effectively reducing Mrs. Jansen's gripes about our "foolish wasting of time."

By our third show, however, the amassing of threadbare kids and even whole families who'd come to watch from a distance caused us to reevaluate our price. Despite Roosevelt's New Deal, scores of folks were still facing hardships. And so we changed our fee to "donations welcome."

As expected, Mrs. Jansen fumed over each red cent that could have added to her son's savings, which was mainly accrued from his shifts at the auto factory on nights and weekends. She was well aware, as we all were, of his hopes to attend college in Grand Rapids and become an engineer. In truth, given his struggling in mathematics senior year, the end goal did start to appear overambitious.

"Now who's the mule?" I mused, finding him at the kitchen table, dressed in clothes from the day prior. On the verge of dawn, I'd awoken thirsty. Or maybe I'd sensed he was still up and hunched over a textbook, grappling yet again with equations by lamplight.

He shot me a peeved side-glance for disrupting his concentration and returned to his paper, eyelids drooping.

On a plate by his elbow sat a curry-egg sandwich, dried and half-eaten. His mug of coffee scented the room, making me wonder how many cups he'd downed to last this long.

"Really though, Arie. You need your sleep."

"What I need," he growled, "is to be left alone so I can figure this out." He erased his work with force, then snatched up his pencil and raked his hair with his free hand.

I sighed. Calculations were my forte, from years of diagramming escapes and tricks, so despite his standard aversion to help, wrapped in my robe, I joined him at the table.

Well, technically the robe was Thea's. Although, sadly, the way Mrs. Jansen tossed her daughter's periodic unopened letters into a drawer, dismissed like last week's funnies, implied I'd be borrowing the garment for quite a while.

It also meant Thea wouldn't be here anytime soon with sisterly advice. Namely the kind that was tough but vital to hear.

"Arie, I've been thinking." I aimed for a tactful approach. "You're whip-smart at so many things, and engineering is fine and good. But maybe you ought to go another direction, one that doesn't rely so much on numbers."

His pencil stopped. I couldn't decipher if he was pondering his math or my suggestion.

I tried again. "You know, with so many specialties out there—"

"The Midtown Hudson Tunnel."

I stared, puzzled.

Then he raised his gaze to mine, no longer aggravated, still intent. "It's going to run a mile and a half under the Hudson, connecting New York and Jersey. For cars to drive through. *Under the river*, Fen. That's why I can't do anything else. I have to be part of something as big as that. To do something that's special and lasting...something..." He was searching for the word.

"Magical?" I suggested lightly.

He shook his head. "Purposeful," he finished, and then I understood.

CHAPTER 22

During my latter years of high school, I had gone to dances with various fellows. Even necked with a few. Yet the only boy I had mooned over was Hendrik, the boy who had grown more than pleasingly out of his lankiness and blunt features. Though we'd shared friendly flirtations in Latin class junior year and in physics as seniors, his high-school courtship never strayed from Nina Dewitt. Shapely and pert, the Home Arts Society president would profusely fuss over him whenever he placed well at a track-and-field meet. Which was often.

Marriage between them seemed a given, until the September he and I crossed paths two years after graduation.

On that muggy morning, I was working at a locksmith shop for close to full wages—a respectable feat for anyone at the time, much less a girl—when he entered wearing a smart brown suit and brimmed hat. His briefcase, suffering a jammed lock, was easy as pie to fix, though my efforts did slow once I casually asked about Nina.

"Actually," he said, "we broke up. Back in May."

"Oh gosh. I hadn't heard. I'm so sorry."

"We just…realized we wanted different things."

I nodded, extending a sympathetic look, my best effort at least.

"At any rate," he said after a pause. "I guess you were the right person."

It took me a second to respond. "Pardon?"

"For the lock." He motioned toward the counter between us, where I'd finished repairing his briefcase without thinking.

"Right. Yes. The lock." I avoided his gaze, feeling my cheeks flush, and slid the case toward him.

He smiled before testing it. "I'm impressed. You're really keen at this." For a skill deemed unladylike, the comment was refreshing. "Let me guess. Training for all those future stage tours."

I was touched that he linked the two, and without a trace of mockery. Then again, as a kid, he did attend a good number of my shows, which dwindled only as Arie became busier with his studies at Calvin College. Supported by an on-campus job and an academic scholarship through a factory connection, he would earn his degree the coming June. I was dizzy to have ever doubted him.

Anyhow.

"Houdini actually mastered locks," I replied, "by working at a shop like this. That's where I got the idea for my earlier jobs too."

"Oh? Such as?" Hendrik set his elbow on the counter, leaning a smidge closer, in no hurry at all.

As I plundered my recollections, I worried I'd absorbed the shop's grease-metallic scent and wished the space weren't so stuffy. "I worked for a carpenter first. He hired me only for sweeping and inventory but said I could learn more from being quiet and watching. Of course, I peppered him with so many questions he finally gave in and let me assist with the woodwork. I...suppose I wasn't very good at the quiet part."

"You don't say." Hendrik's grin made me smile. "And then what?"

"And then"—I hesitated, uncertain how he'd react—"there was my job with a spiritualist."

His hazel eyes went big, but in a captivated way.

"Mostly I helped with her séances—which I know sounds absurd. But it was really quite something. She'd pass along loving messages from her patrons, things they regretted not saying. I swear, you could see their grief practically melt right off."

I confess, I did come to suspect the use of gimmicks: a hidden floor pedal to tremble the table, a magnet that moved sand into messages, a candlewick rigged to self-extinguish. Houdini would have lambasted each of these, having dedicated the latter part of his life to exposing spiritualists as vulturous swindlers. Still, I'd like to think he'd have appreciated the pragmatic lessons to be learned on presentation and persuasion cued by people's tells.

"In any event, I'd have gladly kept the job longer, had it not come to a tragic end."

"How...*did* it end?" He was wary, as though wondering if we'd somehow summoned a demon.

In a way, we did.

"Mrs. Jansen discovered she'd misunderstood the word 'spiritualist.' That it didn't involve teachings about the Holy Spirit. She saw it as witchcraft and just about had a conniption."

Hendrik took this in and burst into hearty laughter.

I too could laugh about the situation *now*. It hadn't been quite as entertaining when every dime I'd earned from that job—including the portion I'd contributed to the family, as I always did—went into the collection basket at church.

"I've definitely got to hear more about this," Hendrik said, easing to a smile.

As I went to oblige, he added, "How about supper on Friday? You know, if you're game, with a little poking around, I bet I could even find a magician's show somewhere."

An official date with Hendrik Smit...

The idea was sumptuous all on its own. Topping it off with a sprinkling of magic?

Nothing, I'd thought, could be dreamier.

On the evening of the performance, Hendrik took me to a quaint Italian restaurant that smelled of stewed tomatoes and roasted garlic. With my hair in a painstakingly elegant twist, I wore my green, scoop-necked dress, chosen to flatter my kohl-lined eyes and girdled figure. I'd packed my raspberry lipstick for touch-ups, as well as powder to fight any glistening from the heat.

None of my preparations, though, aided my attempt to eat gracefully.

Between careful nibbles of my red-sauced linguine, which Hendrik had zealously ordered for us both, I listened to updates about his pals and family and his Midwest travels to sell his uncle's medical equipment to doctors. In turn, he learned of my promise to Mr. Jansen to wait until I was at least twenty-one before moving to a dazzling city like Chicago to find the perfect stage partner and work our way up to a big-time show. Getting a foot in the door might be tough, but I was determined.

What I opted to leave out was that this gave Mrs. Jansen at least three long months to continue urging me to settle down with a suitable match. A futile effort with good intention. Sure, I was bound to marry someday, just not anytime soon. According to my plan.

"Chicago, huh?" Hendrik offered a crooked smile. "I'd better get busy finding you a reason to stay."

Heat again overtook my cheeks. I lowered my gaze and forced down more of my Chianti. Though Prohibition ended back in '33, indulging never personally held appeal, yet that evening, when Hendrik splurged on the wine, I tried for a sophisticated air.

If nothing else, it helped tame my nerves as we sat close at the performance—full of enjoyable if relatively basic acts—and afterward when readying for our drive home. Parked on a side street behind the theater, we were seated snugly in his Model T when he asked permission for a kiss. A subtle waft of his Aqua Velva was even more intoxicating than the wine, the moment as exhilarating as a thousand fantasies I'd had of this very scene.

What followed strayed far from those visions.

Hendrik's kisses were a bit more aggressive than expected—to be fair, we did flirt for years, and my attraction all evening had likely been overt—but that wasn't what startled me most. It was that the reality of the encounter felt starkly empty. Something had doused every spark within me, a frustrating and confusing thing—obviously also to Hendrik, who didn't take long to accept his cue to embark on our lengthy, awkward drive.

Silently I questioned what was wrong with me. I'd spent so much time longing for this handsome, athletic charmer who'd always been out of reach…

Or had that unconsciously been the appeal? Was that why any available fellows had failed to pique my interest?

Maybe, in truth, I was broken after all.

CHAPTER 23

"You're late."

I'd barely entered the house after leaving Hendrik, only to be greeted by Arie. Between the davenport and lamplit window, he stood in undershirt and trousers. His being home wasn't a surprise; he bused back most weekends to work at the factory and help with perpetual house repairs. But typically he wouldn't hover like a sentry on post. "Last I checked," he said, "you still have a curfew."

With his parents gone for the weekend to visit an ill friend, I hadn't fretted over running an hour behind, and now Arie was trying to amuse me by playing the strict parent.

I wasn't in the mood.

"Arie, please don't. It's been a long night. I just want to go to bed." Grasping my purse with both hands, I turned for the hallway.

"First you'll tell me where the hell you've been." His raised voice, underscored by his language, snapped me around to find his expression just as sharp.

Good grief. He wasn't fooling.

"I was…out. On a date. With Hendrik."

"Yeah," he said, impatient, closing in on me. "Saw your note. I want to know where."

Flustered, I tried to remember. "I don't know. Just some restaurant."

"And *that's* what took you all night?" The question was rhetorical, disbelieving.

"We had to drive back—from Brookfield."

A slight slackening of his forehead told me the distance wasn't expected, allowing me a chance to regroup.

"We went down there for a show, and it didn't start till nine." Not that it was any of his business. I straightened. Since when did he become my keeper? "It was a magic show, to be specific. And actually, it was the grandest time I've ever had." I added the jab, knowing that kind of activity was historically ours.

When his jaw clenched, I felt a twinge of guilt before he gave me a once-over. "Well, that's pretty obvious from your breath. Never mind the looks of you."

He'd caught the wine. And, I imagined, a suggestive smearing of my lipstick. Blindly I went to wipe it away, but he stepped forward, looming over me a full head taller.

"If that bastard got fresh with you—pushed you to do anything— you tell me this minute." His seething showed in the taut muscles of his neck and chest, both of which had broadened with age.

It was then that the core of his mood emerged: he was being protective.

Even so, that didn't give him the right to an interrogation. Overriding my undue shame, I jutted out my chin. "Nothing happened that I didn't allow."

His eyes widened. "What's that supposed to mean?"

"It means you're not my father, so stop pretending to be."

He gave a nod, but not the agreeable sort. "You're right. And thank God he isn't here to see *you* acting like a tramp."

I sucked in a partial breath, pierced clean through by the accusation. And yet, like an arrow ablaze, his conjuring of Papa in such a way lit a powder keg within me. It erupted so fast and forcefully that I didn't register the raising of my hand until after I'd slapped his cheek.

Slowly he looked back at me. Through the moisture filling my eyes, I could see his own words sweeping through his head, clearing away the anger, leaving a path of regret. "Fen…" He reached out a tentative hand, yet I backed up, trembling.

"No" was all I could say before rushing off to the solitude of my room.

A good half hour later, as I lay on my narrow bed with my face dried of tears, the kerosene lamp on my bureau flickered a low flame over the room. I'd kept the decor feminine but scant, never forgetting the space belonged to another.

Just then, two sets of taps traveled through the wall beside me, signifying hi.

Literally the word *hi*.

Arie and I had been sharing the wall since junior high, ever since Mr. Jansen collected enough materials to enclose half the porch to build his son a real bedroom. Boys, too, eventually needed privacy. Around that time, Morse code on "SOS" cards, from navy-themed bubble gum packs, had provided the two of us a creative way to chat on sleepless nights; we'd used taps for dots and sliding sounds for dashes. Although we rarely did this past our teens, the method was still ingrained.

Except this time, I had no desire to respond.

He continued regardless.

I WAS WORRIED. AND MEAN. IM SORRY.

I didn't answer.

IM A HEEL

A strong reply in the affirmative was tempting, but so was subjecting him to silence.

AND CHUMP

I still held out.

AND NINCOMPOOP

That one lured my smile. I pushed it down. Determined to stay cross, I sent back:

YES

Several seconds passed before he added:

BUT

Then nothing. I braced myself. If he thought he was justified in the things he said, he was roundly mistaken. I insisted he finish.

BUT WHAT

BUT YOURE

I waited, hands balling.

STILL A BAD MAGICIAN

Thrown off course, I released a snip of laughter. I quickly sealed my lips, regretting he might have heard.

More of his taps followed.

FORGIVE ME?

At the mere question, a powerful combination of two simple words, the last of my resentment slipped from my grasp, elusive as silt through my fingers.

PLEASE

A meager yes would have sufficed. For anyone else who had said what he did, I wouldn't have conceded even that much. But this was Arie.

I gave him my answer, begrudging though honest.

OF COURSE

———————

To make full amends, Arie invited me on an outing. We were to meet after our work shifts the very next evening. He refused to disclose what "big surprise" he had in store, solid bait for any aspiring illusionist. How could I possibly resist a dangling of suspense?

In hindsight, mind you, I should have stopped to think. I should have identified the true root of our quarrel. I should have recognized where it could lead.

And I never should have gone.

CHAPTER 24

When Arie guided me out of the taxicab and up to the ticket window, his secrecy became confounding. The evening excursion was hardly a rarity. We'd patronized the small, aged cinema quite a lot, not just for the low fare but because it clung loyally to silent films despite talkies being all the rage.

Per the marquee, its current showing of *The Invader* neglected to give much insight. I enjoyed Buster Keaton for certain, but not any more than a slew of other stars.

Inside, only a handful of guests peppered the worn auditorium, typical this time of year. Lacking an air cooler, the place offered little relief from the stagnant heat and humidity.

A bit sticky in my sundress, I settled in the seat next to Arie. He set aside his flat cap, then handed over our bag of popcorn and balanced a cup of lemonade on his knee.

I glanced around, wondering what I was missing.

"So…you and Hendrik," he said tentatively. "You're sweethearts now?"

This I wasn't prepared to answer. There was too much to explain, too much I still didn't understand. I simply shook my head.

His brows dipped. "Last night though…"

"I know how it must have looked, after what I said. But no." I sighed. "Trust me."

He nodded that he did. Yet with his demeanor darkening, I hurried to thwart his next natural thought.

"I swear, he didn't do anything wrong. It was nothing but a few kisses. He's a good egg. Just not for me." Anxious to move on, to avoid dwelling, I jerked my chin toward the screen. "Tell me, then. This is your big surprise?"

Expression easing, he reclined and shrugged a shoulder. "Almost."

Before I could probe, the lights dimmed and the projector beamed. Soon the film score played, a familiar tune, and the title screen appeared.

HOUDINI

IN

'HALDANE OF THE SECRET SERVICE'

This couldn't be right. According to the marquee—

I turned to Arie, who was waiting with a conspiratorial smile. "I swung by on lunch break," he said quietly. "Told the projectionist I was in the doghouse. He agreed to help for a little padding of his pocket."

That padding, I suspected, exceeded anything Arie ought to spare. But everything about the gesture was so personal and touching I couldn't help but grin. The picture was an all-time favorite of mine. I must have dragged him to see it half a dozen times before its showings at theaters turned scarce.

A few in the audience weren't as happy about the detour. Based on their grumbles, they preferred Buster Keaton. A crotchety man even pitched a handful of popcorn toward the projection window, calling the teenaged boy up there a birdbrain, then stomped out in a huff.

But the Houdini reel kept on spinning.

I whispered to Arie, "Won't he get booted for this?"

"Nah. His family owns the joint."

All the same, instinctively I sank low in my seat, blending in to deflect associated blame. A short-lived worry. In no time, the remaining attendees were caught up in the film. Really, how could they not be?

Arie too was watching then. I was about to interrupt to express how grateful I was, but of course he already knew. And from that unspoken understanding, my date with Hendrik glared in contrast.

Here I was in plain summer wear, hair casual to my shoulders and makeup untouched since morning, chomping on popcorn with no care about poise. For the person beside me had been there half my life. And not just in presence. More than anyone else, I could rely on him to save me from the clutches of darkness, whether with a reason to laugh or a lifeline of hope. He accepted me with quirks and all, respecting my opinions, of which Lord knew I had plenty. What was more, he'd always had such faith in me and my dreams that it didn't dawn on me to believe otherwise.

On the armrest between us lay his forearm, bare up to the short sleeves of his collared shirt. Compelled, I placed my hand over his. His fingers, roughened from his factory work, angled to curl around mine. The comfort and strength from his hold, as dependable as ever, brought immeasurable calm.

Then he glanced my way, and his smile widened with amusement. Revealing why, he released my hand and brushed something from my chin—a popcorn hull. I might have been embarrassed with any other fellow. Rather, I smiled back warmly.

And in that instant, I felt something between us shift.

As his thumb lingered on my face, all signs of levity left his features. His eyes gained an intensity that hitched my breath. We held that way for an interminable moment, a sudden and distinct sense of longing further thickening the air. At the sight of his parted lips, an overwhelming impulse drew me toward him. My heartbeat quickened as my mouth neared his, close enough to feel his breath.

But then, without warning, he pulled his head back. Retracting his hand, he snapped his eyes toward the film.

Jarred, baffled, I ebbed away from the armrest.

Obviously he regretted showing a blip of attraction—if that was even what it was. Akin to my episode with Hendrik, though reversed in roles, reality might have squashed Arie's interest. Or maybe none of it was mutual, outside of my imagination. After all, I'd leaned toward *him,* not the other way around.

Wishing to crawl away, I sank as far as I could into the confines of my seat. A film that ordinarily went much too fast became the slowest ever played. And for the very first time, I watched Houdini without actually watching.

Only the final frame brought welcome relief—until the cab ride home, which in comparison made the return drive with Hendrik seem a cozy, effortless trek.

———————

After we entered the house, I tugged the chain on the standing lamp by the davenport solely to light the way to my room, not to pursue a strained discussion.

When schoolboys used to razz us, Arie had made clear our relationship was "nothing like that." And I'd agreed, at the time. Since then, flocks of pretty gals had fawned over him in high school, though he'd always been too focused on studies and work and his future to pay them much mind, and now I'd become one of those pitiable admirers.

"Fen…" He removed his cap. It was his first utterance since we'd left the theater.

"Thanks for the date," I mumbled, then caught myself and stammered, "For the outing." A fresh tide of embarrassment crested over me. Dropping my gaze, I headed for my bed, where I planned to remain until his departure for Grand Rapids. In fourteen hours roughly. A lifetime.

"*Fen*," he repeated, insistent.

Nearly at my door, I slowed to a stop. The singular mercy of the evening was his parents' absence for another full day, sparing me from putting on a front for them too.

Pinning on a pleasant expression, I turned around as he approached.

"At the show," he said, "with what happened there, with us, I want to explain."

I was about to feign ignorance when I recalled his overt rejection. All I could do now was patch the rip dividing us with rationale. "Really, there's no need. You don't see me that way, and that's entirely fine. We're fine."

"Please. Just listen."

"We'll talk during your next visit, all right?" And by *talk*, of course,

I meant sticking to any nonmortifying topic, further allayed by the passage of time. With a flash of a smile, I again tried to disappear into my room, but he halted me by grasping my hand. His tenacity was suddenly maddening.

I whipped toward him. "Arie, I already told you—"

All at once, his lips were on mine. I'd only just registered the kiss before it deepened. He tasted of lemon and sugar and smelled of the same, mixed faintly with summer sweat. Then his fingers were at the nape of my neck, in the thick of my hair. Heat roiled through my body. My arms responded by wrapping around him, drawing his chest to mine. I savored the muscles in his back, his shoulders. As if I were stricken by vertigo, the solidity of my world turned groundless and fluid. At the roving of his hands, down my sides and hips, a soft moan rose in my throat.

Given all our years as friends, having stirrings of doubt would have been natural. Even some level of awkwardness. But there was only escalated yearning, so strong it was palpable. As if something bound had been freed.

After a time, with my back pressed against my doorframe, he was kissing my neck when my fingers trailed the collar of his shirt and found the top button. Without thought, I released the binding and moved on to the next. Arie drew his head back, his breaths ragged. He watched me continue down the series of buttons and slip off his shirt. As I went to lift his undershirt, his stomach muscles tightened, but he stilled my hands.

"Wait," he said in a throaty whisper. "If...you're not ready for any of this...it's okay." The desire in his eyes was unmistakable, bordering on primal. And yet at any point, he would stop at the smallest trace of my hesitation. I knew this with total certainty, and that fact only magnified my yearning to be closer.

By way of an answer, I kept hold of one of his hands and led him through my room to the foot of the bed. He asked again if I was sure, searching my face for the truth.

I'd never been surer of anything. For once again, it was just the two of us at night, existing in our own private world where I needn't worry over perception or judgment, propriety or consequence. The entire universe became the room around us.

Free to act on impulse, we soon lay together with clothes peeled away, skin on skin, vulnerable yet safe. His movements, while tender and cautious—almost overly so—filled me with a rush of foreign, indescribable sensations. And through the height of our intimacy, I came to realize what I should have long before then: the reason I'd shunned other boys was never about Hendrik or about part of me being broken.

It was always about Arie.

CHAPTER 25

Crickets chirped outside the partially open window, their soothing tune riding the warm night air. In the shadows on a bed made for one, Arie lay behind me curled on his side, propping his head with his hand. His other fingers grazed my upper back in slow, hypnotic loops and swirls. Even as I teetered on the groggy edge of sleep, I could sense his mental gears cranking.

I teased with a groan, "Doesn't your brain *ever* turn off?"

His caresses paused. No witty comeback. Instead, he slid his hand to my waist, where the sheet draped us both. His heated breaths hovered at my ear, raising tiny hairs on my neck. "Marry me, Fen."

The string of words drifted through me. The instant they took hold, my mind cleared with a jolt. Had I misheard? I twisted to view Arie by a wedge of lamplight from the doorway. The gleam in his eyes provided the answer.

Fragments of a laugh tumbled out of me. "Arie, that's crazy."

He raised up high on his elbow. "Why?"

"Be-because." Apparently I needed to voice the obvious. "It's absurdly fast, for one. I mean, you and I... We only just..."

"Met?" A smile played at the corners of his mouth.

"I'm being serious."

"So am I."

The passionate turn our night had taken, while surprising, felt like a wondrous and perfect next step. But marriage required consideration and planning. Practicality.

I moved to sit upright with the sheet to my chest. "You have college to finish," I reminded him.

"And I will, in less than a year." His chest muscles shifted as he brushed a strand of hair from my shoulder, cluttering my focus.

"That's dandy…for *you*. But I have plans too."

"Which is why," he contended, "after graduation, I say we start our lives in New York. Just picture it, Fen. Out east, I'll build the grandest tunnels and bridges the world's ever seen, and you'll break into the biz and become a huge star. Broadway must have the best stages anywhere, wouldn't you think?"

"Well, yeah. Sure." Performing in New York would be splendid, eventually, but going there straightaway seemed entirely overwhelming. "I've always figured, though, on starting off in another city. Some place like"—I struggled to remember—"Chicago."

He gave this some thought, a chance for me to ground myself, I hoped.

"All right," he said. "Chicago it is."

"Don't be silly. You can't make a decision that fast."

"I just did."

"But…you shouldn't."

"Fen." He sat up fully to face me, his tone firming. "Do you love me?"

I hedged, looking away, exasperated by the diversion. "It's not that simple."

Gently he cupped my cheek, guiding me back to him. "Just answer me. Do you?"

Though it was a truth he already knew, I conceded, "Of course I do."

"Then everything else? They're details."

I sighed, still grappling with reservations.

After a moment, he lowered his hand, and I watched his fingers link with mine. "Tonight, at the show," he said, "that was me being afraid. Afraid of changing what we've had. Afraid of losing you. I've felt like that for a while, but to finally be with you like this… It's worth all the risk."

His thumb caressed my palm, and I couldn't help softening. When I lifted my gaze to his, he went on, "So you see? We can still do all the things we've ever dreamed about, with our careers and big cities. But we'll do it together, someday even with a family of our own. I love you, Fen, more than anything. And I can make you happy, if you let me."

He made it all sound so alluring, so plausible. Easy, even.

"Please," he said. "Say yes."

My heart warmed at his sincerity, but even more at the sight and feel of our interwoven hands. They were a reminder of all we'd survived together, of the many ways our lives were inexplicably joined and, above all, of how much I never wanted that to end.

Besides, given the night behind us, how could we ever go back?

Swayed beyond doubt, I smiled and replied with a single life-altering word. "Yes."

CHAPTER 26

In the morning sunlight, I awoke to a note on the bedside table.

You were too peaceful to wake. Helping a factory pal lay a roof. We'll tell my parents over supper.
  -Your loving husband-to-be

I'd have relished the surreal, endearing sign-off if not for the mention of his parents. A half-panicked survey of the room assured me Arie's clothes were no longer strewn about. Then I recalled that the couple wouldn't be back until evening. Thank heavens.

Still, how would they take the news? Their sustained introduction of me as "Arie's friend" affirmed they never viewed me as a daughter. Yet after they'd cared for me like family, any romance between Arie and me could strike them as wrong—and, either way, his mother could easily rule me an inadequate match. At best, a distraction from his goals. She reliably did the same with any other girl who'd shown interest. Even after seven years of my living with the woman, though sufficiently kind, she upheld a fair degree of distance.

In fact, over the years, I'd overheard her cite an old Dutch saying: *Where two religions share a pillow, the Devil sleeps between.*

Despite all our praying and churchgoing together, perhaps his parents still saw me as far too different.

And Papa—would he have felt the same?

The daunting possibilities mounted until I rolled onto my side, and from my pillow, I caught a scent. Closing my eyes, I breathed Arie in, and with him a wave of tranquility. I could feel him curled up behind me, could hear him whispering that he loved me and that if I loved him, the rest were merely details.

At the thought, everything but the promise of him, and us, fell away.

Practically floating, I ventured out of the house midmorning to buy ingredients for supper. A traditional Dutch meal for Arie's parents just might cushion the shock of our announcement. And anyway, it couldn't hurt.

In line at the market, as I waited to give the shopkeeper a list of items to fetch from the stockroom, visceral flashes of the prior night swept through me. I fought off a grin, conscious of the ladies chatting before me in the queue. I hoped they wouldn't notice the telling flush of my face. Not that it arose from shame, as being with Arie felt the opposite of sinful; it was from giddiness. Sheer bliss.

A frivolity I was about to regret.

For it made me careless in that moment.

I discerned this later upon reflection. If I'd been more vigilant, I could have prepared for the significance of the sounds to come: the squeaking of a stroller being wheeled into the store, the grunts of frustration from inside the carriage, a woman's assurances about going home soon.

None of these on their own were out of the ordinary, certainly not while at a market. But my circumstances had changed, my perspective shifted to that of a soon-to-be wife. If I'd been clearheaded, I would have recognized this and shielded myself before the infant unleashed a tearful wail. It was the sort of cry that, these days, caused me but mild agitation from a timeworn scratching at the door of my memories. Yet when the woman, now behind me, drew the baby to her shoulder and rocked and patted its tiny body, the door within me swung open, pulling me back to the aftermath of the stampede—to a lifeless mother being prayed over, her infant bawling inconsolably.

"Now, now, sweetheart," the woman in the market soothed. "Mama is here. Everything will be all right."

It was a comfort every child needed, even deserved to hear, though such words from my lips would carry no truth. I knew firsthand how fast a kid of any age could wind up alone, dumped in an orphanage like tainted goods in a junkyard. For me to be personally responsible for an injustice within that realm was…unthinkable.

By the time the woman calmed her baby, a painful clarity had speared me to the core: I would never be her.

I could never be a mother.

That reality, I supposed, had long been lurking at the borders of my mind. Unconscious denial had allowed me to avoid picturing myself a spinster. But now at a crossroads, forced to make a choice, the idea of marrying and becoming a parent conjured angst to the point of nausea.

Someday, Arie had said, we'd have a family of our own. He wanted to be a father. All these years, that much was a given, and rightly so. He'd be extraordinary. Not only would he be a kindhearted provider, same as Mr. Jansen, but also a fierce protector hell-bent on keeping his little ones safe. At least he'd try—like so many men in Eden Springs. Like even the father who bore a mountainous build yet collapsed under the weight of that tiny coffin, broken by the loss of three children not even he could save.

If I told Arie where I stood, I knew he'd understand. He would insist it didn't matter, that he'd need only me to be happy.

And he would be lying.

———

I registered very little of the walk home, just that I carried none of the items from the list crumpled in my hand. When I entered my room, the choice before me—the right choice—hit hard as a slap.

All around me, the memory of Arie's touches, his words in the shadows, infused every inch of space. I'd told him I loved him because I did. So much so, the thought of life without him caused a searing pang in my chest.

But he deserved more.

Which was why I needed to leave.

I couldn't wait. If he walked in right then, I'd lose my already tenuous will.

In a sudden frenzy, I rushed to the storage closet and grabbed a large travel bag. Through split-second decisions, practicality rivaling sentiment, I packed my personal belongings and stage supplies. For now, Papa's boots would stay, but his pocket watch would come; my large magic rings wouldn't fit, but trick cuffs and card decks would.

I moved on to my nightstand drawer and stopped. Emotions swelled unexpectedly from the jumble beneath my fingers: a swatch of brown yarn from Mrs. Jansen's knitting lessons; the Christmas ornament I'd made with a shell and ribbons, which I had hung on a tree Arie cut down; a pocket booklet of constellations that, compliments of Mr. Jansen, had kicked off my astronomy-loving phase.

All together they formed a collage of memories, reflecting the life here I had built. One I longed to continue, with Arie most of all.

Maybe he was right about any issues being details...

Then again, even Hendrik and Nita Dewitt, the most idyllic of couples, parted ways for simply wanting "different things." Such *things*, after all, could mean everything.

At my desk, I snatched a pencil and two sheets of stationery. On the first, I told Mr. and Mrs. Jansen how tremendously I appreciated all their years of generosity, how an unforeseen stage opportunity had called me away but I'd soon send an update.

Eyes clouding, I proceeded to the second sheet. I clutched the pencil, desperate to explain, horrified by the assumptions Arie could otherwise make.

But logic stepped in. It argued that my saying too much could lure him to find me, and once back in his arms, my resistance would falter.

For his sake alone, I forced my hand to scribe the meager truth I could manage.

My dearest Arie,
I pray one day you'll forgive me.
Forever, Fen

In his bedroom, converted from a porch, I placed the message on his pillow. I recalled the mornings I'd wake him from oversleeping, how he'd look up at me with bleary eyes. My heart seized at the vision. Shoving it away, I weighed down the folded note with a cherished token. It was the wooden train that had first brought us together. A gift that truly belonged to him.

Tears spilled over as I stood in the entry. Arm draped with my coat, my personal funds tucked behind the lining, I gripped the handle of my hastily stuffed bag. This time unable to mouth goodbye, I slipped out the door and into another life.

1943

CHAPTER 27

Late February 1943
London, England

Much like my move from Amesboro, impulsive yet necessary, my stay in London has been everything and nothing as I expected.

Upon my arrival, I was briefly assigned to a typing pool, perhaps giving the War Office a chance to check my background for any criminal or unpatriotic leanings. Thereafter, utilizing my "unique and innovative skills," as Christopher Hutton put it, I've indeed been tasked with helping save Allied lives—in a secretive manner. As his assistant at Section Nine of Military Intelligence, or MI9, I'm to design escape-and-evasion gadgets for our airmen, POWs, and others covertly fighting for the cause.

Regrettably, my success in doing so has been sorely lacking.

More and more I have to remind myself how, four years ago, my initial months in Chicago were nearly as challenging. In the work arena, the trials and obstacles had similarly taken me by surprise.

That isn't to say I'd envisioned stage careers back then being handed out on street corners like dailies from paperboys. I'd known times were still rough for many, but the insulation of my Dutch community had left me naive about just how many doors would be slammed in my face: theaters, magic societies, variety agencies. I knocked on them all, even willing to start as a backstage maid if need be. The sole offer I received was for a lewd role in burlesque.

I confess, the despicable option did tempt me as I lay in my cold, grimy tenement, fretting over funds, unable to sleep for the police sirens, passing drunkards, and tenants bellowing through walls as thin as those back in the Copper Country. Curled up in a musty blanket, I would think of Arie and weep until drifting off.

It was after such a night that I stood outside Union Station, performing sleights of hand to four or five onlookers for pocket change, when a pale, heavyset cop descended. The hard bill of his hat shaded his eyes. In lieu of ordering me to clear out, as he'd done on two prior instances, in a faint brogue, he declared my arrest, claiming I'd been warned.

More passersby stopped as he went to the trouble of applying handcuffs. A grandstanding move, it seemed. When he bent to gather my prop bag, a woman gasped and several men chuckled. It took the officer a moment to realize I'd slipped free and was dangling the bindings on a finger.

Confused and flustered, he reclaimed his shackles—or rather, those that appeared to be his; already I'd swapped them with a trick set from a hidden pocket of my black magician's coat. My brazenness might have owed mainly to sleep deprivation—or to the overall feeling that I had little to lose—but I presented my wrists in a fashion border-ing a dare. By then, a growing crowd had encircled us. The officer reattached the cuffs, detectably self-conscious over his folly, and took care to cinch them tighter. Not that it mattered to my efforts. For as he turned for my bag, even more easily I maneuvered out again.

Spectators laughed, their faces alight. Between hatted heads, kids stretched for a peek. When I offered back the restraints, the cop didn't hesitate in reaching to snatch them away, only to have them vanish midswipe. His gaze dropped reflexively, scanning the pavement.

More watchers, more giggles, a smattering of applause. We were a Charlie Chaplin act. A Laurel-and-Hardy show.

The officer, having caught on, searched my sleeves, then my visible exterior pocket, and out came the trick cuffs. Glowering, he went to clamp them back on me, unaware I'd flicked a lever rendering them unlockable.

The crowd's laughter from his subsequent attempts warmed me to the core; it seemed a lifetime since I'd reaped such joys. But a flash in the cop's eyes and the reddening of his neck, bright as rising lava, said he'd had enough.

The prospect of a paddy wagon reined in my senses.

I snapped toward the audience. "Ladies and gentlemen, please give a round of applause to this fine sport of an officer who, unbeknownst to you all, had generously agreed to assist with my act, purely for your viewing pleasure."

The policeman startled slightly, and a burst of clapping flowed his way.

I'd lobbed an easy out for us both. Yet I could see his deliberating, a pendulum swinging between duty and pride. I was bracing for the worst when he tipped his hat cordially toward the crowd. A show within a show.

As the viewers dispersed, many tossing coins into my top hat on the ground, the officer whispered hotly near my ear. "I catch ya round here again, and your next stage'll be the cell."

I nodded with a tight smile. Once he strode away, I exhaled with relief.

Only after everyone was gone did I notice a curious contribution to my hat; it was the business card from a dime museum with a note scrawled on the back:

Come tomorrow

The exchange with the officer turned out to be a plain piece of luck. Beyond the retention of my freedom, it led me to a job, albeit meager paying, then to a partnership with the museum's unpolished yet charming contortionist, from which together we paved a path of opportunities.

Until that path diverged.

I've thought of Charles often these past five months. Early on, while visiting the likes of Buckingham Palace, Kensington Gardens, and the Tower of London, I imagined the wisecracks he would make—about Rapunzel being handy or King Henry needing more hobbies, topped off with "royal" puns—and I'd miss the friendship we once had.

I do wonder how he's faring. Most often, I envision him up on a stage, wowing audiences with our reliable acts, maybe a couple fresh ones, all aided by some peppy new assistant.

And yes, I've questioned my choice to part ways: first, during my ship voyage arranged by Hutton, which required zigzagging the Atlantic to avoid German U-boats; and later while hunkered down in myriad air-raid shelters—during which explosions from anti-aircraft shells and the Luftwaffe's incendiaries, thankfully, have been infrequent.

Cellars will never earn my fondness. Nor will crowded stairwells, like those descending into the Underground railway stations all around London, providing safe havens—and practical transportation—when needed. Nonetheless, from repetition and necessity, I've learned to endure them. Conditioned by the blare of air-raid alerts, my brain has come to accept that survival relies on going belowground, not staying above.

It does help that, throughout the sirens, Britons largely stay calm and orderly when filing into those shelters. And despite their tired faces and daily drab attire, many bring along the cheer of games, books, and biscuits. Even tea, naturally. Proof that any circumstance can quickly become one's norm.

Further evidence abounds now as I ride a red double-decker bus through the city, past Hyde Park toward headquarters. A pair of schoolgirls with peppermint sticks settle into their seats; not all children have been sent off to the safety of the countryside. One totes her books, the other a brown box for a gas mask. Across the aisle, a wizened man holds a sack from the market, a routine activity that lies in sharp contrast to the black band on his upper sleeve signifying mourning.

I turn to my window. Past the mesh—protection against blasts—amorous couples at a theater leave a *Casablanca* showing, just next door to buildings reduced to rubble. Beside sandbags near Woolworths, a cluster of ladies yammer the Monday afternoon away, distracted but briefly by a telegram delivery boy zipping past on a motorcycle, no doubt carrying another dreaded notice.

After four years of war, to these people, the sound of that motor is as usual as the screaming and whistling of bombs, the sirens of fire trucks racing toward flames. It's all a way of life, including endless queues and ration books and always doing one's part. Should you forget that last bit for a second, a plethora of posters will be swift to remind you. They're as ubiquitous as servicemen, same as back home, with outfits that sound like high-fashion ensembles: Austin Reed uniforms, Sam Browne belts, Wellington boots.

I know them inside and out at this point, on account of my work with MI9. If there's a fresh, effective way to hide an escape-and-evasion tool in those garments, my job is to find it.

Long before I arrived, in the vein of my handcuffs ploy, Hutton—or Major Hutton, officially—found heaps of crafty ways for airmen downed in enemy zones to elude detainment: tiny compasses screwed into buttons, buckles, and collar studs; silk maps sewn into jackets and stuffed into hollow heels; thin, flexible Gigli saws threaded into shoelaces whose metal tips were magnetized to point north when swung on a thread.

He designed enough devices to fill a catalog he presented to U.S. intelligence, familiarizing his efforts to those like Arie. But several dozen gadgets have since been blown, discovered by German guards at POW camps scattered across western Europe, most of which Hitler still holds with his vicious iron claws.

Each minute of our work, then, is a race against captivity, the stakes being the survival of servicemen. And the outcome of the war. Considered valuable assets, Allied POWs are duty-bound to escape—obviously to provide intel and rejoin the fight but also to drain enemy manpower and resources. Thus, in all my free waking moments, I sketch vigorously in notepads to improve past inventions, my signature skill. That is, when I'm not an errand girl—which is more than half the time lately—delivering sensitive memos, gathering samples, dropping off prototypes. I needn't look farther than the boxes on my lap, piled chest high, to recall the peculiarity and secrecy of my job.

Granted, only the airmen's footwear I designed—innovative, adaptable, and extensively rigged—has earned notable success. The rest of my achievements largely amount to a host of minor modifications. Still, I assure myself that ample opportunities remain, thanks to Hutton's imaginative doing. As tampering with Red Cross packages would violate the Geneva Convention, we've endeavored to create fictional charities. Their shell addresses, borrowed from buildings destroyed in the Blitz, are printed on fancy letterhead with names like the Authors' Society and the Travellers' Association—a daring name, that one. Then into relief parcels, we pack clothing, hygienic items, and pastimes that German guards welcome, believing the activities will pacify their prisoners and distract them from plotting. Ironically so.

Not all our shipped items are "loaded," of course. Gadgets are strategically sprinkled here and there—like *salt in the dough*, Papa would say—and encoded letters from "behind the wire" inform our department of what's been requested, received, and uncovered.

That's how I learned, for instance, the fate of the gramophone records I devised. In a previous version, false identity cards and travel documents were embedded between the disk's two sides; alternately, they held foreign currency for train passes and bribes. My version boasted an expanded cavity, though equally stealth, that could hold all those items plus a tissue-thin map.

Unfortunately, after my boxful arrived at a camp, a postal-room POW dropped the package. A disk cracked open, exposing the contraband. Gramophone records were thereby added to the Germans' watch list, and "Operation Smash-Hit"—a name we thought clever—met the doom of its name.

Other times, my ideas have been ruled out due to materials running low, or they posed too great a risk, as occurred a month ago. Inspired by quick changes for the stage, I'd used my sewing skills to make a British uniform reversible into a German's. But any fabric we could obtain, it was decided, wouldn't pass muster up close and could cause friendly fire from a distance.

Just as disappointing, though more maddening, was being beaten to the punch—and by a fellow magician, at that. Though British illusionist Jasper Maskelyne is in North Africa leading the Camouflage Experimental Section, supposedly hiding whole ships and convoys—with mirrors and painted canvases, I presume—his designs find their way into production at MI9. Among our competing proposals have been double-layered playing cards that split when soaked in liquid, revealing a giant map when laid out as a whole deck. Edging me out, Jasper perfected them first.

Still, I plod on.

What else would I do?

After transferring buses, I reenter the town of Beaconsfield, where my department is headquartered. The driver swerves through another dizzying roundabout, and my unplanned parcel rattles a reminder that soon enough, I'll prove to everyone that my coming here wasn't a misguided error, on both my part and Hutton's.

Fortifying my resolve, I recall his words from this morning. At the inn I've made my current home, his telephoned message was delivered to my room:

Meet at office late afternoon for new
development regarding scheme.

Hutton's suspicion of wire taps has become so heightened I'm surprised by any reference to our work, even if vague. All the same, from his mention of a "new development," I suddenly feel certain that good news awaits, that one of my shelved ideas is about to see daylight, that demonstrating my value, I've at last created something that truly makes a difference.

CHAPTER 28

As per usual this time of day, intelligence activity is abustle at the Wilton Park estate. Requisitioned by MI9, the sprawling property hosts a two-century-old Palladian mansion known as the "White House" and a collection of Nissen huts, all used for work even more hush-hush than mine. There's speculation of a camouflaged bunker as well, rumored to hold enemy POWs, even high-ranking Nazis, for interrogation.

On the property's edge, amid the contrasting serenity of towering trees and rolling parkland, I enter Camp 20. The prefabricated building is where I report regularly to Hutton. Being twenty-odd miles clear of what he calls the "blinkered pen pushers" of Parliament, we're permitted the latitude needed to creatively aid not only escapers and evaders but Resistance groups throughout Europe.

In the entry, service members are sprinkled about, including two from the ATS, the Auxiliary Territory Service being the women's branch of the British Army. Assigned to Hutton's team, his so-called lovelies assist with our packing, shopkeeping, and what minimal accounting is possible with our boss, all while keeping up with the latest gossip. Spotting me in passing, they pause their animated chat. The smiles they impart reflect the common treatment I'm afforded: courteous yet rigid. I return the greeting in kind as I continue on my way.

As an American, and an odd "gadget girl" perhaps, again I'm an outsider.

Down a corridor, the ringing of phones and the clacking of unseen typewriters bounce off the white bricked walls. About to cross my path is Lenora Walsh, one of Hutton's military drivers. A few years my junior, she's willowy in her shapeless British uniform with a billed cap over cropped reddish hair. Though her large eyes and rounded nose comprise a friendly face, she too maintains guarded formality.

"Good afternoon, Miss Vos."

"Private Walsh," I reply pleasantly as she slows to a stop.

"It appears you might be in need of assistance."

A bit dazed from my bus ride, my mind scrabbles for reference.

"With your parcels?" She gestures, a reminder of the stack filling my arms.

"Yes. Right. *Those* parcels." I shake my head with a quick laugh that brings out her smile, refreshingly genuine if brief. "They're really not heavy, so no trouble. But thank you."

Men's chuckles drift from a nearby meeting room, denoting sociable relief from grimmer topics. In that instant, paired with the levity in Private Walsh's eyes, I too find myself yearning for a chat. I could finally learn about her life beyond her duties. Maybe she'd even be game for an outing. While I've no interest in an underground dance hall crammed with hot-to-trot servicemen, catching a film would be far more enjoyable with a companion—as it used to be back home.

I go to suggest as much, yet I'm too late. Already she's moving past me.

And all the better.

I'm here to work, not for leisure.

I march toward Hutton's office in my low-heeled pumps, as plain and practical as my daily dresses. From his half-open door, the room ever resembles a den hit by hefty gusts of wind. Files, documents, maps, and books—several splayed open—form a haphazard maze. Adjacent to a window with a courtyard view, Hutton is seated at his desk. Considering how often he's on the go, it's remarkable to find him planted in one spot. Not to say he's lazing about. Rather, he's hunched over a mess of paperwork, showcasing the thinning of his dark hair. Being "temperamentally opposed to orthodox methods"—as he puts it—he wears not a uniform but a disheveled suit while puffing intently on a cigarette, likely his twentieth of the day.

I knock. At his lack of response, I try again louder, jolting him. He appears disoriented, face drawn and eyes perpetually tired behind his glasses, until homing in on my face.

"Miss Vos. Yes, yes. Come in." He flitters his hand, seeming impatient, but it's merely the pace of his work style. The longer the war stretches, the more ramped his vibration.

I've barely passed his oversized "toy" table, where an array of combs, toothbrushes, and fountain pens lay dismantled for rigging, when his gaze latches onto my top box. At roughly one square foot and half that in height, it's the smaller of my two deliveries and the sole one wrapped. On cream paper, set off with black twine, it's addressed to Carl Howard, a code name used for shipping with initials deliberately matching Hutton's.

"I see it's arrived. Brilliant." He discards his cigarette in an ashtray next to his half-filled teacup. Rising, he accepts the package that clinks when tilted. But instead of tearing it open, he looks quizzically at the larger box, which I rest on the corner of his desk. "Are those the new samples from Gillette?"

"Not yet. They'll be ready tomorrow." The magnetized razors, implanted in military shaving kits to work as compasses, ought to dodge detection from enemy guards. For a time. "These here," I correct proudly, "are a little something I stumbled upon at King's Cross."

He watches as I unfurl the flaps, revealing a medley of strangers' personal belongings: wrist and pocket watches, an empty billfold, solitary gloves, cosmetic mirrors and lipstick tubes, a ladies' scarf and such. I'd spied the boxful while picking up his parcel at the lost-items department at the London railway terminal, the destination we use for confidential shipments. Nowadays Hutton has nearly every package routed there, if not retrieved personally.

"They're from 'Left Luggage,'" I explain. "They'd been there for more than a month, so considered abandoned. I figured the next time Wing Commander Moretti needs tricked-out accessories, they'll already look worn."

Hutton looks pleased, nodding briskly. "A clever idea, Miss Vos."

He understands my reasoning of course. The wing commander, a fatherly type with Italian roots, nicknamed "Gramps" by his aircrew for his wreath of dark hair and ripe age of forty-two, often skirts protocol to obtain our sample gadgets for passengers—agents, presumably—of his nightly ferrying drops.

"I presume they were free of charge?" Hutton says.

"Completely. I simply told the clerk they'd be used for the war effort." From the Official Secrets Act I signed upon first arriving at Wilton Park, I knew not to expound unless necessary and with permission. "He handed them straight over. Both his sons are in the army, he said, so he was terribly keen to help."

Hutton nods again, but with a dimming expression.

Only then do I recall the parallels, with his own son in the Australian Army and another in the Royal Navy, both back in action after recovering from wounds. I assume there was a wife at some point but have refrained from probing, leaving the past where it belongs.

I divert to alleviate the mood. "Sir, from your message this morning, I believe you had news of a development…"

"Hmm? Oh, yes." His demeanor doesn't lighten. If anything, it gains additional weight, appearing to add a slight quiver to his hand as he gestures. "Please, have a seat."

As he resettles behind his desk, the prospect of my celebration slipping away, I lower onto a ladder-back chair across from him.

"Is everything all right, Major?"

"A rather sticky problem has arisen, I'm afraid, as pertains to the boots."

"The boots?"

"Why, our 'Hutton Flying Boots.'"

I knew what he meant, naturally. I just didn't expect them to be an issue. After all, the airmen's footwear had endured extensive scrutiny before distribution, by Hutton included, as a pilot of the Great War. Although they were awarded his name—a decision unworthy of protest, as I'd incorporated several elements he previously crafted, and besides, I was long accustomed to working behind the scenes—I was unabashedly proud of the result. Particularly when they were approved for the entire Royal Air Force, the heavy-bomber crews taking priority.

The RAF's original boots, you see, bore padding that was troublesome in both wet and hot weather. Worst of all, they were conspicuous for evading capture. And so I transformed a comfortable business shoe into an airman's boot, armed with hidden compartments, saw-encased shoelaces, and a cloth loop concealing a razor—for a key purpose. When needed, the tiny blade slices away the ankle-high webbing, detaching the fur-lined leggings to create a waistcoat, and presto! Civilian shoes that blend right in. They were splendidly cunning, many said. Practical. Lifesaving.

"Sir, I don't understand. Whatever has gone wrong with them?"

"By all reports, they are simply not withstanding the cold properly."

"That can't be. The base of the shoe keeps plenty warm."

"It is the webbing, I daresay. On the lengthy flights at high altitudes, the freezing air is seeping right through. Most of the heavy-bomber crews, evidently, have reverted to their old regulation boots."

My instinctive thought, the easiest fix, is to replace the problematic material.

Except it's *not* that easy. Webbing is fundamental to the entire effect.

"Okay, then," I say, striving to seem unfazed. "I'll hop to and solve it. I'll call on the factory today—"

"Such labors," he interjects, "would be for naught. I realize this is a fine smack in the eye. You will no doubt recall, however, the angry screed from a brass hat at the Air Ministry, how we had *encroached* on his ruddy territory. Colonel Crockatt is therefore plainly of the opinion that we not take up the matter."

Crockatt, as the head of MI9 and a decorated war hero who served with the Royal Scots, is a shrewd organizer with no respect for red tape and thus ascribes to leniency. Which is to say, his order for us to move on means precisely that. But then I remember.

"The boots we've sent out. There are already five thousand pairs. What will they do with them all?"

"Don't bother your head, Miss Vos. They might yet be of use to crews of the smaller aircraft. One never knows. Must keep a stiff upper lip, eh?"

If they plan to dispose of them, he might not tell me; where my knowledge isn't required, he often keeps dealings to himself.

Though further deflated, I nod and smile. "Sure enough. I'll whip up something far better."

"That's the spirit." He smiles back, although I sense his disappointment is equal to mine. Likely greater. His namesake boots have been a bragging point for months.

Sure, in all fairness, if anyone should have caught their flaw early on, why not one of the many pilots and RAF brass who examined and tested them out? Still I'm agitated I didn't fully factor in conditions of which I was aware. Wing Commander Moretti has even jokingly asked if I could devise a portable potbelly stove for his nighttime missions, claiming the flights were cold enough to freeze a can of soup.

A stove...

For soup...

My thoughts gradually shift, moving on, as is sensible to do.

Even hours later in the quiet of my room, Moretti's words loop in my head. Combined with a sliver of my past—one bordering on blasphemy by Mrs. Jansen's standards—an idea develops.

I envision a device that's not just innovative but immeasurably useful. For airmen. For operatives. For the Resistance. Maybe even for civilians suffering in the cross-fire.

But first I require a vital ingredient.

While keeping heedful of its risks.

CHAPTER 29

Despite my limited time in a spiritualist's employ, assisting with setups and cleanups and as a participant when needed for a séance circle, I'd learned quite a lot. That included a stern lesson from Madame Esme that now both inspires and worries me.

"This is *not* to be careless with," warned the turban-clad woman after I stumbled upon her bag of a chalky substance. Quicklime. "The smallest addition of water can scorch your precious skin." Therein lay the secret to her illusion, I realized, of warming a glass orb to signal the presence of ghosts.

I'm counting on that ability again. Not pertaining to the ghosts, mind you, but as an effective source of heat. By lamplight at the desk in my room, I prepare to test my latest prototype. Mimicking the telescopic design of the Milk Can Escape, a soup can has been sealed in a larger tin. In the gap between them sits a measured amount of quicklime and, at the base, a compartment of water, potentially creating a self-heating meal.

It's taken me several days to determine the ideal size and type of cans, plus the proportions of the contents. Luckily, Hutton managed to acquire plenty of quicklime for my attempts. Not a shock, I suppose. He possesses an exceptional ability to pull strings. Even my extended stay here at the George, a lovely old coaching inn located in Beaconsfield and just a half mile from Wilton Park, is by his arrangement.

I grip my bradawl, essentially a screwdriver with a pointed tip. Should this fail to work, I have a second sample to try, but no more. Any additions will take days to receive. The manager of a local cannery already granted me a favor by producing these so soon.

"Let's make them count," I say, hopeful.

Near the bottom of the tin, I poke two holes to puncture the water stall, keeping the quicklime safely contained—if my design holds up. I flip the gadget over and cautiously leave it on my desk. There's a trickling sound but no visible leak. A good sign. Then comes hissing, the formation of calcium hydroxide.

My internal clock ticks away the seconds.

Five...ten...fifteen...

I recall my script from the stage: *belief, perseverance, imagination.* Sadly, that combination hasn't yet been enough for me to outdo Hutton's former right-hand man. When transferred overseas, the "charming, energetic, quick-minded" Peter Baker left an impossibly high bar, according to the major's grating reminders: "Young Baker did this, Young Baker did that, and oh, another grand bit regarding Young Baker." Plus, the military's bureaucratic hurdles, often more so for women, haven't helped my cause.

Gauging progress, I grasp the tin. I detect the water bubbling, the container growing warmer. "That's it. Keep going." Self-heating soup would be a feat in and of itself, but to achieve it in under a minute would be doubly impressive.

Forty...forty-five...fifty...

Though it might be too soon, I crank open the tin and inner can. Steam rises, a promising sight. The scent of pea soup offers only slight reprieve from the inn's vegetable stew, meatless and bland, served almost nightly.

I stir the soup with a spoon and take a sip. The temperature is...

"Perfect. I've done it!"

The announcement is wasted on an empty room. I yearn for someone to share it with, and not just anyone. I think of all the evenings I watched Arie fiddling with contraptions or studying how to engineer marvels from scratch, many concurrently practical and extraordinary. I smile and wonder if he'd be proud.

Then realizing I'll never know, I feel a squeeze in my chest.

I try to purge him from my mind, to retain the joy of my achievement, but memories clamor to the surface. To drown them out, I move to my nightstand and turn on the wireless. Another BBC news report on the Berlin bombing raid. Fine news to be sure, though in this moment, I'd much favor a comedic program, like *It's That Man Again*. Even the daily recipe show with tips for reconstituting powdered eggs would do.

I click off the radio.

Wilton Park is generally accessible at all hours, given the urgency of assignments. In Hutton's office, I could fetch gadgets from the work-in-progress table and find distraction in tinkering.

Beyond my blackout curtains, there's no sound of rain. So I throw on my shoes and coat and hustle toward the lobby with flashlight in hand. Blue cellophane keeps the bulb within nighttime regulations. Once outside on Wycombe End, I savor the crisp, cool air that smells of damp meadow.

I'm still all alone but my breaths come easier.

Aided by the moon's glow from a largely clear sky, I tread past inns, pubs, and shops closed for the night. Stars shine brighter due to the blackout, their patterns all the more pronounced. Andromeda. Cassiopeia. Cepheus. When Mr. Jansen gave me a constellation book all those years ago, I became determined to check off as many shapes as I could spy—because why do anything halfway? Every Friday evening for months, I dragged Arie to lie with me in a field. We'd gab and laugh while doggedly searching for—

Oh, enough!

These thoughts weren't supposed to stalk me to the other side of the world.

I concentrate on my steps through a roundabout and plod along a tree-lined stretch. Irksomely I fidget with the metal token on my necklace until recalling its purpose. The engraved identity disc, though not required for civilians, was something I first obtained at Hutton's urging. It's a reminder of the fate that threatens even those out here in the country.

Before long, I note my surroundings. Somehow I already passed through the second intersection, a joining of five roads, where I should have gone northeast to reach the estate entrance. Instead I took a soft right and will now have to double back. I curse my distractedness as much as the scarcity of signposts. Throughout England, many markers were removed to confuse any German troops that might parachute in. The sheer prospect encourages me to hurry back to my route.

But the sound of low voices stops me.

From my right, murmurings drift from a side street shielded by trees. I extinguish my flashlight. It's outlandish to think the area has been invaded. Still, curiosity and imagination lure me to peek, just to be sure.

My vision strains through the moonlit air. Past a thick tangle of branches, I make out two shadowed men in fedoras and long coats. One of the fellows holds a blue-tinted flashlight, which he suddenly aims in my direction. I go still as stone, save for my racing pulse. Does he see me, sense that I'm here?

After a moment, he twists back and passes along a package. Everything about this feels questionable, covert. More garbled conversation follows. Then he picks up the handled bag at his feet and the other man climbs into his motorcar and starts the engine. The headlamps, fitted with slotted masks, softly shine.

I duck deeper into the greenery. Nerves prickle my skin as the vehicle rolls up. It barely pauses before turning right and rumbling off. The motor wanes, but footsteps grow closer. I hold my breath and peer through squinted eyes. Just a few yards from me, the fellow walks by with his flashlight directed at the ground. He's proceeding the way I came.

It's then that I glimpse his face. I know that nose, those specs. That stature and gait.

Hutton's.

A small burst of relief sweeps through me. I'm tempted to jump up and share my foolishness, but then I reassess.

What was he doing out here?

It's no secret he works seven days a week, eighteen hours a day. To the point of obsession. But why meet on a side street in the dark of night, and this close to headquarters, just to hand over...what? The size and wrappings—light paper with twine, from what I could see—have all the makings of a box I know. The parcel from the station. In fact, I've brought him several just like it though have yet to witness a single one opened.

I rise with caution. Ensuring a furtive gap, I trail him toward the intersection, where he veers in the direction of Wilton Park. But as I come around the corner, it seems he up and vanished. I continue toward the entrance and still he's not there.

Not on the street. Not at the gate.

When I arrive at his office, I discover it vacant.

Likewise, the package I last delivered is nowhere to be found.

CHAPTER 30

Crooked. That's how numerous senior officers spanning almost every service branch view Hutton. I hadn't been working at MI9 a week before he informed me of this in a tone more boastful than offended. Apparently, his tendency to discard regulations and protocols ruffles the feathers of some, while a few have even denounced his initiative to use the guise of charities to send rigged packages to POWs, calling it ungentlemanly and "a scoundrel's form of cheating."

Personally, I've considered the latter opinion ridiculous and his bureaucratic infractions worthwhile. And yet, in his office come morning, I can't help but review what I know of the man and his trickery.

As we stand at the toy table, he punctures one of my prototype tins and keeps time on his wristwatch. I could outright ask about his curious meeting, aware my impressions are likely absurd, but not without divulging my surveillance from the bushes.

Instead, throughout the can's trickling, hissing, and bubbling, I steal glances at his desk. No new questionable parcels, just a pile of folders and manila envelopes holding varied documents. On the floor by his chair, his worn leather briefcase bulges with sample materials and notepads of ideas.

If I leafed through the pages, dug through the bag, would I find anything fishy?

"Well, well, would you look here." Hutton is admiring the soup's steam, having opened the outer and inner cans. He sips a spoonful, narrowing my attention to something sensible and known, and his face radiates with delight. "A bang-up job. Superb!"

I can't help but smile. Although I expected him to approve, his validating words reinforce not only my pride but, more important, our collective mission.

"I should like an additional dozen," he declares, "by this afternoon."

As in hours from now? "Major, I'll gladly put the order right in, but the cannery manager did say it will be days yet before they're able to make more."

"*Days?* No, no, no." He waggles the spoon. "That won't do. I shall handle the cannery. And you will plan to retrieve them the moment they are produced. Agreed?"

I've barely had time to answer when he sets down the can and charges on.

"Now. Once they are in your possession, you march half—that's half—of them straight over to the RAF Quartermaster's department. With detailed instructions for use, mark them addressed to these particular chaps." He's spouting this while jostling over to his desk, where he drops onto his chair and swaps the spoon for a pencil to scribble on a scrap of paper. "If anyone gives you what for, merely relate that I insisted they try the gadget immediately and contact me to discuss. The spares can be locked up here in our Pending cupboard. Have you got all that?" When he holds out the note, I hurry over to accept.

"Y-yes, sir," I say as my brain scrambles to keep up.

"Brilliant. I do believe, Miss Vos, we will strike lucky on this." Brightly, he swipes the burning cigarette from his ashtray and takes a puff. But before I even tuck the paper into my coat pocket, his focus shifts to his paperwork.

Our meeting is over.

A celebration short lived.

I start for the doorway, digesting his directives until, off in the corner, an assortment of cloth maps—the boxes holding them, specifically—revives a vision of his nighttime rendezvous.

How nice it would be to move forward without a trace of misgivings, to put any silly notions to rest.

Boosted by our exchange and with a subtle approach dawning, I turn back. "Sir, I've been meaning to ask." He hums in acknowledgment. "The last parcel I retrieved from the station, is there anything in it I should take care of?"

He peers over the rims of his glasses. "The parcel...?" He says this as if attempting to remember.

"From King's Cross. I assume it was samples of some kind?"

"Ah, yes. That is all sorted, but thank you for inquiring." He flits his hand. "There is no time to waste on those cans."

I nod and comply by taking my leave.

As I tread out of the building, a weight descends in my gut, only partially from his ambiguity and haste in sending me away. Mostly, in the midst of his answer, it was the downward flick of his gaze, confirming he has something to hide.

CHAPTER 31

Analyzing and solving: these skills have long been my specialties, as much onstage as in life, a means to achieve order in chaos. Perhaps that's been another draw to my watching more spy and detective films than I'd care to admit. There's satisfaction to be found in the promised resolution of a riddle, from cobbling pieces together through intuition and sleuthing.

I suppose this is what brings me out tonight, but not the only reason. If Hutton's actions are indeed nefarious, I need to know. Lives could be at stake. Not to mention the fate of my own, should my close association be tied to any illicit affairs. Incidents from my orphanage days, of being wrongly accused and penalized, had taught me not to rely on innocence for vindication.

Hidden by trees surrounding headquarters, I wait with a view of the entrance. Hutton's meetings were scheduled until nine. By now, it must be quarter to ten.

A droplet, fallen from an overhead branch, causes me to flinch as it slides past my coat collar. From an earlier drizzle, dampness lingers in the air, along with doubts over my judgment. After all these months of our working together, could I have really missed the signs?

At last he emerges. Alone, hat tipped low. No parcel, but his briefcase hangs from one hand and a suitcase from the other, along with a regulation flashlight that he then clicks on.

I don't dare move.

When he continues around the building, away from the vehicle pool, my suspicions escalate. Again I trail him at a distance.

His winding path lasts a good quarter of a mile before it leads into a field. The space is several acres in size, as best as I can tell by the glow of the moon.

To prevent detection, I keep tight to a long, straggling hedge lining the property. He traipses onward through a meadow that appears desolate save for a tree. A giant oak, I'd guess.

Where is he going and why?

A dip in the soil causes me to stumble. Suppressing a gasp, I catch myself on a rock. It's weather-beaten and lodged in the dirt. A quick scan reveals other stones varying in height and shape, all sprinkled among clustered weeds. By the time I look up, Hutton is gone, vanished once more.

But that isn't what unsettles me most; it's my realization that the stones below me bear inscriptions, barely legible names and dates.

I'm standing in a graveyard.

CHAPTER 32

For the next four days, through my errands and appointments and sketching, I debate my options. Hutton is out of the office, traveling as he often does to meet with suppliers and manufacturers around England and as far away as Scotland.

Or so he says.

I no longer know what to think.

Who takes a leisurely stroll through a cemetery, let alone at night and with luggage in tow, only to disappear? Assuming he's not practicing the occult, what ever was he doing? Of all the places to find privacy for a meeting, a graveyard at night would certainly be among them.

Through a new lens, I consider his paranoia-tinged warnings over phone lines being tapped, his frequent insistence that nothing of importance is accomplished through letters. Have his precautions been truly for the Allies?

The lock on the file cabinet in his office would be easy enough to pick. If caught perusing classified documents, however, I could wind up accused of spying. How would that be for irony?

I could always voice my concerns to Colonel Crockatt. But in addition to having to admit to stalking my supervisor, I've yet to witness anything that can't be denied or explained away. My strongest argument is a hunch that something is off. If I'm wrong, there would assuredly be repercussions.

I don't need to serve in the military to know that falsely accusing a high-ranked officer—of what? espionage, treason?—would bring my role here to an end. In a blink, I could find myself back on a ship, dodging German wolf packs while headed for the States, where nothing awaits my return. No show or partner, no home, no purpose.

Before daring to raise any issues, I'll watch and listen. I need to be sure.

Urgent matter. Report to HQ.

Early Wednesday morning, I both welcome and dread Hutton's phone message passed under my door at the inn, for it occurs to me: he might be aware of my following him, on either or both occasions.

I stow the possibility, hurry to dress, and venture to headquarters.

The building is relatively subdued at this hour, unless compared to Hutton's office, which I find silent and vacant. Framed by the window, sun seeps through the March clouds, casting light through the room. On the desk sits his briefcase. Protruding from the top are a host of folders and notepads.

Within arm's reach.

Offering if not begging to be viewed.

I glance at the door, half-shut, behind me. My pulse thrums as I weigh my choices. My fingers can't resist grazing the bag's unfastened buckle. A peek at the contents could solidify reasons to speak to the colonel—or better yet, provide a rational explanation.

Still, would the invasion of privacy be justified?

"Cecil," a man calls. I whip toward Hutton's voice, echoing from the corridor, and my fingers snag on the briefcase, its handle. The bag tips, spilling half the contents onto the floor.

Blast it! I clamp my jaw, just as a second voice arises.

Hutton is chatting with Crockatt's chief of staff, intensifying my predicament but giving me a chance to recover if I rush.

I scramble to stuff the notepads into the bag, then move on to collecting the scattered papers. I'm attempting to straighten them in their folders when snippets of typed words leap out:

Dutch girl…troublesome…urgent solution needed…

It's a letter signed by Hutton, stamped *TOP SECRET*. My insides coil, tight as a bound wire, as I go to read the full page through. But the men are bidding goodbye.

I shove the papers and folders back into the briefcase I've reset on his desk and step back.

"Ah, jolly good. You've arrived."

I pin on a smile before angling toward Hutton, who swiftly adds, "We must be on our way." He strides past me toward his coat tree in the corner as I steady my thoughts, at a loss over where he'd be taking me.

"Our way—where?"

"Adastral House," he proclaims. "It appears our luck is in with the Ministry. The head of purchasing wants us to look in immediately regarding the self-heating soup."

I'm relieved slightly until I spare a glance at the briefcase. One of the folders is now blatantly cockeyed. As Hutton retrieves and slips on his overcoat, I lean back casually against his desk to block his sight line. "I take it he liked the gadget," I say.

"I am most certain he will, once he knows what it is."

"I'm...not sure I understand." This is the truth but also a prompt to keep him occupied.

"Among the samples we sent, not a solitary one was so much as acknowledged by those blooming clots. Hence, I submitted one of the cans in a form that could not be easily overlooked."

"Oh? How is that?"

He pauses from donning his brimmed hat, looking prideful. "In the wee hours, a monstrous six-foot crate boldly marked *Personal* was delivered to Air Commodore Wright's office. In that crate, I had suspended a single can labeled *Danger*. And wouldn't you know it? His call for a presentation arrived without delay."

My eyes widen, not falsely, at the vision. Yet I think to reply, "My goodness, that's grand. You're right, we ought to be going!" In a zealous motion, I jab my elbow into his bag, just enough to knock it onto its side and prevent suspicion over the folder. "Sorry about that." I cringe. "How clumsy."

He waves this away kindly but then dashes over to grab the briefcase.

And we're off.

CHAPTER 33

With both of Hutton's drivers out on supply runs, he borrows an Austin Utility truck, known as a "Tilly," to deliver us to the Ministry himself. During the half-hour jaunt, or double that—it's hard to gauge from his frenzied weaving around cars—I attempt to study him while mulling over his memo.

Sure, he could be troubled by another Dutch girl, though in all honesty, what are the odds?

Once we've arrived in the waiting area, I sit facing the air commodore's closed door. Its obscure window prevents any glimpse of what awaits inside. Out here and pried open, the crate Hutton sent takes up a hefty portion of the room. A thin rope, frayed from being cut, hangs in the box.

As I learned on the drive, when Hutton received our summons, he was at least gracious enough to inform the clerk over the phone that the tin wasn't in fact dangerous. Why we're still being welcomed to present the gadget is a mystery. Or maybe we're not.

Hutton paces the carpet while puffing on his cigarette. His trembling hand trails ash over the carpeted floor. He looks especially tired and racked from stress.

Previously, I would have presumed them effects of running ragged for MI9. Now I fear it's more. Perhaps I've become one of his worries, an issue requiring an "urgent solution." A firing or reassignment. Or could it be more sinister?

The office door swings open, giving way to a handsome British private, tall as a lamppost and nearly as slender. "Major Hutton, the air commodore will see both of you now."

I rise as Hutton starts forward, but then he glances at his cigarette and frantically surveys the area.

The private pipes in. "May I take that for you, sir?"

"Thank you, Private." Hutton hands off the pluming stub.

As we file past, the private slides me a flirtatious smile until spotting the RAF pin on my coat lapel. Obtained as a favor through Wing Commander Moretti, the "sweetheart wings" that symbolize a courtship dependably prove a deterring ruse. A saver of time and effort for all involved.

The door shuts behind us with a rattle. Planted in his desk chair, an officer with dark bushy eyebrows sports a scowl that appears to be his resting face. He demands without preamble, "And just what the devil is this?"

One of my self-heating cans, labeled *DANGER*, is unmistakably the subject. It stands at the center of his desk, a walnut furnishing that's polished to a shine and as meticulously tidy as the rest of the room. No doubt the potted fern in the corner receives a daily dusting.

Before I can reply, Hutton dives in with a flourish. "Sir, the device before you"—he sets down his briefcase to gesture emphatically—"will prove revolutionary for our bomber crews, keeping them warm and nourished for those night sorties to Hamburg. In doing so, it would be quite the morale booster. And that is to say nothing of its inexpensive cost, efficiency, and ease of use."

Suddenly I recall Hutton's background in the film industry, aptly as a publicity director. I almost expect him to burst out with claims of the gadget's ability to launder clothes and mix gin tonics, all while a musical score plays in the background.

Far into the pitch, there's a tilt to the air commodore's head, his fingers steepled atop his desk. His interest betrays his unmoved expression. "Well?" he says once Hutton breaks for a breath. "Do you intend to simply talk about your invention or demonstrate it?"

Hutton beams, not bothering to correct that the credit should be mine. He turns to me. "Miss Vos?"

My budding offense shrinks away. All at once, I'm back onstage, an assistant taking my cue from the showman. I smile reflexively and whisk a bradawl from my coat pocket, which I thankfully remembered to bring along.

"As you'll witness, sir"—I gracefully approach the officer like hundreds of theater volunteers prior—"two small punctures and a flip of the can are all it takes for a quick, hot meal."

I'm picking up the can when Hutton taps me. "On second thought, why don't we let the air commodore give it a go? He will thereby personally experience its simplicity of operation, a keen benefit for any airman at the controls."

The man grunts his compliance and stands with hand extended. I waver for a moment, ever averse to uncontrolled factors in a trick. I have to remind myself that I won't be in every cockpit, that this is precisely how the can is meant to be used.

After I pass over the bradawl, the officer tentatively pokes holes in the tin where indicated, then flips it and sets it down.

And we wait.

First comes the trickling that leads to gentle hissing. All as expected. But in seconds, an unusual fizzing becomes a gurgle. The noise strikes me as a warning.

The tin is quaking now. It's getting too hot.

Something is wrong, crucially, and I realize the thing just might explode.

I grab Hutton's sleeve. "Get back!" I flail a hand toward the air commodore. "Now!"

Startled, he retreats as we do, an instant before a reverberating blast. We all drop to the floor. With the ferocity of a volcano, scalding liquid flies in every direction, over the bookcase and chairs, the carpeted floor. And not just liquid but flames. The heated waves of red and orange are crackling and spreading.

The door swings open—it's the lean private. "Blimey! It's a fire! A fire!"

My body jerks at the shouts, a reflex from entrenched memories of a near-identical alert. Except this fire is real.

Then come more faces and voices. A team of clerks are hoisting extinguishers and stirrup pumps. Water and chemicals are sprayed every which way until the flames are entirely doused, returning us to safety.

I register the stench as I come to my feet. A nauseating mix of scorched peas, chemicals, and singed carpet assails the smoky air. The potted fern, drooped and pitiful, no longer requires a daily dusting.

My mind races to pinpoint the cause of the mishap. Either the cannery manager erred by adding too much quicklime, or the substance is just that volatile.

The air commodore moves slowly through the room. He pauses at his once elegant and glossy desk, now among the charred casualties. His gaze stalls on me and Hutton, turning sharp as a spear.

Not needing to be told, we see ourselves out.

CHAPTER 34

Visions of the morning's disaster are replaying in my mind when a voice cuts in.

"*Miss Vos.*" The private's tone suggests she's repeating herself. Beneath the brim of her cap, Lenora Walsh shoots me a quizzical look from the driver's seat of the truck while steering us carefully down a cobblestone street in the darkness. Our partially masked headlamps are only so helpful.

"Pardon me?"

"I said, is there something troubling you?"

Has it been that obvious?

I prop up a smile. "Not at all." From the slight gravel in my voice, I realize it's the first I've spoken since leaving headquarters at least an hour ago. In London's East End awaits a large quantity of—I've forgotten—oh, yes, men's grooming supplies. We're to retrieve them from a warehouse once I confirm they've been properly rigged. "I'm just a bit tired."

She's unconvinced by my answer. I detect it in her eyes before they reaffix on the road, but she doesn't prod further. Then again, there's probably no need. After my afternoon of warning the half-dozen recipients of the cans I'd proudly distributed, word of my colossal failure has surely reached the ATS "lovelies." And they're not exactly ones to keep opinions of others to themselves.

Come to think of it...that does make me wonder.

If the two ever observed a questionable act, even by a higher rank, would they let it be known? Similarly, would Private Walsh? As Hutton's driver, she's witnessed many of the man's excursions firsthand.

If I'm ever to probe, this is my chance. My role at MI9 could fast be coming to an end.

"Private Walsh, I've been meaning to ask you," I begin casually, "about your working with Major Hutton. Has anything about him struck you as...odd?"

Her lips tighten, but not quick enough to contain a snip of a laugh.

I laugh a little myself—"odd" being an understatement. "I'll take that as a yes."

I sense her guard lower a notch before she offers, "From the start, Colonel Crockatt did give me fair heeding that the major was rather mad and of my need to humor him."

A savvy answer. She suggested her own opinion without actually giving it. "Gracious, I wish I'd received the same advice." When she smirks, I ask, "Anything else?"

She ponders. "The day I introduced myself, the major informed me that if he's ever in uniform, which he hoped to God wouldn't be often, that he might fling me up a salute, but I'd be forbidden from reciprocating."

"Forbidden—why?"

"He claims it's 'undignified, unnatural, and unwomanly.'" She rolls her eyes, emphasizing the absurdity of what might well have been intended as his show of reverence for femininity. "Likewise, he makes no secret of my driving skills taxing his nerves, saying nothing of Private Leary, who drives like a bloody maniac." She appears to catch herself and awkwardly murmurs, "Excuse the moaning."

"Nonsense." I rather enjoy this peek at Lenora's moxie. At the same time, I struggle to reconcile my recruitment by Hutton, when so many in his position would have opted to hire yet another man.

Is it possible he was intrigued less by my abilities—which, granted, lately have been underwhelming—than the presumption that as a woman, I'd be usefully inattentive, unlike his beloved Peter Baker? Of course, if Hutton now wishes for my removal, his case could be easily made.

"Here we are," Lenora declares abruptly. She parks us in an open spot along the curb.

Rather than tiptoeing around my concerns, perhaps I should just voice them. But she's climbing out of the truck and clicking on her blued flashlight.

I can wait for our drive back.

In the cold, dank air, I join her in crossing the vacant street. Thankfully she knows the area. Given the damage of buildings and the protective boards over windows, let alone the blackout, it's especially challenging to find any location.

I recall we're near the docks. I think of the peninsula of my childhood and visiting the shore with Papa. A wistful warmth runs through me, interrupted by a siren that slices the night.

An air raid.

I inhale sharply and my muscles tense.

Lenora looks around, orienting herself, then speaks over the alert. "There's a shelter close by, at Bethnal Green." She points behind us. "It's a Tube station that way. Follow me."

We turn and I aim for calm while keeping stride beside her. The siren rises and falls as we pass one block after the other. Residents of varied ages are emerging from their flats, like sheep in a storm headed for shelter. Their collective casualness, many toting bundled bedding, affirms this is standard routine. After all, the alerts are timed to give ample notice and the majority nowadays are strictly precautionary.

I'm antsy regardless. "How much farther?"

"Not far," Lenora says. "Wait until you see it. The war broke out before the tracks could be laid. It's like an entire village beneath the city. There are thousands of bunks, a library, a theater. My one time there, a couple even had a wedding ceremony."

I can't imagine ever being *that* comfortable about an air raid. Or an Underground station. Or being anywhere that deep in the earth. But the promise of so much space does slightly reduce my worry.

Around a corner, we proceed onto a street clogged with more figures. Patrons are pouring from a cinema and two adjacent pubs. An older gentleman off to the side, in the uniform of an air-raid warden, waves everyone along. "Keep moving now! Keep moving!"

After another few blocks, the rhythmic wail of the siren ends. But until the solid all-clear signal, a potential threat remains, evidenced by a searchlight illuminating the sky.

Lenora cranes her neck for a view of the street. "There it is."

I stretch upward while walking and look between heads. The station's stairwell entry awaits on a corner flanked by clusters of trees. As usual, I breathe to loosen the anxiety knotting in my chest. In and out, in and out. Once I'm safely down the stairs, all will be fine. Before then, through the inevitable clustering of bodies, I'll focus on placing one steady foot after the other.

The conversations around me swirl with leisure. More folks are carrying bundles. Few faces bear concern. Children ride piggyback or cling to hands. Babies are carried in woolen blankets.

A metallic screech turns my head.

It's the brakes of a bus coming to a stop. Two other buses sit idling nearby. Passengers from each are disembarking, further swelling the crowd.

I breathe deeper, gearing up, summoning Papa's voice: *It is okay, schatje. It is okay.*

We slow to a crawl as those up ahead funnel down the stairwell. I stay close to Lenora and use my opposite elbow to buffer against strangers.

A peculiar whistle and whirring pull my attention. I follow the crowd in looking up. "What is that?" people are saying. "What could it be?"

Londoners well know the sounds of their anti-aircraft guns and certainly the enemy's weapons. Even I sense that what we're hearing resembles neither of these. Before I can contemplate alternatives, a booming roar that verges on deafening ignites a collision of shouts.

"It's a bomb!"

"Run!"

"Hurry, go down!"

All at once, the world devolves into a throng of jostling and yelling and shoving. Loud pinging noises suggest metal casings crashing into the ground.

My heart is hammering, my throat cinching. I'm being moved

forward, the ground wet and slick. The mob is heaving itself toward the narrow entry.

Then a man's bellow: "Back up, back up!" The command is gruff, authoritative, seeming to come from the outer right fringe. But the crowd is still advancing. "Turn around!" the voice says. "Someone's fallen!"

The words latch onto my brain, uncaging a memory, and instantly I'm back in the assembly hall. The flood is again dragging me to the waterfall's edge to plunge me into a sea of bodies and death and darkness. A grip is on my arm—only this time it's Lenora, not Arie. I want to shut my eyes and fold into myself, make the scene disappear.

But no...

This can't happen. *Not again.*

I scour for my voice and manage to shout, "Go back! Everyone, go back!" Faces jerk toward me, but the crowd's panic dominates. People are pushing harder, the pressure growing.

I twist toward Lenora, whose willowy form is being swallowed up. I grasp her hand. "We...we've got to get out," I say. A mix of fright and confusion fills her eyes. "Hold on tight," I tell her, and she nods.

We embark on muscling our way toward the side. When I repeat the order to go back, more folks respond, the rest desperate for shelter. For every two steps Lenora and I achieve, we're shoved back one. Still we press against the current, unrelenting, our hands clutched together so firmly my bones threaten to snap.

For an instant, the surrounding pressure gives. I eke out more steps with Lenora until there's an opening, and we charge straight for it. Breaking free, I suck in gulps of air.

Someone hollers about taking cover across the way, and Lenora tugs me to hurry with her. Under high railway arches—meager protection but it's something—we join amassing stragglers.

We did it. We made it out.

A surge of relief rushes through me. Only then do Lenora and I release our grip.

The baffling noises have stopped. No signs of smoke or damage. No silhouettes of distant aircraft. No engines to be heard. I'm not alone in noticing. A spread of murmurings dissipate fears as more and more from the crowd flee to our space, including children and babies. Thank God.

But then shouts grow from the direction of the Tube entry. "Make way! Make way!"

What's left there of the swarm hustles to clear a path. Gasps ripple through the air. Sudden and ominous, they curl my stomach even before I track the cause.

From the stairwell, a fellow carries a limp form. As he places the woman on the pavement, another body is brought out. An elderly man.

A young nurse rushes to kneel and check for a pulse. Evidently finding none, she moves on to the next. Already a third lifeless figure has been added, this one a child. Then comes another and another. They show no sign of slowing.

Every inch of me quakes. My mind is spinning, a tornado telling me to run, and in a blur, I'm doing just that. Away from the crowd, the ghastly scene. I hear my name, faintly, but don't stop until a wave of nausea rolls through me. I bend over to retch, though only dry heaves rack my body.

A hand is rubbing my back. Lenora stands at my side.

Once my gut begins to settle, she says something about returning to the truck when it's safe and taking me home.

I need no other encouragement. I long for nothing greater than to be rid of this place.

By the time we reach the George, I realize to precisely what extent: as soon as arrangements can be made and logistics permit, I'll be leaving England for good.

CHAPTER 35

A meal from the prior evening sits cold on my desk. It's the latest delivery by the inn's cook, whose concerns over my seclusion are gaining hints of doubt. My claims of battling a seasonal cold must stretch plausibility with each passing day, going on a week.

Owing to her Irish superstitions, she probably wonders if I've fallen victim to a curse. It doesn't help that I'm directly beneath her room, treating her to outbursts from my resurrected nightmares, this time with the fresh nuances of German bombs raining down as I'm trapped in a Tube stairwell, still of course in a pile of bodies.

Blackout curtains scramble my days and nights as I fend off visions, old and new, of limp figures and empty eyes. By lamplight, I spend my waking hours skimming a book or half listening to programs on the wireless: *Music While You Work*, *The Radio Doctor*, *The Glums*.

News broadcasts have captured more of my interest as I seek to evade shame over relinquishing my duties at MI9. The tide of the war is turning, they've said. While bombing raids pummel Germany, Hitler's loss of Stalingrad has delivered him a mighty blow on the eastern front. Even our forces in North Africa, by tightening their hold on Tunisia, are nearing the end of a stalemate with the Axis on the run.

And all without a scrap of my help.

Fine, yes, there's the rest of Europe to consider. But how much difference have I truly made? I'm a cog in a massive machine, sure to be replaced the minute I set sail, if not sooner.

To that end, I'm listening now for the latest updates while curled up in bed. Presented by "Lord Haw-Haw," the Nazi propaganda reports naturally exaggerate Allied defeats yet still help gauge the state of the seas. In an escalating Battle of the Atlantic, Allied merchant ships are being sunk by the dozens, he boasts.

I cringe over the perishing of more lives and selfishly over fears that prevent me from scheduling my departure. As if the prospect of sleeping in the belly of a ship wasn't daunting enough, it now verges on debilitating.

By coming to England, I was proudly embodying my father's bravery, my mother's adventurous spirit. How disappointed they must be, looking down on me here, stuck between worlds, imprisoned by my thoughts—including just what led me to that East End tragedy.

After the bombing of Berlin, German retaliation was logical. With dock areas being a common target, I should have seen it coming. The air raid at least. In that way, I'd become too comfortable, a recurring weakness.

A gentle knock sounds on the door.

My twin-bell alarm clock informs me it's twenty past eight. Monday's breakfast delivery, a smidge early.

I answer from my pillow: "Not hungry, but thank you."

Another knock follows, galling me, rightfully or not. I'm about to assert a reply when the caller announces, "Miss Vos, it's me. Private Walsh."

Internally I sink.

Hutton must have sent her to fetch me, as I scarcely glanced at his phone message from yesterday. Frankly, given my debacle at the Ministry, I'm surprised he would bother. The letter of resignation I left in his office days earlier gifted him an easy out.

As for his questionable behavior, whether I'll report it and how, I haven't the mindset to decide.

"Miss Vos?"

I'm tempted to remain silent, but all things considered, I ought to say goodbye.

On my feet, I make my way to the door. Opening it, I recall I'm in my nightclothes and thus gather the collar.

"Good morning," she says, tentative.

I merely repeat her greeting. The normalcy of her appearance magnifies the lack in mine, causing me a resentful twinge.

"I do apologize for the intrusion, but I've come regarding Major Hutton."

"Yes, I understand. And I promise I'll ring him back at HQ."

After a shake of her head, she pauses. That's when I notice the foreboding in her eyes. "The major has been admitted to Woodside Officers' Hospital. I'm afraid there's been"—she measures how to finish—"an incident."

CHAPTER 36

The drive passes wordlessly. Lenora steers the truck through the drizzling grayness, making no utterance about the ghastliness of our last outing. She could well know by now how many lives were lost, how many were children. Whether the peculiar bombs also caused any casualties. But what good would come from sharing such things?

Certainly none from hearing them.

I fidget with the identity disk that hangs along my collar. For our daunting return to London, I donned my dress and coat with no more thought than the hat over my hastily pinned hair. Through the passenger window, I survey the canopy of clouds. Dread over another air raid looms, rivaling my apprehension over what awaits at the hospital.

Hutton has requested my presence there. That he's suffered a nervous breakdown is all Lenora has told me. It's enough, however, to gouge my conscience. While my resigning is surely but a minor contribution, I can't say the same of our soup mishap. Besides, his increasingly erratic pace, punctuated by his hand tremors, should have caused me some alarm.

To be fair, distinguishing the signs from an eccentric is no simple chore. And this still doesn't explain his nighttime excursions nor passing a package in a manner that—

I squash the rest. The riddle is no longer mine to solve.

Moreover, what harm could the man do now? As treatment for his condition, he could be sedated or even restrained. Verifying as much will render the mystery moot.

Either way, I don't plan to stay long.

In the military institution—formally St. Luke's Woodside Hospital for Functional Nervous Disorders—a nurse leads me toward Hutton's room. Down the sterile-white corridor, my shoes clack on the runway of tiles. Disinfectant permeates the air.

I assured Lenora I'd return by bus, releasing her to other tasks. Part of me wishes I hadn't sent her off so soon.

The nurse, being called to assist with a patient's outburst, directs me to continue the last few yards. I slow at the half-open door, where I'm greeted by the familiar smell of cigarette smoke. Seated in bed, unrestrained and propped against a pillow, Hutton appears to be scribbling on paper. My footfalls draw his eyes.

"At last! Miss Vos, please come in." His lucid state knocks me for a loop. It strikes as particularly incongruent in light of his appearance, with a hospital gown in place of his tweed suit, his face unshaven and hair unkempt.

I venture into the room, a limited space with a curtained window. "How are you feeling, sir?"

His hand shoos away the question as a tired one. "Fine, just fine." His impatience is ever present. "Of greater concern is how to proceed. Whilst the length of my stay is pending, there is still much work to be done."

"But shouldn't you...be resting?"

"After four days here mucking about, I am going positively stale." He grumbles as if cooped up for forty. "Now," he says, "if we are to win this war, I shall require your assistance with our schemes moving forward. More than usual, I might add."

I realize then that my letter never reached him. Or his memory has lapsed since. I need to break the news. But how? Doing so here and now feels cruel, yet stringing him along under a false pretense would be no kinder. And that's to say nothing of my own precarious state. Replacing me is only sensible, above all, for those in jeopardy we're meant to help.

He pauses to point to a chair not far from his bed. "Please sit, sit."

I remain standing. "Sir, I feel terrible if my recent failures added to your predicament in any way," I begin.

"What? Oh my, don't be silly."

While I appreciate his assurance, I forge on before losing my nerve. "Having said that, I've come to believe my efforts are no longer worthwhile at MI9." A mere week ago, he'd have likely celebrated the announcement. Now that he requires more assistance, I brace for a spate of frustration or disappointment, even a guilt-laden appeal.

Instead, he reclines against his pillow with a contemplative nod. "I imagine this pertains to the misfortune at the Tube."

I should have figured he learned of it. Lenora is liable to have shared if asked about my absence.

"I daresay," he murmurs as if musing aloud, "that must have been especially distressing, in view of your childhood experience."

Startled, I blink at him. "How could you know of..."

As my words trail off, he says, "From the vetting for your clearance, Miss Vos. We do deal in intelligence, after all." He offers an amused smile that I don't reciprocate. I begrudge how much he knows of my past, how much he's known all along without letting on.

He appears to detect this and levels his tone. "Rest content, I have it on very good authority that what happened at Bethnal Green shan't be repeated."

A ridiculous assertion. Not masking my view, I laugh under my breath. "There is no way you or anyone else can possibly ensure that."

"Quite the reverse," he states. Then he glances at the door as if to confirm privacy; his paranoid sensibilities now allude to more than eccentricity. "I divulge this in the strictest of confidence." He continues with a rueful air: "Prior to my...episode...I inquired as to what transpired at the shelter, given a lack of news reports on the matter. Parliament felt a media blackout was best—for morale, as it were—on account that the Jerries weren't to blame. Sadly, it was our own anti-aircraft munitions that inspired the panic."

Right off, I find this difficult to believe. The East Enders, of all people, know the sounds of their ack-acks. My mind can still hear the strange whistling and whirring. The thunderous noise and clattering of shell casings were surely the product of German innovation, a weapon we'd yet to encounter.

"I'm sorry, but no. That can't be right. What we heard was distinctly different."

"Indeed it was a new type of rocket, fired for the first time. In an unannounced test, they were launched from Victoria Park, a half mile from the shelter. With the ghastly effects that resulted, I assure you those guns shall be swiftly relocated, if not retired."

I'm about to debate him further when I recall the night's absence of decimation. No visible explosions. No buildings torn to rubble. No signs of any aircraft.

And it all fits.

Hutton shared his insight as a comfort and cause for me to stay. Rather, it delivers a fresh wave of nausea and an even greater reason to leave. For once again, a massive tragedy has proven utterly, horrifically senseless.

No more dithering over my traveling home.

"As I said," I manage, "I've made my decision. I plan to depart as soon as possible. But I do thank you for the opportunity." Unwavering, I start away.

"Miss Vos."

I'm nearly to the door when he says in a rush, "You cannot just leave the country. It will not be permitted."

My steps slow despite my yearning to run.

Is he lying to keep me here? Or is it the truth?

I pivot back to decipher which.

"As yours is a reserved occupation," he explains calmly, "it is the British government's prerogative to bar your departure."

There's no suggestion of falseness in his voice nor his face. Though flailing inside, I summon a semblance of defiance. "Then I'll simply spend the rest of the war in my room. And we'll see how helpful your government finds that."

"Or," he says, "I could put in a persuasive word to aid your case."

I wait, as I sense there's more.

"In exchange for a small favor."

I straighten. Only for the prospect of escaping this island do I ask, "What is it you want?"

"My briefcase. I left it behind unwittingly, just a short hop from headquarters."

When he requests nothing else, I peer at him, dubious. "If that's all you want, why not just send for it?" Then I recall its contents, the ominous memo about the "Dutch girl," the many other documents I haven't viewed.

"Well, you see. The errand is confidential in nature due to its rather...unorthodox destination."

Before he can finish, my memory of such a place creeps back, one linked to Hutton in the most cryptic of ways. And already I know, even if to my detriment, I won't bring myself to decline.

CHAPTER 37

The Tube calamity has decidedly reinforced my aversion to grave-yards. Nevertheless, I find myself retreading a winding path from Wilton Park, headed for a cemetery. At least this time it's by daylight, being roughly half past ten. A break in the rain allows for an easier trek over slightly muddied ground.

As I follow the familiar hedges that straggle along a field, a muffled rumbling halts me. My heartbeat skitters as I look and listen, until I recognize an RAF Spitfire flying between clouds. I blow out a breath, reminded of my goal to leave this life behind.

In a rectangular patch of land a couple acres in size, I warily pass the smattering of tombstones. Their aged inscriptions and surround-ing weeds suggest a disused place of rest, not lessening its eeriness. I continue briskly to reach the meadow in which Hutton disappeared, and now I know exactly where.

A dozen yards from the last set of gravestones stands the same huge oak tree I recall. Its abundant spread of branches provides a strategic cover that beckoned first Hutton and now me to its base. There, purposefully facing the cemetery and disguised as a burial-vault entrance, await stone steps that descend to a door. Camouflaged by turf at ground level, the structure's roof blends impressively with nature.

I try the handle and confirm what Hutton suspected: that based on the last of his recollections from several nights ago, he'd managed to lock the door before walking toward headquarters. Along the way, he apparently found himself out of sorts, his path unrecognizable. Guards found him near the mansion, pacing and carrying on.

I retrieve from my coat pocket the key he lent me. After peeking behind me for anyone in the vicinity, I unlock and open the door. The interior leaves me slack-jawed.

The spacious bunker, a good twelve by twenty feet, boasts all the features of a household den: a wooden floor and rug, a desk and chair, an oil lamp and heater. And on the wall of bookshelves sit hundreds of gadgets. With Arie's penchant for tinkering as a kid, he'd be on cloud nine. Most of the "toys" are a mix of active and blown inventions, the rest evident prototypes in varied stages of development. There are tricked-out dartboards, baseball bats, and badminton rackets; gramophones, lighters, and spools of thread.

When Hutton directed me here, he described it as a vault-like storage room, painting a very different scene. He'd had the place built, he said, to keep his devices from the sticky fingers of servicemen who treated his office as a help-yourself, no-pay gadget shop to amuse their family and friends.

Gazing in awe, I have to remind myself what led me here. These items no longer pertain to my life. Disquieted by the room's underground location and solitary exit, I gear up to seek out Hutton's briefcase.

Within seconds, I locate his bag behind the desk. My mission is explicit, and yet I can't resist. I forgo debating and delve inside, only to find it holds no documents. Just sketches and diagrams of gadgets.

In my periphery, my sights catch on a diversion. Three parcels stacked in the corner bear an appearance I recognize. Cream paper, black twine. Matching the package handed off by Hutton.

Though his graveyard activities are now clear, his nighttime meeting remains a mystery. In my final effort for MI9, I take the liberty of stealing a look.

What I discover results in more questions than answers.

CHAPTER 38

It's late afternoon by the time I return to the hospital with Hutton's briefcase, ending my obligation if not my curiosity.

"Splendid. Well done." He accepts the delivery while seated in bed, eyes alight behind his glasses.

"I locked up, of course, and put the key in your bag."

This doesn't stop him from diving into the contents, surely for peace of mind.

"Sir, if I may, I have something to ask."

"As do I, Miss Vos." He continues to rummage. "Are you aware of the reason I was selected specifically to lead the gadget section?"

The detour gives me pause. "Your...prior service as a pilot?"

"Ah, here we are." Out of the briefcase, he pulls not a key but a billfold, from which he displays a piece of paper folded down several times. "This," he answers his own query. "All due to this very page."

Given his mental "incident," he could well be holding a sheet of doodles and gibberish for all I know. Smoothing it out, he explains, "Amidst my interview at the War Office, I made mention of my early aspirations for the stage. Having piqued the officer's interest, I presented a memento normally carried in my possession." He passes it over and watches me expectantly.

On the creased, well-worn sheet is a standard typewritten note—that much a relief—dated April 29, 1913. I get no farther than the recipient's name before my eyes snap up.

"It's addressed to Harry Houdini."

A small prideful smile plays on Hutton's lips.

"You wrote this? Did you know each other?"

He flits a hand toward the missive. "Read on," he says, and so I do.

In the letter, Hutton proposes that his company construct, in full view of an audience, a sturdy crate to be nailed and roped shut with Houdini inside, dared to escape without demolishing the box. But the six handwritten words at the bottom of the page are the most astounding: *The above CHALLENGE has been accepted.*

I stare back at Hutton. "You…and he…you actually did this?"

Threading his hands on his blanketed lap, he reclines. "After a performance in Birmingham, Houdini offered a hundred pounds to any producer of a wooden box from which he would be incapable of escaping. I was in the employ of my uncle's timber mill at the time. Assembling the packing case onstage, I believed, would eliminate any opportunity for the showman's trickery."

At the cliff-hanging quiet, I urge, "And? Did he make it out?"

Hutton replies with a nod, revealing his own defeat, yet I can't help but grin.

"Precisely how this was done," he says, "confounded me for years. That is, until Houdini revealed his method in private following a show at the Holborn Empire. You see, he bribed our top carpenter three pounds to use almost entirely short nails and to hammer them in such a way that enabled an end piece of the box to pivot. Unaware, I watched with the rest of the theater as Houdini was handcuffed and bound in a sack. Once he was secured in the box that was nailed shut and wrapped with rope, a curtain barred our view. Minutes later, he emerged to a jubilant audience, free of his bindings and without disturbing a single knot on the crate."

As I visualize the escape, each calculated step and earned reaction, an old longing for the stage flutters through me.

"The trick was ruddy clever," Hutton concludes, "although, I must say, scarcely his most daring."

"Well…no. Of course not." The performer's published accounts are imprinted forever in my mind. "That would be his legendary act, the Upside Down. Or when he hung from a crane in a straitjacket. Better yet, his being buried alive. Or being sealed into an airtight box and tossed into the bay."

Hutton raises his forefinger. "And still, there exists one greater. A trick for which he shall never be lauded properly."

My intrigue is baited. Yet just then, a man's voice drifts from the hallway. The patient, shuffling past with a nurse, babbles while gesticulating. It's a glaring reminder to keep Hutton's assertions in perspective, particularly with his tone turning conspiratorial.

He leans toward me. "I trust you to envisage, in the days leading to our last sparring with the Jerries, the benefits afforded a performer of such esteem. Why, he could tour throughout Europe, hauling trunks and supplies, not only free of suspicion but invited to entertain the most powerful leaders in the grandest palaces. Even celebrated for breaking out of their most secure prisons. A celebrity of the like might well accrue some juicy tidbits to share. Would you not agree?"

I study Hutton's face, seeking signs of deception or delusion. He appears genuine and clearheaded. "You're suggesting Houdini was a spy. Against the Germans."

"I would make no such claim," he insists, sitting back. "In the way of officialdom."

I stand there dumbfounded. The theory, while outlandish, is actually so logical it defies dispute.

"So now you see, Miss Vos, the importance I have placed on furthering the critical work of a man no longer able. I would hope you feel the same."

The dual reference—to Houdini and himself—isn't missed on me. In recalling the East End disaster, however, neither is my want for safety, for normalcy. Besides, didn't he recently label me "troublesome"?

"But, sir, you really don't need my help. I think that's become evident to us both."

"As it so happens," he says with a slight hitch before going on, "Colonel Crockatt has informed me that, whilst he will do what he can, given word that I have cracked up, it appears I won't be welcomed back. At least for some time."

"Oh. Oh, I see." The possibility hadn't dawned on me but falls within reason, considering the gravity of our work and its classified nature. Combined with the adversaries he's accrued among the brass hats in every branch, an exception is unlikely. "I'm terribly sorry to hear that, Major."

"No need to be," he replies, "should we continue our efforts together."

"Pardon?"

"I shall merely move my schemes to the background—behind the curtain, so to speak—as you assume the public role on our behalf."

"You're talking about a charade."

"You once applied a similar system to your stage work."

"Yes, I suppose. Although…"

"Then I don't foresee an issue."

"Unless we wind up caught." Fans of magic expect to be fooled; the same can't be said of superiors in Military Intelligence.

"In which case," he counters with a trace of impatience, "I vow to assume full responsibility. Furthermore, unless a security risk, there is no regulation restricting you from gathering outside ideas."

Running low on arguments, I scrounge for another and note our surroundings. "Surely you ought to be resting instead. Taking some time—"

"I'll *rest*," he snaps, "when this bloody war is over!"

At my flinch, he pulls back. The frustration coloring his face just as soon pales. "My apologies."

I accept easily with a nod.

Expelling a sigh, he relaxes his hands on his lap. "With every passing day, ever more of our devices are blown. Our lads behind the wire, the underground operatives, they are all dependent upon our work." He meets my eyes. "The more success they achieve, Miss Vos, the higher chance my boys make it home."

His sons.

Goodness. He speaks so rarely of his personal life that I'd nearly forgotten.

"I understand," I say, though falsely. I can only attempt to fathom the constant everyday worries of a parent, let alone during wartime.

Even so, the thought of his secret shelves of gadgets brings me back to my initial question. To even contemplate his proposal, I need the whole picture.

"Your parcels in the bunker, the cases of jam and marmalade... I saw you at night giving some away. Why?"

He lifts a brow, surprised, then answers sheepishly. "Goods for trading."

"Trading—for what?"

"Priority. For iron, silk, a great many other materials we have required from our suppliers."

Like my tins from the cannery, I mentally add.

"Greasing the wheels," I translate, and he agrees. Again he appears sincere, but I retain my guard. "If that's all it was, why not just tell me?"

Sudden indignance pinches his voice. "The business of compromising ethics is not suitable for a fine lady."

I barely contain a snort; our endeavors pertain to war, not tea with high society. But then, he does tend toward the dramatic. "And the bunker? Which of my ethics would that have jeopardized?"

He mulls over the challenge. "I suppose," he says, "I had grown accustomed to my privacy."

Truthfully, to that much I can relate.

"Major Hutton," a stout nurse barks from the doorway. "It is time for your bath." She sends a glower toward me, an order to exit, just as Hutton touches my coat sleeve.

"Ponder my offer, Miss Vos. Please." His hand quivers, making me question the hazards of him continuing work in any capacity. And yet, he at least deserves a modicum of consideration.

"I will."

CHAPTER 39

In the lounge bar of the George, I wait on the bench along the wall, my mind swimming. Upon my return, the inn's cook, cheery over my moving about, insisted on whipping me up a Spam sandwich. Only then did I realize I'd gone the day without eating. But then, who could blame me?

Presuming the claim of his spy work is true, Houdini raised the act of misdirection to an astonishing level. Now even more, I understand Hutton's obsessive drive, as well as his impetus to recruit me. My own crate trick in New York must have struck him as nostalgic. Perhaps my patter about Houdini even seemed a sign.

My belly growls, interrupting the thought. While embarrassingly loud, the sound is drowned out by girls' giggles. As my only company in the room, the manager's daughter and her two friends—all around eight or nine years old—are playing a board game on the floor. A fire crackles in the hearth, scenting the air. One of the girls flaunts a card that gets her out of jail free.

I smile wistfully, wishing the release of Allied prisoners could be just as easy.

"Pamela!" a woman calls from the next room.

The manager's daughter sits up. "Yes, Mum?"

"Time to feed the animals, love."

The girls squeal. Scrambling from the room, they divvy up assignments for the inn's cat, dogs, and pigeons.

Left to the quiet, I gaze at the abandoned Monopoly game. How differently I've come to view such pastimes, now as delivery mechanisms for war. Dominoes, cribbage boards, chessmen. All those and more have been exposed. German guards are growing ever wise to game sets capable of hiding escape aids, leaving scant new options. Most are too small or thin to rig. Like Monopoly, for instance. There's no compartment to be squeezed into its tiny houses and hotels, its trinkets and slender board.

Or...is there?

Houdini thrived on defying the impossible. While varied in forms, I've been doing the same since childhood, often for survival.

In this instant, I consider a potential reason my life has been repeatedly spared. Could it be to attain justice for the victims of a cruel and callous enemy?

As a young girl, I had no power to retaliate against the anti-union murderer who yelled "fire," or the crooked sheriff and his vicious deputies, or the company management that would have sooner let us starve than pay miners like Papa a decent wage. Maybe I still don't.

But I have a chance now, if even in a small way, to strike back at Hitler for all the horrors he's wrought on the world and families and countless innocent lives.

The revelation draws me to kneel beside the game. Hoping the girls are forgiving, I slide the pieces off to examine the cardboard base. No thicker than one-quarter inch, it couldn't conceal any bulky tools. Yet slim ones just might go undetected, if cut precisely into the liner.

I run my fingernail along the edge of the playing spaces, most named after London's sites and streets. The paper face could be removed, potentially intact, if steamed with care. But how to reattach it after? No chance rubber cement would dry smoothly enough to pass camp inspections. It would have to be engineered from scratch.

That's when I note the maker's name on the box. The company is not only familiar but trusted. A printer of playbills and other amusements, John Waddington Limited already produces our tricked-out cards, as well as color silk maps—the ideal kind, incidentally, to implant in the board since the fabric is thin, compactible, and safe from rustling.

I consider Hutton's unconventional methods. And I don't bother to call for an appointment.

———————

First thing in the morning, I jump on a train headed toward the manufacturer's headquarters in Leeds. Thanks to the company director's recognition of my name from previous shipments, I spend the afternoon in a private room with a skilled engineer, experimenting with boards and decals and an array of escape aids. I apply knowledge from my old carpentry job, commanding a variety of tools with a steady hand for a smooth and seamless result.

By nightfall, we fashion a Monopoly set no different from any other wartime edition of the game—save for its embedded silk map, mini compass, and two files sharp enough to saw through wire.

I deliberate over involving Hutton, for fear of contributing to his stress. But denying the man a clear-cut purpose would surely be worse. For my spirits too, evidently.

When I present him with my sample the next day, spreading it over the foot of his bed, he emits delight but above all relief. He views the prototype as a sign I'm committing to his plan.

And he's right. What he doesn't know is that my latest nightmares, more a motivator now than a burden, solidified my choice. The enemy has never been clearer, nor has my desire to help defeat them.

"As for equipping the game," Hutton says, shifting quickly to the practical, "might I propose a minor improvement?"

I brace against my pride. After all my hours and effort invested, it's hard to imagine an option I haven't explored. "Certainly."

"I should think an innocuous tag, to denote the particular map sealed in each board, would prove useful. This would ensure the games are directed to camps in their correlating regions."

I sweep a look over the center of the board, its contents inaccessible for our double-checking, and humility slides in. He has a fine point.

Borrowing his pencil and pad, I take a seat and we develop a plan: a tiny dot on Free Parking indicates the inclusion of a France-Germany map; one on Marylebone Station signifies a map of Italy, and so forth.

Then to safeguard the loaded games from falling into the factory's ordinary stock, I suggest a seemingly errant period on the box's outer label.

"Also," he interjects, midpuff on his cigarette, "we must include money."

Funds being handy for bribes, food, and train passes, that's actually an addition I had already entertained. "I do wish we could. There's just no room for another false pocket."

"No, no, not in the board. We'll swap out the bound stacks of play money for genuine currency. Reichsmarks or lire, in accordance with the intended camp."

In a rush, my concerns over his judgment return. I lower the notepad to my lap. "You know, I'm not confident that's the best idea, having the real funds so visible." It's a softened statement of the obvious, but he retorts as if I'm the foolish one.

"Naturally we'll place a few bills of play money on the top and bottom of the stacks to help disguise them."

"Yes, but if the board is searched close enough, a camp guard is sure to discover the money."

Hutton winks. "That, my girl, is correct."

Oh heavens. His mental faculties are impaired after all.

"Guards are but human," he continues. "Strained by war and desperation for family, temptation to pocket those funds shall be irresistible. And if that guard fancies another delivery of its kind..."

I realize aloud: "He won't report it to the watch list."

Hutton smirks. "Righto." He takes another quick puff. "Now, before presenting this to Crockatt, you will need to compose a memo, stamped 'Secret,' and send it straightaway to Norman Watson at Waddington's."

Pencil back on the notepad, I scramble to keep up.

"Request a sum of three games with these exact specifications. One each to include the following pictures: an emerald, a double eagle, and a Dutch girl."

I transcribe the instructions, unquestioning, until the last words sink in. "Dutch girl?"

"Ah. Yes. 'Pictures' being maps, of course, each reference is code for a respective region. I shall teach you my terms for all of them."

Reflecting on his earlier memo about an urgent solution needed for a troublesome "Dutch girl"—referring not to me but a map—I can't help but burst into laughter. While Hutton surveys me peculiarly, I resolve to explain in full, recognizing that we would both do well to trust each other more.

The following Monday, on the cusp of evening, the verdict is in. After thrilling over the Monopoly ploy—soon to expand to Ludo, then Snakes and Ladders—Colonel Crockatt remarks on having foreseen the major's need for a respite, and sealed by Hutton's recommendation, he cautiously hands me the reins in the gadget arena.

"A temporary solution," he says, a seeming disclaimer.

In time, I'll convince him the more apt term is *permanent*. For the duration of the war, that is. Regardless, it's a grand reward. Almost as satisfying are the expressions from the ATS lovelies when told the news.

Despite the added burden of responsibility, I practically float out of headquarters. The flaps of my unbuttoned coat could well be wings. I swoop past fellow staff while toting Hutton's briefcase—ours now, really. The piney scent from surrounding trees travels on a crisp spring breeze as I turn for the bunker.

I travel no more than a few strides before a word pierces the air, powerful as a bullet. Paired with the voice, the lone syllable cuts through my core, stopping me cold.

"Fen."

CHAPTER 40

Over the course of my six months at Wilton Park, the potential of this very scenario hasn't eluded me. A dappling of American soldiers from MIS-X, our U.S. counterpart, often frequents our headquarters. At times, a resemblance in one of their profiles, or in a raspy American accent, has steeled me for a confrontation with my past.

I thought.

Now that it's real, now that Arie is closing the few yards between us, nothing within me feels solid. My bones are candles too long in the sun. My brain is sludge, thick and muddled.

"Fen?" he repeats. "You all right?" He touches my elbow as if to ensure stability. His look of concern only adds to my confusion.

"Yes, I…I'm fine. Just…surprised." *Pull it together already.*

Eyeing me from under the brim of his peaked service cap, he nods. But then he glances over his shoulder before tipping his head in that direction. "There's a bench I saw, over by those trees. Why don't we go sit?"

I manage to agree, but as I take a step, he halts me. "Here, let me get that." The briefcase, I realize, barely dangles in my grip. I let go of the handle and gather myself enough to proceed on my own.

My feet guide me past a scattering of service members and around the side of the building to a simple metal bench. Above the treetops, a vibrant blend of orange and yellow saturates the sky, magnifying the surrealness of the scene.

Arie sets down my briefcase and invites me to settle first. The coolness of the seat seeps through my pencil skirt, helping to sober my senses and clear a path for my thoughts.

He joins me on the bench, allowing what little gap is possible. When he removes his cap, his military cut appears a tad longer than I envisioned, the rest of him no less broad or handsome in his olive-drab uniform. Could this encounter actually be happenstance?

"I hope it's okay," he says, "that I came looking for you."

Almost five years apart and he can answer my questions without being asked. As comforting as it is unnerving.

"Absolutely. It's grand to see you." I attempt a smile, not meeting his eyes, dodging the spotlight. "You're here to meet with intelligence, I'm guessing?"

"That's right."

"So...you're stationed in London now?"

"Nah. I'm not staying." Then: "No need for you to fret."

"I...didn't mean to suggest—"

"No, I–I know you didn't." An awkwardness, so foreign between us, wedges in. He picks at his hat resting on his knee. "Just meant I'm flying out tomorrow. First thing."

"Tomorrow," I say. "Going back so soon?"

He hesitates, perhaps not wanting to admit how many days he's been in the area, putting off this visit. Likely debating whether to come. "There's loads of work to be done. You know how it is."

"Of course." I've scarcely registered his presence, much less his departure.

"You look swell, Fenna."

Reflexively I reply, "So do you."

After a beat, he says more pointedly, "What I mean is, you look beautiful."

The full workday has surely faded my makeup and loosed strands from my twist. Still, the sincerity in his tone pulls my gaze to his. What I find there, in the familiar depth of his slate-blue eyes, is something I failed to fathom just how much I've missed: a sense of home rooted in history, in shared memories since childhood, from the one person in the world who knows me better than anyone else ever did or could.

The feeling rings especially true in the muted evening light. As if by magic, it softens his features and our years apart disappear. All at once, we're in my old room, his arms around me, his body curled with mine. It was a night of intimacy and discovery and passion, before he must have come home, eager to share our news, only to find my note...

The guttural sound of propellers—a typical RAF Hurricane in passing—grounds me in reality, where at last I can set things right.

"Arie," I begin, daring to turn to him fully. I push past the emotion gathering in my throat. "About what happened...why I left—"

"Please don't." Firm, not a request. A moment later, his voice eases. "It was ages ago. We wanted different things. I get that now."

There's more to it than that. Although, whittling it down to the barest essence, he's not wrong. Respecting his wishes, the very least I can do, I give a nod. His willingness to speak to me at all is a blessing.

He sheds a breath. "So this job with Major Hutton, I'm glad it panned out."

The diversion is plain, but it does bring forth a question. "How did you know where I was? And about my work?"

"My folks—partly. They reached out, worried, a few days after you rang me. Combined with what you said, it added up."

I should have figured. I phoned them before shipping out and have sent a couple letters since, disclosing what I'm able. "I'm guessing your mother said the same to you as she did to me—that I'm completely out of my tree for accepting the job?"

"She did," he admits.

I can't help but smile, and his eyes gain a glimmer. The warmth in them is just enough to melt a layer of tension. He adds, "Things are going well, then?"

"They are." I consider my day, a welcome contrast to recent weeks. "Particularly well, actually. Not to say I haven't had my fair share of foul-ups."

He nods along, then asks, "You mean like the flaming pea soup?"

I stare at him, befuddled. "But...how? How'd you hear?" Imagining just how far word has spread, I sink into the bench, a flush heating my neck. "Never mind. I don't want to know."

His lips curve upward, almost a grin. "Not to worry. The razzing isn't about you, just the officer at the Ministry. Scuttlebutt has it he's a pompous heel."

I relax only a fraction. "Honest?"

"Honest to goodness," he says. "Moretti tells me you've been doing a real keen job, what with your contraptions and special inks and all that."

"Moretti. As in the wing commander?"

Arie winces and falls mute, the mention apparently unintended. Even more reason to arch my brow and wait, unblinking despite the breeze.

He relents while glancing away. "Every so often, the fella makes it across the pond, ferrying Brit bigwigs. So we'd pal around some. Then back in the fall, I offered him a heap of Lucky Strikes for keeping an eye on the new American gal working with Hutton. A real sport, he insisted on doing it for nothing."

"Wait," I jump in. "*That's* why he pays me visits? Not to bum gadgets for his passengers?"

"Oh, I don't know. I'd wager it's both."

I shake my head, taking this in. Moretti's fatherly manner now seems more targeted than habitual. "You're saying, all this time, you've been keeping tabs on me." It's not an accusation or even teasing; it's a comforting revelation. An awareness that I was never as alone here as I thought.

"Just doing my duty." He shrugs lightly. "Pop's orders."

A plausible enough reason, but there's a flash of care in his eyes that affirms his motives go deeper. With his hand lying mere inches away, I have an urge to reach over and grab hold. Right then, he raises his fingers as if sharing the impulse, only to curl them inward. "Anyhow," he says, "I should let you get back. Must be about suppertime."

Panic grips my gut, a merciless wringing. He can't leave. Not yet.

"We could eat together," I say. "Here, in the officers' mess. Or... at the lounge of my inn. Or anywhere else, if you'd prefer something other than stew." I smile, hopeful. "Your pick and no fuss from me."

He contemplates and murmurs, "That sounds nice." The tension in me loosens as he angles toward me, until I register the graveness in his face. "But I can't."

My heart plunges, dropped through a trapdoor I believed was boarded up for good. "How silly of me," I say casually. "You have an early flight."

He offers a tender smile, playing along. "Yeah, I ought to hit the sack." With that, he rises with hat in hand. Then he picks up my briefcase, and against a sudden weight of dread, I follow him to stand.

As we reverse our path in silence, I catch a glint from a pin on his lapel, a gold sphinx. The insignia of U.S. Military Intelligence. That's when I recall my own lapel pin, tacked to my coat.

Oh no. The sweetheart wings. He might have spotted them and mistook their meaning. But how would I even bring them up to clarify?

Then again, would it change our situation for the better? If anything, perhaps he'll feel entirely freed for another girl, if he doesn't already. I'm tempted to probe, but knowing what he deserves and hearing the details are two different things.

"I nearly forgot," he says, setting down my bag.

I faintly realize we're at our starting point, the area now clear of others.

From a pocket of his coat, he produces an object that fills his palm. A toy wooden train.

Our train.

"This belongs to you." He holds it out for me to take.

I'm astounded he brought it all this way. At least this confirms that his coming to see me wasn't an afterthought. Still, I decline. "It was a gift. Remember?"

"I was grateful to have it," he replies softly. "But it was never really mine." He secures the train in my palm, and I realize then what he came for: closure.

I struggle to hold back a spring of tears as he peers into my eyes. "I'm proud of you, Fen. I truly am." His voice reflects an effort to keep level. "And in case you ever have doubts about us, I need you to know that you made the right choice."

Leaning in, he cups my face and places a lingering kiss on my cheek. My skin hums at the feel of his hand, his lips, a reminder of what we once had.

The reality of losing him, yet again, strikes with torrential force.

I'll tell him I made a mistake, that we could go home together, if he'll have me; that we can make it work for us both—despite knowing that much is a lie.

"Goodbye, Fen," he whispers near my ear. The warmth of his breath brushes my skin. Then he pulls away and leaves without looking back.

CHAPTER 41

Over the many days, then weeks that follow, my most reliable salve proves the same as ever, including for my nightmares: work. I throw myself into designing inventions with gusto.

To prevent suspicion over our partnership, Hutton writes letters to key MI9 staff and our top suppliers, bemoaning his dispirited state and "imprisonment." In truth, his sporadic jitters have yet to fully subside, leaving him tolerant of his hospital stay and conveniently available to meet. And since his eccentricities have long been viewed as madness by many in the military, keeping him here for observation has likely been encouraged.

Together on a vengeful quest, our ideas flow faster than ever.

In the end, my shelved proposal for reversible uniforms wasn't an all-out waste; as an offshoot, we craft a woolen blanket that, when dipped in water, bears the sewing pattern of a civilian suit. This leads us to employing sock suspenders and identity disks to carry small cutters from chain-saw blades. We even pad the lining of heated gloves with banknotes. Phony gold teeth and men's large rings are fitted with compasses. Cigarette holders transform into telescopes, lipstick tubes become flashlights, and a set of baseballs—each stealthily tagged with a single stitch out of place—smuggle the parts for a working radio.

We discover inspiration too in my old stage tricks. A mere cigarette spark turns a square of guncotton to ashes, destroying a map instantly if caught, and my recipe for invisible ink gains new purpose—with adjustments. To view words hidden on a handkerchief, I experiment with a variety of reagent solutions, staying cognizant of ingredients most accessible to downed or captured airmen. I find ammonia to be a fine choice. Yet leave it to a man, Hutton in this case, to point out that urine would work just as well. Not the most pleasant alternative, but undeniably more convenient.

Drawing on my childhood, we even rig smoking pipes and flasks—both being winks to Papa—and on the ribbons of packages, we use Morse code in a printed pattern of flowers and leaves. That one naturally pulls my thoughts to Arie, but I refuse to dwell.

Of course, my working with Hutton isn't always a breeze. Although we've traded enough personal tales to be on a first-name basis—at least on his side, preferring to be called "Clutty" while finding it improper to address me as anything but Miss Vos—my hardheaded independence clashes at times with his conventional if evolving views of female roles and capabilities. More than once, a nurse has shushed our bickering over opinions on a design before we've inevitably found ways to compromise.

In the aftermath of those quibbles, I think of Charles.

I reflect, not proudly, on the countless times I brushed off his input. And now that I'm the showman onstage accepting the entirety of credit, I finally sense how he must have felt: a nagging falsity amid the praise.

Even in this moment, despite the sunny morning that defies the late-April showers, this feeling persists. For as I approach the entrance of headquarters, Lenora stops to offer her congratulations.

"I hear many of your gadgets were just placed in the *Bulletin*," she says, referring to the official training pamphlet.

I hold my briefcase handle snugly and keep my response genial but vague. "I'm just glad they're being put to good use."

She seems to be gauging her next words before two Canadian soldiers exit the building. Weaving around us, they suspend their chat to send flirtatious once-overs, adding to my discomfort.

I'm about to excuse myself for a summons from Colonel Crockatt when Lenora resumes. "I hope, Miss Vos, you don't mind my saying so. But for a time, it appeared you wouldn't be staying. I'm delighted you did."

The remark is surprising, her tone genuine. "Thank you. I

appreciate that." Only half in jest, I admit, "You're giving me hope that others in my department will eventually come around."

"Oh, I'm certain they will. After all, you've long proven—" She self-censors too late.

"Proven…"

"That…you're no Mrs. Bote."

Not understanding, I shake my head.

Then Lenora cracks a smile, as if there's no harm in sharing. "Major Hutton had entrusted Mrs. Bote with the early escape tins— assembling them, that is. As a civilian, she was so pleased to be asked that she transformed the whole of her house, in a village not far from here, into a one-person factory."

Familiar with the pocket-size kit and how meticulously the dozens of survival aids needed to be packed inside, I can only guess how this applies to me. "I take it her finished products were less than stellar."

"On the contrary."

I narrow my eyes.

"Being fond of stout at her local pub, she formed an unfortunate habit of broadcasting details of her tasks. She was out doing just that when Private Leary had to climb through her window so the major and I could help load her supplies onto our trucks. With her neighbors curiously watching, it made quite the spectacle."

Envisioning the farcical scene, I struggle for a moment to identify the relevance. "So the standoffish treatment I've gotten, it's been for fear that I'm another *civilian broad* of Hutton's who can't keep a secret?" At the affirming scrunch of Lenora's face, I muse with a grin. "And all these months, I assumed it was mostly just for being American."

She considers this and lifts a shoulder in her baggy uniform. "Perhaps a spot of that too."

When my laugh slips out, she joins in with a soft giggle, though her gaze just as soon dims.

I encourage her gently. "If there's something more, feel free to say so."

She nods. "It's only that…I never expressed my appreciation, and how deeply I'm indebted to you, for saving my life outside the shelter."

I bristle slightly. Not at the sentiment but the topic.

"We English won't speak of such events. We're taught the stiff upper lip, you see."

It's only logical that the deaths we witnessed would have affected her too. But hearing it verbalized brings me a dose of unexpected comfort.

"There's no need to thank me," I tell her. "It's clear we were there for each other."

Her eyes lighten, a look of gratitude filling them, and she nods again. With a bolstering breath, she says, "Now then. I oughtn't hold you up longer, Miss Vos."

"Please. It's Fenna."

"Only if I'm Lenora," she says with warm sincerity, and I agree.

As she starts to pivot away, I blurt out, "Lenora, would you…be up for an outing sometime? Whatever chums here do for fun?"

She smiles, face aglow in the sunlight. "How about Saturday? A matinee?"

No need to check my calendar.

We're settling details when the business of scheduling reminds me: "Geez, my meeting with Crockatt. I'd nearly forgotten why I'm here."

"Oh my. Off you go." She cheerily ushers me off toward the colonel's office, where—oddly, as I'm precisely on time—the welcome that awaits me glares in contrast.

CHAPTER 42

Seated at the desk in his office, a reasonably spacious room with tidy stacks of files and a European map pinned to the wall, Colonel Crockatt invites me in with a rigid wave. I'm well accustomed to his Royal Scots uniform—replete with tartan trousers, combat decorations, and the Scottish bonnet set on his desk—but not the lack of his trademark wit and agreeable nature.

"Have a seat, Miss Vos."

Over the echo of a phone ringing across the hall, I ask, "Is there a problem, sir?"

His mustache, suavely groomed with a split down the middle, twitches. He gestures toward the twin visitors' chairs across from him. "Please."

His intensity leads me to the only probability I can surmise.

He knows about Hutton. Our charade. All it would have taken was a single supplier, or a nurse more likely, to wise up and sound an alert.

There's a chance it's something else entirely. But treading now toward my seat, I'm daunted by the end of a career that feels just beginning—ironically after having to be coerced into staying. In all honesty, given the colonel's distaste for regulations, his recent comments in passing have resembled verbal winks: *I do wonder how old Clutty is doing. Convey my regards should you happen to see the chap.*

Perhaps I misjudged.

I set my briefcase aside and lower onto a chair, prepared to accept sole responsibility. Not only for the sake of Hutton's recovery but because the decision to go forward was ultimately mine.

A noise from behind turns me. A blocky man in a smart black suit has shut the door, muffling the usual goings-on at headquarters. Was he in the room when I entered, observing?

"Good of you to come, Miss Vos." A low timbre threads his English accent. My gaze follows as he crosses the room. From his slicked wavy hair to his thick eyebrows and cleft chin, he could pass as Humphrey Bogart's brother. He settles before me, against a corner of the colonel's desk, and folds his arms with authority. "I should like to ask you a few questions, if I may."

Curious over the man's identity and position, I glance at the colonel, who only nudges me on with a stolid nod.

I reply to Bogart. "Of course, sir."

"Your association with MI9 began in September. Is that correct?"

"Yes. That's right."

"I will kindly remind you that, at such time, you signed the Official Secrets Act, with full understanding of the consequences of any violation." He waits, despite not posing a question.

Is it possible the office gals have flagged me as another loose-lipped Mrs. Bote?

I answer with growing confidence. "I remember that well. And since joining MI9, I assure you I haven't related a whit of information to anyone who wasn't specifically approved by the department—being vendors and the like. Even then, I divulge the bare minimum."

Then it hits me: Hutton might no longer be considered within the realm of my oath. Could I actually face imprisonment for our continued collaboration?

My nerves stir as Bogart states, "Let's turn the clock back for a moment. Shall we?" He taps his chin twice with a stubby finger. He's well versed in sustaining a placid face.

But so am I, thankfully.

"The evening Major Hutton first approached you in New York, did you ring U.S. Lieutenant Arie Jansen about the encounter?"

Internally I flinch. Then I note that as part of my vetting, my bills and records must have been examined.

"I did phone him, yes."

Crockatt sits forward slightly.

"It was strictly to ask for any general insight about the major, seeing as Arie—Lieutenant Jansen—serves in intelligence, and the two might have crossed paths." Deducing what's sure to be the next query, I add, "He said he'd heard Major Hutton was eccentric…and resourceful, I think. And that was that."

Bogart asks, "I presume he encouraged you to accept the position?"

"Actually, no. I never mentioned the offer." It's a bit rewarding to have knowledge this man doesn't have.

The colonel interjects. "Yet he knew to locate you here on the premises just weeks ago."

As quick as that, I've lost the upper hand. The idea of a staff member observing our reunion through a window unnerves me further. "I imagine the lieutenant simply asked around to find me."

Come to think of it, Commander Moretti likely directed him to Wilton Park, but no reason to pull the airman into the mix. I add, "Arie and I hadn't communicated since the one telephone exchange, but his parents are aware I'm in England to help with the war in some manner. I've corresponded with the couple to put them at ease, always keeping my information vague. You see, I grew up in their home since childhood."

"Yes," Bogart says. "We're aware."

I conceal the gritting of my teeth as he resumes the lead.

"So when the two of you last met, you never disclosed details pertinent to your work here?"

I believe we've covered this, I want to say but think better of it as the colonel sits back, steepling his fingers over his middle. I'm reminded of the air commodore who ruminated in a similar way, right before his pristine office went up in flames—a story, in fact, that Arie and I touched upon. But even on that, I didn't expound.

I regard Bogart with conviction. "No, sir. I didn't."

"Nothing about quantities or locations of shipments? Perhaps agreeing to gift him one of your clever devices?"

Agreeing.

The choice of word clings in my ear. Agreeing, not *offering*. Bogart is implying I was asked. What exactly is he after?

"Miss?"

"Absolutely not. I take security very seriously." I hold Bogart's gaze. After a moment, he nods but then pushes on.

"Do you recollect, at any point, your work papers being out of your possession?"

I'm about to say no again when I register the technical truth, as well as the chances that Bogart already knows the answer. "As a trusted old friend, Arie was kind enough to carry my briefcase for me, but very shortly. And at no time did I reveal its contents, confidential or otherwise."

"You're certain."

"Unmistakably."

Bogart gives another tap to his chin. "Did the lieutenant request anything more of you? Anything at all?"

This line of inquiry, I realize, is less about me than Arie. What ever could he have done to warrant the scrutiny? Particularly in the measly few days he was in England.

Granted, I recall he did make requests—for me to not speak of the past, to move on without regret—but those aren't what this is about.

"I'm afraid I'm unsure what you mean, sir."

"Did he pass you any documents, for instance? A message to forward?"

I resist a smirk at what he's inferring. "Gracious, no. Nothing like that."

But then a memory slams back: his returning of the toy train. It's the object we'd used historically as a courier. For the passage of notes.

Over my urge to redirect, I manage casualness. "Do you mind if I ask the reason for my interrogation?"

"Oh, miss, this is no interrogation. We are only clarifying."

I smile dryly and recognize that if I'm to uncover the core of the matter, I need to be bold—within acceptable limits. A hundred theater hecklers have taught me how to reassume control through a gentle, even humble tone. "Sir, as an American, please forgive me if I'm out of line by saying so. But if I've learned anything from my duties here, it's that the war clock is always ticking, and surely neither of you gentlemen would be wasting your time on a meeting of this sort if it weren't vital."

Although Bogart's face remains stoic, his eyes betray his surprise in where I'm taking this. Even the colonel's brow arches a smidge.

"I must think, then, that the less ambiguous your questions, the faster I might help you unwind this mystery. And trust me, sirs, I want nothing more—mind you, with the well-established understanding that I'm duty-bound to keep in confidence anything you see fit to share."

Bogart shifts his square jaw and studies me. Then the two exchange looks, considerations passing between them. When Bogart lowers his arms and fully stands, I expect him to escort me out. But he slips his hands into his trouser pockets and sends a nod to the colonel, who returns his steadied gaze to mine.

"In conjunction with our forces," Crockatt says, accepting the handoff, "Lieutenant Jansen was assigned a special mission. As such, he was dropped into occupied territory to aid a Resistance cell."

My solace from not being dismissed lasts only until I absorb the words, finding nonsense in them. Arie? Parachuted into Europe?

"That…that can't be right. He was just here several weeks ago. And he's back safely in the States." The claim is scarcely out of my mouth when I note that I have no proof of where he is at all. The notion that England was but a stopover leaves me grasping. "You're certain we're referring to the same Arie Jansen."

Crockatt's tone suggests indulgence. "Quite positive."

The uniqueness of Arie's name does make a mix-up improbable, but his role in intelligence, at least to my mind, was supposed to keep him far from the thick of things. "Where exactly was this mission?"

"The sole element of relevance is that the cell's hideout was blown," Crockatt says, sidestepping my question. "Most succeeded in fleeing, although barely and not without a fight. One not as fortunate was killed." He allows me a chance to process, and through the dread of it, the purpose of this meeting strikes with a wallop.

"And what? You think Arie is responsible for this?"

"The morning of the raid, Lieutenant Jansen was scheduled to meet with the group. He was the only person who failed to appear and has been out of contact since."

I might have laughed at the insinuation if not for my spike of fear. They're saying he's missing—that Arie's missing. I work to keep my voice level. "Obviously something's happened to him and he needs your help." How in the blazes has this not occurred to these men? "He could've been detained or...or he..." I can't verbalize the rest, can hardly think it.

"Indeed," Crockatt says, "that was the original assumption. He has, however, been seen since then alive and well."

Alive and well. Oh, thank God!

Relief pours through me. Only from the remnants of my defenses do I discern the simplest explanation. "Well, then, that's it. He must have been tipped off. He just couldn't warn others in time." No question, he would have done so if he could.

"A distinct possibility," Crockatt agrees, "if not for our contact's report. It seems Lieutenant Jansen has been spotted on several occasions in town but slipped away when approached. Moreover, even through separate channels, he has made no effort to communicate."

I open my mouth to counter with explanations but come up with nothing rational. I can't deny that as a whole, the circumstances don't compute.

"Miss Vos," Bogart pipes in, "is there anything the lieutenant mentioned that might be telling? Any indication why he would betray his country?"

I shake my head, perplexed at first, then adamant. "No. There's nothing. He wouldn't do what you're saying. He just couldn't."

Bogart releases a hitched breath, as if rationing out his impatience. "Miss Vos," he says. The pity in his tone is as comforting as a screech. "To be assigned to intelligence, your friend put forth a great deal of effort to transfer out of the U.S. Army Corps of Engineers. His skill sets in engineering, as you're surely aware, are in exceptionally high demand. Did he ever share his impetus for the change?"

My mind grapples for reasons, any slivers of justification. "He's skilled with languages. And Morse code—way back from his childhood. He likes to help people, to solve riddles." Recognizing the weakness of my points, I contend as if stating a biblical truth, "Working in intelligence was always perfectly fitting."

Bogart goes quiet, unswayed.

Two knocks interrupt, and Crockatt calls out a grudging "Yes?"

The door opens and Lenora appears. "I beg your pardon, Colonel, but it's time we depart for your meeting."

"Yes. Thank you." He turns to Bogart. "Shall we resume this later?"

The response comes swiftly. "I've heard enough at present." With that, both fellows rise, towering over me.

"Wait," I implore, rushing to stand, desperate to make a stronger case. "The Arie Jansen I know could *not* have done this. I've known him practically my entire life, better than anyone. I guarantee it's a misunderstanding."

Crockatt shoots a glance past me. "Private, kindly wait in the truck."

"Yes, sir," Lenora replies.

When the door shuts, I'm still scant on the purpose of Arie's actions—alleged ones, at that—though at least hopeful over continuing to be heard, to explore sensible scenarios.

"Miss Vos, we appreciate your time," the colonel says. Then he motions toward the door, commanding me to exit.

CHAPTER 43

My scheduled tasks for the morning will have to wait. I race back to the inn and tug my curtains closed, perhaps an overly cautious move being on the second floor, but my thoughts are as orderly as a hurricane.

By lamplight, from my bureau drawer, I root out the wooden train, which I buried beneath my winter wear to elude the reach of my thoughts. An effort that clearly failed.

I perch on the edge of my bed and will myself to steady. The toy's compartment could just as likely be empty. Upon reflection, it seems foolish to have not checked earlier, but more than ever, I was anxious to move past the things in life I couldn't change. Or, at the very least, shouldn't.

Finally I detach the cab and look. What I find prompts an instant tremor in my hands: a piece of white paper folded down to a one-inch square.

I set the two train pieces on my lap. Slowly I unfold the page. At a mere glance, I recognize the handwriting, the words.

Because they're mine.

> My dearest Arie,
> I pray one day you'll forgive me.
> Forever, Fen

Confounded, I flip the note over. There's nothing on the back, save for a grid of creases. Blank, like a clean slate. An act of closure.

That was, after all, the purpose of his visit.

But then snippets of our conversation echo in my head: his admission of assigning a pal to look after me, his merciful assurances to lessen my regrets, the solemn finality of his goodbye. Too closely now, they resemble offerings from a deathbed.

Did he never plan to return?

Criminy, this is silly. My imagination is getting away from me.

Even so. His reported actions leave me at a loss, starting with his lie about intending to fly home. Or maybe I assumed as much and he just didn't correct me. Particularly with classified orders.

But orders to go where?

Holland springs to mind, and not due only to his language skills. As of late, Moretti's gadget requests for his passengers—namely postcards and loaded matchbooks and such, printed with Dutch names for hotels or cafés, a clever touch to help agents blend—have indicated frequent drops into the country.

Still, that doesn't explain Arie's transfer from the Corps of Engineers. While his German-related dialect would have made him appealing to intelligence, what had attracted *him*? More important, what if he's hunted down before voluntarily coming forward? Would his captors act in haste before hearing him out?

What if they don't believe him?

Desperate to stop the spiraling questions for which I have no answers, I squeeze my eyes shut. Guilt still finds me. Five years ago, if only I'd let our friendship be, Arie would doubtfully have rushed off to enlist. Sure, after the attack on Pearl Harbor, he'd have joined up. But his promotions would have come later, reducing his connections, perhaps resulting in a transfer denied and an assignment elsewhere.

Cursing a history I can't reverse, I ball my hands on my lap until something pokes my wrist: a corner edge of the train. I grasp its base. As I'd done on so many nights at the orphanage, my thumb finds a home in the grooves. With the train in one hand and farewell note in the other, the two objects symbolically span my relationship with Arie, a reminder of how well I know him. The real him.

In that instant, I draw certainty. No matter the accusations or how incriminating the appearance, I know in the depths of my heart that he's innocent.

The thought brings an old image to mind. A film.

Seared into my memory, *The Grim Game* was our first picture show together. Up on the silver screen, Houdini, as a reporter wrongly imprisoned for a murder, embarked on a harrowing quest to clear his name and secure his freedom.

Almost eerily, the story resembles Arie's predicament. Except this is actual life. And the risks are higher, the costs graver.

After Hitler invaded the Netherlands following the Rotterdam Blitz, even Queen Wilhelmina found it necessary to retreat to London with her government-in-exile. On *Radio Oranje*, a BBC program named for her monarchy, she broadcasts messages to her citizens who tune in secretly on their radios. She can do little more than offer encouragement as the enemy clamps down, the effect of a clear miscalculation.

Not illogically, the Nazis initially figured that as the Germans' Aryan "cousins," most Dutch would be lured willingly into the Reich, but those hopes are withering. Just recently, the slaying of a Nazi collaborator, a high-ranking Dutch official, triggered a succession of German reprisals. Reported among them was the summary execution of fifty imprisoned Allied operatives and raids to seek out more. To prevent meeting a similar fate, Arie needs to make it out of there and soon.

Were our roles reversed, no doubt he'd dive straight in to help— but how?

I skim through our past, times we inherently worked hand in hand. Inspired by that very first film, we performed at the local junkyard for a pocketful of pennies. We played our parts and commanded attention. We made things vanish, then reappear.

Suddenly I see that the goal, of pulling off the seemingly impossible, remains the same.

And so, then, is my solution.

CHAPTER 44

Entering the hospital room, I'm relieved to find Hutton alone. Rumored to be fit any day for discharge, he's at the window in a robe belted over his pajamas, studying the near-cloudless sky while puffing on a cigarette. I've grown as accustomed to smoke from his Pall Malls as to the scent of disinfectant here and barely detect either.

The second I close the door, I launch in without preamble. "I'm in need of your help, Clutty. It's an urgent personal matter."

He turns, peering through his glasses.

Before I can come to my senses, I expound while moving toward him. "The issue pertains to a dear friend in U.S. intelligence. This morning, you see, I was questioned regarding suspicions over—"

"Your lieutenant friend."

This halts me, despite having considered the possibility of Hutton's awareness. "They spoke with you. About me."

"Quite so."

"And…you told them…"

"That I would entrust you with my life, as I believe that has already proven a fine bet."

I ease with an exhale. "Thank you for that."

He waves the sentiment away, shifting on his slippered feet. "Now then. This chum of yours, I reckon you view his guilt as…unlikely." There's skepticism in Hutton's voice.

"Not just unlikely. He's absolutely incapable of what they're suggesting." Pointedly I add, "And I know this because I've entrusted him with *my* life. Far more than once."

At Hutton's pondering, no doubt wrangling with the accounts he's been told, I recall the rationales I assembled on the bus ride over.

"I confess, Arie's actions do appear questionable. But what if his assigned contacts are compromised, keeping him away for safety? Or any number of reasons? If you remember, I had just as much suspicion over *your* secretiveness. Which in hindsight seems laughable. I'm only asking, before someone does anything rash, that he too be given an opportunity to explain."

As Hutton takes a drag on the last of his cigarette, silence drifts through the smoke-hazed air. He twists to dispose of the stub in a cup on the windowsill. When he angles back, it's with an amenable expression. "How precisely would you like me to assist?"

The offer brings relief, though short-lived. I'm fully aware my plan is logical only if one overlooks its odds, perils, and general absurdity.

Then again, the same could be said of war overall. And for that matter, about any trick that teeters between life and death. Moreover, having racked my mind, I see no other acceptable choice.

I begin by acknowledging, "Although you're not with MI9 at the moment, your connections still exist and your input plainly carries weight, with Crockatt at the very least."

"You wish me to speak with the colonel, to voice an appeal?"

"No. Well...yes. But not just about Arie's innocence." My determination solidifying, I take a step forward. "His repeated sightings indicate he's staying in the vicinity for a reason. And I'd wager there are more clues I haven't yet heard." Adopting Hutton's style of Hollywood salesmanship, I lead up to the reveal with a desired conclusion. "In light of all this, I have an idea that can ensure his safety and also lead us to the truth. A strategy in which every party benefits."

He looks intrigued if cautious, as he so often does when I propose innovative schemes. This one by far being my most audacious.

"I'll draw Arie out of hiding and back into contact," I tell him. "By going in as bait."

CHAPTER 45

At first impression, the ploy seems stark, raving madness—to me included. Yet death-defying schemes and orchestrated acts that surpass the imagination are how I've made my living. Plus, the potential negatives are irrefutably meager, at least for the Special Operations Executive.

From the snippets I've collected over my many months with MI9, the SOE, also known as "Churchill's Secret Army," is an intrepid, somewhat slapdash branch of spies and saboteurs who regularly support Resistance cells. Presuming Arie was dropped into the Netherlands, the organization's Dutch unit, N Section, is likely tangled up in the mess and perhaps open to a creative solution with little downside.

According to suspicions, Arie knows he's being sought after, hence even if he and I wound up in cahoots, we'd surely be taken down by one side or the other. And the limited scope of my wartime work would hardly make me a jackpot find for the Germans. Nor a major loss for the Allies.

As for my inclusion, if Arie indeed believes his contacts are compromised, who better to guide him out? And before that, to sight him in a crowd or assess where he's most apt to go? What other Dutch speaker with my skill sets could be spared in such short order?

My main arguments boil down to these, and I hold to them staunchly. While it takes a tide of persuasion to get Hutton onboard, Crockatt requires a tsunami, and even then he agrees solely to give his consideration. But it's a vital step. I couldn't, after all, just march over to N Section's office—wherever that is, assuming one even exists, given their covert nature.

Only after the colonel confers with varied authorities, apart from the major and on both sides of the pond, does he summon me back to his office first thing the next morning—thank heavens, to relate his approval.

Mind you, with explicit conditions:

"Straightaway, you will attend condensed training sessions and debriefings in preparation for your departure." The tempo of his speech matches his steps as he paces between his desk and the chair in which I'm seated. "In addition, you shall adhere strictly to instructions and divulge no details of your mission, under threat of imprisonment for treason."

I nod unfazed, having already taken similar oaths. "And my departure is when, sir?"

"On a night coming shortly, via a flight already scheduled."

"By that, do you mean—"

"When appropriate, you will be notified of the essentials," he states with only a slight pause in his stride.

The deliberate ambiguity swells my impatience. Specifics and careful planning have long been the crux of my careers, my life, and now, above all, Arie's well-being. Still, to prevent the colonel from changing his mind, I refrain from badgering.

"As you can very well fathom," he adds, "particularly in a heavily occupied area, the risks and stakes shall be great. The same must be said of the consequences, should the mission go awry." He stops sharply with a pointed look. "Do you find these circumstances entirely acceptable, Miss Vos?"

Translation: If nabbed by the Gestapo, the German secret state police, am I prepared to be cut loose? The notion brings a lump to my throat. Forcing a swallow, I jut out my chin.

"Fully, sir."

Disappointment seems to darken his eyes, as if part of him hoped I'd reconsider. As if he's acquiescing against his better judgment, perhaps under orders from above.

Then he crosses his arms over his uniformed chest, his posture as sturdy as his tone. "Lastly and not negotiable: You will be escorted by a seasoned agent whose separate assignment shares the vicinity of your destination. Also fluent in Dutch, he is well versed in navigating Holland. Thus, rendezvousing with a contact, he'll acquire more details and areas to target. Integrating your insight, of course. He shall then observe covertly whilst you attempt to lure out the lieutenant."

So my deduction was right; Arie is indeed in the Netherlands. But I know nothing else.

"Furthermore, at the close of your allotted time, whether or not you succeed, you shall be handed off to a courier to guide you along an escape line, which I must warn you carries its own set of taxing risks."

If he's trying to scare me off, it's going to take more than that. "Colonel," I venture, "could you just tell me how long I'll be given once I arrive?"

A strident ring breaks in. He turns to the candlestick telephone on his desk and lifts the receiver and mouthpiece into place. "Colonel Crockatt."

Inside me, pressure compounds from all that's still unknown. I'm a balloon untethered, lacking an anchoring string to keep me from drifting away, from bursting.

"Most certainly," he says. "However, wait one moment to put him through." He muffles the receiver against his chest. "That will be all, Miss Vos."

I straighten in my seat. "First my question, sir. About my timeline in Holland." Aware I'm bordering persistent and obstinate, I hasten to add, "Please."

He huffs a breath, deliberating, before the creases in his forehead soften. "I want you returned to safety in minimal time. Not accounting for return travel from the Continent, you will have a week for your mission."

Already I feel the ticking of the clock. "Colonel, respectfully, with settling in and snooping about, just getting the lay of the land in a foreign area, seven days is scarcely anything."

"On the contrary, it already surpasses my level of comfort. I shall remind you, the territory is highly dangerous and this is not your field of expertise."

"But, sir—"

"The alternative, Miss Vos, is to not go at all." His gaze, solid if not steely, makes clear what I've assessed from day one: he's not the bluffing type.

I gather myself and rise from my chair. "A week will do, sir."

CHAPTER 46

Once more, I begin a new life.

In preparation, when asked about my parents' Dutch roots, I'm embarrassed to confess I know next to nothing. Papa must have mentioned their village or province at some point, but he was never one for nostalgia, and in my youth, I didn't think to prod or commit such things to memory. Now it's a regret that leaves me further unmoored.

But no matter. I'm quickly reinvented.

Normally a drop into occupied Europe requires weeks if not months of training. But nothing about our situation is normal. Wait that long, and any chance of locating Arie will be gone. That this plan is actually going forward indicates how I'm being viewed: uniquely skilled yet expendable. A gamble worth the risk.

In three long, crammed days, I become an artist's assistant named Ida Hofman, complete with a Dutch identity card and passport. My Dutch speech is ruled passable, thanks to years of interactions with neighbors in Amesboro, some of them fresh immigrants, many of them elders set in their ways. Ironically, my dialect gained from the Jansens is deemed slightly stronger than that from Papa, causing me another twinge of remorse.

To cover my bases and any flaws in my accent, I transform into a native of the Groningen province now living in Elspeet, a village in the province of Gelderland, with a full family tree and history. Absorbing these details is a cinch after years of memorizing scripts and acting a role. The information is drilled into me regardless, along with knowledge of daily life to avoid standing out: rationing, customs, transportation, even walking. The British habit of first looking right when crossing the street, a fatal tell in Holland, is one I've mastered since moving to England and must swiftly break. To buffer me against any other distinct norms I could miss, I'm to play a visitor of Utrecht—my destination city—meeting a dear relative on holiday.

As for physical training, I'm permitted to bypass lessons I could literally teach, from escapes and evasions to gadgets and maps. Among the more helpful sessions involve defensive maneuvers and parachute drops—simulations, that is. Strapped to wires in an airplane hangar, and once from a hot-air balloon, I practice jumps with eager recruits from an unnamed section.

I do realize, of course, that my trepidation over a plane ride shouldn't drastically outweigh that of a subsequent leap and plummet through the sky. Nevertheless, focusing on the latter helps sustain my fortitude, as does avoiding related reminders.

Like the unsettling one before me.

Massive on the screen at a cinema in London, a newsreel is showcasing a British bomber. "And look here," the male narrator exclaims. "These brave lads of Tiger Squadron prepare for their voyage on a mighty Lancaster. Oh my... It appears they have created a special gift for their journey." The grinning airmen pose with an enormous bomb painted with the message *Easter Egg for Hitler.*

Less than a dozen hours from my own flight, it's surreal to be enjoying the leisure of a matinee. Truth be told, I'd forgotten all about our Saturday plans until Lenora arrived at the George in her "civvies," with a coat over her skirt and blouse. After my final briefing at headquarters, I was storing my unneeded belongings with the inn manager, who seemed accustomed to Wilton Park guests popping in and out. Despite being packed and ready for my mission, I had half a mind to cancel on Lenora until she dangled a suggestion.

"I fancied we might see *Springtime in the Rockies,* playing at Piccadilly Circus. The musical comedy, you know, with Betty Grable and John Payne."

Compared to an afternoon holed up in my room cursing the torturous wait, the diversion held appeal. I just hadn't factored in the preceding wartime updates, scenes that suddenly strike me as a warning—not to turn back but to brace for failure. After all, scores of our sophisticated planes and inscribed arsenals still haven't secured total victory. How will my abilities alone fare against the Nazis?

My gaze retreats to my lap. These past few days, with my attention narrow and driven, I've managed to skirt thoughts of being captured by the enemy. But now, under a projector's beam, reminiscent of countless picture shows Arie and I shared—with our laughing, discussing, debating—I'm cornered by my fears. None greater than of not finding him in time.

"Fenna…" The whisper drifts from Lenora. "Are you all right?"

I lift my eyes to her concerned expression. Before I can answer, flickers from the screen hook me back, to Nazi soldiers parading in goose-step, the road lined with flag-waving Germans.

"I'm dandy," I reply lightly while craving a reprieve. Moviegoers in a myriad of uniforms dabble every row. "I just need to use the loo."

The instant she nods, I slip out of my aisle seat and stride toward the lobby. In the lounge area of the lavatory, a space wallpapered in pink fleur-de-lis and gratefully vacant, I stand before the vanity mirror. I take a series of soothing breaths, inhaling traces of lingering perfume.

In the mirror's reflection, Lenora steps through the door. She hovers several feet behind, surely perplexed; my distracted reserve, fun as a bump on a log, has no doubt been wearing.

I tell myself to pep up. I'll attribute blame to the stress of work— which technically isn't false. But as I pivot to face her, given the potential perils of my mission, namely that I might never come back, I'm seized by a desire to be as candid as allowed.

"I'm sorry, Lenora. There are just some things happening."

"It's quite fine." She tenders a faint smile as I continue.

"It involves someone I care about, deeply. A person caught up in this mess of a war, and I'm…desperately fretful and anxious to help." I'm tiptoeing through a minefield of oaths and secrets, wishing I could say more.

Appearing to comprehend this, she goes to speak. But then she hesitates and peeks into the lavatory as if to confirm we're alone.

That's when I notice that, really, she's been as quiet as I have since we departed Beaconsfield on the bus.

"What is it, Lenora?"

She angles back to me but doesn't meet my eyes. "At times, as a driver, I am privy to fairly sensitive conversations. In the colonel's office the other day, you talked of a certain lieutenant's quandary."

She'd caught the tail end of my argument, I recall. For her to bring this up would seem an intrusion of privacy for most Englishwomen. Paired with her caution and mood, I realize: "You've overheard something else. About my friend Arie."

Her silence only confirms this.

"Lenora, what did you hear?"

One of her hands begins kneading the other. "I was in the truck this morning, awaiting the colonel. He was approaching when a suited gentleman engaged him in a rather tense discussion. Now, I've no inkling of details," she inserts, either a defense or disclaimer. "I only know, however you're involved, your purpose...isn't as you think."

I shake my head, trying to decipher. "What does that mean?"

Her continued hedging is plain and justifiable, but so is the reason she's inclined to relay anything. It's less likely for our friendship—frankly, in the early stages—than out of a compulsion to repay a perceived debt.

In usual circumstances, I'd insist again that we're square over the air raid. Instead, I strain to withhold my frustration. "I beg of you, Lenora. It's critical that I know, for Arie's safety—and mine. What did they say?"

Her hands go still, fingers clasped together as she ekes out her answer. "Reports indicate that your friend's actions are more problematic than you may know. When you make contact, if you do, your assigned agent is not tasked with guiding him in."

My bafflement over the implication is brief, overridden by a revelation so horrifying that my stomach lurches even before she finishes.

"The order," she says, "is to take him out."

CHAPTER 47

Panic surrounds the outskirts of my mind, walled off by a single fact: I have time. I've got several hours yet before my night drop. To think, to plead, to negotiate.

Although, what trust would I have in any assurances I might garner?

At a briefing just this morning, Bogart—not his real name, but that's who he is to me—reiterated that all would go as arranged.

I want so much to believe Lenora misheard. Yet she's fiercely convinced she didn't, and the potential risks from discounting her claims are a thousand times greater than accepting them as truth.

On our return bus ride, having skipped out on the picture show, I'm festering with anger—at Bogart and Crockatt and whoever else chose to twist my role so deceitfully. Repulsively. Was this the only reason they'd accepted my proposal? At the very least, I deserve an explanation of what firmed their misguided conclusion.

But I can't worry about that now. I have to stay clearheaded enough to make my own plan. Because whatever they *think* Arie's done, based on the details they shared or more, he needs a chance to present the truth. The pure truth, not filtered and distorted through another's mouth out of ignorance or idiocy. Or malice.

"What will you do?" Lenora is finally able to ask once we disembark in Beaconsfield, no longer hindered by the presence of passengers. In the bus's wake, petrol fumes pervade the afternoon air as I scrounge for an answer.

"Quite honestly? I haven't a clue yet."

She's quick to reply. "You'll figure something out. You will."

While I've sworn to keep her disclosure in confidence, the possibility that she's jeopardized her career isn't lost on me.

"Thank you, Lenora. For telling me."

She offers a heartfelt look. "Godspeed, Fenna."

As we go our separate ways, I think back to my old standby lesson—how I need only belief, imagination, and perseverance to solve any given problem.

Now more than ever, I hope that holds true.

CHAPTER 48

The place was designed by an illusionist.

That's according to the serviceman who chauffeured me here, and a tenable theory. Shielded by trees, north of London—Tempsford, I gather—the moonlit airfield with its crisscrossing runways masquerades as an expansive farm. Fleets of aircraft are tucked away somewhere in the darkness. Clusters of remarkably disguised buildings give no indication of the equipment and munitions surely stocked to the rafters. The farmhouse too is well utilized, hosting preflight receptions, like the one I completed upon arriving.

On a sofa chair in the sitting room a smidge past ten, I now wait alone. Beyond the blacked-out window, a buzzing noise grows. I envision a Lysander charging along a runway and up, up into the blackened sky.

Just as my own plane shortly will be...

I busy myself to mute the thought. On the lap of my travel pants, I root through my unbuckled satchel, triple-checking items in both the main and hidden compartments. Among them are a nightgown and a few interchangeable outfits, a select handful of well-disguised gadgets, two forms of relevant maps, and added just tonight: Dutch wartime guilders for food and accommodations, a worn ration card, and all my round-trip paperwork and passes needed for a holiday getaway with my cousin. That reason being fictional, of course. Same for the cousin.

How strange to at last venture to my parents' homeland, where any actual familial ties were severed before my birth. Even Papa's talk of the old country was so rare and removed the place seemed barely to exist. I can only pray that my ancestral journey isn't meant to end there.

"I daresay the hour is upon us," the suited man declares, entering the room. I know him strictly by his cover name of Bram.

He's the one.

My escort.

Fair-skinned, his hair the color of mud, he gestures toward the entry. "Shall we?"

Already my performance has begun. Smiling, I rise with my bag and coat. "Gladly."

When we first met tonight, I took fast note of his solid frame and the scar at his temple yet his lack of otherwise sinister bearing. An encouraging surprise. My mind pounced on the possibility that Lenora was mistaken, or maybe the higher-ups had reversed course since she'd heard. However, as Bram informed me of the last details for my role, his eyes revealed a truth, an internal callousness I'd encountered many times since childhood, from the mines and orphanage to the tenements and tough Chicago streets.

He's a survivor willing to do whatever is needed to reach his goal.

I follow him to a lamplit barn to complete our being "kitted out," as they say. Already tonight in a nearby Romney hut, military staff gave each of our garments a final inspection, even turning out our pockets. A British train stub or receipt could prove deadly. All my clothing, on my body and packed for the trip, are well worn and authentically Dutch. Pristine hems and fabric might raise suspicion; a foreign collar and buttons could prompt my arrest.

We now meet up with the two male agents joining our trip. Like Bram, they appear to be in their twenties. Both have light hair, their features pleasant but nondescript. A factor, I would guess, in why they were chosen.

Staff members proceed to bandage our ankles and insert rubber cushions in our shoes for a safer landing. They then fit us with camouflage coveralls, baggy enough to accommodate civilian clothing—even a baby grand, a fellow jokes. One of the agents, incredibly, has jammed a whole briefcase into his suit jacket. We're further layered with matching foam helmets, long leather "gauntlet" gloves, and canvas overboots that cover our shoes. Last of all come the parachute packs. Snug in our harnesses, we're bundled so comically, I might have laughed if not for the reality of our journey.

Our "dispatcher," a British jumpmaster, has just completed testing our release mechanisms, several times each, when an airman peeks into the barn. A member of the so-called moon squadron.

"Righto, Joes! This way to your chariots."

A "Joe" is how they refer to agents—which, of course, I am not. I'm cheese in a trap, a worm on a hook. But no need to clarify.

In a jiff, we're funneled toward a pair of idling motorcars, their blackout-regulation headlamps aglow. My vision races to adjust to the moonlight. I trail Bram toward the closest vehicle, both of us carrying travel bags soon to be strapped to our legs. I'm nearly at the car door the airman has opened for me when, several yards beyond the hood, a passing figure slows. Blocky in his bomber jacket and peaked cap, he angles toward us and halts. It seems odd for him to stare; departing agents, I'm told, are largely kept isolated here as a security precaution.

Then I see his eyes. Beams from the headlamps glint softly off his gaze, aimed directly at me. It's Wing Commander Moretti, clearly stupefied by my presence. Let alone my jump gear, I realize. I'd wanted to avoid this run-in, not only since his fatherly manner would almost guarantee he'd worry but because no one else needs to be bothered. Particularly over a mission I can't divulge.

For Arie's folks, I scribed a note, to be mailed by Hutton if I don't return. Suddenly I regret not doing the same for Moretti. All these months of his friendly chats and gadget requests, he's looked out for me—as a favor to Arie, but still. I should have expressed my thanks and shared, ambiguously, that it was my turn to serve as a guardian.

But it's too late to explain, and others are present. I sneak a small wave before clambering into one of the motorcars with my bulky pack. The instant I shut the door, we're swept away like thieves on the lam, and a stunned Moretti dissolves in the distance.

Our jump group is delivered to a heavy bomber painted with layered circles that, for my taste, too narrowly resemble a bull's-eye. Up close, the four-engine Halifax, modified for drops, looks positively monstrous. Multiple turrets armed with protruding machine guns make it all the more formidable.

Safer, I tell myself.

A crewman directs us to the entry on the side of the fuselage. Our dispatcher climbs the drop ladder to continue preparations.

Bram gestures to me. "After you."

I need a moment to bolster my will.

"You go on ahead." I fake a need to adjust my jumpsuit.

He takes a breath, saying nothing more. He knows the flight is my first. Reluctance can't be unusual.

One by one, the agents climb inside with the assistance of an airman.

When I can no longer delay, I edge forward with lungs tightening and hazard an ascent. Halfway up the ladder, I'm able to view the illuminated, cavernous interior, a moderate relief. I've taken refuge in air-raid shelters smaller than this. What's more, working in Hutton's bunker has further expanded my tolerance for such a space.

Although...not while thousands of feet off the ground.

"Having second thoughts, luv?" Bram's voice tips toward concern. Surely it's not all selfless; my fear and inexperience could cause him grave consequences, as they could me.

A whisper of temptation says I can bow out. I can retreat to the barn, give back my supplies. With or without me, the group will proceed.

But then, so will Bram's mission.

Stifling my angst, harboring my disdain, I resume my climb and get ready for takeoff.

CHAPTER 49

Flying unescorted and without exterior lights, the pilot periodically changes altitude. I persist in clutching my seat, positioned along a curved wall of the hull, where air from every crevice of the bomber unites in a barrage of wind. For well over an hour, a red interior light has glowed eerily like a warning.

I breathe rhythmically to the tunes in my head. "The White Cliffs of Dover." "That Old Black Magic." "Serenade in Blue." Anything to distract me from the shaking and rattling that with every passing mile brings us closer to occupied territory.

If we make it that far.

The dispatcher, with his sharp features yet easy manner, sits nearby sipping from a thermos. Hot tea. He offered me some, casual as can be while we crossed the Channel through a brief but grueling hail of gunfire. *A German welcome party*, he called it.

I hum another song: "Don't Get Around Much Anymore." If my jaw wasn't clenched, I might smirk at the irony. All the while, my assigned plan circles in the back of my mind, with personal modifications.

As it is, our group is to rest at a safe house not far from our drop site; come morning, as the nameless agents go their separate routes, I'm to sit and wait for Bram's noon return from his meeting with another contact—for a separate mission, he's said. Then we're to bus westward to the city of Utrecht, where a newsstand vendor possesses the latest clues for finding Arie.

Of course, I have every intention of reporting to that stand, just not with Bram. Once I slip away to grab the earlier bus, based on the pocket schedule I was issued, I'll have a two-hour lead to track down Arie first.

I'd prefer days to hours. But it's something and, so far, the best I've got. Outside of a weapon, that is, which I pray I won't need for anything beyond the practical.

Stored in the smallest of my jumpsuit pockets, my folding knife is sharp enough to free me of my parachute if tangled in a tree. I suspect the other operatives were assigned weapons of their own. Unlike me, Bram was also given a spade with a removable handle for burying our gear. Similarly, when we were issued special pills tonight, I received only two of the three types he received. Supplies were mistakenly short of the white ones, I was told. The "knockout drops" would put a person to sleep for a solid six hours.

Could someone suspect I might use one on Bram?

The red light now shifts to amber.

My pulse skips a beat.

The dispatcher half cups his mouth with his free hand. "Over target in ten minutes!" he projects above the engines' roar, then sets aside his thermos as the agents swing into motion. Evidence they've all done this before.

Our packs and straps are rechecked—there are no reserves, after all—and we each hook onto a static line to ready our chutes for self-deployment. Where the ball turret originally lay, the dispatcher unseals the floor hatch dubbed the "Joe Hole." Cold, deafening air blasts through.

"Action Station Number One!"

My nerves heighten to an all-new level as I follow the men's lead in queuing up. The first agent sits on the floor and, despite the airstream, hooks his legs over the rim of the short cylindrical opening. The second agent lowers behind him, prepared to scoot forward, followed by Bram, then me. With trembling hands, I confirm my satchel is secured to my leg. Meanwhile, the dispatcher positions a large metal capsule near the edge to be dropped with its own chute. No doubt the container is chock-full of weapons and tools requested by the Resistance, or even by the operatives here.

Perhaps it holds the very gun meant to take out—

"Remember, now," Bram hollers to me. "I'll be down before you, so I can assist if you've had any trouble with the landing!"

I nod, a stiff motion.

Through each bump and drop, every fiber in my body tenses. It's nearly showtime on the largest stage imaginable, with limited planning, countless variables, and a mass of uncontrollable parts. I recall the trainer's instructions, directed at the women as we learned to jump: *Keep your knees and feet together, just like your mothers taught you!*

The remark had received a mix of giggles and rolled eyes, my reaction being the latter. Now I'm grateful for the memorable phrase, as well as for the promise of soon being on the ground, released from this enclosure.

The notion brings me a trace of comfort until the plane banks left. I feel it descend to avoid anti-aircraft detection and flak—to as low as four hundred feet if matching our preflight rundown. The trade-off is our closer proximity to German eyes and ack-acks. Perhaps electric pylons and unseen mountainsides.

Stay calm, stay calm.

"Running in!" the dispatcher warns.

I swallow hard. We're closing in on the drop zone.

The engines throttle back and the aircraft shudders. We're slowing down, in contrast to my insides, which are roiling.

I visualize my drills in the hangar, my jumps straight down with chin tucked. My perfect landing from the hot-air balloon. *You are quite a natural,* I was told. And now I'm squeezing from the remark every ounce of confidence I can muster. At a low altitude, there will be no room for error.

The light goes green.

On cue, the dispatcher shoves the capsule through the opening. "Go! Go!" he shouts. The agents rush to follow one after the other, including Bram, who leaves me with a semi-salute that says: *See you on the ground.*

To ensure we'll land reasonably close, on my rear, I scurry into place as quick as I'm able in my bundled suit, only to gaze down into an abyss.

Don't think, don't think, just drop.

But then the plane jerks hard, throwing me sideways across the floor. On reflex, I grab a metal bar attached to the wall. Possibilities ricochet in my head—we've clipped a tree, lost an engine, been sprayed by bullets.

I look to the dispatcher. Knocked to his knees against the wall, he clambers to right himself as the Halifax levels off, engines still roaring. No explosions. No shooting.

"Turbulence," he yells, an explanation. Frantically he waves me toward the hole, urging me to hurry and catch up. "Go now, go!"

Though disoriented, driven by a spike of adrenaline, I do as he says. And I jump.

CHAPTER 50

An icy grip snatches the air from my lungs. Slung through the sky, I lose all sense of reality. Then with a clap of thunder, the world snaps back. My chute released by the rip cord, I'm yanked fiercely upward, a puppet on strings. My harness straps cinch around my chest and thighs. A loud rustling fills my ears, wind flapping fabric. Above me, the nylon parachute is an instant blossom, and I'm floating.

Only from the fading sounds of a bomber's engines do I recall precisely where I am, what I'm doing.

And with whom.

I quickly survey the area below, tucking my chin, my mind clearing. Moonlight casts the earth into a surprisingly detailed sketch. Tree lines thickened by undergrowth separate fields and meadows. A couple lone barns denote scatterings of farmland. Amid a pasture, the capsule's chute is strewn on the ground. Vertically staggered, the silhouettes of the agents' parachutes, each in turn, are about to touch down. From the delay in my drop, it appears I'll end up in a pasture quite a distance away. I'll have no immediate help from Bram.

I concentrate on the mechanics of my landing.

All too soon, the earth rises up. I meet it hard with my feet, collapsing to my thigh and hip to distribute the impact. Following my training skills, I scramble to stand and immediately work to reel in my parachute, still partially inflated. The consequent noises make me cringe, but they're better than being sighted by Nazis.

Once out of my harness, I assess my surroundings. All is still and quiet but for a breeze rustling the fields.

With landscape features obscuring the agents, a question forms:

What if I don't wait to sneak away? Already separated from Bram, I could embark on my head start now.

Except, no—there isn't a bus until morning. The whole point of my scheme is to find answers and, together with Arie, decide the next move, but before I'm ruled an enemy. Perhaps even a second target.

Best to keep to my plan.

I detach my satchel and sling it across my torso. Taking my bundled parachute to bury it with the others, I start my trek to reunite with the group. With every few strides, I glance around, hyperalert. Even the scents of dirt and meadow are intensified.

After I walk what seems a hundred yards, a fuzzy halo of light emerges up ahead, from beyond a wall of blackberry bushes, paired with a man's voice. I stop.

Seasoned agents wouldn't dare use a flashlight nor speak above a whisper—would they? Or are they just so confident the vicinity is clear?

Crouched down, I creep toward the side edge of the thicket. When I stretch for a peek, I shudder at the origin of the beams. Roughly thirty yards away, two sets of partially obscured headlamps shine dimly on the agents. The three men are facing the vehicles, still in their coveralls. With their hands behind their heads, they're being forced to kneel by rifle-wielding soldiers in bell-shaped helmets.

German troops.

Oh, God in heaven, no, no, no.

I jerk my body out of view, though for the life of me, I can't steer my eyes away.

An officer, distinctive in his peaked hat, walks toward them with an awkward gait. He halts before the middle captive—Bram—and speaks. Indecipherable from a distance.

Did the Germans spot our low-flying plane and radio ahead to track us?

The officer gives a wave of his pistol, a signal. A soldier marches over. Beside Bram, he raises his rifle high and at an angle, then swings the butt of it toward the agent's head. Surely this all occurs rapidly, but in that instant, fear slows all movement in my mind's eye. In detail,

I see Bram shift out of the weapon's path and jab his elbow into the soldier's groin. As the man contracts, Bram immediately grabs hold of the rifle, as if his instigation was deliberate, strategic.

Then a blast rings out.

Yet the spray of blood emerges from Bram, a bullet having tunneled through his skull. The officer shot first.

Bram's body crumples just as a neighboring agent lunges for the pistol. The officer's extended arm leaves it vulnerable. The two fight for control, a struggle that ends with another blast of a gun—this time from a soldier's rifle—and the agent collapses.

There are barking sounds, muffled by the screaming inside me. Outwardly I'm frozen. My limbs are anvils, which is fine, just fine. As the scene can't be real. It's a film on a screen. I'm watching from the safety of a theater. Shortly we'll have an intermission and a change of reels.

"*Herr Hauptsturmführer!*"

The officer—a captain with the SS, I believe—responds by turning to the approaching caller, a broad soldier lugging a large cylindrical object. It's the capsule with parachute dragging. Behind him, another soldier escorts a German shepherd snarling on a leash. As the officer confers, a moment of collective distraction, the third agent sneaks to his feet. He dashes furtively toward the shadows, until the dog erupts with ferocious barks.

The soldier who'd been guarding the agent turns. "*Halt!*"

Let loose, the canine charges after the runner. It leaps at the man's back, toppling him. Rifles are taking aim but the captain orders not to shoot. This is their last detained operative, and certainly they could use his information. But then the dog yelps and goes limp. A blade glints in the agent's hand. When he again scuttles into a sprint, defying more orders to halt, two shots meet his back. He arches from their impact before sprawling on the ground.

The captain pulled the trigger. Still, he bellows in frustration. He marches over and uses his pistol to smack the face of the negligent guard, hard enough to crack a jaw. Then he turns to his troops. "*Finde den vierten!*"

His German words filter in pieces through my brain. Their translation shakes me from my trance.

Find the fourth.

Could they have seen me jump? Mistaken the capsule's chute to be mine? Terror bolts through me. I need to move. Legs, you need to move *now*.

"*Suche!*" he adds, and all five soldiers disperse to search in various directions, weapons ready.

Managing to back away, I begin to reverse my path. My parachute… I'd forgotten it's still in my arms. Silently in the darkness, my pace gains momentum before a shallow ditch causes me a light stumble. I spare a glance over my shoulder. Glows of flashlights are encroaching on the bushes. The growling of waking engines indicates the vehicles will be facilitating the hunt.

A long dirt road runs parallel to my left, so I cut right and race toward the nearest cluster of trees. The leaf-filled branches might be structured well enough to hide me.

I round the undergrowth to the backside of the cluster. At the first promising tree, I shoulder the parachute, reach up, and grip the lowest solid branch. My foot seeks traction on a knot at the tree's base. Heaving upward, I slip on a strap of my dangling harness. I try again, slipping once more but on a slick stretch of nylon. Drat! The chute and strings will surely snag on branches all the way up. Yet discarding the gear anywhere close would leave a glaring trail.

Flashlights draw closer, as do headlamps. Wheels slowly crunch gravel.

My heart rises to my throat. Time and options are running thin. I recall the knife in my jumpsuit and, underneath, an item in my coat. Stowed in the tiny pouch I'd sewn in, a pocket within a pocket, are my military-issued pills, including a single L-pill. *L* for lethal. A grim choice to be made.

Then again, the small blade is obviously measly against guns, and the cyanide is for only the worst of scenarios. Which as of yet, I decide, this can't be. It isn't. Not with the waist-high shrubs maybe twenty feet away. They squat in a dense row along the border of a pasture. If I hurry, I could stuff my parachute into the greenery. But can I manage to do that and still climb fast enough—and isn't a tree the first place they'll look, the most obvious?

Never was I more in need of misdirection.

An old trick comes to me—the sucker effect. Let the audience think they're seeing something by mistake, a faux reveal, only to guide them to the actual illusion with greater impact.

Could it work?

What better option do I have?

Staying low, I spread out the parachute as if someone landed and abandoned it in a rush. I toss my helmet on it for good measure. Then instead of shimmying up the tree, I dash to the shrubs. Working my way in, I serpentine my body horizontally, careful not to disturb the top layer. The added bulk of my satchel makes the task more challenging. But soon I settle in the tangle of branches, thick but breathable. And I wait.

It's a deceit based on a presumption, as I'd once taught Charles. A twist on a story that viewers convince themselves to be true. After all, no spy would be foolish enough to stick around when given a chance to run.

The seconds tick away.

Fifteen…thirty…forty-five…

There are hints of walking: a rustling of trousered legs, footsteps on farmland. Someone is getting close.

I see nothing through the shrubbery. I pray the obscurity works both ways. And if not, that true to my name, adapting like the Arctic fox, a creature built to survive, I'm indistinguishable from the background.

"*Schau mal!*" Excitement boosts a fellow's voice, the pride of finding a treasure. In this case, a parachute. "*Komm her!*"

More rustling, more steps. A second voice joins in, his murmured words interweaving with clinks of the harness. Then silence.

My heart, still lodged high, presses into my windpipe. I ration breaths, in and out, envisioning the soldiers scanning the area, peering up at the trees, their rifle barrels hungry for another target.

A smattering of light penetrates the shrubbery. My eyelids drop to shield the white of my eyes, and I escape into the haven of a memory. The leaves around me are patches of my childhood quilt. The branches are my mattress, cozy by the potbelly stove. Papa is asleep in the next room, snoring after late-night drinks with the strikers.

I fill in the setting with every detail I can plunder, fending off images of Bram's spray of blood, of the Nazi soldiers but a few yards away.

There's a swooshing now. From fabric. Clinks.

They're gathering the chute.

After several tension-racked seconds, the murmurings resume, yet fainter. Same for sounds of movement. I ease my eyes open, just as the soldiers call out. I flinch.

A vehicle revs closer, rolling over gravel. When the engine idles, I brace for the troops to return on a more scrutinizing search.

That doesn't come.

Their hunt continues but farther and farther away, until it's only me, left cocooned in the darkness with the daunting choice of what to do next.

CHAPTER 51

During our final briefing, I received directions to the barn that would serve as our safe house. *We're to meet there,* Bram told me, *should anything go astray.*

Bram. My alleged adversary. Although he's gone, my relief is scant given the scene I witnessed. A ghastliness I can't afford yet to process.

I spend the next couple hours cautious in the shrubs, squelching the images as best I can, along with my plans involving the barn. In their ongoing search, the Germans could be surveilling any structures in the area. Not that Voorthuizen, the sole village within walking distance, promises to be much safer. But my bus stop is there, and I have no better alternative.

In fact, for both me and Arie, I have only greater reason now to catch the earlier pickup, the first of the day to Utrecht. Watchful Nazis aside, once the British hear what occurred, who's to say they don't reassign Bram's duties? Perhaps to an operative already nearby and without including me. A saving grace of the situation is the military's tendency to piecemeal information, covert work even more so by design. Battles and distance, I figure, could also delay communication, giving me the upper hand.

For a few days at least.

All in, I have a week here—not even. I'm to depart by train Saturday morning to rendezvous with my escape guide, leaving me but six full days to find Arie—or "Frans." That's his field name, I've learned.

Anxiously, I climb out of my hiding spot. I remove all my jump gear and, minus my knife—which I store in my hidden pocket—cram it into the shrubbery. Seated close, away from the road, I'm prepared to serpentine back in if needed. To fend off sleep, I ingest one of my two blue Benzedrine pills, and through the side effect of a light dizzy wave, I listen for sounds.

At dawn's welcome light, I change my clothes. Since pants on women are considered brazen here, I pull on a plaid day dress, as subdued as my lisle stockings made of gray cotton. After refastening the buttons and belt of my coat—also gray, though charcoal—I rid my hair of debris while tidying the pins. Less out of hunger than to pass the time, I snack on the licorice and biscuits I received before the flight—both deliberately Dutch brands.

Since Papa's pocket watch is American made, with *ELGIN* printed right on its face, it could expose me if seen in the open. But like a lucky charm, it had been with me through all my journeys, so in my bag's hidden compartment it will stay. On my wrist is the quiet watch I've been issued, Dutch with a simple leather band and dainty hands that I proceed to check incessantly.

Not a single person passes through the area. Sunday mornings for the Dutch, thankfully, are spent sleeping longer and occupied with family.

At last, the time comes to head out for the first bus of the day, set to depart at 10:48.

Staying off the road, I grip my satchel strap over my shoulder and traipse northward through the countryside. The sun sends a honeyed glow over the array of trees and expanse of meadows. The beauty of the Gelderland province invites one to forget about the lives cut down in these fields, the souls spilled on this very soil.

Vigilant, I scan the area and sneak periodic looks at my silk-printed map. The mile-and-a-half route is already embedded in my mind, yet I'm adjusting my pace for a well-timed arrival. Cutting it close could mean missing the ride; too early and I'll have to stand around and linger.

On a roundabout path, I enter Voorthuizen. With a breath of courage, I start down the main street of the sizable village. The farther I wade, the more I appreciate the moderate amount of bustling, given the sprinkling of German soldiers. I can only hope they're posted here for standard spot checks and aren't the same troops from last night, still hunting.

Time now: thirty-seven after ten.

I tread along, gazing down at the cobblestones. In this, I'm not alone. All the civilians in my periphery appear to have learned this is best, to move through town as if anticipating a dropped coin. I'm certain the shopfronts are lovely and charming, straight from the sketches of a postcard, but my concerns lie only with the pair of black boots just ahead on my left.

A soldier with a rifle strapped to his shoulder is checking the identity papers of a gentleman with a slight stoop. In a small park across the street, another soldier does the same with a young woman who towers over his height.

I manage natural strides in passing.

None too soon, I reach the bus stop at the center of town. In alignment with my briefings, it's located directly outside a tobacco-and-vegetable shop, next door to Hotel de Vergulde Wagen, where a decorative wagon atop the roof confirms I'm in the right place.

I pocket some guilders from my satchel, ready to pay upon boarding.

Six minutes to go.

With eyes lowered, I steal occasional glances at my watch.

Two minutes left. Then one.

Schedules being a priority to the Dutch, it's hard to imagine any transports running late. But now it's three minutes behind.

Where is it?

No other traveler to ask. I'm still the only one waiting. A clerk at the hotel might be able to assure me it's coming.

I head into the place and hustle the few strides toward a small reception counter, behind which an oafish man is reading a book. He's the lone person present. Gratefully.

I continue to listen for the bus's engine.

"Pardon me, sir," I say in Dutch, and it hits me: this is the first test of my speech in the Netherlands, where regardless of my "passable" accent, I'm to refrain from being chatty, to not borrow trouble.

"Could you tell me if the bus to Utrecht—the ten forty-eight—runs a bit late at times?"

Engrossed in his book, its edges so tattered it might have been read by the entire village, he mumbles in reply, "Sunday."

"Uh, yes...for today."

"On Sundays, the first bus to Utrecht is the twelve forty-five."

It's the one I was to take with Bram. I suppress a rise of angst as the clerk looks up at me without inclining his head.

"Fuel cuts." He states this as if I should have guessed. As if it was common knowledge.

"Oh, right. Of course." Internally I curse the schedule from headquarters in need of an update—although perhaps this explains why our planners had chosen the later time. "Instead, sir, do you know when a *train* would depart for—"

"Station is closed."

How could a railway station just shut down for the day?

"Six years ago," he clarifies, my confusion seemingly detected. Hopefully not to a suspicious point.

I uphold a pleasant expression, and despite my dread over the wait, I reply, "Thank you, sir."

CHAPTER 52

The vacant lobby is no place for me to stay. I'd be as good as prey in a trap.

I venture back outside. The soldiers down the street continue to question passersby. I bat away worries of being unprepared, all unproductive thoughts, and seek a means to squander the time. But the stores appear closed. Too early, perhaps, for even the few allowed to operate on a day reserved for worship.

That's what they're doing, I realize. Streams of people in black dress and hats, a tradition of strict Protestants, are heading toward a tall brown steeple. Though without a tolling bell—likely melted down for cannons by the Germans—it serves as a beacon for a communal assembly. The service should last a whole hour, maybe two.

I debate joining. Even with my acceptable dark coat, I'm apprehensive of standing out among the regular flock. Then I recall Houdini and his greatest illusion: aiding the Allies by spying in the open.

And so I flow into the crowd that funnels into the large church. A mix of light body odors and exhaustion hangs in the air as locals exchange greetings.

I'm troubled nearly as much by the funeral-like sea of black as I am by the absence of a clear second exit, particularly in this circumstance. Still, from the inner aisle, I slide into the fifth pew from the back and tuck my satchel under my seat. Beside me, an elderly man nods politely, his spectacles thick as jam-jar glass.

It takes tremendous effort not to constantly turn and gauge the entrance, even as a minister appears at the front and welcomes the congregation. I reach for my necklace to fiddle with the disk but find it missing. As instructed, I'd left it with my valuables at the George, yet only now do I feel fully stripped of my identity. Should an ill fate befall me, no one here would know the truth of who I am—or was.

The minister requests that everyone stand to sing, a timely diversion.

My neighbor struggles to rise, negotiating his cane and hymn book. I'm lending him a hand when I sight a uniform. A fair soldier in the outer aisle, helmetless, is keenly surveying the room.

Panic splinters through me, darting like pinballs every which way. I edge back, using the man beside me as a cloak.

The congregation launches into "How Great Thou Art."

Assessing when and if to run, I join in softly: "When I in awesome wonder—" I catch myself. I'm singing in English.

The elder shows no sign of noticing, perhaps hard of hearing. Despite my quivering, I offer to hold the book for us both, not simply for the verses but to sidle up beside him in a display of accustomed familiarity.

Abruptly, the soldier raises his hand: an alert to a person unseen.

My feet shift toward the center aisle, about to tear away when the soldier breaks into a smile. From a far-forward pew, a uniformed pal waves him over to attend the service.

I ease out an exhale. My fears abate, to a limit. The fellows are young, unarmed, and seem genial enough; they're Nazis nevertheless— all that matters—and now they'll hamper my ability to sneak out early if needed.

I try not to think of this as the service plods on. Through prayers and more hymns, I remain friendly with my pew partner and ever more grateful to the Jansens for helping me blend, specifically for expelling my old Catholic habits. A genuflection or the sign of the cross could have given me away.

By the time we sit for the sermon, the air is warm from body heat. I find myself sinking into the minister's tone, as lulling as a spell. Sneaking a blue pill from my pocket is tempting, but it's my only one left. I refrain and pinch my leg.

My blinks grow longer.

And longer.

When my chin drops, I realize I've dozed off. For seconds or much more? I can't say.

My pulse races as I peek at my watch: 12:33 p.m. Just twelve minutes until my bus. While I haven't missed it, I have to slip out. The service could last another hour.

I'm contemplating how to evade attention when the minister commences a final prayer, a timely reward, though his blessing stretches cruelly in length. Upon the "Amen," I grab my satchel and trail the congregants ebbing toward the doorway. I keep to the middle of the stream.

Finally outside, I cast my eyes downward and walk with casual purpose. At the glimpse of a bus idling by the hotel, I bridle my urge to sprint. Several folks are queued up to board. An armed guard is checking their papers. Fumes from the engine grow in pungency as I approach.

I assure myself I've been supplied with foolproof forgeries. Retrieving them with a steady grip, I review my lessons in London meant for exactly this scenario. Were those really just two days ago?

Ida Hofman, I am Ida Hofman from Elspeet.

The young soldier is unfocused. Combining German and improvised Dutch, he's flirting with a girl standing off to the side with her bike. Her flowy peach dress punctuates the surrounding drabness. As her chirpy giggles float over mauve-painted lips, a lean suited man in a brimmed hat lines up behind me. I have no intention of skipping out, yet there's a troubling sense now of being locked into my spot.

When it's my turn to hand over my identity card, the burden of its falsity lessens from the guard's preoccupied state. He skims and returns the document, clearing me with a flick of his hand, eager to keep chatting up the girl.

After such a buildup, the simplicity of my entry almost causes me to laugh, the release of tension like a wave breaking then washing over the shore. Containing the impulse, I board, pay my fare, and start toward an empty row. And that's when I hear the sputtering of engines. Louder, closer. Swooping in, a military truck parks before the bus. A blockade.

My stomach plummets, a boulder dropped within me.

Then a motorcar arrives and its driver lets the officer out. He steps forward with a limp, a gait I recognize from the field. It's the SS captain, adorned with insignia on his tunic, an iron cross dangling at his collar. All at once, more soldiers are circling and someone is yelling and the flirty guard is ordering all passengers off.

Could the hotel clerk have reported suspicions? Perhaps a shrewd congregant?

More troubling yet, had the Germans somehow known we were coming? *Find the fourth* was their order even before discovering my chute. Were they waiting in the field from the start, and if so, how much detail would they have? Indeed, my itinerary would have led them straight here.

A tremor in my legs threatens to betray me as I disembark with the seven or eight others, including the driver. We're instructed to spread out alongside the bus.

The captain, whose thin, brown mustache centers on a chiseled face, lights a pipe while we scramble into place. I land at the end of what resembles a police lineup, our gazes glued to the ground. Soldiers clutch their rifles.

I do the same to my satchel hanging from my shoulder, snug as a harness, and a conversation returns to me. The dispatcher explained the less obvious reason for tightening the straps of our parachute packs: the Gestapo's practice of checking suspected spies for bruises to the thighs and chest. I hadn't noticed any forming, but are they there?

The officer makes his way gradually down the line. He exhales smoke with the leisure of reclining on a veranda at sunset. His boots brush the ground, creating contemplative sweeps. And it dawns on me that he lacks specifics of the missing fugitive, that his strategy has been to wait in the lurch, ready to pounce on the departing transports and screen for shifty, nervous characters.

My name is Ida Hofman. I am on holiday to visit my cousin Martha.

Fixated on my low-heeled shoes, purposely weathered and faded black, I notice a spot. A dirt-brown smudge. Soil from the fields I neglected to wipe off.

He pauses before me. Does he see it too? Is there shrubbery on my clothing I somehow missed? Will he inspect my skin for bruising?

The smell of pipe tobacco, normally a comfort reminiscent of Papa, only emphasizes the officer's proximity. I feel his stare. It bores through my hair, my head, as though he's attempting to pick through my brain. I yearn to close my eyes, disappear, pass through a trapdoor onstage.

"*Herr Hauptsturmführer,*" a voice hollers. "*Schauen Sie, ein Problem hier.*"

The troops surrounding us undoubtedly finger their triggers.

After a beat, lowering his pipe, the captain swivels and strides toward the caller. My shoulders don't dare slump. Without moving my head, I see the young guard by the front of the bus. He's waiting with papers from the lean suited man. Save for the crinkling of the pages, there's only quiet.

Soon comes a noise: a sharp slide of metal, punctuated by a click. The chambering of a round.

My face snaps up. A Luger is pressed to the civilian's temple, his fedora now lying on the ground. The captain peppers the man with what I believe to be questions. To my mind, they're barely audible, as the earlier executions have returned in flashes. My muscles clench, waiting for the blast. The blood. The crumpling of another body.

Then the captain tilts his head. All goes silent until he sneers.

A decision made.

He jerks his pistol toward the truck. At the directive, soldiers hustle to the suited man and escort him onto the back of the vehicle. He's been spared. A cause to rejoice if not for imagining what might await him. Possibly no better for those of us left.

The officer confers with the guard. From what I can tell, he's asking if the remaining passengers have been thoroughly checked. The soldier replies in the affirmative—too boldly and swiftly, I fear. I stare back at the ground, preparing to be grilled.

There are more puffs from the officer's pipe. A torturous pondering. What follows is a nod, presumably, because in a burst of shouts, the guard ushers us back onto the bus as if herding cattle into a pen.

By the time I lower onto my seat, still fighting to control the quaking in my limbs, the other vehicles are rumbling away. Only the man's hat remains, the solitary clue that anything happened here at all.

Tears rush to my eyes from shameful relief but also from potential blame, over a chance he was mistaken for the wanted fourth.

Quivering breaths draw my ear. Across the aisle, a matronly woman presses a hand to her window. I trace her attention to the other side of the street. Among the onlookers, the peach-dress girl stands with her bicycle, fist over her heart and smile wavering. She appears to say goodbye, her purpose as a distraction served.

It's strangely comforting to know with certainty that I'm one of many here playing a role, harboring secrets, and with every reason to be petrified.

CHAPTER 53

During the hour-and-a-half long ride to Utrecht, doubts gather like storm clouds, dark and ominous. The fact I made it out of the village isn't enough to ensure I'm in the clear. Since meeting with my contact might now be riskier, I consider a delay of hours. The longer I wait, however, the greater the chance that word of the field incident will surface and spread, potentially losing Arie in every way possible.

My decision is plain.

Toting my satchel, I disembark at Utrecht Centraal, the main railway station of the city. The proximity of several German-military institutions, headquarters, and installations is instantly evident by the number of service members walking about, notably higher than in the village. Posted signboards appear to give instructions and warnings, all in German. Expected though most startling, swastika flags hang on buildings, staking territory in the colors of death and blood.

I stifle a shiver as I enter the station as originally planned, minus a companion. With armed guards posted at each door, I continue directly on a path memorized from a diagram. Silently I review the coded phrases Bram and I were supplied at our final briefing.

Past the ticket lines, I round the last booth and there it is, tucked in a far corner: the designated newsstand. As eager as I am apprehensive, I maintain a natural pace. In an adjacent waiting area, presumed travelers are parked on long benches, among them soldiers and suited gentlemen immersed in periodicals and teenage girls in conversation. An older couple shares a snack while an agitated woman struggles to rein in a pair of youngsters. In shorts and knee-high socks, the kids are attempting to play tag.

Few in the group spare me a glance.

The last newsstand customer leaves as I approach. Behind the counter, a woman shuts her till box and turns to me. She's around sixty, her cocoa-brown hair streaked with silver, shadows underscoring her eyes.

My greeting stalls. A man is to be my contact.

Or was that my assumption?

"Well?" she says, more an order than a question. Her Dutch speech reminds me to use the same.

"Could you tell me, ma'am, are you the usual vendor here?"

A furrow splits her brow. "Always. Why?"

Wary of surrounding eyes and ears, I rush to assemble a reason. "I was just wondering which paper you recommend most."

Her shrug of apathy resembles a twitch. "Whatever you choose. It is no difference to me."

I nod, smiling tightly. Neither had I expected my contact to be this brusque.

Swiftly I scan the display, each headline boasting a Nazi victory. Propaganda parading as facts. I swipe two issues at random, hurrying before another customer can approach. "These will do." I set them on the counter and fish for coins in my coat pocket. "I'm curious, by the way"—casual though annunciating, I segue to Bram's coded phrase—"is Park Lepelenburg a short walk from here?"

Yes, it's a nice spot to watch the ducks, the vendor is cued to say, to which I'm to add, *I am sure it's even lovelier in the summer.*

"Not far," she states.

Then...nothing.

My script was to serve as a key, but for a lock that apparently won't budge. Did I deliver Bram's line in error? Or is his mere absence triggering her caution? That must be it. To communicate the change but stealthily, I'll simply open the lock with an improvised—

"Are you paying or not?"

"Sorry," I say. "Of course." Her expression softens marginally as I hand over my coins, guessing at the total. As she fetches change from her till, I mash together clues to tip her off. "You know, it's one of the reasons our dear friend Bram insisted I come. 'Ida Hofman,' he said, 'you must visit the park.' He was supposed to have joined me but got pulled away unexpectedly." Remembering how, I charge through a tightening of my throat as the woman drops her attention to a hangnail, possibly meant to look inconspicuous as she listens. "He said you might have fine activities to suggest, such as watching the ducks at Park Lepelenburg. You could always write down the ideas as a great help to me."

When her eyes flick up, a promising sign, I press her with my thoughts, begging for details I desperately need.

But her furrowing returns, now with indignance. "I don't know this Bram you speak of. I am not a tour guide. Buy more papers or go." Her volume threatens to attract an audience, including a Nazi officer approaching the display rack.

Under pressure, I retreat with my coins and papers, trying to understand. I'm confident this is the newsstand where I was directed to go. The officer's presence might well have scared her off. And yet she could have spoken prior to then. Perhaps she's aware of the agents' murders and disengaged to be safe. I was, after all, the only one to get away.

Wait… Could they suspect I was in on it?

I entertain the notion for only a second before it's ousted by the most likely scenario.

The newsstand was never part of the plan, much less the coded exchange. My knowledge was no doubt skewed to suit my role.

So what to do now, where to go? Would the boardinghouse where I was set to stay truly be safe? My head is muddled from stress and lack of sleep, the rest of my body quickly draining energy. I'll regroup and find a solution, possibly revisit the vendor.

It's too early for despair.

Outside, on my memorized route, I head toward the center of the city, where I'll seek out my own accommodations. Better paranoid than sorry.

Bicyclists whizz by in every direction as I avoid passing eyes. Once more, I appreciate the camouflage lent by the populous streets, if not the company. German soldiers, sailors, and airmen are scattered all around, as well as civilians with armbands of all kinds. Straight-arm salutes with "Heil Hitler" greetings are traded with disquieting normalcy.

Dom Tower, with its gothic belfry that reaches several hundred feet into the sky, assists as a navigational point. In another time, I'd gaze in awe at its intricate beauty; same for the medieval architecture and cathedrals and monuments strewn about. Instead, I stride over the cobblestones as if these sights are nothing out of the ordinary.

Beside a long stretch of businesses closed for the day, I pause to discreetly orient myself. A small cluster of armed soldiers appear at the corner, ribbing one another while ambling my way. From the other direction, a black Mercedes Benz pulls over to park. Swastika pennants flank the hood.

Residual panic simmers in my gut, worsened by a sense of enclosure.

I detour by crossing the street. Near a small bridge, two ladies emerge from a staircase. The steps lead down to the Oudegracht, the "old canal" that runs from the original moat of the fortified town and through the center of Utrecht. The walkway below, vacant and dappled with trees, offers a chance for reprieve.

As I descend, an elderly fellow drifts past in a rowboat. I proceed alongside the water, feigning a casual Sunday stroll, unwinding a string of breaths.

"Miss." The voice in Dutch turns my head.

But the speaker isn't the rower. It's a man around my age, at the base of the stairs. In an overcoat and tweed cap, he boasts a perfectly Aryan face. One I recognize. On a station bench, he'd been reading the paper. The realization he's trailed me all this way isn't what chills me most. It's the intensity of his stare.

On impulse, I increase my pace slightly. Too quick and I might draw additional attention. I'm hemmed in by the canal on my left, a stone wall to my right. There's no way to cross without a boat—unless at street level. Past several trees up ahead, a brick bridge arches over the water. From the walkway, a staircase must lead upward for access.

"Miss Hofman." Implicit in the tone is a command to stop. "Ida Hofman."

My cover name…

I glance back, tempted to slow as he strides closer. But then I recall announcing my name at the newsstand—perhaps not in its entirety, though I can't be sure in this instant—and the Germans might have already had that information.

"Please," he says, more insistent. "We should speak about your friend."

My friend—does he mean Bram?

Being wrong could prove fatal. The thought doubles my desire to run, right as I pass the last tree and stop short.

There's no staircase to climb. The base of the bridge creates an impassable wall.

I'm cornered.

Heart racing, I spin to face him. He's a mere few yards away, but his cobalt-blue eyes are raised toward the street. Thrown off, I trace his focus. A man in the gray uniform of an officer stands above us, turned away from the canal.

I brace for my stalker to holler up to him. Instead, his voice drops to an urgent hush as he moves in. "If you want to live, play along *now*." His sudden English with a Dutch accent stuns me. All at once, his hand is on my hip, his other cradling my cheek, and he bends to nuzzle the side of my neck.

"Go along," he whispers, "if you wish to hear of Frans."

I'm jolted as much by Arie's field name as by intimacy with this stranger. But with the officer rotating in our direction, I close my lids halfway and let my satchel slide to the ground. Applying a breathless smile, I run my fingers along the back of the man's neck, over the soft blond stubble above his collar. We carry on this way for a full half minute, the seconds ticking in my head, and I glimpse the officer observing us. His toothbrush mustache, mirroring Hitler's, sets my stomach to curl. I throw him an intentional peek, and he looks away discomfited, a markedly relatable feeling.

"Is he there still?" The question is warm on my neck. I go to whisper yes, but then a stylish woman appears at the officer's side. Arm in arm, they saunter off together and out of sight.

"He's gone."

My forged companion—evidently, my actual contact—glances up and sighs. "*Goed.*"

I let go and step back, feeling flushed.

After straightening his cap, he says quietly, "Come, then, for us to speak." He offers his elbow to continue our charade as a couple.

I hesitate, my mind and senses whirling.

"You wish to stay alone?" Not a true question, a dare. His smugness pulls me back to myself. Sure, his quick thinking helped, but I'm entirely capable of making my own way, learning and adjusting regardless of the dangers.

Except that isn't why I'm here.

With a deadline looming, I clutch my bag and accept the crook of his arm.

CHAPTER 54

Through the city's hustle and bustle, we wind down one street after another until arriving at an alley. A quarter of the way in, my mystery guide stops at a cockeyed, weather-beaten door. By the handle, he hefts it open and peeks inside what appears to be an empty storage building. A sweep of his hand invites my entry.

At my deliberating, his lips slant at a wry angle.

"If I were a *mof*, you would not be here."

The Dutch slang for a German—deeming them musty, evidently—is no more complimentary than calling them a Hun or a Kraut. And though his point is valid, it doesn't rule out my being used as a pawn. I'll have to *play along* to find out.

With a concessionary look, I step into the cool, stale-aired meeting spot. The series of windows are dust-coated but numerous, inviting decent light while hindering the view from anyone who happens into the alley. Granted, the same in reverse puts us at equal disadvantage.

A metallic scrape from behind causes me to flinch. He's bolted the door.

"Care to rest?" He nods toward a solitary wooden chair off to the side, its white paint chipped and back uneven.

"I'm fine standing."

He gives a small shrug and goes to claim the seat for himself. His distance from the door provides minor relief, as does the open expanse of the space. Strewn about are paper scraps, some tattered boxes, and sprinkles of sawdust. Markings on the concrete floor suggest long tables once populated what seems an abandoned workshop. In a back corner, cobwebs mostly veil a four-legged hulk of rusted machinery. A shroud over a forgotten life.

I ask at last, "Would you mind sharing who you are, now that we're...otherwise acquainted?"

From his coat, he produces a metal cigarette case and lifts it opened toward me. When I shake my head, he slips a hand-rolled smoke into the corner of his mouth. The shortage in Holland suggests it's cheap homegrown tobacco or a black-market buy. "Willem."

A traditional Dutch name. Presumably his cover.

"Are you with a network here, or were you sent by London?"

He lights his cigarette and snuffs out the match. "*Ja.*"

"So...which is it?"

"I am a messenger of information only."

I'm aware languages are well studied in Dutch schools, at least in the cities; still I might have complimented his English, if not for his hint of arrogance.

"Fine, then. Your message for me is...?"

The leisure with which he finds tobacco on his tongue and flicks the speck away is irksome. "But, you see, my instruction was for delivery to you and one other."

"Indeed," I agree, "it *was*. Only there's been a change of plans, requiring me to continue on my own." Honest yet vague, it's the explanation I prepared when I'd planned to arrive early at the station—which would have been pointless, I now realize, assuming Willem hadn't been there all morning.

"Oh? And what is this change?"

"I am unable to say more, I'm afraid." Also the truth. I can't have him wondering if his orders to help me should be rescinded.

He expels a ribbon of smoke, contemplating. Likely for his own safety. Finally he nods in acceptance. He's about to speak when a whistle spears the air.

My attention flies to the window, then back to Willem, who sits upright with hand raised, a signal to halt and listen. The shrill alert repeats, louder and closer with a man's hollers, suited to an officer of some kind.

Willem waves me toward a front corner of the room. I rush over and press my back to a plastered wall as he hurries to stand beside a window. Cigarette parked between his lips, he reaches under the breast pocket of his coat—for a weapon, I imagine.

I'm reminded of my own. Nerves again heightening, I grab my folding knife within the concealment of my pocket. I think of my single lesson with a dummy torso, stabbing its neck, heart, stomach. Each just enough to get away.

Willem leans to peer through a glass pane, a semi-clear spot.

Soon come more shouts, gradually waning in volume.

When the quiet returns, Willem's broad shoulders drop and his hand slides free. Yet the implication of his weapon remains.

The vast room suddenly feels smaller.

"You said you know of Frans," I prod, my patience now low.

Willem rotates toward me.

"Have you been in communication?" I ask.

He removes his cigarette, gives it a tap. "From a distance. For the passing of a note."

"And since then?"

"He has been very difficult to contact, this man."

Seeking any hints of deceit, I venture closer. "Do you know where I can find him? At least where you saw him last?"

Willem takes a drag. "I see him on Domplein, the cathedral square, several times. Always through crowds. Once, I follow him north. Every time like a mouse, he gets away."

I shouldn't feel pride under the circumstances, but it's hard not to, given how Arie learned to slip in and out of spaces under the scrutiny of an audience in broad daylight.

"When was the last time he was spotted?"

"It was…two days ago."

"Do you know"—I hesitate but need to ask—"if he's in any sort of danger?"

Smoke puffs from Willem's mouth, a short cough from a laugh. "Aren't we all?"

"From anyone in particular, I mean?"

He shakes his head. "I have heard nothing."

"Then why ever is he steering clear of you?"

"Again, I do not hear of it."

"Well, why do you *think* he is?"

Willem stubs out his cigarette on the wall. He too is losing patience. "As I say, I am only a messenger. He was to make contact with his people; that was my assignment. But you are here. All business with Frans is no longer mine. Now"—he sighs—"I must go." He peeks through the window before hefting the door, this time to unbolt it.

My mind scrabbles for what more I ought to ask.

"Goodbye to you, Miss Hofman."

As he opens the door, I urge, "How do I find you? If I need anything else?"

He doesn't answer nor look my way. But neither does he leave.

"Please," I say. "I'll trouble you only if necessary. I promise." I reach out and touch his sleeve, a mindless emphatic act. However, fresh off our encounter by the canal, the heaviness of his gaze on my hand sends tingles up my arm. I pull away.

There's a debate in his eyes but also an air of gentleness at his core. The latter appears to win out when his jawline softens. "A café is closed for the war. Called Menno's. Directly ahead of the pass-through of Domtoren."

"The bell tower?"

At his single nod, I envision the gothic structure, tall enough to be seen throughout the city.

"Leave three small stones on the outer windowsill. Word will reach me. If I can, I meet you back here. If two hours pass, I am not coming."

"Of course. I understand."

He lifts his chin toward the alley. "And beware of the Dutch police. Some are worse than the *moffen*."

In my prepping sessions, I'd been warned of the same. "I will. Thank you, Willem."

"*Succes*," he murmurs, a Dutch wish of good luck, and then he's gone.

CHAPTER 55

The boarding room sits on the second floor atop an *apotheek*, or pharmacy. Powdery-blue walls surround an armoire, a chair with standing lamp in the corner, and a pair of single beds divided by a night table. Hung in a simple wooden frame, an amateur painting of three children in a fishing boat with a windmill in the background provides the sole dash of personal decor.

When seeking accommodations in the vicinity of Domplein, a task made more challenging due to commandeering by the Nazis, a voluble street sweeper directed me here. Until last month, he said, two of the druggist's three sons were attending Utrecht University, a portion of it located on a corner of the sprawling square. But students' protests against a Nazi loyalty oath ended with the school's total shutdown. All three boys were apparently since "recruited" for factory labor in Germany, leaving their two bedrooms available for let.

One of which I promptly confirmed to be unoccupied.

The druggist's wife, Mrs. van der Meer, isn't overjoyed my stay will be brief but has agreed regardless, swayed by a week's prepayment. And gratefully so, as the view from my window spans a good portion of the L-shaped public square. Awning-adorned shops and various other businesses line the central area, which runs between the bell tower straight ahead and, to my left, Dom Church.

In my doorway, the middle-aged woman with sharp features and tired eyes strokes the gray cat on her arm. She's explaining how a central nave once connected the two structures before it collapsed in a storm a few hundred years ago.

Frankly, I could do without visions of any calamity, let alone one in the focal area of my search. "That's very intriguing," I reply kindly in Dutch, anxious to regroup. "Well, I should be all set now."

But she doesn't exit. "You already saw the bathroom is down the corridor?"

"I did, yes. Thank you."

"As soap is limited, I do ask that you use it sparingly."

"Certainly."

"Also, we launder on Wednesdays. Tell me, when shall I expect your cousin?"

To best account for my lone visit, I've stuck to my tale about Martha, whose ballet studies in The Hague make this an ideal halfway point for a sojourn.

"Within a few days. Just as soon as her rigorous training permits." Beyond that, a minor misfortune will have to cancel the poor gal's trip. "In the meantime," I add brightly, "I plan to thoroughly explore the beauty of your city."

The cat hisses, as if detecting my half fib. Mrs. van der Meer lets the animal down on the wooden floor, saying, "Oh, I nearly forgot. Before my food shopping tomorrow, we must coordinate use of your ration coupons. I do have a small plot in a community garden, so your room fee will cover any vegetables from there."

My stomach belts out a growl, either coincidentally or advocating for itself, and diverts the woman's speech. "You must be hungry from your travels," she says.

If only she knew how truly far I've come.

"A bit." I smile.

"I will bring you a snack if you'd like."

The thought of being slowed by a meal makes me even more restless, but I do need to eat. "That would be lovely."

She nods. "Now, should any needs arise at night, my living quarters are on the third floor." Behind her in the hall, the cat's slinking movements snag a portion of my focus. "Between breakfast and dinner on workdays, you can call on me downstairs, where I manage the pharmacy while my husband is stationed away."

Stationed? The choice of word, unreflective of forced labor, recaptures my attention. Did I wind up with a detrimental host?

I interject, conversationally, "He's with the German military, then? Your husband."

She pauses but a second. "His medical expertise makes him quite valuable to the war effort." Her statement emits pride while also seeming rote, making the situation challenging to assess.

Either her husband and sons have been forced to assist the Nazis and she's wary of grousing to a stranger, or they're serving voluntarily and she's guarded against judgment.

"Well," she says, "I'll leave you be." She reaches for the doorknob, taking her leave—which is what I wanted, until this moment.

"I do hope he's back soon," I assert. It's a subtle invitation to share more. But she just nods and shuts the door, giving no hint to where her loyalty stands.

I could still switch accommodations. Yet how, without raising the very suspicions I'd be trying to avoid?

Brushing off the idea, I ponder the great number of Dutch civilians opposed to the occupation. Even more so these days, given the *Arbeitseinsatz*. Hitler's labor draft. With German workers forced into the armed services after the Stalingrad defeat, Dutch men in their prime—largely the unemployed but others too now, apparently—are being shipped off as replacements to Nazi farms and factories. Those with connections or with the many jobs deemed "essential" are considered safe, but as Germany's defeats accumulate, even that could rapidly change.

I imagine the many husbands, fathers, and sons living behind walls and under floorboards, desperate to avoid being imprisoned or rounded up in raids, called *razzias*. By that very reasoning, though, I wonder: What actual odds do I have of tracking down Arie when it seems that he, likewise, wishes not to be found?

According to Crockatt, Bram's assignment to Holland was initiated for a separate mission. This makes a night drop of a replacement agent all the more probable. The realization boosts my need to not only succeed but to do so quickly.

Aided by my mini-telescope, smuggled within a cigarette filter and powerful for its size, I observe the city square from my window—most of it anyhow. A dotting of chestnut trees thick with foliage does cause some obscurity. Thus, after my snack—and confirming my fortunate lack of bruising from my harness—I forgo the safety of my room and venture out to Domplein. Only then do I notice a soldier high in the bell tower. Though he seems to keep lookout primarily toward the sky, his eagle's vantage point remains unsettling.

And so I use a tree for partial cover and settle at its base with my notepad. Slowly, absently, I sketch features of the landscape, a defendable reason for constantly scanning my surroundings. Two separate painters—one facing the belfry, the other the cathedral—help me blend in as I seek out a familiar face and even hope to be seen. By one particular person.

My identity card is checked, of course, though by a Dutch patroller. This time, it's astutely examined yet still passes muster. Soon after, a German soldier pauses his stroll to compliment my drawings. His wife is an artist, he says with marked affection, and it jars me to remember the enemy is also human.

Growing antsy as the day wears on, I walk the entirety of the square and the adjacent cathedral garden. I broaden my search slightly by heading north, based on Willem's clues. Between the city's accommodations for canals and its row-house-style buildings, the paths Arie can take are limited. I perk at a few hopeful encounters—a glimpse of a face, a posture from a distance—but none last beyond an instant.

Come dinnertime, I return to the boardinghouse to gobble down a plate of *boerenkoolstamppot*. The traditional mashed potato-kale dish is enhanced by a small spoonful of gravy, a wartime luxury, and a slice of grain bread. Around the table are Mrs. van der Meer, eating quietly, and the newlywed boarders, whose gentle, average looks are clearly transformed into MGM-level knockouts in each other's eyes.

Between Dirk's stories from his workday at a motorcar-maintenance shop, one commandeered by the SS for truck repairs, auburn-haired Klara alludes to hoping to be in the family way soon. Considering the state of the world, this seems genuine madness, yet I politely listen and nod.

Inspired by a mention of my ballerina cousin, Klara shares that while ballroom dancing is forbidden by the Nazi occupiers, local folk dances are held every Sunday despite the shortage of boys. "Mostly girls dancing with one another, of course, but still an amusing time," she says, her nose sweetly crinkling.

Swallowing my last bite of bread, I register the excuse to head back out. "What a fine idea," I reply. "If you happen to know where, I'd love to take a peek before curfew."

Mrs. van der Meer is lost in thought, making it all the easier to excuse myself.

Treading the same areas, I study every male face for recognizable features. April's extra daylight here eases the task, but alas I come up empty and have to retire in time for curfew. Due to a recent crackdown on Resistance activities, this currently means the early hour of eight o'clock.

I admit, it was wishful thinking to imagine I'd somehow feel my parents—Papa at least—here in their homeland, looking down, guiding me. Still, I curb a gnawing of discouragement while lying in bed. It's been barely a day, after all, if a tiring one. My eyelids grow heavy at the soft glow of the jarred candle on my nightstand. I'll let it burn as I drift off, a reliable childhood comfort. I'm on the cusp of sleep when I detect a noise.

A low-pitched droning.

Then a siren wails. An air raid.

I spring upright to sit.

The flyovers are practically nightly in the Netherlands. This tidbit was indeed included in my blur of briefings. But secondary to my concerns over Arie, the prospect of Allied bombers passing at exceptionally high altitudes, simply en route to such targets as Bremen or Hamburg, seemed fairly inconsequential.

It doesn't feel quite the same now.

I scramble to my feet, not knowing where to go. I should have thought to ask! My heartbeat accelerates, as it's prone to do from such warnings, but even more than usual as the humming grows, resembling a nudged hive.

I rush to the neighboring door in the hall. I'm about to knock when Klara swings the door open, and we both gasp. But then she smiles. "Come and we'll take you to the shelter. It isn't far." Her calm demeanor is moderately reassuring.

I hustle regardless to put on shoes and fasten my coat over my nightclothes. Led by Mrs. van der Meer, the newlyweds and I emerge on the square, where searchlights streak the sky, crisscrossing their ghostly white beams. We funnel with the crowd along the street and into a large, well-lit underground shelter.

There, we settle on the floor. Edgy among strangers, I watch Dirk shuffling a deck of cards. Another couple has asked him and his wife to play bridge.

Klara turns to me. "Would you like to play too?" She manages to project over the humming that has swelled to a flight of a million bees. "If so, we could always pick a different game."

Explosions echo from German flak, of which I'm to look accustomed.

I pin a smile over my dread and kindly decline.

Eventually the all-clear signal sounds. As patrollers order us all back to our homes, I think of Bethnal Green station. How once again I face the unwitting threat of being killed by my own side.

CHAPTER 56

The day that follows, I decide, calls for an expansion of canvassing. Since Arie has reportedly passed through the square multiple times, he's obviously traveling from a starting point to a destination.

I take brief breaks from Domplein to snoop around canal areas and cinemas, given his passion for bridges and enjoyment of picture shows. Not that I expect him to be lazing about, but I have to be resourceful. Proactive. I've never been good at sitting back and waiting for things to come my way.

All around Utrecht, German warning signs and swastika flags are ceaselessly disturbing. Yet ever more troubling is the frequency of three posted Dutch words:

Verboden Voor Joden. Forbidden for Jews.

News of segregation laws, then mass deportations to work camps, have long been filtering over the airwaves. The only Jews anymore in Holland, people say, are detained or living in hiding. But with assertions so extreme, part of me figured the reports were propaganda.

To see traces of evidence firsthand now tears at my heart, leaving me to question how far the Nazis' cruelties have gone.

Unable to wrap my mind around it all, I channel my thoughts away, back to my mission. What I came here to do.

Throughout the city, I watch and listen, simultaneously vigilant over being discovered and trailed by someone other than Arie. It's a tiresome undertaking with so many faces, especially on a Monday now with businesses open. Lines stretch everywhere for everything. The market, the bakery, the greengrocer. Certainly at the butcher's, for those hoping for a bit of sausage, or at least minced horse meat to spare.

Meanwhile, another day of searching goes by. Another dinner, air raid, and evening walk—with girls I met at the dance, I claim—and still no trace of him.

Doggedly, I charge on through Tuesday. I wall off a pooling of doubt, though with each passing hour and cumulative mile, cracks in that barrier form and grow. The slow leak of grimness seeps through, by nightfall becoming a steady stream.

On my fourth afternoon, resting my throbbing feet in the square, I pause my sketching at the sight of a woman. Her colorful dress and turban-like headscarf remind me of Madame Esme, bringing me to a thought: given all my years with Arie and the bond we long shared, one might suggest he'd sense my presence from a channeling of energy. A fantastical idea, maybe sheer nonsense, but I'm willing to try almost anything.

Closing my eyes, I strive to mute the noise of the square: the chatter, the footsteps, the lone street organ playing in the distance.

Arie, if you can hear this…please, trace my voice…here to this spot…

A hand touches my elbow. I jump and my eyelids fly open.

There's a fellow before me but wrinkled and silver-haired, a vendor with a flower cart. He holds out a wilting bouquet for me to consider. I manage a polite shake of my head.

No longer theoretical, my plan feels downright absurd. This is a city, not some little town. By now, it's even possible Arie has heard about Bram, whether of the agent's fate or goal, and altered his route. That's assuming a replacement for Bram hasn't arrived, tracking down Arie first and—

I squash the thought and promptly replace it. If anything, Arie has finished his own purpose here—whatever in heaven's name that was—and fled the vicinity, maybe even the country, to a place of safety.

In which event, and in all likelihood, I'm chasing but a shadow.

CHAPTER 57

In my boarding room that night, I contemplate not by lamp but candlelight, as the power companies periodically cut resources to conserve power for the German war industry. I'm too restless to retire into my nightclothes, never mind to sleep. Only two full days remain before I'm to travel an hour south to my contact in Tilburg, my entry to the escape line.

Seated on my bed, I leaf through the false documents meant to deliver me on trains through Belgium and France, then into neutral Switzerland by a guided hike.

With Arie, I'd hoped.

I cringe at the idea of abandoning him—again. As if once wasn't already unforgivable. But how long before all my roaming and sketching raise suspicions by observers?

Klara and Dirk are less worrisome at least. Last night, the opening four notes of Beethoven's Fifth—resembling *dot-dot-dot-dash* in Morse code, as in "V" for Victory—introduced the BBC news faintly through our adjoining wall, the broadcast here illegal. In contrast, the druggist's wife inquired about my cousin this evening with growing skepticism; after all, girls my age don't typically jaunt around cities alone, during wartime even less so.

Oh, I've been meaning to share, I replied. *I phoned Martha from the post office, as I was concerned over her delay as well, and discovered she's fighting a terrible cold. But she's hoping to recover and still join me.*

Klara responded with sympathy, whereas Mrs. van der Meer barely nodded. The excuse might not hold up the whole week.

I clutch my paperwork, frustration climbing.

Back at headquarters, I'd been so assured of my proposal, touting my insights from knowing Arie best. The truth of the matter is, I still can't explain his evasive behavior, why he took a field assignment in the first place, or why he transferred into intelligence at all.

After our years apart, much about him could have changed. Even the little things. Maybe his favorite radio program is no longer *The Burns and Allen Show* nor his usual drink at the drugstore a butterscotch malt. Maybe he'd moved on from curried egg sandwiches and whistling Benny Goodman tunes, or his old habit of staying up late, or—

The parade of memories skids to a halt.

He'd been a night owl since boyhood, often venturing out while others slept. With the enforced curfew here, a nocturnal trek might be unlikely but not impossible. Moreover, if he realized he'd been followed by Willem, particularly amid daytime crowds, he could be using nighttime as a magician would a cloak. How ridiculous not to consider this before.

I trade my papers for my telescope. Anticipating a long night, I swallow my last blue pill and blow out the bedside candle. The plunge into darkness stiffens me on reflex. Blindly, I hasten the couple steps to the window and find reprieve past an edge of the blackout curtain. Once my vision adapts to the moonlight, aided by a spread of stars stippling the sky, I quietly move the chair from the corner and settle in before the window.

It's roughly two hours post-curfew. A few patrollers are monitoring the area, noticeably fewer than earlier, consistent with the expected. I dive in by alternating between my telescope and naked eye, scanning for movement.

As the next hour drags by, patrollers become more and more sparse. Eventually the square appears vacant, though the belfry likely maintains a lookout.

By my watch, midnight passes. The absence of creaks indicates a sleeping household. I'm singing a tune in my head to stay alert when a shadow stretches over the cobblestones to my right. I lean forward as a figure emerges. Bridling my hopes, I use my telescope to home in.

It's the back of a suited man. His hair is light, trimmed short.

My breath holds while I seek his face. I glimpse a woman behind him, clutching his hand. They slow alongside the bell tower, a stone's throw before me, and peer up toward the guard. Could a romance be the reason Arie strayed from his sworn duties?

But then I examine the man's build. Narrow-shouldered and long-limbed. Not at all like Arie. Disappointment and relief wash over me in equal waves.

The fellow extends his head around the tower, perhaps assessing the length of Domplein. As if by a starter's pistol, the couple dashes off in unison. They cut across the square's width, leaving the cover of one tree to gain that of another. Past the cathedral, they disappear.

The hands of my watch soon mark one. I shift in my seat.

At last another figure appears. My spine straightens as I use my lens. From the far-left corner, the person rounds the bronze statue near the University Hall building and strides my way along the perimeter. I needn't so much as squint to make out a German helmet. Although... for the chance Arie could be in disguise, I look closer, only to verify the structure of a stranger's face.

The minutes go on ticking. I shake my head recurrently to sustain my focus. Even so, at some point, my mind drifts. I check my watch. It's a smidge past two. From a glance to my right, I discover a new silhouette at the base of the bell tower, nearing the square. I scramble to raise my telescope.

Again it's a man, alone, but a civilian based on his overcoat and trousers. A fedora obscures his head, yet his form and gait are stagger-ingly familiar. Or do I just want them to be?

Look this way, look this way. At the coolness on my palm, I find my free hand splayed on a glass pane. Recalling my plan to slide open the window and call out—in a stage whisper, of course—I stand to release the lock on the sill. Maddeningly, it won't budge.

How could I have not tested it? Evidently I hadn't had faith the actual need would arise.

At the corner of Dom Tower, same as the couple, the man peers around the edge. I'm terrified he'll race away before I can see his face, before I know.

He looks up toward the belfry, then swivels to retract against the wall. Now toward me, he reveals his features from the nose down, all of them familiar.

Could it actually be him?

I tap a pane, too lightly. Tap again louder, in spite of my household. The fellow lifts his head, only partly. But like all those many years ago, when from my window in Eden Springs I'd spy my friend on his moonlit walks, I know in my gut.

It's Arie.

A thrill bursts through me. But before I can act, he takes off toward the cathedral. I stop myself from thumping on the glass. Rather, I hurry from my room with coat and shoes in hand, throwing them on at base of the stairs, having descended with the softest but quickest of steps.

I crack open the front door as laughter floats down from Dom Tower. The two Germans posted high above appear distracted with conversation. Arie is lost from my sight but can't be far. I slip out, pulse hammering in my ears, and rush the short distance to sidle up to the bell tower. Umbrellaed by branches, I again mimic the caution I've witnessed before stealing across the open space between trees, past the cathedral, and out of the square.

Up ahead, the street splits like a Y. Which path did he choose?

Blast it.

Arriving at the divide, I locate his silhouette down the bend to the left—thank God. He's rounding a corner in the distance. It takes every ounce of my will not to yell his name. Surely some patrollers are in the area, making rounds at all hours. I recall Willem's warning about the Dutch police. If either of us is caught, if we're arrested, no doubt our identity cards would be further scrutinized and—

My ID. I'd left it in the room.

I hate to imagine the penalty for the combined infractions, of where that could lead, but turning back isn't an option. Barreling forward despite the odds of stumbling, I cast around glances for patrollers. The cool air seeps through my woven blouse. There's no time to fasten my coat.

Lining both sides of the street, potential gazes bear down from blacked-out windows. I sprint away from the thought, keeping near silent on the balls of my feet while following Arie around the corner. Where once more he's vanished.

Still, he can't be far.

I hasten down the road until reaching another split. I look both ways, straining to locate him through the dimness, not finding him.

North—Willem said he went north. But then what? And which direction am I even facing? Staving off panic, I hazard a guess and go straight. At the next corner, I glance left, and I see him!

Joy shoots through me. But with just as much power, it shatters in an instant. Posted outside a building on the right side of the street, a German soldier gazes off while smoking a cigarette that glows orange at the tip. Moonlight glints off the rifle strapped to his shoulder.

I hug the building beside me, shifting out of view. The Nazi is as close as thirty yards away. I long to shout for Arie even more than before, now to alert him. I steal a look. He's heading right for the enemy. How does he not see that? What the devil is he doing?

As if he's heard my warning, he pauses. He's seen the soldier, but too late. The German grips his weapon, turning toward Arie, who immediately raises both arms.

No—not both. One, sharp and straight.

A *Sieg Heil* salute.

I stand utterly frozen as he greets the soldier. Their words are indecipherable but there's casualness in the exchange. Even smiles of being well acquainted. Then the German releases his rifle, letting it hang from his shoulder, and opens the door to invite Arie inside.

CHAPTER 58

Desperate for solidity, for reason, I press my back against the building, safe from the guard's sight. I must have misinterpreted what I saw. I'd made such an error before, with Hutton, thinking his alarming behavior amounted to more than it did.

Of course, that didn't involve a German soldier, and certainly not a Nazi salute. Then again, Arie could be *pretending* to work for the Germans. As a double agent. But if so, why wouldn't he pass on word to London? Why risk them believing he'd betrayed his own people?

Maybe, just maybe, it wasn't Arie I followed. That would explain everything. And yet the pit in my stomach affirms it was him, begging the questions: At what point do I stop dismissing the obvious? When do I quit scraping for excuses?

I peer around the corner and find the soldier still guarding the building. Several stories high and made of light stone, the place could be Gestapo headquarters for all I know.

I can't deny that secrets are nothing new for Arie. Starting as a young boy, he became fully adept at keeping activities from others—sneaking out at night, even taking secret jobs to pay for surprise gifts. Now, with an icy shudder, I wonder how much else he's been hiding and for how long.

Given the threat of patrollers, it's unwise for me to stay. But how can I leave until understanding what I saw?

Finally, the man reemerges. While chatting again, he strikes a match to light the soldier's cigarette. By the glow of the flame, there's no denying Arie's identity. Then he steps in my direction but quickly angles back when the German adds something more. Their shared laughter crawls under my skin.

Any second, Arie will resume his walk.

I act on instinct and speed back the way I came, my legs carrying me, my eyes surveying for patrols. Upon turning the nearest corner, through the haze of my thoughts, I wrestle with my options. The safest is to flee to my boarding room. The most desirous is to confront him.

The fact I'm unsure if he'd be honest shakes me to the core.

Suddenly disoriented as to precisely where I am, I'll default to trailing him for now. Perhaps his next stop could explain much more.

Across the street, partially outlined by the moon, a large decorative feature adorns a pub entrance. I dash over, lacking time to think. It's a wooden barrel stood upright. I crouch behind it, tight as a ball. Regulating my breaths, I wait.

Soon come light footfalls. They travel past me and continue on. I peek just over the barrel to find him rounding the corner. A reversal of his route.

I accelerate in his wake down the vacant street. At the next corner building, I stretch my neck for a cautious look.

No sign of him.

I listen for footsteps, hear nothing. He could have slipped through another doorway. Or he's hiding from a patrol. Not that he'd need to, apparently. It's no wonder he's violating curfew, while I'm brazenly pressing my luck.

With soft steps, I proceed past another shop and around a brick column. That's when something covers my mouth, yanking me back, a hand from behind. The shriek that leaps from my throat is muffled by a grip. An object presses into my side. The muzzle of a gun. Held in the cove of a doorway, I feel a man's chest tight against my back. My breaths pass in and out of my nose, fast and audible.

A terse whisper meets my ear. "*Niet schreeuwen.*" Don't yell.

It's Arie. He's Arie…

But sensing his finger on the trigger, I muster a nod, as much as his grasp on me allows.

"*Wie bent u?*"

Who are you? he wants to know. His hand loosens for my answer but hovers at my chin, poised to clamp down.

I state clearly, "It's Fenna."

There's a flinch through his body, then for a moment stillness. His lowering of the weapon allows me to breathe easier before he turns me around by the shoulder. Our faces mere inches away, his shadowed features gain distinction.

"Fen?" Shock filters through his rasp. "What...what the hell are you doing here?"

Though still recovering, I straighten. The role of interrogator is mine, not his. "It's exactly what I'm here to ask *you*."

Beneath the brim of his hat, his eyes are darting back and forth between mine, seeking to comprehend the situation.

I'm about to push harder when a noise echoes in the distance. We both whip toward it.

Only quiet follows.

Arie gauges the street, the gun tight to his chest. But then instead of leading me off, he clutches my elbow and pulls me farther into the doorway. A pair of brick columns creates a shallow screen.

"Listen to me," he orders, his tone hushed. "I don't know how you ended up here, but you need to get out."

I jerk my arm free. "I'm not leaving until you share what's going on. Because let me tell you, there are plenty of people doubting which side of the war you're actually on." *Including me*, I nearly add.

A sound from his throat signals irritation. "Cripes almighty, Fen. This isn't a stage show or some kind of spy game."

"Really? Because you seem to be busy playing one."

His mouth opens, a wordless stammer. From our various jousts through the years, I recognize the fleeting gap in his armor of stubbornness. To pin him down, I can't let up.

"Of course, if you'd prefer, I could just have a chat with that Nazi pal of yours. Maybe he'd care to fill me in."

His stare hardens. Contrary to his claim, a game has indeed ensued: one of chicken. But I'm not about to yield.

He shakes his head and curses under his breath. Then he rechecks our surroundings and shoves his gun into the back of his waistband. "Stick close, and don't make a sound."

CHAPTER 59

We retrace Arie's winding path down the streets and on through the square, stopping twice to avoid patrollers. He scopes around corners using a small special mirror—made for spies, it seems—and scans behind us intermittently. The combined tactics are presumably how he confirmed I was on his trail.

After but a few more streets, he slows at a narrow break in a series of row houses. A cautious survey of our surroundings and he leads me through a brick archway into a small courtyard with a smattering of trees. On the back side of the building to our right, he scuttles down concrete steps to unlock the door. Our relative proximity to my boardinghouse would astound me if not for my hailstorm of far more crucial thoughts.

When he waves for me to enter, I wince, ever averse to basement-like settings. But since dawdling as an open target appeals even less, my reluctant steps deliver me to the doorway.

"Don't worry," he says. "I'll light a candle in a sec." After shutting us in, he does just that by striking a match and illuminating a pair of candles in tin cans. Both are set on a small wooden table beside a lone chair.

I relish that he knows me so well before recalling my newfound uncertainty over how well I truly know him. Still, I confess, I find comfort in the familiarity of his movements as he sheds his hat and overcoat onto a simple wooden bureau. In his dark suit, he strides to the far corner and crouches at the potbelly stove. While he tucks his pistol up inside, I observe his room to glean insight.

A washbasin stands beside a half-open door that reveals a small commode. High on a brick wall to my left, blackout curtains denote a window at street level, perhaps allowing for detection of footsteps. Hung off in a corner, a laundry-draped clothesline indicates he's been in this spot for days, if not his full several weeks in the country.

With candlelight sending winglike flutters across the garments and his unmade bed, memories arise of the last time we were alone like this. In a bedroom. Together.

I shift back to my purpose. "So tell me, then." I speak quietly, unsure how loud is safe here. "Explain how things can't possibly be how they look."

Arie remains squatting at the stove, his reaction unseen.

"Swear to me you didn't actually betray the cell you were sent to help." I hear in my voice how very desperate I am for a denial.

Twisting back only partially, hair mussed over his temple, he replies, "I can't."

The two syllables fall between us, jagged as teeth and even more cutting.

That wasn't supposed to be his answer.

I struggle to understand, all good reason lacking traction, as if scaling an icy slope. "When questioned, I–I said I knew you better than anyone, that you could never do the horrible things they were saying. How could..." Muddling through, I manage to demand: "Why?"

Arie closes the stove door firmly and rises. He goes to a nearby box on the floor and rummages through the contents, surely for an object that will help support his actions. Something to justify them all.

He produces only a flask. With suit jacket unbuttoned, he kicks off his shoes and sits on the bed with his back against the brick wall. His unreadable expression further unnerves me. As he unscrews the lid of his drink, he seems on the verge of responding. But then he props a knee up and simply takes a swallow.

I plant a step forward. "Arie."

"Do you remember the letters? The ones from Thea."

I gape at him, exasperated by the use of his sister to dodge, or oddly to reminisce. At least his normal volume assures me I don't have to whisper my retort. "After everything I've risked, coming here to try and keep you safe—"

"*Her letters*," he says with a slight hitch in his voice. "Do you remember?"

He's answering me, I realize, though I scarcely see how this pertains. I supply what he already knows: "Your mother would toss them in a drawer, unread."

"Yeah. I thought so too. After about four years, apparently the stamps and postmark switched—not from Wisconsin anymore, the Netherlands. At some point, my mother gave in and read one. Wouldn't write back, on account of pride of course, but wound up going through them all."

Having lived under the family's roof during that time, through all those letters and years, I admit to him, "I had no idea…"

"None of us did. The thing is, Jacob—that's Thea's husband—he first came to the States with his brother. By the time the market crashed, the brother and wife had two boys. They tried to stick it out, but as the Depression dragged on, Thea was struggling to have a baby, so probably welcomed the change. Anyway, Jacob's old man was an importer in Holland, a widower. When he fell sick, the group sailed back and the brothers inherited the company once he passed. All real sensible, right?"

Arie ingests more from his flask, and I envision Thea. Frozen in my memory, she's a teenage girl with a honey-blond ponytail, a sweet smile, and a playful wink. Not a married grown woman.

"How did you learn of all this?"

"Over supper, a couple years ago. Pop and I were yammering on about Hitler and of Europe being on the brink of another war. I was already in the Engineers, bridge building at that point. Out of nowhere, Ma blew a gasket. She finally told us about the letters and how Thea and her husband moved over there—here, I mean—and even had a little girl. Evelien. That bit struck Pop awfully hard."

I briefly forgot where we are just now, and it dawns on me that Arie came to the Netherlands to help them. But before I can ask, he says, "Then fear grabbed hold, for all of us, with Jacob's family being what they are."

"What do you mean?"

His eyes level with mine. "They're Jews, Fen. That's why my parents had refused to give their blessing."

The cause of Thea's estrangement gains instant clarity, and an old Dutch saying from Mrs. Jansen drifts back: *Where two religions share a pillow, the Devil sleeps between.*

She wasn't speaking of me but of her daughter. One potentially now in peril, given the treatment here of Jews. I tense from apprehension before I recognize that if the worst had occurred and Arie knew, he'd have no personal cause to stay.

"Right away," he goes on, "Ma had me write to Thea. I told her how Pop insisted he'd cover the return passage for them all to come home. She was real grateful, but they'd started a family, a new life, she said, and besides, the government had a neutrality deal. Then Hitler invaded, and her letters stopped. So Ma started writing Thea herself. We heard nothing back, but folks in town said it was the same for them, that the mail just wasn't getting through."

The fact I wasn't there for the family through all this stirs me with guilt. But then I recall what I witnessed tonight, and with it, my need to be objective. I find an excuse to distance myself by settling on the chair as Arie downs another gulp. Regathering my queries, I latch onto one posed by Bogart—validly, it now seems. "So you transferred into intelligence. They say from the Corps of Engineers, that's no easy doing."

He shrugs in agreement. "My language skills helped, learning some German too. Still took plenty of persistence and rubbing elbows to get the okay. I just figured an intelligence post was the best way to at least keep tabs on the area."

"To gauge if your sister's family was safe."

He nods, resting his flask on his lowered knee. "With my level of clearance pretty limited, I wasn't going to find out much. But it was better than doing nothing while we waited for word from her."

"Did you? Hear from Thea?"

"Eventually did, yeah. Got a smuggled letter about their going into hiding."

My delight over the letter's arrival swiftly dissipates at the idea of the families living in such fear. Impatiently I prompt, "And then…"

"And then, I went to Moretti for a favor. In addition to looking out for you," he clarifies. "I asked him to sneak a letter to Thea through an agent on one of his drops. Told him I needed my sister to stay strong, to hear she wasn't forgotten."

While the sentiment is sound—even through their separation, Arie always spoke of her fondly—a gap in his recount tugs at me. "How'd you know, though, where to send the note?"

"She told me. In her letter."

"That…seems terribly risky. Don't you think?"

"Would've been, if she hadn't used a code of sorts. She was always real smart like that."

Intrigued, I raise a brow automatically, spurring him to explain.

"She wrote about us playing hide-and-seek as kids, using the basement of a brewery. Except there was never any brewery," he says. "I got the hiding part. The rest stumped me until I ran it past my folks, and Ma remembered from earlier. Thea had written a few times about a fella named Brouwer, a shipping associate of Jacob's father. He and his mother would come for dinner on occasion. So you see?"

He waits for me to decipher the link. I consider the Dutch surname, descended from brewers of ale or beer. And now, evidently, it extends to a hider of Jewish families. Clever. "You're saying this man, Mr. Brouwer, passed your letter to Thea."

"I could only hope—which wasn't easy to do when compiling reports every week of Jews being rounded up, sent off to godforsaken camps, and—" The rest snaps off, dropping away. "My parents wouldn't say it, but we were all going batty. If my sister needed help, we had to find out, even if it meant learning it was too late. Just to keep dwelling, left with no answers…" He pauses, reflecting. "There's nothing worse."

He's referring to Thea. Not to me or us. Still, for leaving him in that very state, I'm singed by a flare of shame. I do my best to focus as he resumes.

"That's the reason, anyhow, when some British brass came to DC, I broke chain and made an appeal to one. I'd been applying for a field position for months. Told the guy it was as good a time as any to team up with us Yanks, what with the crackdown on cells. Also said I had locals in Utrecht I could trust. I never let on it was personal, of course. But then another officer pulled him away from the conversation. I assumed I was out of luck, until what do you know"—Arie raises his flask—"a month later, I was called in for training."

From his mention of local connections, in earnest I finally deduce, "So Thea and her family are nearby, hiding in Utrecht. That's what all this has been about?"

After another swallow of liquor, he loosens his tie with a couple jerks, his nod almost imperceptible. "My orders, after my night drop, were to lie low before reaching out to my primary contact and helping the Resistance. It was perfect, I thought, having a few days to spare. In the meantime, I told my greeter I needed false papers to get some *onderduikers* out."

It takes me a second to translate, "under divers" being those hiding from the Nazis.

"When the guy pressured me about how I knew them, to be sure of the risks, I didn't see a choice. I confided they were family. For some extra dough, he was in. Said he'd bring a camera for their ID photos. Only problem? It was all a setup."

My eyes widen, my nerves spiking.

"Turns out, I wasn't actually assigned a greeter for my night drop. I got wise to the rat, but not soon enough. We'd just reached the Brouwers' and Gestapo pulled right up."

"Arie...no..."

He looks directly at me. "They weren't there," he says, correcting my assumption, "Thea and the rest."

I lean forward in my chair, trying to sort it all out. "You mean, Mr. Brouwer *hadn't* been hiding the families?"

"Oh, he had. For a time. While I was being arrested and praying to God they weren't found, the house was getting ransacked. Brouwer's mother came flying out. Told the Krauts to check their files. Said the 'dirty Jews' had forced themselves in, and she'd proudly turned them over just a week prior."

My hands rise to my neck, where fear and revulsion are gathering, a solid mass.

"See, late that night…" Voice gone thick, Arie pauses. He throws back more booze, and it occurs to me that the liquid fire has been burning a pathway for his words. He wipes his mouth and his attention affixes on a distant view. "There I was, going nuts over whether Thea's family was alive or dead, when my cell door swung open. I was expecting thugs to come soften me up. Only it was a *Sturmbannführer*—an SS major turned Gestapo. Bastard named Ziegler. I wasn't about to confess a thing, but then a guard brought in a little girl. She was hunched up, sniffling from crying. And my heart just about stopped, because she was Thea. A five-year-old version of her."

I'm motionless in my seat, picturing the terrified child. Arie's niece. Of all the things I might foresee, this wasn't among them.

"Ziegler says there's good news. That my family had been imprisoned nearby, waiting transport to a camp—fortuitous, he called it. And how he'd arranged for me to see them. I hadn't a clue what to make of that till a guard put a step stool under a barred window."

At the sudden welling of Arie's eyes, dread courses through me.

"Down in the courtyard, they were marched out into the lights, lined up against a wall—Thea and Jacob, his brother's family, their boys grown. When I saw the soldiers with their rifles, I started shouting for Thea, trying to yell through the glass that I was there. She couldn't hear me, of course. Then a soldier blindfolded her and the others, and…and I…"

Arie's neck muscles go taut. He brings his trembling flask to his lips before discovering it empty, and his knuckles blanch. I sense his urge to scream, to hurl the flask at the wall. His effort to keep from crumbling threatens to undo me.

My tears come in a burning rush. Unable to stay away, I move to sit on the bed facing him. For a moment, as we'd done countless times while the rest of the world slept, we say nothing amid the candlelight and lingering scent of gin. Gently I reach for the flask, the way I used to for Papa, and Arie lets me take it. Only then do I notice the quaking of my own hands.

"I was just staring at them lying there," he rasps. "Till a voice shook me out of it. All loud and sweet-like, Ziegler was inviting Evelien out into the courtyard." Arie's gaze jumps to mine, and I realize I've gasped. "The bastard, cool as can be, asks me: 'What is she worth to you?'"

The depth of such cruelty is too enormous to fully digest.

"So I did it," he says. "I told that sadistic Kraut I'd do anything, give up anything, if he'd just let her go." Hatred seethes through Arie's voice, threaded with something else. A note resembling shame.

I fail to see how anyone with even a scrap of humanity could possibly blame him. And yet...paired with his evident release, his alleged wrongdoings suggest a troubling scenario. But to what length?

"Arie," I venture softly, tentative, "what sort of deal did you make?"

He squares his shoulders, an instant defense. "I could see it in his eyes, all right? The man liked toying with people. He didn't have to bring my family there, and after he did, he could've killed Evelien with them. It was a game."

I ask, despite being afraid to, "Which means?"

"It means," he says, "I played along. Upped the stakes till he agreed to keep Evelien safe—no prison, no camps. And if I came through, he'd let us flee the country with ID, travel papers, and all."

I'm dumbfounded. "He actually said that?"

"Sure. And I pretended it wasn't a bare-faced lie."

It's a logical take, though my thoughts and emotions are positively brimming. As moisture dissipates from my eyes, same as his, I find my way back to my question. "What was the compromise?"

"For one thing...I convinced him that when I connected with my main contact, it'd look suspicious to show up with nothing. My case of weapons wasn't an option—obviously. But I did get to keep half the money I brought and some ration coupons and maps to pass along."

A fine feat, considering. But these benefits, I notice, are all one-sided. I nudge again, "You haven't said what you promised in return."

He hesitates, and that hesitation makes painfully clear he's indeed been skirting the answer. My grip tightens on his flask as I wait.

"Intel," he admits at last. "Supplies. Resistance plans." Then adds, "To give up the leaders of several cells."

I stare at him, shaken. "You did all that?"

"It was a bluff, Fen. It was meant as a bluff."

I must have a reaction to the word *meant*, because he leans toward me, saying, "Just hear me out. I needed credibility. Mixing truth with lies, I had to keep feeding Ziegler with something."

"Like…?"

"False info—all tough to verify. And some real intel that I knew had just been intercepted." The last word drags with a hint of a slur. "Since that wouldn't be enough, I gave up some of the underground's weapons. The local network had a munitions cache, in a shed for drying flower bulbs. I was supposed to add my case to the pile. So tipping off the storage location also gave me an alibi to explain my missing stash. In the large scheme, it seemed a small price."

By that rationale, I can't deny that the trade comes off as palatable. Regardless, he does, and will, have more to account for. "At HQ, they said a cell's meeting was raided. That you were the only one who didn't show up."

"It wasn't a cell," he corrects, not impatiently. "Like I was saying, it was the top leadership of several from around the country. Our saboteur groups had all taken hefty hits, which is where I came in, to aid coordination and supplies. Controllers usually keep disjointed for security, but forming a national effort, sharing resources and plans, the networks could all benefit if done right."

I take this in, comprehending. "But if that meeting were to be raided," I muse aloud, "in a single swipe, leaders are wiped out, others deterred. Morale squashed. Networks face collapse."

He nods. "All of which Ziegler would love to take credit for."

No wonder the commander was willing to bargain, up front anyway. Again though, how far did Arie's concessions go?

"Did you do it?" I persist bluntly. "Did you tip him off about the meeting?"

A brief, unsettling beat. "I gave him the date and time—"

"Arie," I breathe.

"But a false location," he stresses. "I needed Ziegler out of the house. His wife barely lets Evelien out of her sight. But his house-keeper swore the wife would be gone at an event. And with the cook away at the market, I'd have a chance to snatch Evelien back."

The implications induce mental whiplash, a single one dominating the rest. "He kept your niece? At his home?"

Arie struggles to answer, plainly having said more than intended, and my heart twists. "She's fine there," he says. "For the time being."

Registering his use of the present tense, I challenge, "How do you know?"

"Proof. It was a requirement of the deal. I pass him info, and I get a glimpse of Evelien up in a window." Discomfort underlies Arie's tone, justifiably so. This commander indeed treats people as pawns in a warped game. Even greater reason to get her out.

"What of the housekeeper? You persuaded her to help you?"

"We have an arrangement," he says. "Besides, she knows it's the right thing." Fairly vague as answers go, but I concentrate on a more pressing point.

"Well, something went wrong or you wouldn't still be here." I hold his gaze, demanding he elaborate.

With a gin-laced exhale, he sits back against the wall.

Years of experience tell him I won't relent.

"The big meeting was set for two weeks ago," he says, slightly grudging. "Night before it, I received word about a prisoner, a guy with the underground. News was, he'd spilled all about the gathering, including the actual location. I couldn't have Ziegler realizing I'd lied. Straightaway I raced over to his house. I pretended I'd just learned about the change of plans. The date and time I'd given him still lined up, so he was skeptical but seemed to buy it. Said to meet him there— which, of course, I had no intention of doing."

I relax, if marginally, factoring in the admission by the prisoner. Technically, the full tip-off came from *him*.

This doesn't mean, however, that Arie won't face a barrage of questions in London. "Was there any way you could have warned them? Sent word somehow?"

"Don't you think I tried?" His voice turns gruff, not specifically at me. "I paid a boy to leave a signal at the designated park. At a checkpoint on the way, he saw Krauts arresting a guy they'd just beaten to a pulp. Kid got scared."

I ward off yet another ghastly image and offer, "You're saying your warning..."

"Never reached the group. But I didn't know it," he says. "I figured Ziegler and his goons would end up raiding an empty room. Meantime, I headed to Ziegler's house, making sure I lost anyone who might be trailing, like usual. But when I got there, I found out his wife had taken Evelien to the ladies' breakfast with her. Like trotting out a doll. A damn pet."

I pass over his bitterness, mystified by the woman's flaunting. "I don't get it. How could a Nazi officer's wife possibly take—" I stop, realizing how terrible the rest would sound. But Arie hears enough to reply.

"The girl's only half Jew and frankly doesn't look even that." He shows no offense, thankfully. "Plus, it might've been Ziegler's idea if he suspected at all what I was up to. Or, I don't know...maybe it was his wife's call. Housekeeper said the woman's always wanted children. Who knows what her husband told her about Evelien? About where she came from and why."

A thought pops into my head: that maybe the wife suffered from similar troubles as Thea. I don't dare voice this. Instead I ask, "Has the poor girl been told? About her parents?"

Arie swallows before answering. "Housekeeper says she knows they're gone for good. That's all."

It's somewhat shocking that a man so evil would spare her the details. I suppose the alternative would mean subjecting his wife to a less pleasant child. "And...you think his wife wants to keep her?"

Arie blurts out, "Who *cares* what she wants?" At my outward startle, his expression, suddenly tight, tapers.

No need to continue the topic.

I give him a moment before detouring to issues still murky. "Back at MI9, when they told me about the raid, they said someone was killed."

"What?" He squints at that, his eyes increasingly glossy. "No. All but one got away. Ziegler's henchmen nabbed the gal. But she's alive."

I stiffen from surprise. I want to trust him, but the discrepancy deserves scrutiny. "You know that for sure?"

"She was my primary contact." It's as if that alone should suffice, before he adds, "We'd met once about details to set up the big meeting. On the day of, when I found Evelien gone, I hauled off to the meeting spot. I knew it was risky, but to keep the girl safe, I had to salvage the ruse with Ziegler. Like I said, I was still thinking the leaders got the message and wouldn't show. So here I am, ready to try and convince him that the schedule got switched a second time, honestly doubting he'd believe me. Instead, I get there and learn the group was actually raided just minutes earlier."

It's a relief, at least, to hear they all survived. A small miracle really. "And where is the woman now? Your contact."

Lips parting, he pauses and changes course. "I think you've heard all you need to."

"You're wrong," I reply, not to be obstinate. "This is what HQ will be asking us both. And if you're aware of which prison she's in, maybe they'll coordinate with contacts here to help break her out."

He glances around as if growing restless, eager to end this. If by not sharing, he's trying to protect me, it's too late for that. Perhaps recognizing this, he concedes, "She's at a hospital. The one you followed me to."

"A hospital?"

"She was shot in the shoulder, took some baton hits to the head. Gestapo are waiting for her to recuperate."

The last bit seems odd after what I witnessed in the field. "But why would they bother, assuming they're just going to torture her, or worse?" It's a grim question, legitimate nonetheless.

He expels a breath, as if perturbed by a gnat he can't shoo away. "I told Ziegler she has intel too vital to miss. And that only I can coax it from her. It's given me time to work on a plan to spring her out."

Much more of the puzzle is fitting together, including his walk tonight to a guarded destination. "Does she know the truth? About Ziegler and the rest?"

"She knows enough."

Unlike Bogart. Or Bram. Or any replacement they might send to pursue Arie—if they haven't already.

Reminded of what's personally at stake, I wonder which of his peculiar actions, without context, ultimately ruled him unworthy of a gamble. "London has been trying to track you down," I tell him at last. "We need to get in touch so they understand what you're doing."

He seems unsurprised. "No dice," he says. "There's a good chance communication's been compromised."

"What makes you think that?"

"From being set up, right after landing."

Oh gracious. In that light, it's very likely how the Germans were waiting on the night of my own drop as well. Yet another reason for us to make it back soon, to prevent them from sending more agents straight into a trap.

I'm about to voice as much when Arie maneuvers his legs off the bed as if they're weighted. "Now," he says, "you know enough too. And you'll shove off from this mess of a country however you planned. It's far too dangerous for you to be here."

"Just...hold on," I insist. "What about your niece? I presume you have another plot in the works to get her back."

Arie rises to his feet, not answering.

"Maybe I can help."

"Yeah. You can." He spares me but a glimpse. "By getting the hell home. I've got plenty on my shoulders without worrying about you too." Stepping away, he sways a tad as he picks up his overcoat from the bureau. "You keep the bed. I'll take the floor."

"Arie, the whole reason I came here—"

"You know"—he slows in rolling his coat into a pillow-like ball—"why did they send you, Fen?" As if contemplating a sudden riddle, he rotates, shadows dragging over his face. "You've all but said HQ thinks I've been turned. It doesn't add up, them recruiting you for this."

"Because they didn't. I volunteered," I correct, the pride in my voice inadvertent.

He tilts his head, waiting for me to go on.

"I said I'd come as bait."

He narrows his eyes. "Bait."

"To help find you, I mean. To straighten things out."

"You didn't come alone...did you." Not a question, yet I hasten to answer.

"An agent was assigned as my guide, but he was captured upon landing, right after our night drop—"

Arie huffs a humorless laugh, as if I've validated his point about the dangers. But then he returns to the topic. "And you think this guy wanted to sit down with me, just chat it out over coffee?"

Arie has already arrived at the same conclusion as Lenora, without even being privy to the conversation she overheard. I do feel somewhat naive in hindsight, made worse by the look he gives me—as if I couldn't be denser. Maybe a product of the booze. Still unwarranted, given all I've done to be here.

I speak through gritted teeth. "My plan was to find you first," I begin, but he's not interested.

"Tomorrow, we'll get you pointed home and into safe hands." He adds in a leaden tone, "Then I want you out of my business. Forever."

CHAPTER 60

Sleep comes in ragged stints. Aside from my Benzedrine wearing off, there's too much to absorb for a peaceful rest. Snapshots loop mercilessly on the pages in my mind, of executions and raids and a little girl thrust into a lonely, frightful world.

I realize only from the drag of my eyelids that eventually I'd succumbed to a spell of decent sleep. A slice of light, past the blackout curtain opened an inch, alerts me of dawn's arrival and Arie at the washbasin. In undershirt and trousers, he stands lost in thought with cup in hand. Through my groggy vision, as in so many of my dreams, the sight of him brings a mix of serenity and yearning, until reality—of us and the war and our setting—grips me with the force of a riptide. Then comes the recollection of our last exchange, renewing a swell of resentment.

If not for a sense of obligation, above all to his parents—oh mercy, his poor unknowing parents—I'd grant him his wish by leaving this very moment. Instead, I sit upright, fully dressed within his bedding.

The rustling interrupts his daze. With face and eyes weary, hair and clothes mussed, once more he reminds me of Papa after a night of indulgence when occasionally too much was said.

"Do you really want me to leave?" I ask this flatly, as I'm aware of the answer.

He downs his drink, this time much needed water no doubt, and pours another cupful from a pitcher. "I think we've been over this." His voice is matter-of-fact, at least absent of his previous harshness.

"Then tell me your rescue plans."

He gestures toward the box near the stove. "If you're hungry, there's bread and a bit of cheese. Grab what you want, then I'll give you a safe route through the streets to wherever you're staying."

"Arie."

"Ziegler could have a lookout in the area. Best to slip out the bathroom window." He adds, refusing to face me, "I would hope it goes without saying not to tell anyone you've found me."

"*Arie*," I repeat.

He dries his hands on a towel as if I've said nothing.

I bridle my reaction. "Regardless of your refusal to hear me out last night, I'm telling you, you can trust me with your plan."

"And I'm telling you," he intones, "I got everything handled."

I openly scoff. "Well, if that were true, I wouldn't be here. Would I?" At last he spins toward me, but I head off a rebuttal: "I'd wager a hundred dollars your scheme needs improvement."

His expression constricts. "You haven't even heard it."

I nearly smile. "You think I'd have to?"

A dry laugh slips from his mouth, and he promptly seals it shut, amused in spite of himself. He tosses the towel aside and jerks a nod toward the floor. "Grab your shoes. Time to get a move on."

"Criminy, you're being ridiculous." I cross my arms, seated solidly against the wall. "Arie, you *know* this is my specialty. It's what I've always done—dissect illusions and tricks, and now gadgets. I make them better by figuring out what could go wrong. I'm an expert at escape and evasion, for goodness' sake."

"Oh, believe me," he mutters, "I know that much." He stops and shakes his head, appearing regretful of the barb. It's a personal one that would gouge me deeper if not for my current resolve. "Listen," he says, hitching his hands low on his hips, "I appreciate the offer. I just don't need your input on this. All right?"

At my silence, he presses me with a stare.

"Fine," I say.

He nods with relief—too hastily.

"How about Evelien? Could she use it? What about your contact, the one trapped in the hospital? Are you so terribly certain your plan can't use improvement, even with all your lives at stake?"

He looks away, and quiet swoops in between us. Although clearly perturbed, he's not countering my points.

More gently I prod, "Well?"

After a mumble and sharp groan, he jabs a finger in my direction. "You give your feedback, then you're gone. Nothing more. You hear me?"

"Yes," I stress, "I hear you."

It's a genuine reply, my choice of words entirely deliberate.

CHAPTER 61

To conceal my overnight absence, I sneak back into the boarding-house to show my face at breakfast. The morning meals thus far have consisted of bitter ersatz coffee and bread. Today it's porridge, a child-hood favorite of Klara's.

Why, oh why couldn't it be anything else?

Staving off memories of the orphanage, I force down a bowlful, barely. The thick glop lacks even a grain of sweetener, sugar naturally being a rare treasure. But I keep a pleasant expression, some of my best acting I'd say.

For this feat, I'm soon rewarded—by an idea. When Mrs. van der Meer leaves us to clear the dishes while she opens her store downstairs, the fact it's a pharmacy plants in my mind a seed, one that takes root by the time I return to the quiet of my room.

I've promised Arie suggestions after contemplating his plan. He intends to rescue his contact and Evelien, in that immediate order, two days from now. It will be the date of my departure, though many hours after I've left. That's when Ziegler and his wife will attend a late dinner across town for some Nazi hotshot's birthday. With the cook off for the night, Evelien will be alone in the care of the housekeeper, who for the occasion is due to stay the night.

The couple isn't expected back until late, Arie explained. There's a good chance, I figure, they won't notice the girl's missing till morning. By then, Lord willing, we'll have made good headway west, hoofing it to the countryside.

And what then? I asked.

A farmer there, near Gouda, quietly takes people in. The hope is that he'll allow us to stay for the duration.

Arie acknowledged it isn't ideal, again relying on others to hide out. But aside from his temporary identity pass that exempts him from the labor call-up—issued by Ziegler and barring all travel beyond Utrecht—he lacks papers to protect him and Evelien. His options are therefore as limited as his time line, with Ziegler growing increasingly impatient over the recovery of the wounded Resistance leader.

Her code name is Nel. *A real brave and strong woman,* Arie said of her.

The admiration in his tone did make me wonder if something more lay between them. If so, it might even be bolstering his drive to rescue her and—

I quell the thought. It's entirely his business.

All that matters is that to save her and Evelien, along with himself, through quick thinking, he'd appealed to Ziegler's self-interest. Arie told him that Nel has knowledge of a high-ranking officer, a man from the old German elite, engaged in undermining Hitler by feeding intel to the Allies. Such a level of betrayal could earn Ziegler accolades if uncovered; a demotion, at best, if missed.

Arie went on to relay: *I told him that, even if tortured, Nel wouldn't give up the traitor's identity. Not to a Nazi, anyway—but just maybe she'd confide in an established contact. One dressed as, say, a hospital janitor under the guise of preparing for her escape.*

This in reality, he's sworn to me, is exactly what he's doing. Under Ziegler's authority, he's been allowed access to a janitor's uniform and Nel's room, where she's been buying time by feigning incoherence. And though the plausibility of her condition lessens with each day of her healing, Arie has been seeking a discreet exit point while scouting the nighttime staff and schedule.

Would any of the nurses be willing to help? I ventured, recalling his luck with the housekeeper.

Nel's nurse on the night shift is plenty friendly, he said, *but she's dating a Nazi officer. And I haven't sensed I can trust any others.*

It's understandable why he'd rule them out. Still, even with the hospital apparently within a mile of Ziegler's home, I noted a glaring problem.

But while you're racing to get Evelien, the nurse could quickly figure out Nel's gone. With an alert sounded, it'll be harder for you all to get away.

Well, yeah, he said. *The question is how the heck to delay that discovery.*

Or, I proposed, *you could get Evelien out first.*

In fact, I was surprised this wasn't his plan until he explained.

I can't just leave her outside the hospital, Fen. And besides, the Zieglers' party is at seven thirty. If they run behind in leaving, even if I still manage to get Nel, Dutch police will be patrolling the streets for curfew. We'll all be good as caught.

Have you considered waiting until late at night, when the Zieglers are asleep and there aren't many patrollers out? I almost didn't ask that one, as it seemed too obvious.

Yeah, and that's a no go. Housekeeper says Ziegler sleeps in fits and starts, so he's often up working. And with the curtains, I wouldn't know where he is until I'm in.

That's when I remembered the white pills I was never issued, knockout drops that could put Ziegler into a heavy slumber.

Taken when I was arrested, Arie replied when I asked about his own supply. *Even so, it would've meant having to knock his wife out too, and no way the housekeeper would've agreed to try. Blaming an armed invader for taking Evelien gets her off the hook. Drugging the couple herself is a guaranteed death sentence.*

Of course, I told him.

At that point, I realized just how many options he'd already explored, and the best way I could help was to improve his current plan—a possibility of which now dawns on me.

Although drugging the Zieglers isn't an option, what about the night nurse assigned to Nel? To delay her from sounding an alert, an effective means might be well within my reach—almost literally. In the pharmacy below me, there must be a supply of sleeping pills. By crushing them up and slipping them into the nurse's food or drink, Nel's room could be left unattended for hours.

My hunt for any such pills will have to wait, mind you, until my household is asleep. Hence for the moment, I circle back through Arie's scheme for other issues to solve.

Like his qualms over hiding out till war's end.

Suffice it to say, the ideal would be to eliminate the need altogether. To do so, I realize, might actually be possible...

True, the solution would require someone with special skills and resources, and with little time for turnaround. All of which could amount to a long shot. And that's to say nothing of entrusting a person I barely know, a man I've met only by his code name. In short, the chances of success seem low.

Given the dangers of the alternative, however, I'm willing to try.

The abandoned workshop is surely as cool and musty as before, though I scarcely feel it. I'm too consumed with the seconds, minutes, and now two full hours that have passed. I check my watch for the twentieth time and picture the trio of small stones. As directed, I'd placed them on a windowsill of the shuttered café, a signal for Willem's help.

Indeed, I recall his disclaimer: *If I can, I meet you back here. If two hours pass, I am not coming.* But I promised to call on him strictly if necessary. Could he really ignore the plea, or might he be unaware?

I suppose, despite my careful placement of the rocks as I pretended to steal a glance into the café, at least one could have rolled off. Or a well-meaning tidier could have brushed them away. Far worse, an informed collaborator might have alerted the Gestapo, who could burst through the door at any moment.

Arms folded tight, I resist the scenarios.

Five minutes—no, ten. I'll wait another ten.

Both come and go, further leaching my hopes, before a silhouette fills the frame of a dust-covered window. Wearing a hat—or is it a helmet?—the fellow passes the next set of panes, closing in.

If I could hide as a precaution, I would. But the room's shabby boxes are too sparse for cover and the hulk of machinery sits too close to the wall. Should I have muscled the door to bolt it? Too late for that.

The cockeyed door wobbles, an attempt to heft it open.

My knife. I reach for it in my pocket, just as the door opens to expose the man's fair and angled features.

"Willem," I blurt out. "Heavens. I'm so glad it's you."

He shuts us inside, not returning my smile. "What is it you want?" The tone in his English isn't cold, but neither is it warm. A touch unexpected after our last interaction.

He is, nonetheless, here.

"I need your help. Only once more."

When he doesn't respond, I dare to cut to the situation. "Two friends are in grave danger. They need ID cards and travel papers, like mine, to get to Switzerland along an escape line." A vision of the three of us traveling together sweeps through my mind. As if sharing the view, Willem's stoicism wavers.

"*Ach*. That is all? Let me look." He makes a show of patting his coat pockets, a smirk passing over his lips. "Sorry. I must have forgotten my extra set."

As with Arie, the mocking is galling, though just slightly more reasonable. I know from MI9 how often we shipped forging supplies—passable stamps, inks, paper materials—to POWs and Resistance groups throughout the Continent.

"Please, you *must* know someone with access to resources. A leader in the underground, maybe a sympathetic clerk."

His spark of levity dims. "I do not wish to be more involved."

Then why ever did you come? I want to say. But cautious of putting him off, sensing his readiness to leave, I delve swiftly beyond the personal. "The agent I dropped in with—Bram—the one you asked about—"

"He is dead."

"You knew?"

"I have heard."

I shouldn't be surprised; at some level, word must have spread in the days since. Perhaps my prior withholding of that information is adding to his guardedness. "Well, what you might *not* have heard is that the Germans seemed to know we were coming. Given similar occurrences, it appears intelligence has been compromised. That's why it's even more vital my friends and I get back to share details, so London won't keep sending operatives."

"But already," he says, "these are stopped."

"How do you mean?"

"There are no more drops. Not of people. Therefore, your headquarters must already be informed."

I want this to be the case, I do—particularly after what I witnessed in the fields. I just wish it didn't weaken my cause for Willem's help. "That may very well be true. To be safe besides, if there's any way you can still assist—"

"As I told you, I am a messenger of information only."

"Yes. I know you said that—" This is all I get out before he turns to exit, and apprehension grips me. "Willem, stop. I beg of you! I'll pay you all that I have!"

Hand on the doorknob, he pauses. "It is not a matter of money."

"What, then? What would change your mind?" Encouraged when he looks back at me, I rush to emphasize, "There must be something I can offer you. *Anything*."

Even before seeing it in his cobalt-blue eyes, piercing beneath the brim of his cap, I recognize the implication. An overt link to our first encounter. Suddenly I'm back at the canal, his mouth hovering at my neck, his hand intimate on my hip.

He appears to remember the same as he shifts to face me, his attraction clear.

I yearn to set him straight, that my intent was strictly proper, but then a grim vision intercedes: little Evelien huddling in that monster's home, trapped until the couple grows tired of their pet or a Nazi friend uncovers her heritage, and she meets her mother's fate. Maybe worse.

I needn't meet the child to know this truth: mere minutes of impropriety couldn't possibly outweigh an opportunity to save her fragile life. Countless others have sacrificed much more, and for less.

In all candor, it's not as if I have the purity of fresh snow. I can do this. I can.

Before I'm able to reconsider, my hands find the belt of my coat. As I undo the knot, Willem watches me with an intensity that shoots a tremble through my knees. Still, I proceed with the buttons. I slide free the first one and the next, and my coat falls open.

He advances with slow, purposeful steps.

Just imagine it's a dream, I tell myself, not because the man isn't handsome, as he assuredly is, but because he's not...

A pointless thought.

I move on to my blouse. I'm unfastening the buttons when Willem arrives before me, delivering a light waft of tobacco. His hand layers mine. His fingers brush the hollow of my neck, and my insides contract. Gradually he lowers my hand. I close my eyes, waiting for him to take over.

I can do this, I can.

Through the motionless moment, I imagine his gaze lazing over me. How I wish he would hurry.

"*Zo ben je niet*," he says. "*En ik ook niet.*"

This is not you. Or me.

I open my eyes.

He was only stopping me.

Humiliation floods my veins, coursing through every limb. I angle away and fumble to reassemble my blouse. In the deafening silence, my face flushes with heat. This was all a mistake. Not bothering with my coat buttons, I start for the door.

"These friends," he calls out, "one is Frans?"

The reference to Arie reflexively slows my feet. Against my desire to leave, wary of being tested, I answer simply over my shoulder: "Yes."

"It seems maybe he is not to be trusted."

The suggestion is enough to turn me around. "That isn't true." I'm assertive despite the nuanced truth; the rightful core is what brought me here. "As I said—and you've heard—intelligence has been compromised. People have been getting the wrong information. But I know him. Personally. And his intentions are only good. He came to this country, risking his life, to help those who desperately need it."

Willem's expression gives away nothing. At his silence, I switch to the practicality of my mission. "My orders," I state, "are to assist in getting him home, and that's what I'm going to do—either with or without your help. Thereafter, any questions about his assignments will be sorted out with London."

I remain unflinching as Willem studies me, his lips a firm line.

At last he says, "There is a forger. However, like many, this person is growing scared."

My first instinct is to sway Willem with phrases of reassurance. But in honoring Arie's family, as well as any others involved, I reply candidly. "They have every reason to be."

He scratches the back of his neck, deliberating. Just as before, when he offered protection both through actions and words, there's a sense of him caring. For even a virtual stranger. "How soon is your need?"

My embarrassment has ebbed, making way for a margin of hope. "I'm aware it's not much time—"

"When?"

"Saturday."

"In two days?" He snorts a laugh, for which I genuinely can't fault him. "They will need different documents and identification for every country. The Dutch papers alone are more difficult to copy than the Germans'."

"I know it's a lot to ask. But, Willem," I say, "the other person is just a child, and she absolutely must get out."

He reflects on the insight pensively, its implication evident.

I think to add, "Even by dawn on Sunday could work." The more time for him, the better, obviously. And if it results in acquiring the papers, a small delay in fleeing would be worth the risk.

Glancing upward, he sighs as if annoyed with the ceiling. I figure the irritation is actually with me until he responds, "All right." And I realize it's most likely with himself.

I strive to contain my hopes as we discuss particulars. We start with the forger's access to photos of others who could potentially pass for Arie, our best bet with limited time. As Willem is already familiar with Arie's physical traits, I need only to provide my knowledge of Evelien's description.

After which, he tells me, "For children of her age, even crossing borders, a birth certificate will be enough, I think. But having also a baptism document might be better."

"Please, then, whatever is safer."

"The forger will know this. As I said, I am a messenger only."

I smile at that, as he's obviously extending beyond his usual duties.

"If I get what you require," he says, "and that is only if, I will leave them...there." He points to a gap between the floor and the base of the cobwebbed machinery.

I nod that I understand. "Thank you, Willem. I have every bit of faith you'll try your best." I say this not meaning to pressure him. Oh, who am I fooling? Of course I do.

Appearing to sense this, he tips his hat without another word and slips out the door.

CHAPTER 62

My idea of escaping together, the three of us, wouldn't come without complications. There are train connections, safe-house stops, and a mountain hike to consider, as well as the logistics of linking up with my guide.

As it stands, on Saturday, straight after my morning train to Tilburg, I'm to relay scripted lines to a bookshop clerk—who, I now realize, probably isn't even my contact. Mirroring Willem's, that role will more likely belong to an inconspicuous listener, which means I can't delay my arrival. And since Evelien's escape isn't possible until that evening, I'll be spending a long day and night in Tilburg, just praying she and Arie will follow on the first train in the morning.

That is, if by then the Gestapo isn't scouring Utrecht's transportation hubs for the pair of them...

Oh, bother. None of this will matter if Willem and the forger don't come through.

For now, I'll refocus on a problem I can actively solve. Namely, devising a way to delay an alert at the hospital once Nel is freed.

Years ago, I witnessed an impressive trick that just might prove key. I was living in Chicago when a showman stopped through. Onstage, he disappeared in a poof of smoke and reappeared almost instantly in the balcony, dazzling the audience, me included. I attended the performance twice more to puzzle and analyze. When finally I noted a change in the man's face, his chin gaining a powdered scar but only while in the balcony, it hit me: the fellow had a twin, or some other kin who could pass as him.

Needless to say, I'm not counting on finding Nel's doppelgänger, much less in two days. A similar swap, however, could be an option. Nel has a room to herself due to security, her door being guarded round the clock. What if her nurse, made to doze off, was tucked into bed to pass as the patient? With Arie there for misdirection, Nel, in a nurse's uniform, could conceivably walk right out of her room, then the hospital entrance.

By my estimation, given the staff's lighter workload at night and the hospital's mazelike layout from being a commandeered school, the real nurse wouldn't be missed for at least a few hours. Likely more, thanks to an inattentive supervisor, by Arie's description. In fact, if the entry guard believes he saw the nurse leave, a search very possibly wouldn't start until the following day.

For any of this to happen, of course, we'll need sleeping pills. Fast-acting and potent.

I'm pondering this in my lamplit boarding room, the return of electricity a welcome treat, when I hear the clanking of pots. Upstairs, Mrs. van der Meer is busy preparing dinner. Klara and Dirk too are preoccupied, laughing next door.

Since my goal is purely reconnaissance at first—in case Mrs. van der Meer keeps a close inventory count—I consider going now. It could be even safer than waiting for the quiet, late hours. Seizing the chance, I throw my rigged hairpins and tricked-out lipstick into a deep pocket of my cardigan. Then I tiptoe through the hall and down the stairs, avoiding creaky planks.

At the base, two doors greet me. The one straight ahead empties into the square, and that to my left offers a side entry into the pharmacy, which is the knob I try.

Locked as expected. With my hairpin-disguised picks, I navigate the aged mechanisms with ease despite my humming nerves.

Once inside the darkened shop, I illuminate the flashlight built into my lipstick tube. I shut the door without sound and move past the windows covered in cardboard blackout squares. Beyond the counter, I reach the back room—also locked. Again, I rely on my picking skills to enter. With the space too closet-like for sealing myself in, I leave the door open a crack.

Beaming my light, I scan the U-shaped configuration of shelves. Only partially stocked. Bare sections, empty jars. I'd venture to guess the Germans have raided supplies, hoarding all but the basics. I investigate what's left.

Various herbs, petals, and roots sit segregated among glass bottles of myriad shapes and sizes. A mortar and pestle further evidence the crafting of homemade remedies. Among the smaller jars thankfully are pills. But with all of them white, they look practically the same. Most are labeled in a messy hand. Of what I can read, nothing indicates a sedative. Abbreviations and medical jargon, in a combination of Dutch and Latin, fail to ease my task.

I resort to inspecting powders, with no added luck. I even sniff bottles of liquids, the most pungent causing me to wince. After pressing through a wave of wooziness, I still find nothing recognizably useful.

Leaning back against a shelf, I groan. "Somewhere in here, there has to be—"

A scratching noise jolts me. I whip toward the door just as it swings open. My heart stops at the sight of two eyes, the pupils bright from my flashlight.

But only inches from the ground…

Thirza. The house cat.

"Jiminy Christmas. You scared the wits out of me." I pat my chest as the beats within it restart, now racing as if to make up for those that were skipped. The gray feline lets out a whiny meow and winds around my leg, tail curling.

Relieved, I kneel and give her head a rub. "Let me guess. You managed to sneak in with me?" She meows as if affirming, clearly craftier at spy work than I am. "Well, come here. Let's get back upstairs." With plans to try again, late tonight and alone, I lift her up and carry her from the back room. I'm just past the counter when a lofty voice sings out.

"Thirza?" The side door is opening. A voice calls in Dutch: "Are you here?"

I duck to scramble into hiding, covering my flashlight. But the store lights flare and the animal bolts, clawing my hand. I suppress a scream as Mrs. van der Meer stares. Straight at my face.

"What are you doing?"

My heart is still racing. I'm formulating an answer when she swoops up the cat protectively, her eyes accusing.

I must look like a thief of her cherished pet. Oddly, honesty seems safer, to an extent.

"I was looking for some medicine is all. Something for sleeping well."

"The truth," she hisses, "or I'll ring the police."

"It is the truth. Sincerely."

The cat purrs, snuggled up to the woman's apron-clad bosom, but even this can't prevent the deepening of Mrs. van der Meer's scowl. "Just like the claims of your cousin? Her illness, her visit?" Her tone matches that of a teacher from my youth whose every query, whether academic or disciplinary, made clear she knew the answer.

It's equally fitting now, I realize, from the mother of three grown boys.

Before I can respond, she adds, "You came to rob our supplies, but for what? The black market?"

I blink at where she's gone wrong. "Gosh, no. It's nothing like that."

Ignoring me, she heads toward the counter, beyond which a wall telephone awaits.

"Please, don't. I'll pack up and leave this instant." As she's about to blow past me, I blurt out, "That isn't why I came. I swear it on my papa's grave." Sincerity infuses my plea, succeeding in giving her pause, but only that. Like Arie, I've schemed with a mix of truth and lies, and she's gauging which way the scales tip.

I vacillate over how much to say, unsure of her loyalties. But from clues I've caught when she believes nobody is watching—the annoyed shifting in her seat at dinner through Dirk's tales of friendly soldiers at the repairs shop; her subtle glares and mutterings toward patrollers on the street after air raids—I take a gamble, relying on my gut.

"Mrs. van der Meer, I promise, I'm here only to help loved ones in unspeakable danger. To do that, I was seeking sleeping pills, not for myself." I tread carefully. "For your welfare, it's best you hear little else. Just know, from what I've gathered of your family, I believe in my heart you'd approve."

She continues to eye me for an excruciatingly long moment before setting Thirza on the floor. With a shake of her head, she resumes her march around the counter.

I glance from the phone to the door, wishing I'd brought my satchel.

"Don't run," she commands. Bypassing the telephone, she reaches below the counter. Blocked from my view, she appears to jostle a drawer and shift objects around. Is she accessing a hidden compartment?

The notion of a gun assails my thoughts, a weapon to keep me here until the authorities arrive. I debate defying her order.

But then there's a soft clinking of glass, and she again maneuvers the drawer, seemingly back into place. She sets on the counter two small bottles, one clear, one amber. Then she collects her cat and strides past me the way she came. No words or explanation.

"Ma'am...is that..."

The lights click off. Leaving the door slightly ajar, she disappears into the house.

CHAPTER 63

As a precaution, I circumvent Arie's front door. Obscured by hedges, I crouch and send a signal as instructed on his bathroom window. *Tap-tap-slide-tap.* "F" for Fenna.

Curfew is still an hour and a half off, yet I wait anxiously, leery of any henchman possibly lurking. Though Ziegler requires regular check-ins by Arie, I was surprised he permits Arie to roam at all, until considering that the alternatives—keeping him detained or openly guarded—might raise more alarms with the Resistance, a detriment to the officer's goal.

Then, of course, there's the darker logic: *He's got Evelien,* Arie explained. *And Nel. The bastard's given me plenty of ideas about what would happen to them both if I skipped town or double-crossed him.*

I banish those imaginings as I signal again.

Tap-tap-slide—

A corner of the blackout paper peels away, just far enough for Arie to peek, before the window opens. He shoves something into the back of his waistband. His pistol, I'd say. "Sit and put your feet through," he whispers, "then grab onto me."

With my hands on his shoulders, he grips my waist. As he guides me downward, I feel his muscles shift beneath his cotton shirt and my skirt rise to midthigh. Our faces land so close his breath brushes across my skin. His hold around me stalls. But then breaking away, he mumbles something about a discussion of plans and continues into the main room.

Heat lingers on my sides from his touch. And I'm reminded of what I was willing to do with Willem. I push away the shame-tinged thought and step into the room alight with candles, where Arie is stowing his gun under his mattress. Then he strides toward the potbelly stove, where a round tin smells of broth.

"Hungry?" he asks, blunting the awkwardness.

"Not just yet."

A quick nod, and he diverts to conversation while stirring. "So I've got news," he says. "I lined up a fella today for a handoff by the hospital."

I'm trying to track the relevance, still collecting myself. "Sorry. This is for…?"

"For Nel. You asked how I'd get her to safety fast, before I'm able to grab Evelien."

"Sure—of course."

"The guy is Nel's uncle. Her usual connections are all up north. But she sent me his way, so no reason not to count on him. I met him just briefly, but he seems okay. He isn't part of the network, but for her, he's willing to risk it."

"Well, good. That's splendid, then." I extend a smile, which Arie reciprocates. When he returns to stirring, I go to sit on the bed but think better of it and detour to settle on the chair. "Speaking of news"—recalling the main reason I've come—"I actually have a bit of my own." In the candle's glow on the table, I present the two bottles from my cardigan pockets, not with a stage flourish but close. "I believe these ought to be useful."

"Oh, yeah? Whaddya got?" Abandoning the soup, he strides over and attempts to read their smudged labels. I save him the trouble.

"The clear one's for anesthesia. Ether, I'd guess. And the amber one is a sleep tonic." Mrs. van der Meer might have intended for me to choose between them, but the combination seems ideal to knock a person out quickly and for a lengthy stretch.

At Arie's bewilderment—likely figuring they're for the Zieglers and thus ready to discount them—I plunge into my idea: about Nel and a dozing nurse swapping places, along with their outfits. It's a classic trick of hiding in plain sight, I tell him, and better than his existing plan of using extra bedding to pass for a body.

"And yes, I *know* that worked at the orphanage," I say, preempting his pushback. "But a hospital's a different story. I wasn't being guarded and checked on at night. As you've said yourself, the longer you can delay the search for all of you, the better. You could even hide in the city till morning if need be."

I don't delve into why that option might be preferred. One topic at a time. Instead, I wait for him to brighten with approval.

A response that doesn't come.

He holds the bottles up between us. "Where the devil did you get these?"

Expecting the question, though not his intensity, I trip a little through my reply. "A pharmacy, from the owner—well, his wife. I've been renting a room from her on an upper floor."

"Does she know what it's for?"

"Of course not—not specifically."

"What do you mean 'not specifically'?"

I aim to stay calm, even as he triggers my defenses. "She simply knows it's to help people and that I couldn't tell her more."

He huffs and glances away, muttering, "That's just swell." Sharply squaring to me, he returns the bottles to the table, not slamming them, but neither is he gentle. "This is all the evidence she needs to turn you in. You realize that?"

"She won't though," I insist, reflecting on the encounter, how she volunteered the offerings. "I know it."

"You don't know that." He bends to loom over me, hand planted on the table. "Think of Thea and her family. After almost a year of hiding and caring for them, just like that, the Brouwers tossed them out like meat scraps to a pack of wolves."

I loathe feeling like an admonished child, and the Brouwer family's betrayal still seems peculiar. Nonetheless, his point is impossible to counter.

He adds, "At least tell me you haven't spoken of Evelien—to anyone."

I open my mouth to fire back that of course I wouldn't have, but the protest catches in my throat. Because it isn't true.

"Fen," he rasps. The fear in his voice reaches his eyes. "Who did you talk to?"

I fight the impulse to shrink into my chair. After all, Arie himself just secured help from a stranger. I answer, mustering confidence, "Willem. He was my contact. One of yours too, he said. He's actually how I knew where you'd been spotted when—"

"I don't *know* any Willem."

I gape as Arie stands warily upright.

"But he said…you two communicated…"

"When?" he presses.

I'm trying not to panic. I could describe Willem's looks—except that a tall blond with blue eyes describes half of Holland. "He told me the other day. When I first met him."

"No, *when* did he say we communicated?"

My mind scrabbles for purchase. "I don't know… He didn't say exactly." I'm questioning if I've been fooled, how many details I gave him, and what he'll do with that information. "He only said he passed you a note, from a distance. And that just this week, he was trying to find you, to get you in touch with London."

Arie relaxes a fraction. "It's Anton," he says, a conclusion to himself.

I'm suddenly reminded that resisters, same as formal operatives, claim various code names. But there's no time for relief as he demands, "Did you tell him where to find me? 'Cause if he's thinks I'm a collaborator, I could wind up floating in a canal."

Even without Arie's prior warning, I understood as much. "No. Absolutely not."

"Well, what did you tell him?"

"Scarcely anything," I contend, despite my intuitive sense Willem can be trusted. "Just what he needed for the forgeries."

Arie blinks hard. "What are you talking about?"

Presented in jumbled order, my news meant to fuel optimism is having the opposite effect.

"It's what I came to tell you." I lean forward, and he rears back a step. It's an emotional reflex I choose to ignore. "He's working on getting IDs and travel papers for you and Evelien. Then hopefully we can all go back together, as far as Switzerland at first, and on to London with some finagling."

The neutral Swiss government, technically, was to hold for the duration all able-bodied Allied servicemen who reached its soil. I've heard, however, that our boys regularly repatriate by sidestepping those rules, whether diplomatically or by escaping from there. And anyhow, we can tackle that obstacle later.

"This way, for the rest of the war," I tell him, "you wouldn't have to worry about either of you being discovered at a farmhouse or anywhere else."

Arie stays quiet, digesting the reasoning that should deflate the pressure. And it does, but not entirely. "You should've asked me first."

His permission. This is his prime concern?

"I wasn't aware we had unlimited time."

"We won't need the papers," he says. "Evelien and I aren't going."

If not so stunned, I'd laugh, particularly given the risks Willem and I took to even meet up, and that's to say nothing of the forger's bravery.

"Why? Because staying behind is so much safer? After everything that's happened to you and your family, I would think—"

"Because I can't go back," he says gruffly. "If I do, I'll be tried and convicted as a traitor. And who knows where that'll leave the child."

"Arie, that's *not* going to happen. You already said the raid wasn't your fault."

There's a pause. Then a tensing of his jaw. "I never said that."

Daunted as much by the inference as his demeanor, I sink back into my chair. Now I'm the one instinctively wanting distance. "What haven't you told me?"

He replies but without looking my way. "Truth of it is, I–I gave up more than ammo, all right?" I'm hesitant to breathe as he begins pacing the floor, rubbing his temple. "From my intel, I knew that one of the underground fighters was running a scam. He'd been taking money from Jews, telling them he'd smuggle them out, but wouldn't follow through. He was robbing these people blind, even boasting about it. Who would they complain to? The police?"

"You're saying…you handed this man over?" I'm comprehending, not accusing, but he becomes more guarded.

"Like I said, I had to give up enough information to keep the ruse going. And it was disgusting what that lowlife was doing. He deserved prison, and that's what he got. I just…I didn't count on him knowing details of the big meeting."

By the flickering candlelight, Arie moves in and out of the shadows. I watch him absently while distilling the situation, connecting how Ziegler learned of the correct location. A consequence, for sure, but unintended and seemingly unforeseeable. In all fairness, isn't that the essence of war? It's a constant stream of ramifications from impossible decisions, compromises, and sacrifices. Some more harrowing than others.

As it stands, if our scheme goes well, Evelien and Nel will both be freed and safe.

I want to offer Arie encouragement about clearing his name after all is set right, but his agitated movements are making me jittery. I rise and calmly catch his arm. "It'll be fine. Once we get back, we'll march straight to HQ and explain it."

He stares as if I'm mad to even suggest it. "Explain what?"

"The whole story. How you tried to warn them."

"It's the military, for crying out loud. Won't matter squat to them." He gives me no chance to argue. "Listen, you wanted to help, and you did. But that's enough. The problems are mine, not yours. Now I want you out of it."

I heave a sigh, exasperated, though I am not about to give up. I'm reminded of the many nights in high school, back when he'd struggle through math formulas, similarly resistant to my help, as if that made him less than. "We can surely solve this together. Arie, if this is about your pride—"

"I said it's *enough*," he erupts, and my body retracts. He flicks a glance toward the window, appearing to remember that sound travels, and tempers his volume yet not his mood. "You told me you'd give your input and wouldn't do anything else. Instead, you go and put yourself in more danger, and maybe Evelien too. But hey," he smirks, "what was I expecting? You always do as you please, regardless of what I think or feel."

And there it is. The pain of a history never actually addressed, a wound left to fester from the unsaid.

I scramble for my thoughts, trying for a steady reply. "Arie, I'd understand if you're upset about the past—"

"You're damn right I am," he seethes in an undertone that somehow makes the words more cutting. "I loved you, Fen—for near half my life. I put my heart out there, giving you everything I had, and you threw it away, you threw *me* away, all because things got a little too scary for you."

My tears are instant. They fill my eyes as emotions charge through me, unleashed without warning. "That is not what happened."

"Yeah? Then what? Tell me what I missed."

His challenge is searing. Still, I gather the will to straighten, recalling how my every intention was to protect *him*, so he could find the happiness he deserved.

"You wanted children," I say, at last confessing. "After the stairwell, the tragedy—seeing those kids and parents, the babies, I just couldn't. I couldn't give that to you. And I loved you too much to rob you of that." I fight fiercely to keep my tears from spilling. As Arie regards me, I await the softening of his bearing, a sign of his grasping a long-veiled truth.

Then a syllable cracks the air. "No."

I stare at him.

"You don't get to do that. You don't get to play the martyr."

Breath knocked out of me, I feel speared in the heart. I recognize his desire to lash out, even his right, but that doesn't cushion the impact.

"The sheer fact is you were scared, and that's it. Sure, about being a mother, but just as much of being with me. About putting yourself out there to risk getting hurt. So you took the coward's way out. Well, guess what? I was scared too, Fen—terrified actually of something ever happening to you, let alone of being a father and losing my kids. Of being destroyed by that kind of loss…"

Trailing off, he turns his face away, moisture pooling in his eyes. What he's picturing at this moment couldn't be clearer. The broken fathers, the procession, the funerals. Visions I should have realized we still shared.

I grapple for what to say. "Arie. I didn't know..."

He speaks under his breath. "How could you have? You didn't stick around to find out." With a half shrug, he angles back. "Who knows, maybe it would've been just a little less scary if we'd faced it together. But none of that matters now, does it?" Beyond his wall of bitterness, in the depth of his gaze, I'm struck by the pain I alone caused. A reflection of what I too have worked so hard not to feel.

A merciless quiet stretches between us.

Though battered, I surrender to an urge and reach for his hand. My fingers barely graze his before he recoils as if burned. Repulsed.

"I need air," he says.

I stand there, every part of me pinned in place, as he grabs his coat. Then he's through the door and gone.

Only at that point do my tears pour over.

CHAPTER 64

Through the many twists and turns in my relationship with Arie, one constant remains: he never lies to spare my feelings, even when I wish he would.

Back in my lamplit boarding room, I'm the one pacing, assaulted by second-guessing, thinking myself a coward.

But no. Had I stayed and indulged in the fantasy of a blissful marriage and family, I'd have only prolonged the inevitable, and to a crueler end. Even tonight, he suggested we could have overcome our fears together. As if with some nudging, I could have been swayed.

That isn't to say I don't ache to the point of feeling gutted from thoughts of him hurting, tracing back to even his youth. Yet here and now, what can be changed? I'll respect what he wants and steer clear of his path. Come morning, I'll head for Tilburg. Being a day early, I'll simply rent a room if needed and wait out the time. Better there than here.

Wishing to be on that train this instant, I shove my belongings into my satchel. At the feel of my travel papers concealed inside, I recall Willem's mission.

Criminy. Do I summon him again to call it off? What if the forger has already agreed? Then again, Arie has been adamant. He's done with my help; his plans are handled, and it's time for me to go.

Frantic barking emerges from outside. Dropping my satchel on my bed, I go to the window and peek past the curtain. Under the dimming sky, patrollers are clearing the area for curfew, an evening standard. Yet a unique addition catches my eye. Led by a Nazi officer, a small knot of armed soldiers marches through the square in the direction of my building. Their leashed German shepherd releases more barks, unnerving echoes from the field executions.

A knock rattles my door, and I jump.

"Miss Hofman?" Mrs. van der Meer's Dutch greeting is recognizable, her tone, however, impassive. "Are you in?"

As the soldiers draw closer, I'm gripped by Arie's warning. He was right. The woman reported me.

She knocks again.

Eyeing the doorknob I've locked out of habit, I listen for the clink of a key ring.

Since my very first minute in this room, as is my habit, I identified a secondary means to exit: out my window, I could scale down the drainpipe. But that plan, while viable given a fire, would now land me in full view of the soldiers.

From the square comes a shout, baritone and forceful: "*Aufmachen!*"

The German order to open up is accentuated by pounding, rifle butts on a door. It shakes the windowpanes, and my heart pumps with matching force.

My gaze darts to my nightstand. Amid my valuables not yet packed sits my mirror compact, rigged with a compartment for secretive notes and, currently, my L-pill. I transferred the pea-size tablet from the convenience of my pocket, having no intention of ever ingesting cyanide; still, I couldn't bring myself to discard it, given the memory of Bram's words.

Hardly a sin to just keep the bloody thing, he urged at our final briefing when I balked at the offering due to my Catholic roots. *Believe me, there are situations worse than death.*

Stronger poundings reverberate. There's a scuffling in the hall and a floorboard creaks. Footsteps move away. Mrs. van der Meer is clearly adhering to the command. Perhaps she's ruled me collateral, a trade to bring her family home. Personally handing me over could ensure her credit. While she descends to the entry, I'll dash to another room in search of an alternative exit, at minimum a hiding spot less obvious than inside an armoire or under a bed.

At my night table, I sweep the stray items into my satchel with a hurried hand. Her footfalls sound on the stairs. I inch open my door and begin to creep into the hall. I startle at the feel of an object beneath my shoe—a tray?

On it are a slice of dark bread and a spoon. A bowl of stew sloshes with chunks of sugar beets, carrots, and cabbage. Dinner. I'd skipped it when I returned, food being the least of my cares.

Mrs. van der Meer's footsteps, I notice, aren't moving downward but up. Back to her residence. But what of the soldiers?

I close the door and race back to the window. The troops are still below but joined by a civilian in handcuffs. The man wears his shirtsleeves rolled up and hair tousled, as if interrupted while relaxing after a workday. A woman in a headscarf rushes out, calling to him as he's led away at gunpoint. It's then that I comprehend: the soldiers had paid a call to the neighboring building.

Tears return to my eyes. This time, born equally of relief and fear, they're a glaring reminder of the dangers all around, a message reinforced.

It's time to go home.

CHAPTER 65

The hours drag their insufferable feet. I toss fitfully in my bed, fending off visions of Arie crossing the square on his route to the hospital. Or reporting to Ziegler. Or doing whatever else he does during the night. As he always has.

The notion revives thoughts of his parents. According to Arie, they're aware only that he's using his military position to find his sister, not to what extent nor the distance he's come. How much, if anything, am I to tell them? Such a cruel duty couldn't possibly be mine, could it?

From my bedside candle, the orange flame casts a haunting dance over the walls. The sight takes me back to the orphanage. Instinctively, my thumb rubs the side of my finger, an old soothing pattern absent of wooden wheels.

The rhythm must eventually lull my mind because at some point I'm in a dream. My awareness that it isn't real is a welcome comfort on account of my surroundings, being the assembly hall of Eden Springs. Unlike so many nightmares of this place, I'm gratefully free of the stairwell and the terrors it holds. Rather I'm standing in the vacant main hall, where toppled chairs sprinkle otherwise neatly set rows.

Then I hear it: a baby's cry.

Through the hazy air, I trace the sound to an infant being soothed on the shoulder of a shaded figure. I remember this actual scene and think to look downward to locate the mother. There, lying on the floor in her yellow dress, she stares toward the high ceiling. Eyes open, lifeless.

Where is Father Lawrence? He needs to gently close them, letting her soul rest, preventing it from remaining stuck between worlds.

I walk over to the mother and kneel to assume the duty. I'm midreach when I observe her features.

She's not a stranger—she's Thea.

With a gasp, I scramble backward and bump into the side of the shaded figure's legs. In the person's arms is no longer a baby but a young girl, held protectively. She peers down with blue eyes as vibrant as Thea's, making clear she's Evelien. Then the face of the shaded figure turns to me. And in that instant, before my scream launches me from sleep, I realize I'm staring at myself.

CHAPTER 66

Being that it's Friday, the next morning train for Tilburg leaves at twenty to ten. From Utrecht Centraal, it travels down through Den Bosch to reach my destination, just north of the Belgian border.

For me to make that departure, however, is impossible on this day. Because already it's past nine, and I find myself returning to Arie's room. After I again pass stealthily through his bathroom window, his feelings over my presence are etched on his face. With his shirt untucked and only partially buttoned, he places his hands in his trouser pockets, not casually but rather as if to ground himself.

"Fen, look." He dives in before I'm able. "I appreciate your coming all this way—to Holland, I mean—and what you've done to try and help. But I can't have you ending up like the others. So I'm telling you once more: take the train, meet your contact, then stick with a guide to get you home." A degree of aggravation belies his message, my own emotions similarly at odds.

"I first need you to hear me out."

He expels a breath. "Please—not now." His tone is beseeching. "Yesterday, I shared a lot more with you than I'd ever planned. I'm sorry if it came out harsh, but I can't think about any of that today."

"Believe me," I tell him. "That's not why I'm here."

Although he quiets, morning light slipping past the curtain accentuates his still-tense jaw, speckled with shaving cream missed by his razor.

"I have an idea, specifically about transporting you and Evelien to safety."

He barely prevents a roll of his eyes. "I told you already. We can't go back to London."

"I'm talking about out of the city. To the farm. Only it could be in a fraction of the time it would take on foot, and without you dodging patrollers and checkpoints along the way."

Interest can't help but seep into his demeanor.

He just as soon shoves it down. "We're good as we are."

"Arie, she's a little girl—I assume with little legs. Any area around Gouda has to be, what…nine, ten hours away. And I'm guessing that's a straight shot. Are you planning to carry her there?"

"If I have to? Absolutely."

"While loaded up with enough food and water?"

"I'll pinch a bike if I need to."

"And what if you have to keep stopping, even camping out to avoid getting caught?"

With a slight hitch, he states, "I'll figure it out."

"Good grief, you're being stubborn." I add in a mutter, "And you call me a mule."

He yanks his hands from his pockets with fingers curled. Before his temper can further rally, I leap to the point. "The Brouwers."

The name hits him like a wall. Then molten steel enters his gaze and drips into his voice. "What about them?"

I wouldn't mention them unless wholly necessary, so he knows to keep listening.

"I was up last night thinking about Thea." After my nightmare, I had ample opportunity. "And I still couldn't make sense of it. Why would the Brouwers, after all this time, just suddenly turn the families in?"

He contemplates a mere instant. "Who cares why? I was there. The woman called them 'dirty Jews.' Said they forced themselves into the house."

"But that makes no sense. If it were true, she could have handed them over a year ago instead of taking huge risks by helping them hide. Not to mention feeding and caring for them all. Arie, there has to be another explanation."

The rationale settles on him, rendering him mute. But then he shakes his head as if to shed the theory. "Even so, what difference does it make now?"

"You said Mr. Brouwer deals in shipping."

He gives a shrug, more of a puzzlement than dismissive. "And?"

"Shipping companies are allowed to travel. Who knows how far they can haul cargo without raising suspicion?" For me, it's a question made rhetorical by Houdini's tours, moving freely about Europe with supplies in tow. Perhaps secretly with even a person or two. "At any rate, I'd say it's worth a visit to Mr. Brouwer. And if by chance he's willing, we could decide what to do then."

I wait as Arie rubs the back of his neck, frustrated. "I don't know. Maybe. I'll chew on it." He peers at me. "Either way, this is my responsibility, my family. I can manage from here."

"You're wrong." Before the remark can be misread, I assert, "It's my family too, Arie. The only one I have left." I'm immeasurably grateful he doesn't argue. "How could I ever face your parents knowing I could've done more?"

"Fen, I assure you, the last thing they'd want—"

"Above all, I owe this to Thea."

He stops and looks at me askance. But I'm not reaching for excuses.

"Without her realizing it, she left me a spot in a home with a bed and meals and folks who cared, keeping me safe." I'd slipped into Thea's shoes, quite literally, while her own journey took a heinous, undeserved turn. "Her daughter needs those very things now. Once I have a better sense you'll both be okay, I'll leave. I give you my word."

There's another reason, of course, which I choose not to voice—two, in fact, instilled by last night's dream: my yearning to protect a motherless child, to the point I'm able; and from the woman in a yellow dress, a reminder: when amid a tragedy of many, sometimes you can save just one. So regardless of the costs, you do.

Arie, surely comprehending this already, submits a nod.

CHAPTER 67

The cerulean dome of sunlit sky should induce tranquility. Instead, apprehension slinks through me as, once again, the minutes count down. Together yet separate, Arie and I left his rented room and rode the streetcar across the city, or "tram" translated from Dutch. With directions set to memory, I then followed him at a distance to a back alley. Behind the building that neighbors the tall brick structure housing Brouwer Transporten, I wait, obscured from the street.

Swear to me, Arie said before heading in. *If you don't see me in twenty minutes, you're gonna scram. Not a second past. I need you to swear it.* The sternness in his eyes befitted the risks he was about to take. Mind you, those risks shouldn't be his alone. We'd come here because of me; regardless, on this condition, he wouldn't budge. Thus, I agreed.

Now, by the hands of my watch, only seven minutes remain, and I'm still waiting for his signal.

This morning, though begrudgingly, he booked an appointment with Mr. Brouwer. Half past two was the earliest available. To ensure a private meeting, Arie claimed to be a "potential client with sensitive matters." Then he packed his pistol, stolen from a public bathhouse frequented by Nazi officers, I'd learned. And now I can't shake a vision of it pressed to Brouwer's skull, a coercive tactic if met by a refusal.

I recall the feel of that muzzle myself. Just two nights ago, before Arie knew it was me trailing him from the hospital, he'd threatened my life in similar fashion. He'd relented at my voice, but the question persists: How well do I really know him anymore? Our dynamic has changed. He's changed. Hardened, understandably. But to what end?

Then again, my theory on the Brouwers could be mistaken. What if they've genuinely sided with the Reich? By now, the gun could well have been wrested away and aimed back at Arie, the police already summoned.

I stare at the space that divides the two buildings. He'd taken that route to reach the front entrance, and for an instant, I fear it's the last I'll see of him.

A rustling from behind spins me around. A rat. It's foraging in a toppled barrel of trash. The rectangular loading area, hemmed in by a concrete wall, suddenly feels smaller.

Then comes a whistle. I turn. Arie is poking his head from a back door at Brouwer's. With fedora in hand, he waves me over, a grand relief. Though what occurred inside?

I peek down the alleyway that leads to the street, where a motorcar rumbles past. I hurry across to reach Arie. "Well? What did he say?"

"Not out here." The fact he ushers me through the door seems promising. As he shuts it behind us, I take in the warehouse that stretches to a high ceiling, where yellowish light bulbs shine from metal beams. Dominated by hammering, a pair of male voices echo through air that smells of cut lumber from the surrounding rows of crates. The containers range widely in size, the smaller ones pillared like toy blocks. The large ones are precisely what we'll need.

"Gosh, these are perfect," I exclaim quietly before noting Arie's lack of enthusiasm. "What is it? Was I wrong about the Brouwers, about their betrayal?"

He lifts a shoulder as if unsure but then shakes his head, the combination amounting to a soft *no*. A reason for relief if not for his pensive air. Most likely he's reflecting on the events that had followed. I fight an instinct to reach for him, given his rejection of my last attempt.

"And you believe him?"

Arie glances down briefly. As if irked by his own judgment, he supplies a low but definitive "Yeah."

I smile, encouraged. "That's good, then." I venture to press. "So he'll help us?"

Another shrug. "Your idea with a crate, he says it won't work."

Bewilderment tempers my indignance. I almost laugh. "I've used the trick onstage a hundred times. Did you share—"

He shushes me, alerting me of my growing volume. I lower it: "Direct me his way, and I'll gladly explain it myself."

Arie sighs and replaces his hat. "I warned him as much."

With that, he turns and leads me through a labyrinth to reach the base of an open staircase. "Got workers in view. Keep your head down," he says, then continues up the single flight toward what appears to be an office overhead.

From a quick survey, I trace the hammering to a couple fellows down below, assembling crates of various shapes. Near them, white sheets drape a chest-high statue—evident from an exposed hand made of stone—and sizable framed paintings lean against a wall. When one of the hunched workers stands to stretch, I heed Arie's warning, angling my face away until we enter through the door on the landing. There, he encloses us in the room with a lean suited gentleman. In his midforties and parked at his desk, he's staring off toward the shuttered windows that overlook the warehouse.

"*Meneer* Brouwer?" I prod.

He twists toward us and rises. Eyes woeful between his slicked chestnut hair and a handlebar mustache, he greets me in Dutch. "I am so sorry, miss, about your family. I dreaded that would happen, but still I was hopeful..." Clearly Arie has updated him, with an overview at least.

"Thank you," I say, though tentative; I'm not the one owed an apology. I regard Arie, who nods in my direction, indicating Brouwer's words aren't new to his ears.

"I beg of you not to blame my mother," the man continues. "The pressure had simply taken a toll. Our house was searched twice already, and she was struggling to eat and sleep." His insistence borders on a plea. "I was here at work when our neighbor's home was raided. Caught harboring Jews, they were marched into the street and—" He stops, the rest better left unsaid. "She was told there would be leniency, for any Jews also, if the surrender was voluntary. I was utterly heartsick when I learned—"

Arie interjects, stepping forward. "You told me you want to help." There's a restrained clip to his voice, an aversion to the topic, a lingering of resentment.

Brouwer can sense it. The guilt rides the creases of his face, the timbre of his reply. "I'd drive the truck for you myself, without question. I have clients scattered about and therefore travel papers for deliveries." He gestures toward the maps thumbtacked to the walls, red and blue lines suggesting routes. "But a crate concealment, I can say with confidence, regretfully is doomed to fail."

I try my best to be polite. "Sir, boxes with false bottoms are long proven to hide things, including people."

"Indeed. As the occupiers have well discovered," he adds gently. "I assure you, they have become exceptionally shrewd at comparing the inner and outer depths of containers, for that very reason."

My spirits sink, but only a degree. If my time with Hutton has taught me anything, it's the benefits of collaborating and of not giving up. "In that case, we'll have to craft something they haven't thought of. We'll put our minds together, for Evelien's sake." I look for agreement from Arie, who appears torn. Under the circumstances, we're far from his ideal team. I'd wager it doesn't help that an adequate design would result in tremendous dependence on Brouwer, including his discretion.

After a moment, Arie murmurs as if coaxing himself, "More than one solution to any problem..." The reference stems from our magic days, a callback to a time of our friendship, of trust. The memory equally warms and stings me as he exhales and turns to Brouwer.

"Got pencil and paper?"

"Yes. Yes, of course," the fellow says, his energy gathering. "Please have a seat while I lock the door." His face lightens with optimism, determination. An opportunity for redemption.

Perhaps for us both.

CHAPTER 68

The best illusions, remarkably, are rarely complex in design. They merely combine the three principles of magic: disguise, simulation, and distraction. Pulling off the escape we've devised will require a seamless balance of all three.

After a hefty bout of our strategizing, Arie rises from his chair, clutching his hat, itching to wrap up. He peeks past the blinds to see down into the warehouse, a safety measure, as Brouwer and I review the final sketch while seated at the desk.

Rooted in concepts from the Goblet Escape and even the classic sawing-a-lady-in-half, our plan will have Arie and Evelien fitting into a space that appears too small to hold a person, let alone two. The result will capitalize on presumptions, much like escape aids buried in boots and records. Shaving kits. Monopoly boards.

Earlier, as I pondered my prior schemes for inspiration, that last word emerged as a key factor. *Boards.* Not the gaming type; the kind made of wood. Our design therein took shape. Assisted by Arie's engineering skills and Brouwer's materials, we arrived at our "disguise."

What will appear a staggered pile of lumber—no more than a foot high, three feet wide, and imperceptibly bound—will hold a compartment for Arie and Evelien to lie closely together. Their small cut-out entry will require them to climb in as if sliding into a sidecar.

But how to conceal that opening? With misdirection, naturally.

Directly above, furtively bolted to the lumber, will sit a medium-size crate. After all, if a crate is sure to draw suspicion, we'll use that to our advantage: a predictable focal point. By sight alone, a guard would easily deduce that the box is far too short to smuggle a person. Meanwhile, the same way Charles would hide beneath the stage, Arie and Evelien will lay tucked in the boards below. Like a trapdoor, the bottom of the crate will be spring-loaded for removal. In essence, an access hatch.

Once the two are secured in place, Brouwer will stuff the box with artwork and shredded paper used as dunnage. Other small and medium containers, all bearing similar contents, will be piled on the boards and throughout the delivery truck. As an added precaution, stamps of *Fragile* or *Heavy* in both German and Dutch will mark every box. This should deter inspectors from ordering the vehicle to be unloaded.

Fortunately, Brouwer has a delivery due in Bodegraven, just north of Gouda. Pretending to get a bit lost while driving—hence, our "simulation" element—he'll stealthily drop off Arie and Evelien as close to their destination as is feasible.

"What's more," he stresses to me with significance, "I will include a case of brandy."

"Brandy? Why is that?"

Arie turns from the window. "For Germans who get nosy at checkpoints."

Brouwer nods. "Nowadays the value of money is less, but brandy can be bartered. Or drank."

Greasing the wheels, I recall. Hutton employed the technique to entice not only British suppliers but also German prison guards tempted by gifts.

And now we have our "distraction."

"Shall we go over the pickup details just once more?" I ask Brouwer.

"Most certainly." He's aware this is our last shot.

I ignore Arie's impatient fidgeting as Brouwer rattles off instructions, which can't be put to paper. The day after tomorrow, once the morning curfew lifts—as a night drive isn't an option—Brouwer will commute here from home, and under the guise of a VIP artwork delivery, he'll drive the loaded truck to pick up Arie and Evelien. The pair will be waiting at the deserted workshop. My idea. Conveniently located for Arie's purposes, it's discreetly accessible and lockable. And by then, it could hold the forged documents, no doubt useful even for fugitives who stay within the country, whether for everyday outings or in the event of a raid.

Today, thankfully, Arie isn't objecting.

"We really ought to go," he states and shoves on his hat.

I glance at the wall clock, confirming he's right. It's a quarter to four. Brouwer has warned us that a soldier will be swinging by in about an hour to pick up a shipment.

For Arie, limiting interactions with Brouwer is likely as much of a motivator.

"Indeed you should," the fellow replies pleasantly, and we both stand. "Rest assured, only one trusted worker will assist me with building and loading the contraption. Beyond that, he will be privy to no details."

Arie asks, "And what of your mother?" Despite his controlled tone, I detect an underlying resentment.

"She too will hear of nothing, for everyone's safety."

At Arie's lack of response, I chime in to sustain cordialness since we need this man on our side. "Thank you, Mr. Brouwer. I know you're taking an immense risk."

"I would do much more if I could. Your family, they are very dear to me."

Skipping genialities, Arie angles toward the door, but Brouwer thrusts out a hand. "Until Sunday."

Arie pauses at the offering.

Take the man's hand, my mind implores.

If only I could step in for him, but I can't.

Arie shifts a foot, as if to continue his exit, but then slowly reaches out and accepts the handshake.

Brouwer softens with relief, as do I.

The plans are set, my work complete.

Oddly, however, I feel no sense of closure. For it's a foreign and troubling thing, constructing an illusion I won't be present to perform, the reward for success being not applause but survival.

CHAPTER 69

At the rear door of Brouwer's building, Arie and I slip into the late-afternoon shadows, and I realize that this, right here, is where we part ways.

I rake my thoughts for anything more to review, not wanting to miss a detail.

Not wanting yet to leave.

"If you'd like," I say, "we can go over the plan again."

He shakes his head. "I appreciate that, but I've got it down pat. Besides, we really shouldn't dally around here."

Although reluctant, I nod.

He asks, "You sure you'll be okay, getting to Tilburg on your own?"

I think to answer: *It's me, remember? Going it alone is my specialty.* But I don't trust myself to express that with levity. From last night's discussion, a part of me remains bruised, defensive, ashamed.

"I'll be fine." I apply a smile that he fails to return, not unkindly; rather he meets my eyes with conviction.

"You be safe now. All right?" Reflexively, I'm about to reciprocate when he adds, "And thank you, Fen. For all of this."

The sincerity of his words, the care in them, moves me unexpectedly.

"It's the least I could do."

While burdensome to leave the unspoken between us, the alternative could wind up more damaging. I strive to keep the moment light. "Who knows? Maybe after this war is long over, I'll tour through Europe, and you and Evelien could come to a show."

Would they still be here?

I choose not to ask.

"I'd bet she'd like that." He smiles faintly, noncommittal. It matches his reply and suitably so. Our strained relationship aside, there's no guarantee the escapes will succeed, particularly when relying so heavily on others. The housekeeper, Gerda, for one.

Their "arrangement," Arie has divulged, began soon after Ziegler took Evelien. Seeking potential assets among the house staff, Arie trailed the cook on several occasions, only to discover her to be a devout champion of the Führer. In contrast, Gerda, he learned, regularly sneaks food from the Zieglers' to family and friends, evidence of her compassion and selectivity of Nazi laws.

In exchange for her help, aside from not reporting her crimes, he gives her food from the black market, enough to share. I'd still be wary of anyone in Ziegler's employ, except that two weeks ago, when Arie swung by her home to drop off food, she warned him of a message couriered to Ziegler: news that the Resistance member, the sham smuggler Arie handed over, had confessed the real location of the big meeting.

That tip-off very likely saved Arie's life. Possibly Evelien's too.

I pray the woman will come through again. I'd meet with her myself to make sure, but my meddling was to end here. So unless Arie requests otherwise, I refuse to once again break my word.

"About your folks," I say, nearly forgetting to ask, "how much do I tell them?"

"I got that handled, but thanks. I'll try to update them when I can."

Surprisingly, the exclusion leaves me more dispirited than relieved.

"Well," he says. "We should start for the tram. You ready?"

"As I'll ever be."

We both linger awkwardly, faced with how to say goodbye. A handshake, a shoulder pat. Those somehow seem worse than nothing at all.

"I'll scope out the street first," he offers.

Before I can respond, the rumbling of an engine catches my ear. At the squeak of brakes, our attention swings toward the side alley. The bleating of a horn precedes the sound of a car door shutting. My body stiffens.

Arie signals for me to stay put. He sidles up to a back corner of the building and hazards a peek. Hastily he retracts his head, nearly knocking off his fedora. "Krauts," he whispers, and my stomach folds.

The potential that Brouwer betrayed us hurtles through my mind. But then, why would the driver honk, declaring his presence? Early. The soldier arrived early.

Arie is scanning the surrounding concrete wall, a good nine feet high, when another door slams and a man barks out, "*Wer ist da?*"

The obvious German demand, asking who's there, indicates Arie was seen. Perhaps only the brim of his hat.

The driver didn't come alone. How many more are with him?

Boot steps are approaching.

We each have passable papers, yet how to explain our lurking back here? If Brouwer is questioned, the scheme could be ruined and Evelien's fate sealed.

"Let's go," Arie urges in a hushed voice. "I'll help you over the wall."

I nab his arm. "There's no time," I whisper, and besides, where would that leave him? He'd be hard pressed for a plausible reason to be prowling here alone. Suddenly a memory zips back, of being trapped by the canal with a similar excuse needed, of an SS officer turned abashed when caught staring.

I command Arie, "Play along." Willem's phrase.

"What are you—"

"*Trust me.*" As the boot steps draw near, I throw my arms around Arie's neck and pull him close. At the meeting of our lips, he flinches, his instinct to resist apparent. But recognizing my intent, he drops his shoulders and rests his hands at the sides of my unfastened coat. He kisses me back, fulfilling his role. My pulse quickens—a reaction, I note, purely from fear, as the amorous act feels starkly dutiful, detached, robotic. No rekindling of what was lost. Just performers following a script.

"*Was macht ihr hier?*"

Resembling Dutch, the question of what we're doing here announces the soldier has emerged. Arie and I break apart. We allow our feigned embarrassment to answer his query.

The soldier appears a bit startled, the desired response.

"*Bitte, verzeihen Sie uns,*" Arie replies, sounding of an apology. He goes on to say something about thinking we were alone. It's both fascinating and unsettling to hear him speak German so well.

The soldier, with his round face and ears protruding from his cap, looks exceptionally young—surely a plus. He continues to grasp his rifle but lowers it as he treads closer. When he lands before me, I expect him to hold out his hand for my identification. At his delay, I attempt to hasten the process with a phrase I've memorized, offering to show him.

At glacial speed, he surveys the front of my dress, down the length of my body. "*Ich will mehr als ihren Ausweis sehen.*" He's clearly saying he wants to see more than documents. He's pegged me for an easy girl.

I yearn to close my coat, but I sense he'll take the liberty of reopening it himself. My heart now thumping, I avoid his eyes. He drags his tongue across his bottom lip, slow and suggestive.

Arie steps forward.

In a swift motion, the soldier points his rifle at Arie, who interjects with an offer, it seems, to show his ID first. His tone is casual, yet I detect the clenching of his jaw.

The soldier studies him, sneering, basking in the power of his German uniform, his regulation weapon. But he's not the only one armed. I recall this as Arie, awaiting an answer, hovers his right hand over his coat pocket. Both his pass from Ziegler and loaded pistol are within reach.

My thoughts scramble over how to intervene, stopping him from what he surely longs to do. To make it out of here, to save Evelien, he needs to stay calm.

"Hahn!"

The soldier jerks at the name hollered down the side alley. Presumably the voice of another German. But Hahn doesn't reply. Gaze fixed on Arie, he wants to pull the trigger, perhaps his first kill. He's silently begging for Arie to give him an excuse. It's horrifyingly clear, as is Arie's thinning restraint.

I don't dare move an inch.

"Hahn! *Lass uns gehen!*" The German order comes louder.

Agitated, he yells back, "*Ja.*" He glances my way, his lips curling with disdain but also disappointment. A cat forced to free a mouse. Then he spits at the ground, barely missing Arie's shoe. "*Haut ab!*" He flicks his rifle, a brash command to clear out. With an arrogant stride, he proceeds around the building and out of sight.

I let out a breath, recovering. Arie is staring after the soldier, fists at his sides. He's still holding himself back.

Once the motor revs and fades, he walks, resolute, toward the side alley. He rechecks the area and confirms it's safe for us to leave. But there's no celebration, no regaling over our close call, only the simmering of his fury from being helpless, yet again, to react.

In doing so, of course, he likely saved us both. But my saying as much will do little good.

He tells me, "Go back to the closest stop and catch the tram. I'll join you on the next stop."

In the same manner as we came, we'll travel together but apart.

I nod, welcoming the chance to flee what had become a partially walled-in trap, and hurry off without another word.

Only when I climb aboard alone does it dawn on me that neither of us said goodbye.

As if but strangers, we sit on opposite ends of the transport. No interaction. No eye contact. Nothing to connect us.

The tram jostles and rattles down streets. Passengers get on and off, obscuring Arie from my periphery. When at last we approach his block, I grip my hands on my lap. Folks shuffle off, others on. Then the tram lurches forward, and I sneak a glance at Arie's seat. Another man has taken his place.

An ache sets in, a recurring throb. I refrain from looking out the window for reasons beyond caution.

The tram continues on its tracks.

From pondering what's to come, the dangers awaiting tomorrow, it takes me a moment to register the sound.

A blaring wail.

An air raid.

How can that be? It's daylight yet. Is it only a drill? Even if real, the alert is meant to give plenty of warning. But passengers are craning their necks out the windows, searching the skies.

The tram shudders to a halt, and I notice a hum woven into the rise and fall of the siren. I jump up and join the crowd pouring into the street. Amid the confusion, I trace the path of fingers pointing upward.

Dots. So many. Hundreds. A thousand. Sunlight reflects off what appear to be bare-aluminum bodies, suggesting American bombers. In their wakes, streaks of white vapor plow the blue sky as the buzzing grows.

Headed west, they'll drop their payloads on Hitler's factories. But not here. Here we're safe.

This is what I tell myself a split second before the scream. A woman gestures frantically to a bomber broken from the swarm, descending in a steep dive as if on a mission. Objects are falling from its underbelly, plunging toward the earth.

Bombs. Targeting the city. Civilians.

A man yells to take cover as a distant explosion reverberates. Smoke billows on the horizon, and panic sweeps through me.

The crowd is scattering. I need to find the closest shelter. But where?

Anti-aircraft guns are firing, the buzz surging. The planes and their contrails are blotting out the sun.

Through the commotion, someone grabs my hand, and I turn.

Arie.

"Come with me," he says, and so without thinking, I do.

CHAPTER 70

Through the blur of passing people and streets, I soon find myself ushered through a doorway. The siren has ended, if not the threat. Arie shuts us in, muffling the aircraft engines. We're back in his room, I realize. While largely below street level, we're not far enough underground for protection from impact. Yet he's striking a match at the table, lighting the candles as if to settle in.

"Arie, no. Stop. We have to get to a shelter."

"We'll be fine here," he assures me. "Honest."

Holing up with a horde of strangers could be a risk, more for him than me, though is it worth the chance of being blasted to pieces or buried by rubble?

And then I think: "The Zieglers'—do we rush there to grab Evelien?"

His extinguished match releases a waft of sulfur. "She'll be okay. Gerda said they use their cellar for air raids, and their guard goes in with them." He abandons his hat on the table and hurries to the window.

Unless vitally called for, never stray from the act. It's long been my mantra. But that was before an impulsive detour literally dropped me into Nazi-ruled territory, now being attacked by my own country.

Arie reaches up to slide his blackout curtain closed, though being spotted should be the least of our present worries.

"Didn't you see them out there? They're bombing the city."

"Nah, Fen. I saw them," he says, "but it looked like a B-24 just lost its engines."

"What are you talking about?"

He jerks his chin toward the window. "Listen close. What do you hear?"

Though incredulous, I strain to detect anything beyond the droning hum and anti-aircraft fire and finally grasp a sound. Specifically, the lack of one.

"No bombs exploding."

He nods. "Seemed the pilot was lightening its load over the edge of the city, trying to get home. The rest are flying out of ack-ack range, too high for any intended target."

Could he be right?

What if he's wrong?

As though reading my thoughts, he says, "Don't worry. If things get hairy, you'd better believe I'll be hightailing it to Ziegler's to go after the girl." Then shrugging out of his coat, he turns away. His words are a source of relief.

In theory, that is. My legs are still trembling, heart racing. A dizziness envelops my brain. Desperate for a grounding in every way, I find solidity against the nearest brick wall. There, I lower to sit on the floor, walloped by a culmination of adrenaline spikes and plummets, of nights scant with sleep, of emotions and memories exhumed and jumbled.

"Fen," I hear. "You okay?"

I'm tempted to burst into a mix of laughter and tears. Considering our current predicament, my scale of "okay" has become farcically relative.

He crouches before me and asserts gently, "I'm telling you, we'll be just fine."

I mean to nod but am unsure I do. He glances at my fingers shaking on my knees. Unable to still them, I wrap my arms around my middle, hands curled out of view.

"Hey," he says, "c'mere." He settles at my side and, without pause, places a strong but caring arm around my shoulders.

I detest ever appearing the damsel in distress, with Arie above all, yet I can't deny the comfort that flows through me in an all-encompassing wave. His velvety tone alone wraps me like a blanket. When I relax my head onto the curve of his collarbone, my heartbeat slows and shaking ebbs.

We sit that way for a good while, even after the rumbling of war fades, our inhales and exhales linking in an old, paired rhythm, like partners reunited in a long-ingrained waltz. The candle's flame sways over the walls, almost hypnotic.

That's when a revelation comes to me: how deeply I wish this moment would never end. For after fleeing a home, a state, even countries to protect us both in different ways, I wound up right here beside him, amid unspeakable dangers, unable to recall the last time I felt safer.

"Arie?" I keep my eyes down, not wanting to falter.

"Yeah."

"Tell me a story...will you? The way you used to."

Given our ages, let alone our surroundings, the notion must seem absurd. But his breath drifts out, suggestive of a warm laugh. "About pirates, you mean?"

I shake my head *no* against his shoulder, and I imagine he's scouring his memory.

"Knights and dragons?"

"A story about us."

His arm on me tenses, indicating I should stop there. Instead, with little left to lose, I close my eyes and describe the scene rolling through my mind, vivid as a film flickering on a screen. "A story," I tell him, "of the morning I'm about to walk out. How you come home early and refuse to let me leave, not without explaining. And because you're there with me, I find the courage to tell you why. Then you take me into your arms, and that overwhelming fear of mine, it all falls away."

I hear my voice splintering yet continue to push through. "When your parents get home, we burst out with the news because we can't possibly wait till supper. And the very next day, we dash off to the courthouse, just the four of us. It's nothing big or fancy as we exchange our vows. But everything about the day is beautiful and perfect, and we live happily ever after, together." Tears pool in my eyes as the vision fades. Still, I dare to lift my head and meet

Arie's gaze. His eyes too are glossed, which only adds to the emotion thickening my throat.

"You were right," I say, "about my being scared. Over losing you most of all. You always knew me better than anyone. Better than myself." And then I verbalize what should never have required such hardships to utter: "I love you, Arie—with everything in me. I always have." A tear slides down my cheek, trailed by another.

"Fen…" he says with a rasp. No words follow, but he moves a wisp of hair from my forehead and wipes my cheek with his thumb. The tenderness of his touch sends a flush over my skin. He bends slightly toward me as his hand cradles my face. He stills for an instant, our mouths just inches apart. I can barely breathe from the anticipation of his lips on mine. He's leaning closer, when suddenly he flinches and looks toward the window.

It's the sound of the all-clear signal.

The raid is over.

We sit unmoving through the solid alert. At its end, the silence between us expands, an invisible force pushing us apart. He withdraws his arm in an awkward motion. "You, uh…you should go. To keep safe." He's no longer meeting my eyes. "We'll use the window to be cautious, with folks back outside."

I struggle to respond as he stands. "Come on, then," he says softly. I hesitate at his extended hand. Against the weight of my thoughts, heavy as cast iron, I accept and manage to rise.

Promptly releasing me, he turns to lead me to the bathroom. I gather myself enough to swipe the moisture from my face and tread in his wake. While there's no time to untangle what just occurred, I do sense a lone surety: despite the outcome, I'll never regret the truths I shared.

Arie grips my waist, preparing to lift me from behind. Same as before, I'm to open the window and scan the area before climbing out.

"You ready?" he says, and I nod.

And wait.

At his delay, I listen for an outside noise, a voice, a reason for caution.

But then his grasp on me tightens and he draws me against him. His head lowers to mine. "Damn it all," he says, a murmur at my ear. The warmth of his breath seeps through my hair, sending blazing tingles over my neck and down my spine.

In his hold, unthinking, I rotate toward him, and all at once, we're kissing—deep, raw, and hungry—a feverish longing taking over. His hand in is my hair, the other running down my side. With my chest pressed to his, I feel the pounding of his heart and the burden of the layers dividing us. Guided by his steps, we move into the main room while shedding our clothes, both each other's and our own. The passioned frenzy soon delivers us to his bed, where skin passes over skin, as heated as our quickened breaths.

Until he stops.

He stares down at me, and I fear he's had second thoughts, come to his senses. Instead, what lies in his eyes is desire intertwined with something more powerful. Surpassing even forgiveness, it's pure, unbounded acceptance.

Threading my fingers with his, he raises my hands over my head, gently pressing them into the pillow. Braced by his forearms, slowing to an almost torturous pace, he leans down and places kisses on my neck, one after the other, a path to my lips. It's in this way that we savor every movement and emotion, each breathless sensation and indescribable connection, as if we have all the time in the world. As if in this moment, lost somewhere between day and night, between a dream and reality, a war isn't happening just beyond the door.

CHAPTER 71

Curled on my side, I drag my eyelids open and gradually register my blunder. At the sight of Arie in front of me, reclined in bed against the wall, I groan, having failed to keep awake.

"Was I out for long?"

"Not very."

"I don't even remember getting sleepy."

A corner of his mouth slides up. "Personally, I took it as a compliment." Candlelight accentuates the gleam in his eyes and the toned contours of his upper body, free of the blanket we're sharing. He continues to stroke my hair. From the lulling rhythm, no wonder I dozed off.

"Stop that now, or I'll fall back asleep."

"And what'd be wrong with that?"

The answer forms on my tongue, but I hold it there, swallow it down. Based on the withering of his smile, as if he's just recalled the reason, it needn't be said. I rest my arm across his middle, wishing I could forever anchor us to this spot.

"It's all right," he says. "It's only seven. I'll wake you in time to get back."

An hour left before curfew. The fact it will be here soon—too soon, along with tomorrow morning's train—causes a sinking in my chest. Over the quiet stretch that follows, I catch his gaze tracing the profile of my face, the curve of my neck, as if etching them to memory.

But none of that would be necessary, if only he'd reconsider.

I edge upright to sit, the grogginess clearing. "Arie, we don't need to go our separate ways. Not anymore. Come back with me—

you and Evelien both. We can work things out at headquarters. I'm certain of it."

While he doesn't concede, he's contemplating, a positive sign.

"We could ask Willem to vouch for you. Or Nel maybe?"

"No." Swift and firm. "Not her."

The possibility of an attraction, even feelings, between them sneaks back into my mind. Normally I'd avoid asking questions whose answers I feared, including Arie's. Particularly so. Yet absolute honesty has since shattered the barriers dividing us.

"Could I ask…if there's something between you two? Because if so, you could tell me."

His brow dips briefly in puzzlement. "Nah, it's nothing like that. She's a devoted wife, mother of three. Her husband's off at a German war factory, sabotaging parts. What with her capture, I just can't ask her for anything." He amends: "I won't."

I admit I'm relieved, about Nel if nothing else, until he adds, "All that besides, the escape line's out for me. It's dangerous enough for you, but for Evelien? Hiking the Alps, the steep inclines? The snow and cold, the rocky terrain, patrols. Just can't happen."

Good gracious. From my whirlwind preparation, I don't recollect such daunting specifics. Not that it would have deterred me from coming—or leaving. Toting a little one, though, changes the situation, and thus my conclusion.

"You're right."

He chuckles. "Can I get that on record?"

"Which is why," I tell him, "I'd like to stay." I'm merely expressing a desire, technically adhering to my promise. Still, his dimple vanishes.

"Nuh-uh. No."

"Just listen to me."

"I heard you, and I'm saying no." He drops his feet onto the floor and yanks his drawers on. As he starts toward the washbasin, I center on practicality.

"You *know* you could use a lookout."

"Yeah, got Nel's cousin for that." Without turning, Arie sips from a cup of water.

"Well, sure," I say, "from what he's told you. But you just met the guy. What if he doesn't show? And even if he does, what about at Ziegler's? If all goes to plan, Nel and her cousin will be long gone."

Arie sets down the cup and rounds to face me. "For pity's sake, Fen. This isn't like one of your dang picture shows."

"Actually, it's very much like those. Lucky for you, I've watched them a thousand times." I'm joking of course—mostly.

"You couldn't follow me even once without my knowing."

About this, he isn't wrong, though it does wound me a little. It also reminds me that I never got around to asking. "How *did* you know I was there? That night by the hospital."

He glances off with a roll of his eyes, the topic not a priority. "In front of the pub, when you were crouched in hiding, I saw a corner of your coat on the ground."

I wince. A rookie flub for one who deals in concealment.

"Look," he says, "that doesn't matter."

"Okay. What does?" I mean to corner him, causing him to stammer for an answer. Instead, he comes back with fervor.

"If anything happened to you, I couldn't live with myself." His eyes, the sheer worry in them, make me pause for an instant.

"Then I promise you that nothing will."

"You can't possibly promise that."

"Actually," I reply brightly, "I just did."

Cocking his head, he gives me a half-hearted glower. "You're insufferable."

"Not among my most flattering traits, but yes. I am."

His lips verge on a grin, but he battles it down. When he rakes his hair, angling away, I wrap myself in the blanket and stand. Moving toward him, I say, "Arie, I'm not about to leave you. Not ever again." Then vitally and in all sincerity, I add, "Not if you'll have me."

He releases a breath, softening. With the back of his hand, he caresses the length of my cheek and rests his thumb at my chin. "There's no guarantee our scheme will even work, Fen. It's just a plan. A hope."

While all that's a given and perfectly valid, I remind him, "So was coming here to find you." I have to smile, admitting, "In some ways, that might have been nuttier." This much earns his agreement, conveyed in a scrap of a laugh. Then his eyes lock with mine.

"You sure about this?"

Against the alternative, of potentially losing him again, I couldn't be surer of anything. For although happily-ever-afters rarely occur in reality, facing whatever lies ahead together will be more than enough.

By way of an answer, abandoning the blanket to the floor, I kiss him in a manner that makes this abundantly clear.

And I know right then that there will be no train ride in the morning. My unspoken understanding with Mrs. van der Meer further squelches my need to return before curfew. So here is where I'll stay for as long as I'm able.

As if sharing the thought, Arie takes me in his arms, and an irony settles over me. Despite embarking on the journey of a fugitive, I feel as though, for the first time in my life, I'm out of hiding. I'm free.

CHAPTER 72

The morning comes too quickly and passes just as fast.

How I wish I could stay in this room with Arie for another day, another week. But there's Evelien to consider, and Nel and her family.

Arie helps me into my coat, then guides me to face him. "Fen, listen, about tonight…"

I almost make a joke—about wishing I had a nickel for every time, during even the last few hours, he's had us review the plan *just once more*—but his heavy expression stalls my words.

"If anything goes wrong," he says, "if I'm not out of the hospital by seven thirty, I need you to go to Ziegler's."

Now comprehending, I shake my head to stop him, but he charges on. "Get Evelien to safety if you can. Just find the unlocked window we talked about. Once you're in the house—"

"There's no reason to tell me all this," I cut in. "We'll be going there together."

He pauses and brushes a stray hair from my eyes. "Remind me, what's the surest way to need a backup plan?"

I'm suddenly resentful of the dratted old stage lesson. Yet aware of its wisdom, I surrender my answer: "Not having one."

When he half smiles, I gear up to absorb every detail that remains, guaranteeing I won't have to use them.

In theory.

After I've repeated the new instructions back to Arie, twice, we share a kiss, not quite long enough to convey goodbye. No doubt a deliberate choice by us both. Then he helps me climb out his window. I stay crouched while peeking from the hedges.

The area is clear.

As I turn back, he reaches up and squeezes my hand. "Be careful out there."

"You do the same," I reply, not lightly. We each have preparations to complete, all carrying their own set of risks, before reuniting this evening for his plan—our plan.

Thus, savoring one last look at him, I let go of his grasp.

———

Arie would rather I limit my tasks, but he couldn't deny that my stopping by the abandoned workshop could be worth the trouble. Considering all the variables tonight, there's always a chance an obstacle could detour us to a different hideout. This would leave the IDs from Willem, if any await, out of reach.

As soon as I arrive, I go straight to the machinery and kneel to peer underneath. A thorough search produces nothing.

"Dang it…" Although Willem could yet come through, those odds are waning.

I suppose, either way, so long as we make it safely to the countryside—with Evelien and Arie below the crate and me in the passenger seat, acting as Brouwer's secretary or some such—we'll all be fine. Who knows? The farmer might have a forgery contact of his own.

More important at present is Arie's trip to the black market. Aside from quality cigarettes for distracting the entry guard, Arie intends to procure top-notch coffee for Nel's nurse. Spiked with sleep tonic, a small thermos of the brewed drink should prove irresistible to the gal, as she often complains, Arie said, about the bitter ersatz version she endures throughout her shift. Soon after, while they're still in Nel's room—and with Nel's help if needed—Arie's ether-soaked cloth will draw the nurse into a peaceful nap.

I confess, at moments, the idea seems overambitious. At one point, Arie questioned the same, before recalling the many news stories through the years of kidnappings and robberies performed in such a way. And mind you, while not ideal, should all fail with the nurse, one way or another, Evelien will be rescued.

For now, I revert to being hopeful—though a bit on edge.

As I approach Domplein, headed for my boarding room, a bell trills from across the street. Over my shoulder, I trace the ringing to a young girl on a bicycle. But it's a figure beyond her that ceases my steps. A tall fellow in a tweed cap looks quite a lot like...Willem.

A tram rolls between us, blocking my view as it stops. Passengers hustle on and off. And I realize: he must have arrived with the papers just as I left, spotted me in the distance, and set out to catch up. The tram now pulls away.

But he's gone.

Did he hop onboard? I survey the area. No trace of the man. Was it simply a case of wishful thinking? With features commonly Dutch, even partially obscured by a hat, he could have been a stranger. Most likely so, considering his disappearance.

A pair of armed patrollers, the mere sight of them, jars me back to my mission.

I forge on through the square.

Once settled in my room, I freshen up and change my outfit, readying for travel. While repacking my belongings, however, I'm slowed by distraction. The painting on the wall, featuring a trio of boys fishing—the van der Meer sons, I'd guess—reminds me of the many art pieces being packed and transported by Brouwer's company. The likes of which make me wonder...

Given the trials of wartime, who would splurge on such extravagance, and with what funds? Unless, that is, the collectibles were commandeered. Stolen by Nazis, like so much else.

I recoil from the probability of Brouwer's complicity. Yet in light of his help, which I too am depending on, who am I to condemn the concessions?

Another maddening gray area of war.

Through the gap beneath my door drifts the scent of boiling vegetables, affirming it's almost time. Fully packed, with travel documents concealed and gadgets reassembled, I store my satchel in my armoire. I check my watch and think through the plan. Again.

Scheduled for six on Saturdays, dinner upstairs will be served very shortly. Several bites into the meal, citing a queasy stomach and an early-morning train, I'll bid my goodbyes and declare a retirement to my room. A partial truth: food sounds entirely unappetizing due to the stress of the night ahead. Then with my belongings, I'll sneak down the stairs and out of the house for good.

At half past six, Arie and I are to meet Nel's cousin near the hospital, timed to coincide with the end of patients' meals and the start of the shift for our targeted nurse. Padding ourselves for curfew, we should have the benefit of traveling with ease as a group.

Before all that, of course, the dinner table here needs set.

I'm opening my door when Klara emerges from her room. Back from work, Dirk is loafing on their bed with a handcloth over his shoulder, having freshly scrubbed the engine grease from his fingers.

"Ida." Klara smiles. "We missed you at breakfast."

I smile back ruefully. "I'm just as sorry to have missed it." I'm preparing to deliver an excuse when a pounding noise interrupts.

"*Aufmachen!*"

Our faces swing toward the front door. The muffled command to open up is underscored by additional pounding, firm and rapid. A matching description now for my heartbeat. Rushed footsteps bring Mrs. van der Meer down from her floor. She shoots a troubled look our way before descending the next flight, confirming the knocks this time aren't for a neighbor.

Bolted upright, Dirk orders Klara into their room. As she dashes inside, I rush back into my quarters and shut the door. My mind spins. I fear again that Brouwer betrayed us. Or was I trailed here from Arie's?

Was the man by the tram indeed Willem? What if he agreed to help me just to locate Arie's hideout? After all, the communication line was compromised; why not by the contact assigned to us both?

Gunshots echo from a place unseen. With my curtains partly open to a mottled gray sky, I peek through the window. Spread throughout the square are men in the dark-green uniforms of the Ordnungspolizei. The German Order Police. They're barging into more buildings than ours.

It's a *razzia*.

Though not solely for me, it's still a raid.

I scan my room, noting its bareness. Too bare for a guest staying overnight.

Overlapping boot steps thud up the staircase. At least two men are charging this way.

I grab my satchel, toss out garments to look naturally strewn about, then heft the bag aside.

"*Ausweise!*" The call for our documents booms through the house. Fear scaling, I wrangle my identity card from my coat pocket. The hall floor creaks a mere second before my door flies open, and I suck in a breath.

The policeman is brandishing a rifle. He jerks the barrel toward the hallway, ordering me out.

I hustle past him and join Klara and Dirk. With backs to the wall and papers in hand, we stand before an "Orpo" officer. Bearing a widow's peak and prominent Adam's apple, in Dutch thick with a German accent, he demands of Mrs. van der Meer: "Your marriage booklet?"

She appears laudably composed. "I store it in my room, sir. Upstairs."

Trouwboekjes, listing marital details and lineage with children's dates of birth, are being used to sniff out *onderduikers* through discrepancies in count. I've heard that some police, at the slightest suspicion, shoot randomly at walls and floorboards to test for anyone in hiding. Just as likely to torment for amusement.

No doubt aware of this, the woman adds, "My husband and sons are all in Germany, sir, proudly serving the Third Reich."

From the start, I'd taken the claims about her family for fact, but are they? Nowadays everyone seems to have a secret.

The officer studies her, his eyes like a pair of black marbles, his holstered pistol within short reach. I brace for the verdict.

He orders the rifle-wielding policeman to go and check. The directive sounds more cursory than dubious, lessening my anxiety a fraction. As Mrs. van der Meer is escorted up the stairs, the officer turns back to us. "Any copper or brass in the house? Candlesticks, door handles, serving ware?"

"No, sir," Dirk says. "Not to our knowledge." A marginal hedge.

Klara reiterates with a shake of her head, gaze half-lowered. I do the same as two more "green police" arrive. Testing our denials, they plunder the couple's bedroom, seeking metals needed for ammunition. One rips through drawers, throwing clothes into a heap. The other upends the mattress and sifts through bedding.

I think of the visible remainders in my satchel, the gadgets packed among the clothing, all meant to withstand typical scrutiny. Praying they will, I glimpse Klara's quivering fingers. And I remember their listening to the BBC news on their wireless, risking imprisonment.

Are they hiding other crimes? Contraband, weapons? Acts punishable by death.

As the officer inspects our papers, noises from overhead—clunks and thuds—convey rummaging of the uppermost floor. How is it that copper, the insatiable thirst for it, has found me here, bringing more perils to my life?

Dirk clasps his wife's hand snug to his side. He too must have noticed her trembling.

"Exempt, I see," the officer reads with interest. "You must be a special man." He almost seems sincere before he inclines his head, skewering Dirk with a glower. "Special men deserve special jobs. Do you not agree?"

Through Dirk's silence, a spate of foreboding swamps me.

"How fortunate for you, I will ensure you have just that. In a factory in the Fatherland. I will even wait while you pack."

"No!" Klara bursts out, and the officer snaps toward her.

"What did you say?"

Dirk intervenes with strained placidness. "My wife is surprised, sir, that is all." He angles toward her, clutching both her hands with his. "It's okay, darling. We will get this sorted. I'll be back soon."

"Dirk, no…no, please," she begs, cheeks reddening, tears brimming.

I'm not entirely sure why I do it. Maybe it's the officer's flagrant malevolence, far too reminiscent of the soldier in the alley. Perhaps it's Klara's aspirations for a family, despite being absurdly idyllic—or because of precisely that. Maybe it's the couple's haunting resemblance to how I imagined Jacob and Thea lined up against a wall, lives teetering on the whim of another monster.

Whatever the reason, I interject regardless of all I stand to lose.

"Sir, you are positively right."

The faces of all three turn to me. The couple's eyes seem to ask: *What in God's name are you saying?*

"He is indeed a special worker," I clarify, "being a skilled mechanic who keeps trucks moving for the Führer." The static tension in the air implores I go further. "As such, even high-ranking SS officers in the area view him as indispensable."

The man shifts back to Dirk. Dry lips curling, he issues a cynical once-over. "Indispensable, they say?" He's awaiting a firsthand response. Dirk has mentioned compliments by service members whose rankings I'm unsure of, but he appears to comprehend that to agree or disagree would be taken as equally wrong.

"Sir, I simply do my best."

The officer's gaze lingers, then slings back to me. "Who?"

My mind stumbles. "Pardon me, sir?"

He overenunciates, sharpening each syllable. "To which high-ranking SS officers are you referring?"

The fear inside me is no longer just scaling but clawing, particularly as the two other policemen move on to pillage my room.

The officer presses, "I trust you have specific knowledge to make such a statement."

The detriment of not having an answer is as clear as his skepticism, even as I hear my furnishings being ransacked and my satchel shaken empty.

I push out the sole name in my arsenal, my mouth dry as dust.

"Sturmbannführer Ziegler, sir. For one." *Of course, how would I, a Dutch civilian and lowly woman, possibly know this?* "From what his wife has shared," I add, "at a recent ladies' breakfast."

The effect on the officer is slight but immediate. His scowl retracts with a twitch.

I could leave it at that, though better to give him a prideful way out. "This appears, sir, to be a simple, well-intended misunderstanding. I only wish that my friend here can one day make his mechanical skills just as useful to you."

He's assessing me, my bearing, my alleged connections.

In my periphery, hope seeps into the couple's faces still bent with confusion, now for a different reason.

At last, wordlessly, the officer hastily returns our documents. Dirk won't be transferred, it seems. A relief.

But then a policeman yells from my room, a German phrase I don't catch. The officer stares at me for a beat, my ID barely in my skirt pocket. Then he motions his head toward my door. "In. All of you."

Sweat prickles my scalp over what might have been said, what was found. Knowing nothing yet, I feign mild intrigue before complying with heavy feet. Klara and Dirk trail virtually on my heels. I don't dare meet their questioning eyes.

Another gunshot blasts, distantly. My hands ball up.

In my now-ravaged room, the officer strides past us. He traipses over my clothes, my undergarments among them, though I'm in no state for embarrassment. A few gadgets have rolled to the edges of the room: my cigarette filter and lipstick, both intact. He accepts a palm-size object from the taller of the policemen.

What is it? *What have they found?*

Suddenly I recall my pocket watch. I envision the American brand printed on its face. But if they uncovered that, they'd have everything—my papers and silk map, none of which I see.

Don't panic.

The other policeman observes us keenly, clutching his rifle, trigger finger ready. Finally the officer pivots toward me, and the discovery sets my heart to thrashing.

Whether dropped or stepped on, my powder compact lies in pieces, exposing a secret compartment, made evident by its contents.

"Explain this." More seething than an order.

The few scraps for notes inside are blank—thank heavens for that—but there's no rationalizing the L-pill. Or doesn't he have it? I don't see it in the compact nor in his hand. Where did it go?

I exaggerate a sigh, stalling, improvising. "Goodness, that is awfully unfortunate. It was such a handy contraption."

As he skulks toward me, I manage to trace the pill. It's a single stride from me on the floor. Yet should the officer take only two more steps, he's bound to crunch it under his boot. If he doesn't find it otherwise.

A clanking breaks out upstairs: pots and pans, a search through the kitchen.

An opportunity to misdirect.

I gasp and send my attention toward the ceiling. Instinctively the group looks up, rifle barrels following. A discreet flick of my shoe sends the pill under my bed frame.

"I apologize." I wince sheepishly. "Gunshots make me jittery."

Aggravated, the officer shoves the damaged compact toward me. "What is this?"

With an abashed shrug, I weave an answer threaded with truth. "Surely it will sound silly to you, sir. But the fact is, it's for magic."

He blinks, not expecting that. "Magic?"

"Yes, sir. My cousin planned to visit and enjoys the little tricks I do." I elaborate since the specifics can't be disproven. "By slipping a coin or button inside—even her name written on notes—I make them disappear. I would have gladly shown you if, well, if it weren't destroyed."

He arches a brow, his mouth an instant line against the inference of blame.

"Which is just fine, though, naturally." Scrambling for a mollifier, I glimpse a plausible prop amid my scattered clothes. "After all, I still have my playing cards for other tricks. As you can see there." I gesture, redirecting focus to my boxed sample deck—the map-embedded version. Thanks to Hutton's long-held insistence that a map is an evader's most valuable tool, I tossed it in as a backup and suddenly couldn't be more thankful.

"A performer," the officer scoffs. "Of card tricks. You?"

A measly girl, he means.

"Actually, I've always possessed quite a knack for them."

His eyes narrow to slits, and I recognize that the mocking I'd endured since girlhood has ruffled my defenses, an inane reflex.

Dirk intercedes, emphatic and chipper. "It is quite true, sir. The tricks she does are astounding. Isn't that right, darling?"

Klara responds with a touch of a stammer. "Yes...yes, that's right. While playing bridge in the evenings, she often performs for us. Truly she's...astounding!"

Their zealousness only adds to the officer's disbelief. He addresses me with a sneer. "Show me, then, if you are—as they claim—so *astounding*."

The couple trades quick, troubled looks; their repayment of my help has put all our lives in jeopardy.

But strictly if I'm proven a liar.

"Happily," I reply. I walk over to retrieve the deck, wishing I could tell them there's no reason for fretting. Although, my own confidence teeters when I slide out the cards and comprehend my challenge.

At the nightstand, I shuffle a full three times, to stall again, to think. Not only has it been several years since I specialized in close-up sleights of hand, it's been even longer since I've performed with cards not meant for magic. Marked Bicycle decks, Svengalis—these were central to my dime-museum tricks. And soon after, on our tour, Charles took over even those parts in our show.

Speeding through the dusty files of my mind, I hunt for a trick that requires no setup. I happen across one yet temper my joy. I still have to pull it off, and the technique poses more risk than I prefer.

To bar any quivering from my hands, I envision the Sugar Plum Fairy, my old preshow tactic to infuse grace and calm into my movements. With a measured flourish, I fan the deck facedown and extend it toward the officer. "Pick any card of your choice, sir. Then memorize it, and privately show others if you would like."

He hands my compact back to the tall policeman. Curiosity

encroaching on his skepticism, the officer does as I say, though shows no one. I square up the remaining cards.

"Now if you will, please tell me when to stop." I use my thumb to riffle a front corner of the deck, held seemingly out of my view. Roughly three-quarters through, he stops me. In the span of a blink, I use the edges of my vision to peek at the exposed card, thereby learning that the seven of clubs will sit just above his choice. I direct him to insert his selection into the spot he chose. Once he's done, I launch into overhand shuffles.

Each pass, despite my mixing the stack strategically in clumps, increases the gamble of separating the pair. But shuffling too little will raise suspicion.

The policemen watch in cryptic silence. I'm accustomed to working for the hard-won approval of servicemen in an audience. Just not any who are openly armed. Nor willing to kill me at the smallest provocation.

Maintaining my calm, I turn the deck faceup. Slowly I thumb through the cards. I alternate a hard stare between each one shown and the officer's face as if straining to read his thoughts. Through my hemming and hawing, I avoid Dirk and Klara, whose nerves can be felt clear across the room.

I'm halfway through the deck when I see the seven of clubs, indicating that the card directly preceding it—the four of hearts—*should* be the officer's pick.

"I believe that... Yes, I am sensing, sir, that *this* card is yours." Dramatically I slide out the four and display it for all to see.

There's no collective gasp, no applause. The officer is the sole person aware if my guess is correct. If he lies, only he would know.

A trace of amusement teases his lips—or is it a smirk?

"Give them to me." He holds out his hand, a startling order.

I pass over the deck, struck anew by the damning images it harbors. He examines several cards, holding them up, flipping them over. Surely he's just determining if it's a trick deck I used. I tell myself the map is undetectable, that my experimental sets required being soaked in water to reveal their hidden printings.

Not that samples can't have flaws.

Mustering a genial expression, I present my palm, gently inviting a return of the cards. But he keeps them in his clutches and issues a command without leaving my gaze.

"Take her outside."

CHAPTER 73

Women's cries are the first thing I hear, a mix of sobbing and pleading, when I'm marched out the front door. Storm clouds fittingly darken the sky. Through the square, a good half-dozen fellows are being led at gunpoint and loaded into a truck. Onto another, confiscated brass and copper items are tossed on a clattering heap. Loved ones—wives, sisters, mothers—struggle to reach their men, kept at bay by "green police" who belt out orders while shaking their fists and weapons.

I shiver in spite of my coat. Tied yet unbuttoned, it's the one addition I was instructed to take as Klara and Dirk watched with anxious eyes. "Don't worry. I'll see you soon," I told them, a repeat of Dirk's assurance. It felt just as false.

"Wait here," my escort says. He steps away to confer with another policeman, and a single word tears through my mind.

Run.

But armed police are spread about, not to mention soldiers high above in Dom Tower. How far could I get before drawing a spray of bullets despite the apparent shortage?

"Go." The guttural command comes from the Orpo officer, who suddenly appears at my side. He points me toward the truck, opting to accompany me himself. Apparently, any connection I might have to Ziegler's wife is too tenuous for him to fret over. That or he's concluded one doesn't exist.

I force my legs to cooperate even as my knees threaten to buckle. We pass the wall of women. Their desperate wails turn faint in my mind, smothered by my imaginings of likely destinations. Scheveningen Prison. Sachsenhausen Camp. The details I've heard, the horrors of them, revive a heeding from Bram. *There are situations worse than death,* he said, swaying me to carry a pill now gone, as is he.

The officer raises his hand, a signal. From behind the steering wheel, a driver nods. Then both trucks barrel forward, leaving exhaust fumes in their trail—and us.

I wonder if he's changed his mind, but he ushers me onward. I'm being taken elsewhere. Maybe only to be questioned. It's possible, isn't it? A wisp of hope rises through me.

After the winding stretch of two streets, heading south from Domplein and away from Arie—*oh mercy, Arie*—the officer guides us into a small alley.

My feet stop. I haven't a clue where we are, but it's not a police headquarters.

Is now the time to run?

"In here." He clutches my arm and steers me through an inconspicuous door.

It's a home, I realize, as we cross a narrow foyer. The parlor we enter abounds with Germans—all officers, it appears. But they aren't alone.

In unbuttoned tunics, they lounge on chairs and settees, kissing and fondling ladies scantily dressed. The women's lips are painted red. Other couples are pressed up against walls. Sickly sweet perfumes clash in the air. Straight from a decanter, a gal pours liquor into the mouths of Nazis. Underlying the chatter and giggles, a gramophone projects a warbly song in French.

My head aches, squeezed by the pressure of why I'm here. A barter for my freedom? Extortion for the Orpo officer's findings in my cards?

Perhaps, in truth, he found nothing, outside of an excuse for what I'm about to endure.

As we wade deeper into the room, the plum-colored walls close in. What will Arie do if I don't show? Will he bypass our hideout, Brouwer's pickup included, for fear our plan has been blown? Will he stay to search for me?

Evelien's safety needs to come first. He must know I understand that.

Still, there has to be a way out, something I can do…or use. I slip my hand into my coat's hidden pocket. My fingertips brush the folding knife. The small blade, while useless against a houseful of Nazis, can debilitate a lone man. If he doesn't see it coming.

Play along, I think.

Once we reach the far corner of the parlor, the officer opens a door. Dread surges through me as he stares, waiting for me to enter. I dare to inch forward, and though I'm delighted it's not a bedroom, the setting yet confounds me. Flanked by book-lined shelves and a mantled fireplace alight with flames, two officers sit at a table for four…

Is one of them Ziegler? Perhaps I'm being delivered as a test of my claim.

Then I recall the dinner party he's attending shortly, and I surmise—I hope—it would be near impossible for this to be him. Though why else would I be here?

My escort declares in German something involving boredom and refers to me as "*ein Geschenk.*" Two Dutch-like words.

A gift.

At the depraved implication, a dire voice screams in my head: *Why didn't you run?*

The duo turns our way, the yellow shade of a standing lamp tinting their pallor, before they wave me off.

But my escort prods me forward with a small shove and shuts the door. Then he shoves me again toward his comrades. "*Zaubertricks,*" he stresses, as if correcting their assumptions.

And it all becomes clear. *Magic tricks.*

The fellow with a double chin perks with interest while his companion, oval-faced with a broad nose, exudes indifference. They could almost pass for the comedy team of lean, grumpy Abbott and heavyset Costello—if not for the SS uniforms. Between them sits a chessboard, its white king toppled, and pint glasses half-filled with what looks to be beer.

As I reach the table, calming slightly, the Orpo officer pulls my cards from his pocket and tosses them onto the board.

"Entertain us," he says to me. The command doubles as a warning. He takes a seat between his friends, who eye me expectantly.

I'm a trained monkey performing on demand. In that light, even circus chimps are rewarded for pleasing a crowd. If, likewise, I manage to delight them, who knows? I just might make it back to Arie. Or make it out of here at all.

I paste on a smile for my audience and begin by recycling my previous trick, except with Costello choosing the card. He remarks only in German but seems to understand enough Dutch to follow my instructions. I use accompanying hand gestures to be safe. This time, confirmation of my success comes from the man's satisfied nod.

"Go again," Orpo says. "Something different now."

"Yes, sir." As I shuffle, I resist checking my watch. Added pressure will do me no good. I leaf through my mental files, my fate again hinging on my alleged skills, and an early trick returns to me. Its difficulty level rates quite low but will have to do, spiced with charm.

"In this case, gentlemen, there is no need for you to choose a card, since the next one will choose you." With deck in hand, I display what appears to be the top card. "The king of spades," I announce, concealing the card behind it, a classic move called the *double lift*. Briefly I rest the pair on the deck while adapting my patter.

"Unfortunately, as in real life, it can be difficult to control a king." I grandly slide the true top card into the middle, saying, "No matter where I place him, or how vigorously I move him about..." I riffle shuffle the deck thrice through, keeping the king subtly in place, then hold the deck toward Costello. "Even after a few firm taps to keep him down"—which the man does, indulgingly—"the crowned fellow always rises to the top." With that, I reveal the top card. Presto: the king of spades!

The officers murmur in moderate amusement, save for Abbott. When Orpo notes his friend's unimpressed yawn, I register the need to step up my act—while not coming off as professional. Thankfully, more tricks are flowing back. Thus, I dive right in, trying not to ponder the time or envision Arie waiting.

After a quick fanning of the deck, I invite a card selection from my uneager spectator, far from the first I've battled to win over. When he places his memorized pick on the deck, I secretly palm his card and request he do the honor of shuffling. "To make certain I'm not cheating," I explain, overly light, my hands deliberately in view. Once he stolidly obliges, I ask him to locate his card in the stack, which naturally he fails to do.

"That's rather odd." I motion toward his uniform. "Would you care to check your pockets, sir?"

His eyes betray his ascending interest, mirroring that of the other men, as he searches the pockets of his tunic and pants.

"Not there?" I mull. "Well then. Perhaps somehow——"

Abruptly, sounds from the next room——laughter and talking and Parisian music——crescendo from the opening of the door, turning us all.

Orpo encourages the guest, another officer, to come and join, then flaps his hand at me. "Continue!"

The door shuts.

I'm recalling where I left off when I notice the new arrival's gait, and my breath catches. His limp clues me in even before I recognize his face, chiseled and dashed with a thin brown mustache. The SS captain from the village. The cold-blooded *Hauptsturmführer*.

All at once, I recall the field executions, the lineup at the bus. Would he remember me from the morning after the night drop? Who's to say he's not still hunting the missing "fourth"?

"Go on, go on," Orpo says, impatient for my reveal.

Nearly dropping my palmed card, I aim to steady my hands, my voice, to resume with Abbott. "Perhaps, somehow…your card landed in my own pocket." I give my coat several pats, all while making my hands look empty. "How strange," I say, as the captain takes a seat at the table. "It *must* be in the room somewhere. It couldn't have simply vanished. Or could it?" For a mere moment, not dragging out the buildup, I concentrate on a spot in the air and lurch with my hand, snapping the card into view as if appearing out of nowhere.

A partial smile edges out of Abbott, boosted by chuckles from his first two pals. Yet their approval is suddenly the least of my concerns.

As the captain packs his pipe with tobacco, a compulsion bolts through me: to clear out of this room, to avoid his gaze.

"I am terribly sorry, gentlemen," I say regrettably, "but I really ought to return for dinner." I'm fast to add, "If you'll permit me."

Orpo responds as though I've not spoken. "Give us more."

But Abbott, then Costello weighs in, speaking German; they seem to have greater matters to discuss. As the captain lights his pipe, further choking the air with each smoky puff, Orpo ruminates. "One last trick," he grumbles, conceding. "Make it good."

In another time and place, the stipulation would mean little. Here, reinforced by the sight of his hand resting on his pistol, disapproval could end with a bullet to the head.

And so I begin to shuffle. I need to work fast while looking calm, perform well but not excessively so and, as much as possible, divert attention from myself. It's this last thought that spurs me to fumble, dropping half the deck onto the table.

A deliberate flub. I audibly gasp to help sell it.

The misdirection will allow me to set up the rest of the deck by flipping the bottom card in my grip while, reliably, at least one spectator— Costello in this case—reaches reflexively for the dropped cards.

Typically I hurry to regather the deck and continue with the trick that dazzled many a street crowd in Chicago. For once, however, I don't get that far.

In my rush, I neglect to identify a crucial factor: the pint glass in Costello's path. Seemingly in slow motion, the toppled beer spills an unhurried wave that spreads over the table, splashing the chessboard, drowning the cards.

It takes but an instant for me to grasp the situation, the disaster about to unfold.

Instinctively I lunge for the cards, but Costello holds me off, insisting all is fine. As an amends, surely more for his comrades than on my account, he swipes a linen napkin from the table and proceeds to dry off the casualties.

Trepidation mounts in my chest, not only from a vision of the cards peeling at the corners—revealing their markings of cities and towns, rivers and borders—but from the weight of a stare. Out of the corner of my eye, I catch the captain tilting his head, studying me as if I've struck as familiar, but from where?

I angle my face away, as much as I can without increasing suspicion.

Amid the quiet, flames crackle in the hearth. The rising heat permeates my skin, sending fine beads of perspiration from my pores.

At last Costello hands over the cards, and I smile, genuinely grateful, until I recall Orpo, who may very well demand I finish the trick. I turn to him, gripping the rigged deck, not knowing how it—or I—will survive another act.

"If it's all right with you, sir, with their being damp and, well, harder to maneuver—"

He huffs in annoyance. His decision could go either way. He could order a couple more tricks. Five. Ten. Not that the cards could last that long.

After an excruciating pause, he shoos me off in a pestered manner. "Go."

I fight the impulse to dash for the exit. With a quick bid of good night, still dodging the captain's gaze, I turn to leave as the men engage in their own conversation, my presence already discarded.

"Halt." The word, projected in my direction, pulls me to a standstill. I stare at the door an arm's length away, rooted by dread. Behind me come the sounds of a limping approach.

The captain remembers me.

Granted, any related details could be vague. And besides, I tell myself, there's nothing to connect me directly with the agents.

Unless any of them lived, that is, and confessed.

I need to keep calm, steady. Arranging an impassive face, I force myself to pivot back. I gauge his eyes for an awareness, but they give away nothing as he continues closer, one boot brushing the floor in small sweeps. Drops of sweat grow along my hairline. One of them slides slowly along my temple. I fight an urge to wipe it.

He stops just before me with pipe in hand, bringing a waft of smoke that assaults my nose. In a sudden motion, he raises an object in his other grip. I go rigid, remembering his pistol, his firing without hesitation.

"*Hier ist dein Karte,*" he says.

A card. It's only a card.

Producing a smile, I attempt to accept the offering. But he doesn't let go.

Between my fingers, I feel the edges of the card separating. Has he already noticed? Did he recognize the markings of a map?

Same as beside the bus, his gaze bores through me as if to root out thoughts I've stowed away, secrets for safekeeping. My pulse is so loud in my ears I wonder if he too can hear it.

Then the corners of his mouth creep upward, and he continues in German. He's insisting I do something again. Perform, I gather. I don't comprehend all his words, but I do catch these: *für mich.*

For me, he's saying. Not *us.*

He holds on to the card a full second or two more before relinquishing his grip.

I sustain my smile and nod politely. "*Danke schön, Herr Hauptsturmführer.*" In thanking him, I address him by his emblazoned SS rank as any respectful Dutch civilian would do. When I swivel to leave, I sense him watching me walk away. Fear burdens my every step as I close the door behind me and pass through the parlor, a single room that lasts a mile.

After making it to the street, I constrain my pace to a natural one until reaching a vacant stretch. My breaths quicken and hands shake, reactions my body withheld to keep me alive, to not raise alarms.

I long to rest and recover. But a glance at my watch affirms there's no time.

It's nearly a quarter to seven.

Through the dimming evening light, I look around to situate myself. Then in Arie's direction, prepared to use caution only when needed, I run.

CHAPTER 74

This time, I make sure something as foolish as my coat won't give me away. Entirely out of street view, I stay crouched beside a large metal container. A refuse vault by the looks of it. Nestled between shops, it sits in a rectangular inlet catty-corner from the intersection that leads to the hospital. As before, I wait in the shadows for Arie to appear, but now without the benefit of late-night darkness.

I'm not the sole anxious one here.

The man squatting next to me continues to murmur in Dutch. "Where are you, where are you?" With coat collar pulled up around his face, he looks ready to spring forward at the first sight of Nel. Understandably. Arie was hoping to be out by seven. It's sixteen minutes past. Only a bad sign, I tell myself, if he'd gone in precisely as planned.

He's already inside, Nel's cousin reported when I arrived. *He waited too long for you as it was.*

I didn't bother to explain my tardiness; it makes no difference at this point. Neither, I decide, will I worry about the contents of my satchel, all now irretrievable, including gadgets useful for the countryside— never mind my treasured pocket watch, my last remnant of Papa. Currently I have the wherewithal for just the issues at hand.

A rustling movement turns me. The cousin is standing and peering over the bin.

I demand in a whisper, "What are you doing?"

"I'm getting closer," he hisses.

We've been tasked with staying hidden from sight and watching for patrollers, so that when—not *if*—Nel emerges, we're to slip out and distract them while pretending to window shop, a rare if defendable activity past closing.

I start to remind him, but he hauls off across the street. It's vacant, fortunately, yet only at the moment. And though the police might be occupied with raids, a hospital guard will be posted.

I rush to intercede, barely remembering to snag the duffel Arie left for me. A sprinkling of rain dots my face as I catch up to the cousin, who slows at the corner and peeks around the building. "Stop," I whisper-shout. "If you're seen, you could endanger them both."

Almost an hour remains until curfew, but with most sensible folks already at home for both safety and weather, any activity can fast draw scrutiny.

He doesn't go farther, which reassures me until I note his hand in his coat pocket and the butt of a pistol in his grip. A surprising possession for someone not with the underground.

Or so his story goes.

Could he actually be a member? What if they've definitively ruled Arie a traitor? After Nel is freed, her cousin could have his own set of orders...

Then again, maybe, hopefully, Arie is right about my seeing too many picture shows.

The cousin checks his watch. I resist doing the same. Not that it helps. I feel the ticking of every second. Dutifully, I surveil our surroundings while clutching the duffel. At the thought of its contents—namely the travel food and escape aids, all hidden beyond Arie's personals—our discussion from this morning drifts back.

If anything goes wrong, Arie said, *if I'm not out of the hospital by seven thirty, I need you to go to Ziegler's. Get Evelien to safety if you can.*

That countdown now is going much too fast.

To combat my nerves, same as I did during our shows as kids, I visualize him completing each of our calculated steps. I imagine him in a janitor's coveralls, knocking out Nel's nurse with tonic and ether, dimming the room for the night, switching her uniform with—

"There he is." The cousin is peeking again around the building.

I refrain only briefly before hazarding a look past him. Arie is just outside the hospital entrance, back in his dark suit and hat, though without his overcoat. Assuming he wore it going in, either he forgot it or discarded it while rushing, a potential sign things didn't go smoothly.

But no, he's acting as planned, presenting a pack of cigarettes to the armed guard. The rationed tobacco is highly coveted next to the usual homegrown sort. When the guard reaches out, Arie purposely drops and spills the open box.

My deliberate fumble with the cards crashes back at me. I fear a similar disaster as Arie kneels with the soldier to collect the cigarettes, but right on cue, the door opens and a nurse walks past. When the guard glances up, Arie corrals the guy's focus onto their task.

Beside me, the cousin's murmurs—"Hurry up, go faster"—confirm the woman moving toward us is Nel, though I could gather as much from her steps. Stiff and wobbly, they resemble those of a person attempting a sober facade. Or, in this case, recovering from a head injury after weeks of confinement in a bed. The closer she gets, the more unstable she appears, and the faster my heart thrums.

If she collapses, even stumbles onto the cobblestones, what would we do?

Her cousin lifts his pistol to midchest. He seems to be gearing up for those very scenarios. Holding off the guard, however, would leave Arie stuck between.

Don't fall, Nel. Whatever you do, don't fall.

She has fewer than fifteen feet to go. A lock of dark hair slips from her nurse's cap as she trudges toward us.

Ten feet...

Five...

One...

The instant she rounds the corner, the cousin grabs hold of her, keeping her upright. She greets him with a weary smile, her face strikingly similar to typical mothers at the market, on the buses and trams, unsuspecting. Then I spot Arie starting our way, and a small burst of hope tunnels through my apprehension. How I wish he could break into a sprint without attracting notice.

In recalling my role, I gauge the street behind me. Still empty, both ways.

When I turn back around, Nel is leaning against the wall. Her cousin, no longer supporting her, has raised his pistol again. Finger on the trigger, he's readying to aim around the corner toward the guard.

Or is the target Arie? There's no way to know until he shoots.

The debate clashes in my head. If I delay intervening, I could be too late.

"*Halt!*"

My eyes dart toward the voice. It's the guard—except now there are two, and they're clutching their rifles. In the doorway, a man in a white coat is gesturing frantically. A doctor has discovered the swap.

Arie freezes with hands up, his back to the soldiers. Shock traps my breath as they proceed to advance on him.

Nel's cousin whips toward me and Nel. "*Get down.*" I can scarcely react before he booms toward Arie: "Run! Now!"

An eruption of firing obliterates the quiet. I drop to the ground and crouch with Nel. Our arms cover each other, a reciprocal shield. The bullets blast in both directions—*pop-pop-pop*—echoing like firecrackers prior to the war. I feel Nel trembling; maybe it's me. Surely it's both.

At the sound of shattering glass—a window nearby—I hug her closer, eyes down, breath held. I vaguely remember Arie too has a gun, just as the popping falls away.

In the silence, the shots resonate in my bones and reverberate in my ears.

"We go," the cousin orders and helps Nel to stand. She sends me a glance over her shoulder as he spirits her away, leaving me here alone.

Where is Arie?

My insides clench, wrested by panic. I scuttle to my feet. Stepping toward the corner, I run into a towering form. I gasp, expecting a guard.

But it's Arie.

Past him, halfway to the hospital, the soldiers are sprawled on the ground, either killed or wounded. Arie's hat sits solemnly, abandoned.

I throw my arms around his neck, propelled by relief. He retracts, for good reason. "We gotta go."

He's right. The gunfire alone is surely drawing German troops.

We turn for our planned path, and again I remember: "Your bag." I reverse and snag it, then charge forward while scanning the streets and windows. As he clutches his pistol tight to his body, I listen for yelling, for shooting, for sirens. A scattering of civilians, on bicycle and foot, are fleeing the area. Soon I spot a staircase.

"Down by the canal." I point. "We could stay off the road a ways."

Arie quickly deliberates through an exhale and nods.

When we reach the steps, finding no one below, I take the lead toward the boatless water. At the bottom of the stairs, I realize he's lagging, almost stopped. What does he see?

My gaze sweeps the canal, the bridges and walkways. "What is it?" I whisper to him, and that's when I notice.

He's leaning on a rail, struggling to descend. I hurry to his other side and assist him down. "What's wrong? Are you hurt?"

He doesn't answer through the last of the steps.

"Is it your leg? Your foot?"

From my hold on his upper arm, my fingers are warm and damp. I stop at the base of the stairs, registering the red smears on my hands. "Arie, you—your arm. You've been shot."

"It's just a graze. We've got to keep going." He tries to move past me.

"Arie—"

"I'm *fine*. We need to get to Ziegler's. When word of Nel reaches him, we'll never get Evelien out."

My mind races, seeing his logic, yet also my own. "I can at least put pressure on it. This will only take a second." Not waiting for his agreement, I set down his bag to search for a makeshift bandage, just as I once used on Charles for a gash during a rehearsal. But I don't get that far before glimpsing the belt on my coat. I untie and pull it off, then with wool socks from his duffel as padding, I wrap Arie's left arm over his jacket, covering a pair of small holes: one toward the front, the second toward the back. An indication the bullet passed through. That's a good thing, isn't it?

He grimaces from the knot.

"Does it feel like it'll stay?"

A sharp nod, and a breath.

"This is more than a graze, Arie." But I suspect he already knew that.

"It'll be all right. Let's go."

The faster we retrieve Evelien, the sooner we can get him proper care. Somehow.

Duffel in one hand, I grasp his elbow with my other to lend support. Along the canal, we stay tight to the weathered brick wall. He keeps pace as best as he can, clearly boosted by fortitude and adrenaline.

Eventually, a bridge blocks our path. We angle for the closest staircase, though I pause with a thought. "Arie, wait. You don't have to come."

He replies, slightly winded, "Look, I'm not up for arguing—"

"I can do it. Without you. It's not far, and you already gave me the instructions. I'll bring her down to you here, then we'll decide what to do."

He doesn't take time to ponder it. "After everything that's happened," he rasps, "I can't sit this one out."

In truth, I understand. For the same reason I first refused to go home, it's about repaying a debt, setting things right.

Albeit it's also maddening.

Together, then, we begin to climb the stairs, though halfway up, I tell him, "Stay back for a sec. I'll see if the area is clear." I am, after all, supposed to be the lookout.

Ascending high enough for a view, as a precaution, I wipe off my hands, thankful for my coat's dark fabric. In discreet fashion, I scan the dim street. A few civilians in the distance. No immediate sign of patrollers. The rain is picking up.

I turn to go back to help Arie, but he never stopped climbing. The stubborn man.

Once I resume my place at his side, he stores his gun in his pocket. Snuggled close, we tread forward like an amorous couple while concealing his belt-wrapped wound. With every passing building, every minute, I tamp my worries by trying to solve the problem: how to find a doctor. Rather than waiting for Brouwer to come to us, we could go to him—tonight. Except that we can't make it there by tram before curfew, and the walk is much too far, specifically in Arie's condition. How much blood would he lose by then?

"Hold on," he says. We wait for a man with a dog heading toward us to round the corner to our right. I realize we're in front of the large church Arie described. By my watch, it's twenty-four minutes to curfew. We had hoped to have Evelien already.

When the stranger is out of sight, Arie whispers, "At the next street, peek to the left and get a look at the house. It's the second one on your left side. See if there's a motorcar parked out front. And a posted guard."

I nod and hustle past the church and along the side of a neighboring house, each window covered for the night. Cautiously at the corner, I survey the specified home. Two-story and brick, it's impressively wide amid the narrow houses in the area. No motorcar, a good thing. Per the housekeeper, the Zieglers planned to leave for the party at a quarter past seven. Their armed guard, leaning beside the front door, whistles softly while staring off.

Ironically, worse than his presence would be his absence, leaving his whereabouts in question.

I return to Arie and report my findings.

"All right, then. Through here." He guides me on a narrow pathway between two sections of the church. After a few turns to round its smaller buildings, we squeeze through a damp wall of arborvitaes and enter an area adorned with trees and low hedges. We're in a private courtyard, enclosed by three walls of a C-shaped house. It's the back side of the Zieglers' home—one they've stolen from a local family, at any rate.

"There's the signal," Arie whispers. In the far-right upper window, a small mound of white cloth sits on a corner of the sill, subtle yet visible against the blackout shades. The go-ahead from Gerda is welcome yet daunting. Venturing illegally into any place, let alone one dark and unknown, would be unnerving even if it weren't a Nazi commander's home.

I follow Arie's trek to a window, the one farthest left on the main floor. "The bindings," he says, flicking his gaze at the duffel, a request. I put down the bag, and from the hidden compartments, I produce the pair of scarves and two strips of rope, noting his added challenge. How will he handle these using a single arm?

He stifles a groan as he struggles to slide the window open. "Help me, will you?"

I do, though I hesitate at the contortion of his features from the pain he's attempting to suppress. When he reaches for the supplies, I pull them to my chest. "No, wait."

"For what?"

"Arie, you're in no shape for this."

He clenches his jaw, impatient. "Hand them over once I'm in." Without letting me respond, he glances between the drapes, then tries to climb in with one hand. Almost immediately, his body contracts, rendering him breathless.

I cradle his face and angle it toward me. "*Please*, Arie, just think. I know what to do. And it will be faster if I go, and safer. We're a team now. You need to trust me. I can get her."

His reluctance remains, but his determination is wavering, pride yielding. I detect in his eyes that he finds sense in what I've said and, more than ever, that I have his trust. "I'll watch for the guard," he submits. A small relief.

As he moves out of the way, I stuff the supplies into my coat pockets and strive to level my nerves. I take my own peek and, by the slant of light I'm letting in, confirm the vacancy of a library. *Five minutes*. This will all take five minutes.

Pushing past the blackout drapes, I climb through the window and barely miss a wheeled cart. A collision with its decanters would have been disastrous.

I inhale a breath, and with it the scent of leatherbound books from the expanse of shelves. In the corner, a large globe hulks between two wingback chairs, huddled together like ancient scholars.

"Fen."

I spin toward the curtains, held open by Arie.

"Quick but quiet."

I nod, and he lets the drapes close. Vision adjusting, I cross the wooden floor and pad over an area rug to reach the door. I grip the ornate knob. At its squeak, I bristle.

And listen.

No consequential sound.

I resume my task, half an inch at a time, and open the door a smidge. Illumination from a distant room gives me pause. But again no noise. No indication of a worrisome presence.

Out of the library, I tiptoe through the hall. A trace of sweetness floats in the air. A recently baked pastry. It's a luxury denied most people and a reason to despise the Nazis even more, if that's possible.

French doors ajar on my left suggest a darkened ballroom. Following the diagram in my mind, I continue into the foyer. Blacked-out windows flank the front door, a mere slab of wood separating me from the guard. I push away the thought and turn for the lavish staircase set off from the parlor, in which a dimly lit chandelier highlights the room's finery.

To minimize noise, I tread up the side edge of the steps that after a short landing bank left. At the top, I hook right to enter a hallway and startle at a ghostly form.

My own, I realize, and breathe. It's only my shadowed reflection in a gilded mirror at the end of the hall. From beneath the last door on the right, the glow of a lamp marks my destination.

Quick but quiet.

I forge on, every tiny creak of the floorboards stalling my heart, until I grasp the doorknob. Hoping to high heaven this is the correct one, as there's no other way for me to verify it, I turn the knob slowly. The door opens a crack, enough to reveal a bedroom. My gaze drops to a figure on the floor, where a little girl sits on a rug. A pink bow hangs from the back of her dress.

Feeling more assured, I open the door wider. She twists and looks up from the doll in her hands. From her honey-colored braids to her sapphire eyes, she looks so much like Thea—a five-year-old version of her, as Arie said—that I can't find my words.

"Who are you?" a voice snaps in Dutch. Not from the girl. My attention jumps to a woman by the window. She's rising from a chair with a pinched face. A frilly maid's cap covers her hair.

And I remember: the housekeeper is expecting Arie.

"You're Gerda?" I say in her language, the question perfunctory. Or calamitous if the answer is no.

The lift of her head qualifies as a nod, barely.

"I've come for Evelien," I explain. "Her uncle"—unsure which name she knows Arie by, I default to ambiguity—"he's waiting outside."

Her skepticism is palpable. Perhaps she truly cares for Evelien. Either way, given the risks on Gerda's part, any deviation from the expected merits alarm.

"You can check for yourself." I try to speed this along. "Look down at the courtyard if you'd like."

Evelien watches Gerda. Past the shade, the woman strains to find Arie, who I suddenly realize could be hiding among the hedges, looking out for the guard.

When she rotates back to me, it's with a white cloth in her hand. Is the signal no longer needed? She doesn't say, just moves to the rug and kneels before Evelien. The long, gray skirt of Gerda's uniform pools between them. "You're going to go with this nice lady now. Understand, child?"

Evelien's gaze skitters between us, the scalloped collar of her floral dress nearly hunched to her ears. Gripping her doll, she launches herself at Gerda. The poor girl must view me as yet another stranger threatening to rip her from the life she knows.

Which I suppose I am.

She has every right to be wary, but with the guard out front, a hospital alert surely issued and, just as urgent, the need to tend to Arie's wound, we don't have time to waste.

I bend down and summon my cheeriest Dutch voice. "Want to know something, Evelien? When I was only a little older than you, I lived right next door to your mama and uncle. He's here, actually. Would you like to come see him?"

Her head swivels partway toward me. She doesn't move otherwise, just gauges me through the corner of her eye.

It occurs to me that her sole encounter with Arie was brief and frightful, and in a prison cell for that matter. But from stories and photographs, she's known of him all her life, the same way she's learned of her grandparents. This is according to Thea's letters, Arie has said, and I borrow that knowledge now.

"Eventually, your grandparents even let me live with them. And they became like a family to me, which means you and I are like family too." For emphasis, I give her shoulder a tender squeeze.

She only withdraws farther.

I scour for another tack. For years, my interactions with youngsters have largely been limited to those at my matinees, on the other side of an orchestra pit and with their parents at their sides. Although, I do recall how onstage as volunteers, they'd often beam from feeling in the know.

"I could be wrong," I muse, "but I'd venture to guess you're a big fan of secrets. Want to hear a splendid one?" Heartened by the flash of curiosity in her face, I lean forward and cup my mouth by her ear, not only to seem sly. It's best if Gerda doesn't know more, just as much for her sake.

I impart in a whisper, "Your uncle Arie and I are going on a thrilling adventure, to a place that's lovely and safe. We'll be staying at a farm with lots of space to run around. And loads of animals too, I'd bet. Do you like animals?"

I lean back to collect her answer. Her cupid lips twitch. Then she ekes out a nod.

"Well, marvelous." I smile. "Because if you come with me, you can see them too. How does that sound?" Encouraged by her pondering, I dare to reach for her hand. She accepts, thank goodness. As I draw her toward me, however, she recoils with a squeal.

Gerda is fast to soothe her. "It is all right, child." Then with an undertone of angst, she presses, "You need to go. Be a mindful girl."

Evelien clings even harder to Gerda and the doll.

I'm fighting back a rise of panic. Arie is waiting. What am I to do?

We'll never make it out if she explodes into a tantrum. I scan the room for a solution: a bribe, anything.

Rather, I'm jarred by the array of frills, so colorful and vibrant amid the grayness of war. The wallpaper of ivy and sunflowers, the chest of dolls and toys, the quilt-adorned bed sized for a child. I find myself wondering, in an elegant home scented by pastries, her clothing as neat and clean as her face and hair, could she be better off as she is? The world beyond these walls is far from paradise.

Just as soon, of course, I recall the horrors that led her here, the frailty of her position, the risks inherited through her blood. That's to say nothing of Ziegler's wife and the twisted nature of a relationship that crawls over my skin.

With tentative care, I reach for Evelien again, only to provoke another squeal.

In this disguised prison, she brings to mind a similar girl. Poppy at the orphanage. How she too feared leaving the comforts of her cage, needing just the right nudge, a small incentive to break free.

I don't have a magic book at my disposal. Perhaps second best is the very trick that first delighted Poppy, earning her initial trust.

Willing to try, I exaggerate a gasp. "Why, I almost forgot. I brought my special button." I yank the lowest button from my coat, and Evelien watches from behind her hunched shoulder. "Would you like to see what makes it special?"

I don't bother waiting for a reply that may or may not come. I simply dive into a quick succession of sleights of hand, making the tiny disc disappear and reappear, each time luring out more of Evelien's interest and the width of her smile. When it comes to the button dropping from her nose, eliciting a stifled giggle, I pray I've baited her enough.

I let out a forlorn sigh. "I'm afraid it's time for me to go now." Her brightness dims as if on a switch. "But," I tell her, "if you come with me and your uncle, I'll not only let you guard the magic button, I'll also teach you how to make it vanish. Would you like that?"

The girl is tempted, debating.

Gerda chimes in. "Your real mother would insist that you go. You may even take Marie with you."

Evelien studies her doll. After a moment, she eases away from Gerda and once more accepts my hand. This time, to my grand relief, she doesn't change her mind. As Gerda assists with the girl's coat and shoes, I stuff the bed with clothes to mimic a body. Should Ziegler's wife peek into the room tonight, as I suspect she's prone to do, any delay of discovery would help.

Then in the neighboring bedroom reserved for Gerda, I race to support her alibi by binding her ankles and wrists with rope. I hope it's enough to keep her safe. Following my short but heartfelt thanks, I use scarves to cover her eyes and mouth.

At last, I close the door and return to Evelien. I whisper as we move toward the staircase, "To be superb at magic, and especially escapes, you must first learn to be quiet as a mouse. Can you do that?"

She nods up at me in earnest, protecting the doll in the crook of her arm. This is precisely where it remains as I carry them down the steps on the balls of my feet to best prevent creaks. We're just past the landing when I hear it.

A rumbling motor, paired with a slam.

A car door.

My stomach leaps to my throat.

"Heil Hitler," a man greets, just outside. The guard.

I hold Evelien closer and sprint down the remaining stairs. I'm wheeling around the newel post when a rattling sounds, a fumbling of the doorknob.

The library is too far away.

Against the wall under the staircase sits a telephone table. On its far side, away from the entry, I crouch low in the shadows with Evelien in my arms. I press my finger to my lips, a silent *shh*, just as the front door bursts open.

It's Ziegler, I presume, glimpsing his black boots and wide breeches through the legs of the table. Abruptly I fear that Evelien might call out, even run to him. He could have tricked her into thinking he's a kind, fatherly type.

Then he hollers, "Gerda!"

And the girl shrinks into me. Her little limbs shake.

He hasn't fooled her at all.

I know right then: I'll do anything it takes to keep her from his clutches.

But why is he here? Was the event canceled?

He cusses in German as his boot steps cross the foyer, striding in the other direction. "*Wo ist das Geschenk?*" he shouts.

That word again. *Geschenk.* Now it references a different type of gift.

En route to the dinner party, he must have circled back, preferring tardiness to an empty-handed insult. He marches into the parlor, searching for either Gerda or the present. Regardless, this is our chance.

Holding Evelien tight, I dash toward the library—*quick but quiet.* Once inside, I set her down and close the door just to the frame, not latching it, remembering the squeak. At the open window, I cautiously peek past the drapes. "Arie," I project in a hushed tone, scanning the hedges.

"You got her?" he asks, jolting me. He's already in place.

"Ziegler's back. I'm passing Evelien through." I turn around to grab her.

But she's gone.

The door is open, her tiny figure barreling toward the foyer.

"Gerda!" His voice ricochets off the walls. He's growing angry. His footfalls verge on stomps.

If Evelien refuses to leave, how can I force her? I consider climbing out the window without her, but for only a split second. Instead, I steal across the room, chasing after her. I make it into the hall just as she picks up something by the telephone table—her doll. Then she flips around and hurries back in my direction.

"*Gerda!*" Ziegler is coming back this way.

I scoop Evelien up and run back into the library, this time going straight to the window. Arie is waiting there, anxious, with his good arm out.

"Go to your uncle," I whisper to Evelien. I try to pass her feet first, but one of her shoes gets caught in the curtains. I'm reversing her body to lead with her shoulders when a light flicks on. I cast a glance through the glare. In the doorway, beneath a peaked visor cap, the man's eyes are wide with shock.

"*Was mach ihr da?*" he blurts out, a demand to know what we're doing. His build and face appear unnaturally square, as if made of cinder blocks. It seems his feet are too, given the weight of his steps as he suddenly bounds toward me.

All at once, my neck jerks back. My scalp is screaming. I reach up and feel his hand in my hair before he yanks me aside and throws me to the floor. Rigged cards fly from my pocket, scattering around me. I look up and see Evelien disappearing through the window. Arie managed to hold onto her waist. But Ziegler is lunging into the drapes.

I scramble onto my knees, disoriented, trying to stand, and spot my pocket knife on the floor. I swipe it and open the blade as a muffled shriek passes through the window. Ziegler has a grasp on Evelien's leg. She's kicking hard, yet he refuses to let go.

Sheer instinct overrides any training I've had with a weapon. Lurching toward him, I raise the knife high and swing it toward his shoulder. I feel a piercing of skin, a burying of the full blade. A sharp groan bursts from his mouth and his elbow flies up, hurling me backward. He reaches for the knife protruding from his neck. Evelien is gone, saved.

The blade clatters to the floor. Ziegler turns to me with eyes black as ink, hand on his neck, blood flowing over his fingers. With his free hand, he draws his pistol from his holster.

In that moment, when the world shifts to an impossible slowness, the muzzle of the gun angling toward my face, I realize that it's over, that this is where my journey ends.

Then come the blasts. Two in a row.

My lungs suck in a breath, and Ziegler drops his gun. He steps toward me, staggering, before falling to his knees, then facedown on the floor.

"Fen...Fen..." The voice seeps into my ears as if sieved through cotton.

I turn to the window, where Arie is calling to me, struggling to wave me out with his gun in hand.

Registering the urgency, the need to leave, my mind gains enough clarity to clamber out the window. Evelien is standing nearby, clinging to her doll. I pick her up and rush away with Arie. "It'll be okay," I tell her as we pass through the courtyard and back toward the church, away from a man now shouting—the guard, no doubt—and a woman screaming. Ziegler's wife.

Through the shadows along the street, we travel as a knot. Carrying Evelien, I strive to support Arie, whose breathing grows heavier while navigating our path. Raindrops are thickening, coming faster.

Soon we arrive at a split in the road. We begin to veer right but stop.

Dutch police are gathered in the distance, perhaps just clearing the area for curfew. Though by now, authorities could be searching for Arie and Nel.

We change course and go left. We continue past homes and shops. Once again, there are police ahead. These ones are Germans.

We can't go forward. We can't go back.

A siren blares, an alert of the Gestapo coming for us.

But suddenly there are people. From every direction, they're filing out of buildings and onto the streets.

The alarm is an air raid.

Arie looks at me and swallows. I squeeze his hand, a signal of hope. Folks are heading to shelters, seeking out safety. Unaware, they'll serve as our personal stream of camouflage. If we hurry.

CHAPTER 75

The undulating siren, layered with the drone of passing planes, fades slightly when I heave the door closed. No indication of explosions—thus far. With a slide of the bolt, I secure the three of us inside the abandoned workshop. Dusky light through the windows creates a haunted aura.

Evelien stays at my side as Arie works his way to an adjacent wall. He settles on the floor with effort, half suppressing a groan, stoking my concerns.

The girl gives my hand a small tug. "Where are the animals?" Her Dutch words are taut. It's the first I've heard her speak. I brush droplets from her hair and face, gathering an answer.

"We'll be heading to the farm tomorrow." I infuse far more certainty into my tone than I possess. With Arie hurt, our plan calls for adjustment; to what length, I need to determine. "We're just going to rest before our travels. Okay?"

She chews on her bottom lip, her doll kept close, and nods.

It's a testament to her youthful innocence that she's still able to trust anyone, much less me. A practical stranger. She even grips my hand while accompanying me over to Arie. When I guide her to sit nearby, he gazes at her with a smile that emits both gratitude and pride.

"You're safe now." He sounds tired from our hastened trek. "You're going to be safe."

Surely bewildered by all that's happened, she simply regards Marie on her lap. As she smooths the doll's dress, I kneel before Arie and confer in English so as not to alarm the girl.

"The belt on your arm, is it tight enough? I can get something else, if there's anything you've packed in…" I glance around for the duffel, and my stomach sinks. "Oh no. Your bag—it's in the courtyard."

"I'm fine… The belt's plenty tight."

There was no time to do a single thing but race away. I'm frustrated, nonetheless, by my inability to better contain the damage. "Now we need to find you help."

"And we will," he agrees, "at the farm."

For a second, I think I've misremembered the timeline. "That's not till tomorrow."

He doesn't respond.

"Arie—"

"Check for our papers," he rasps. "Will you?"

"What?"

He raises his chin toward a back corner of the room. "Papers. Under the machinery, you said."

Indeed, they're one of the main reasons I suggested coming here, but our priorities have since changed. "Yes. But first, we need to figure out—"

"Just check. *Please.*" His priority—Evelien's safety—plainly remains the same. And really, it's taking longer for us to quibble than for me to tackle the request.

"All right." I stride over to the machinery, discernible from the lightness of its cobweb cloak. I squat and thoroughly search the contraption's underbelly, just as I did earlier today—a period that feels like ages ago.

Same as then, I find no packet or papers waiting.

I can't say I'm surprised. In fact, given my recent second-guessing of Willem, even coming here seems a risk. Although, where else would we go?

Again I lower onto my knees before him, empty-handed. "I'm so sorry."

He assures me with a tender smile, face glistening from the rain. "Worth a try." Shifting his body for comfort, he muffles a gasp, then closes his eyes and lays his head back against the wall.

From my desperation to do something, anything, an idea comes to me.

"Mrs. van der Meer—the druggist's wife. She'll be at a shelter now, but when the air raid is over, I bet she can send me to someone."

"No."

"By that, I mean any doctors she knows in the area—"

"Who could all be on alert," he finishes, eyes still shut. "Even trying to bring one here is bound to get us caught."

I yearn to dispute his points but can't, frustrating as they are. "Then I'll...I'll go to Brouwer."

Arie sighs as though weary of my badgering. He lifts his head to look at me. "After the shootings, Krauts will be scouring the streets. If Gerda cracks when she's questioned, if she gives up any descriptions, you'd better believe they'll find you."

I think of the officers at the brothel-like house, now well acquainted with my face. The SS captain among them. But still...

"Fen, you need to listen." Arie grasps my hand, rests it on his knee. "You promised me you'd try to get my niece to safety. Even without me."

My heart twists at his tone, one of preparing me for the worst. An outcome I'm not about to accept. I pull my hand back and correct him. "Only *if* you didn't come out of the hospital. But you did, and you're here. And we're staying together. That was our deal." I hold his gaze for a long moment, unfaltering. I'm gearing up to argue more staunchly than I've argued anything in my life when he replies.

"Okay."

The tension in my chest releases a fraction. "Okay?"

He smiles and touches my cheek. "Okay," he echoes. No doubt aware I'm about to press for particulars, he adds, "When Brouwer gets here, we'll see if he knows anyone to patch me up."

"But...that's still hours from now."

"It'll all work out, I promise."

This is a compromise, I suppose, not waiting until the farm. Grudgingly I admit, while not ideal, it's perhaps the most sensible choice. And anyway, I have no better suggestion.

I quickly remind myself of soldiers who have survived far worse. Among the Great War veterans I've met in London, some still carry around bullets in their aging yet otherwise healthy bodies, a peculiar bragging point at the pubs.

When at last the all clear sounds, I turn toward the window.

One threat over, leaving plenty of others.

"Evelien," Arie says and reverts to Dutch: "You enjoy games, don't you? Like playing hide-and-seek?"

The girl looks to me. I give her a small smile, encouraging her to answer, before I recall the significance of the reference. A code in her mother's letter for hiding.

Evelien responds with a nod.

"Well, good," he says. "Because for the trip we're taking, to get there, that's what we're going to play."

So that's what he's doing; he's preparing her for the crate. An important step I should have considered.

But then, together that's always been our greatest strength, balancing each other, bridging the other's gaps.

"All right, you two." Arie leans his head back against the wall. "Come over and try to get some sleep. Big day tomorrow."

Though still anxious about our plan, I find my home at his side. His right arm enwraps my shoulders, holding me close. I turn to Evelien to persuade her to join, wanting to keep her warm, but already she's scuttling over. Embracing Marie, she lays her head on my lap.

From the rhythm of Arie's breathing, woven with Evelien's and mine, I savor what comfort I can while bracing for the hours ahead. An endless night of sitting and waiting and eyeing the obscured windows for warnings.

CHAPTER 76

The blast of a gun jolts me awake.

Was it real or from a dream? My gaze zips around the room. I strain to remember where I am. No longer in Ziegler's house with a pistol pointed at my head, I'm here safe beside Arie, who's dozed off, same as Evelien. On the floor, the girl is nestled at my side like a kitten.

Dawn's early light hazes the air. I urge myself to relax against Arie, grateful to have survived the night uncaptured, before I glimpse my palm. It's coated with a rusty-brown substance—Arie's dried blood from earlier. But I'd wiped that off by the canal. It must be Ziegler's. Or gracious, is it mine? My memory flashes on the knife I'd swung, the bullets that flew, my hair grabbed and body thrown.

I tug back my coat sleeve, tracing smudged streaks down the underside of my forearm. Frantically I pat my limbs, then my torso in search of wounds I somehow missed.

There are none. A relief, until I think of Arie's left arm. I rush to assess it, terrified of how much blood he might have lost. But the makeshift bandage, though tainted, remains in place, snug and knotted.

Glancing down, I notice a hole. At the left side of his jacket, it's the kind created by a moth. Too closely, however, it resembles those in his sleeve. Bullet size.

Apprehensive, wary of disturbing him—as surely it's nothing—I slowly lift the bottom flap of his jacket. Removed from his trousers, suspenders encircle his waist, holding a wadded undershirt tightly to his side. The cotton fabric is soaked with shades of red and brown.

I sit upright, comprehending a second wound. He'd added pressure to it himself, but how without rousing me in the process? Unless he did it at the Zieglers', aware that all this time he was—

"Arie…" My voice scarcely amounts to a whisper.

I give him a nudge.

His eyes are serenely closed, his cheek set comfortably on his shoulder. But there's a difference about him. A paleness that churns my stomach.

I prod a bit stronger.

Nothing.

With trembling fingers, I touch his face. His ice-cold skin causes my hand to retract.

No…

No, no, no.

I grasp the collar of his coat for a shake, only to note the unnatural heaviness of his body. I probe his neck for a pulse. *Where is it? Blast it, why can't I find it?* Past a merciless wallop of shock glares the unconscionable:

Arie is gone.

My hands fly to my mouth, fending off the screams erupting in my head. My lungs are shallow. My brain is pounding.

This isn't happening.

It can't be.

I squeeze my eyes closed, needing this all to be a dream. Another nightmare from which Arie will wake me. At my bedside, he'll sit with me in the dark and spin stories until we tire. Then we'll find peace in the silence before drifting off, and a new day will start with the rise of the sun.

Though how could it? How will it ever? Without Arie on this earth, the world can't possibly keep turning.

A noise cuts in, and my eyes snap open. For it must be Arie; I'd simply made a mistake.

But it's the door shaking. A person trying to enter.

Evelien stirs beside my leg.

Vaguely I recall why we're here and the dangers lurking outside. My breath catches as the caller, abandoning the door, peers in through a dusty window.

Yet I know that face, the tweed cap. Willem came to help after all. Oh heavens…

That's precisely what we've been waiting for: help for Arie. Maybe it's not too late, if only we can find a pulse.

Any doubts about Willem no longer matter a whit.

Gently, swiftly, I swoop up Evelien. She's confused, drowsy with sleep. Her cheek rests on my shoulder. Her doll remains in her arms even as I hurry to unbolt the lock and usher Willem inside. He's barely closed the door when I launch into my plea, quietly in English to prevent frightening the girl.

"He needs your help, Willem—" My voice breaks. "Please."

His gaze slides to Arie, and all bemusement drops away. He hustles over and crouches before the tied-off arm.

"Under his jacket," I urge, "by his waist." As Willem investigates the hidden wound, I keep Evelien facing the other direction and feverishly battle back tears. "If only he'd told me…before Ziegler's, after getting Nel out…or during the air raid or…" I'm rambling, wrested by fear and guilt and hope. I need to stop, allowing Willem to better listen; he's pressing his ear to Arie's chest.

At the sight, an old scene flickers back: folks after the stampede trying to resuscitate those lined up on the floor. Some attempts even successful.

Still, I barely keep myself from interceding. I want to burst into shouts, order Arie to wake up, forbid him from leaving me.

And Evelien.

Us.

Willem turns back. Following a grave pause, he shakes his head.

Just that. A few inches of motion. It's a gesture people perform dozens of times a day, maybe more, with little thought or consequence. In this case, it confirms what part of me, perhaps near all of me, knew to be truth, and yet the message hits like a sledgehammer.

"I am terribly sorry," Willem offers.

I stare at Arie sitting alone, slumped and lifeless.

In my periphery, Willem rises and contends, "I will see to it that he is well cared for."

The finality of those words should reduce me to a blubbering mess, a heap on the floor even with the child in my arms. Instead, something inside me shifts. Separates. Turns off.

"Ida." Willem advances, after how long, I don't know. "The *moffen* are searching the city. With soldiers shot and a Gestapo officer dead— this Ziegler—if you are involved, they will not give up until they catch you. You must go."

Go...

Go where? Anything prior to this moment is mired in a fog.

Willem transfers an envelope from his coat pocket into mine. "Here are the papers, which they"—he amends—"that the child will need. But you must not depart from Utrecht Centraal. They will be inspecting everyone there closely. You have your own travel papers, yes?"

Depart. Inspecting. Travel papers.

"Ida," he persists.

A memory filters through, of being ushered from my boarding room by police.

"My...Dutch ID. The rest I had to leave."

He sighs and glances away, though he doesn't bother to delve. "It is fine," he decides. "Once you make contact with the escape line, they can handle it from there."

The references are coming to me, of Tilburg, the rendezvous I missed. The escape route Arie ruled out.

"We can't." I remember distantly. "I was to meet yesterday. They could be gone...and the mountain crossing, she's a little girl."

"Trust me, if you do not find them, they will find you," Willem assures me. "And no doubt they have helped many children, even younger. These are risks, yes, but now for you both, staying in Holland would be worse."

All sensible assertions. Even so, Arie had another reason for our avoiding the line: those involved might believe he betrayed the underground and...

The thought dissolves. The deterrent no longer exists, as neither does Arie, an unbearable notion that a force within me immediately stomps out.

Willem's expression abruptly hardens. Not at me but the windows, from the hum of an engine. He waves a silent warning to clear out of view. I oblige, robotically, as he takes up post by the door. Soon, a truck reverses into the alley, and a reminder burrows through my mind.

To care for Evelien.

Get her to safety.

Still carrying her close, I strain through my daze to watch the vehicle park. The driver climbs out and scurries toward the door. His lean profile, topped with a brimmed hat, streaks past the glass. Willem readies a knife from his coat, and a command tumbles from my mouth.

"Wait."

He ceases and stares. His eyes demand whether I'm sure.

Despite not feeling sure of anything—barely feeling at all—I issue a nod.

Willem retains the weapon though low at his side. He opens the door only partially.

The suited man with a handlebar mustache is indeed Mr. Brouwer, who, noting my unforeseen company, appears flustered. Without preamble, he whispers in Dutch, "I am afraid I do not have room for four."

Logic. Practicality. I too seize on these, somehow managing a level response. "It will be just me and the child."

Brouwer looks puzzled. Then surmising, or perhaps from a glimpse behind me, he extends a voice of compassion. "My dear…"

I refuse to hear the rest; the meager strands keeping me intact will otherwise snap clean apart. "We are now going to Tilburg."

"But," he says, "I thought—"

"Will you take us?"

Thrown off, he stammers. "I-I would gladly…yet I have no present clients in that area. Checkpoints will already be a gamble, but that close to the border will raise extraordinary suspicion."

Evelien raises her head. Lured by his voice, she rotates sleepily, inducing Brouwer to sigh. "Well, hello, little one." Smiling tenderly, he gives her arm a soft squeeze. Her choice not to recoil reminds me of the friendship and protection he long provided her family. Then a sadness mists his eyes, a tragedy mulled.

His gaze returns to me. "Den Bosch," he says. "It is less than an hour south. While driving, I can alter the paperwork just enough, and you could take a short train ride from there."

I regard Willem, who answers me without needing asked. "Before word spreads that far, it should be sufficient. You have funds for the train?"

He is right to wonder; those too were left behind in my satchel. Yet I happen to recall the hem of my coat, where I'd sewn in guilders before my night drop. A lesson owed again to Papa.

I'm about to supply a yes when Brouwer's face whips toward the street. The rumbling of a vehicle, several rather, grows somewhere in the distance. "We must hurry," he says. "Come." He waves me forward and heads for the truck.

I intend to follow, but defying their cue, my feet stick in place, cemented. They seem to acknowledge before my consciousness the colossal, irreversible effect of crossing the threshold. How do I bring myself to leave? Deserting Arie, let alone like this, is a scenario beyond conception.

"Don't," Willem warns. "If you wish to honor his sacrifice, you will go, and you will only look forward."

He understands. There's a peril in my saying goodbye, an utter undoing that would resign me to surrender and worse. I'd be useless to Evelien, and all would be for nothing.

At barest minimum, however, I need to ensure this:

"Swear to me, Willem, that he...that you'll..." I'm incapable of finishing.

"I swear it," he says, a vow to lay Arie properly to rest.

I nod, trying to relay gratitude in a glance. Then with Evelien in my arms, steeling myself, I push past the door that Willem immediately shuts. The sealing of a tomb.

Once more, there's no going back.

CHAPTER 77

At the rear of what resembles a large milk truck, I lift Evelien inside and climb in after her. Brouwer closes the door immediately behind us. Visibility dims but slightly, maintaining light from the windshield up front.

I trail Brouwer around piled cargo to reach the crate, our sketch brought to life. Marked as fragile and heavy and appearing too small to hide a person, it sits secretly bolted atop boards fastened in a stack. Their fresh-lumber scent permeates the space. Surrounding cases, several stamped *BRANDY* in German and *BRANDEWIJN* in Dutch, serve as diversionary props.

With the crate lid set aside, Brouwer pulls out objects shaped like vases and small sculptures, all wrapped in white fabric, along with cushioning dunnage, to reach the false bottom. Below this lies the rectangular compartment that will deliver Evelien to safety.

But first...

First, she needs to be prepared.

Limited in time, I reorder my thoughts, focusing strictly on what's ahead. As she rubs her eyes, I conjure a mask of normalcy and kneel before her. I nearly forget to speak Dutch. "For our trip...there have been some changes."

A tiny crease splits her brow, and her gaze raises to mine. "Will there still be animals?"

I hesitate, but then I think of the array of pets kept at the inn in Beaconsfield. "There will. And there are fields to run around in too. But to get there requires"—words from last night float back—"playing a game. Like hide-and-seek. Remember?"

She bobs her head *yes*. But will her agreement last the whole trip?

I recall a reliable incentive. "On the drive, if you're again quiet as a mouse, I'll let you keep the magic button as your own. Would you like that?"

She considers this and nods again.

Brouwer announces, "It is ready." He holds the false bottom at an upright angle, antsy to depart.

I peek inside. The exposed sidecar-like entry is just as we designed.

"All right, then," I say to Evelien. "Up we go." By her sides, I easily swoop her into the crate. I instruct her to slide into the compartment, but she merely clutches her doll. "Not to worry. The ride isn't all that long. And I'll be just up there"—I indicate the passenger seat—"close by the entire time."

Brouwer interjects, startled. "You won't be hiding with her?"

"Well...no." It occurs to me he didn't even know I was coming until he arrived; there had been no opportunity to share. "That is, I figure I'd ride along as a secretary, or perhaps a curator of sorts."

"But this is out of the question."

I'm about to assure him that I, specifically, am not being hunted, for now anyway, when he explains, "We cannot put the child in alone. At the checkpoints, a single peep will compromise us all."

Oh gosh. The reason, naturally, is sound, one I'd surely have contemplated in any other circumstance. Not that it would change my body's reaction now. The mere prospect of lying in the compartment, dark and enclosed, triggers a hollowness in my chest.

I scrounge for an alternative. "She can join me up front. I could be a niece of yours and she my daughter. Or a friend's daughter—"

Before I'm even done, he rules with a shake of his head.

"But she has papers," I insist.

"If she is known to be missing, it is still too risky, at least in the city."

Of course, there is no *if*. Her absence is well established.

Once more, I survey the wooden compartment suddenly reminiscent of a coffin, and the air steeply thickens. "There must be another way."

He appears less frustrated than befuddled. "The specifications of the compartment, they are just as you requested."

True. Though they were never intended for me.

"In small spaces, I—I just can't."

He seems to grasp the gist. Though when he exhales, it's laden with regret. "I deeply apologize, but you *must* ride inside with her. I cannot do this otherwise."

Every additional day that we stay, every hour, escalates our danger. And besides, going back into the building isn't an option.

Evelien chimes in with her small voice. "Is my uncle coming?"

The question slices through me, sudden and biting as a winter gale. I fight to keep steady. Centering on the apprehension in her eyes, I muster through only what's necessary. "He dearly wanted to. But I'm here. I'm here to protect you."

As the words leave my mouth, I'm reminded of my duty. My promise to Arie.

My final one.

Brouwer presses gently, "We could gather again later, to formulate a new plan—"

"No."

He blinks, uncertain, and I meet his eyes.

"I'll get inside."

Denying myself even a second to reconsider, I climb into the crate with Evelien. My breaths shorten as I step into the opening. Foreseeing the darkness ahead, I yearn for my lipstick light. Now gone. I turn to Brouwer. "A flashlight, do you have one?"

He thinks. "Nothing here," he says. More regret.

I can do this, can't I?

Oh, what if I can't?

A response emerges in my head: *It is okay, schatje. It is okay.*

Papa's words reassure me, bolstering my will. Before it can fade, I slide into the compartment and lie fully back. The boards cover me only to my hips. Brouwer assists in guiding Evelien to lay alongside me. All will be fine, I decide. This is all the two of us have to do. Just lie here for a bit.

But as Brouwer lowers the bottom slat, every inch of me goes rigid. Panic springs from the chasms of my mind.

I close my eyes to send my soul elsewhere. Any place peaceful and open and bright. Yet only nightmares come flooding back, of being trapped in a stairwell, a basement, a casket. A grave, buried alive.

An impulse shoots through me to scramble and jump out while I'm still able.

Right then, a hand grasps mine. Arie offering comfort.

Except he's not here.

It's Evelien, and her little hand isn't extending comfort but seeking it for herself. I catch the worry in her face an instant before all goes black. I feel her trembling, hear her quickened exhales. They persist through the rustling of the contents Brouwer is returning to the crate.

I bring our clasped hands to my chest. "Shh," I soothe raggedly. "Easy, now. Listen to my breaths. Just breathe." I detect the quiver in my own voice. Still, I force my breathing to slow. Gradually it submits, coaxing hers to do the same. I find the crown of her head and stroke it the way I imagine Thea would have done. "That's it," I assure her. "We're hiding together. See? Just playing a game."

Moments later, noises affirm the replacement of the lid. Then comes a thud and sliding. A case set on top, trapping us further. My heart contracts.

Brouwer asks, "Everything all right in there?"

Just breathe, I tell myself. *It is okay, it is okay.*

I have to be okay for Evelien.

I manage a "yes" that I'm not at all sure is audible until he says, "Then we are off."

Within seconds, the engine rumbles and we're rolling down the alley. The lumber around us vibrates and squeaks. A light clinking of glass travels from elsewhere in the truck. Our sway to the right suggests a left turn. Once straightened, we bump and rock over the first of many roads that will deliver us to Den Bosch.

If all goes as it should.

"Nice and calm," I murmur recurrently. To Evelien as much as myself.

The heat of our breaths turns the compartment humid as the drive continues, the route unseeable, the path unplanned.

This—all of this—so flagrantly defies my meticulously honed

system: testing, practicing, improving. Crafting a backup. Repeating the steps. Doing them again. Rechecking every tool and prop. Calculating for probabilities of success.

And yet here I am, in a last-minute slapdash scheme. Literally along for the ride. Equally unnerving, I'm doing precisely what I pledged to myself I would never allow again: I've placed my fate wholly in another's hands. And not for just my survival but Evelien's too.

"Checkpoint ahead." Brouwer is slowing the truck.

This is it.

I whisper to Evelien, "No sound, no movement. Or we lose the game. Understand?"

She nods on my arm. Our hands remain clasped despite the sweat dampening our palms.

When the vehicle stops, there's a voice. Presumably a guard. Hard to make out, same for Brouwer's words. Then a door opens and closes, and soon they're by the rear of the truck. The door swings open and their voices grow.

The exchange is friendly.

They know each other.

A remark from Brouwer—about a personal delivery to a high-ranking officer—reminds me that he isn't new to these drives, particularly for prominent clients.

A flipping of papers follows, a cargo manifest, I'd guess. Then silence. The guard must be surveying the boxes to reconcile them with the list.

I hold my breath as Evelien continues her soft inhales and exhales, all seeming amplified in the small, dark space.

The door slams.

Was that it? Could it have been that easy?

Brouwer climbs back into the front and shuts the door. The next thing I know, we're driving away.

"All clear," Brouwer proclaims.

A tiny part of me eases, though true relief won't come until we're free of this box. Rather, when we're safely through the mountains.

In the meantime, more rocking and bumping carry us onward.

Stretches of smoother roads come intermittently, each a lulling respite if not for our surroundings.

Once more, too soon, Brouwer gives the alert. "Checkpoint."

I direct Evelien to keep playing our game.

After we slow to a stop, a conversation follows, muffled as before. The door opens and closes. Brouwer has stepped out. But this time, as we await their arrival at the rear, Evelien grows squirmy, tired of being constrained.

I plead with quiet urgency, "Hold still now. Only a little longer."

She manages to comply just as a projection of voices confirms the opening of the back door. More flipping of papers. More discussion, the tone not as friendly. Then the truck sways.

Added weight.

Boot steps.

The guard has boarded. "Open these." His Dutch, tinged with a German accent, is razor sharp.

My panic springs back, further fueled by a revelation: harboring a fugitive is crime enough; one tied to the murder of an SS major could warrant a punishment worse than death, for everyone involved.

The truck sways again: Brouwer has joined.

Lids are removed, contents examined.

"What is here?" The guard thunks our crate with what sounds like a baton.

"Collectibles, sir. Rather valuable."

"Show me."

The lid is removed, then the artwork. The guard orders them unwrapped. He's checking for smuggled contraband mere inches above us.

I tell myself we're safe, that the false bottom, clicked into place, keeps us concealed deep inside. But the thought, meant to be calming, only shrinks the walls. I mentally push against the enclosure, stopping the boards from crushing us both.

The baton strikes the floor of the crate, testing, searching, just above Evelien. From the jolt, her shoe meets wood.

"Halt," the guard barks. "What was that?"

I lay my finger on Evelien's lips, demanding she go still, begging her.

Brouwer answers brightly, "Pardon my clumsiness." A wooden tap sounds, his attempt to replicate the noise. "I just thought you might care for some brandy." I envision him presenting a bottle from a case. "Today I so happen to have extra." His voice carries a faint strain that hopefully only I detect.

The guard doesn't reply. He's listening. For us.

Again, as Evelien's breathing continues, I withhold my own. But now a tickling rises in my throat. I fight the urge to clear it, even swallow against it; any of that might be heard.

Finally the guard responds. "I do not drink." He sounds bitter, as if appalled by the vice. Or maybe by the very offer, seeing it as suspect. A distraction. A bribe.

"Of course," Brouwer says. "Well. I will just pack this away for another—"

"Although"—the guard seems to reconsider—"the father of my girlfriend *does* choose to partake."

"Splendid!" Almost too excited, Brouwer bridles his tone as I continue to suppress a cough. "Here you are. Guaranteed to earn you the utmost approval from your future father-in-law."

A pause. "You think I need your gift for approval?"

The comment, clearly meant to be playful, invoked just the opposite. I imagine the guard's glare, sharp as the silence that now descends.

What if Brouwer is taken in? Arrested? How would we help him? What would become of us?

"I daresay," Brouwer replies, "if he is even the slightest like a typical German father, any fellow courting his daughter would certainly stand to benefit. Even the Führer himself."

The silence endures, cold as frost.

The joke was a great risk, blasphemous some would say. One that could get a man shot.

Then a soft sound arises. The guard's breath. A chuckle. And a moment later: "You may go."

CHAPTER 78

After the strenuous series of checkpoints, on a vacant side street near Station Den Bosch, we prepare in the truck to part ways. I pocket funds from the hem of my coat as Brouwer pats Evelien's head with affection. "You were so good and quiet, little one, yet again."

She smiles with a touch of pride while embracing her doll. I consider how often her family must have hidden from the enemy, requiring a great many risks by Brouwer.

Come to think of it, we never discussed how he'd handle the deliveries not initially planned for this area. I ask him, "How will you manage the drive back, what with all the cargo you have?"

"I have some ideas," he assures me. "And all include taking a vastly different route."

A necessity, I realize. The same checkpoints could be problematic.

He adds, "I am just sorry I cannot take you farther."

"Please don't be. Your help has been tremendous."

"It is small in comparison to what I wish I could do. But thank you." While his eyes remain pensive, a hint of relief rides his exhale. "Now then." He checks his watch. "A train from Utrecht should be coming through soon."

The prospect of what awaits, a gauntlet that spans all the way to Switzerland, tempts me to keep myself and Evelien right here in the truck. Of course, any such safety would be fleeting.

"We should go," I announce, more for me than anyone. "Thank you again, Mr. Brouwer."

He offers his hand with a caring look. "May our paths cross again," he says, "in a better world."

It's impossible to envision any future beyond the immediate challenges ahead. Still, I accept his handshake, grateful for the notion.

———————

Beneath the arched cover of the station platform, shaded from the morning sun, a pair of teenage boys sprints past to catch a departing train. The sweep of air causes me to shudder, sweat still dampening my scalp. Blindly I tuck errant strands of hair into place. I'd have applied powder and lipstick to lessen my dishevelment if I could.

Then again, a blander look is wise. Who knows how soon an alert of Evelien and our murder involvement will spread?

As it is, I'm wary of any stares. Given the Germans' Gilze-Rijen Air Base located just west of Tilburg, numerous airmen from the Luftwaffe are among the travelers awaiting our train. At my side, Evelien holds Marie in the crook of her arm while fiddling with her newly prized button, a token the girl has well earned. It was one of the few items still in my pocket, perhaps anchored by the last of my ale-soaked cards. Or maybe it's magical after all.

One can hope.

A dog erupts into barking, and Evelien grabs my hand. On a neighboring platform, the German shepherd stands leashed by a guard. Even after quieting, the animal appears eager to attack. Same for any number of soldiers patrolling the station, stopping people at will.

In my left pocket, I fidget with the tickets I've purchased, ready to show them to a train conductor when called for.

Evelien lets out a tiny groan, looking up at me. "I'm hungry."

Once more, I lament the belongings left behind, including the snacks for our trip. *Crud*—my ration coupons too. I glance about, weighing a desire to search for food at the risk of missing our transport.

I tell her, "The ride should take only twenty minutes or so. We can find something to eat when we get there. You'll be okay, won't you?"

Though reluctant, she nods. I summon a smile to thank her, giving her hand a tender squeeze.

I struggle to remember my own last meal. Despite a profound sense of emptiness, I find no appeal in the idea of food.

At last, our train chugs toward the platform. Folks prepare by folding up newspapers and gathering bags.

While walking here from the truck, I presented Evelien with her temporary name in the event she was asked. I retest her now. "Ready to go, Elisa?"

She nods again, this time with a knowing glint in her eyes.

After passengers disembark, I force a casual pace and guide Evelien to board, the button protectively in her fist. We settle into our seats. The air smells of perspiration. Following a slog of minutes, the locomotive pulls away.

A chance to relax, I think—wrongly. For right then, a couple of German soldiers enter the coach and scan the rows. I drop my gaze, matching many of the surrounding civilians. My nerves hum from another trap, a targeted search with nowhere to hide.

As the soldiers stride forward, they chat among themselves and claim seats at the end of the coach. They're traveling. Nothing more.

Their presence still provides reason for tension, though a bit less.

Then another soldier arrives, tall with severe features. I expect him to join the others. Rather, he yells for our papers, and the inspection begins.

An idea forms: a potential way for Evelien to dodge any questions he might ask.

The less talking, the better.

I lean toward her. "How about a nap, Elisa?" I issue a wink, signaling another game. Thankfully she takes the cue. Curling up with her doll, she lays her head on my lap and closes her eyes.

The soldier moves closer, bringing into view the silver metal plate that hangs from a chain around his neck. Shaped like a third of a moon, it features a golden Imperial Eagle underscored by a single word: *Feldgendarmerie*. German Military Police.

I manage to remain calm as the MP closely examines documents. Incredibly, he scrutinizes even those of German servicemen, confirming they're traveling with permission and within their limits. He doesn't take his duty lightly.

The train clacks and rocks over the tracks.

In preparation, I reach into my pocket for our papers. I leave those meant for Arie tucked away. The act sends a pang through my chest, intensifying to a stab when I glimpse the coloring on my wrist.

Arie's blood. Still there. Streaked down my arm, smudged across my hand. A tide of nausea and loss and fear crashes over me.

The MP inspects passengers just two rows ahead.

Madly, discreetly, I try to wipe off the marks, rubbing hard with my thumb.

The blood won't budge. My hands are shaking.

But they can't be. Not now.

I think of *The Nutcracker*, the Sugar Plum Fairy, the ease and grace in the dancer's movements. Yet my trembling continues. I can't make it stop.

The MP is a single row away.

That's when I hear the voice. A man's words in French. An intonation I recognize.

It yanks my attention over my shoulder. I find the back of the fellow who's speaking as he slides into a row. Ebony curls peek from his fedora, and for an instant, I'm sure I must be hallucinating. A product of exhaustion or desperately wishful thinking. Yet I recall the syllables I helped refine, transforming a rougher Cajun dialect to a suave European accent, in a crafting for the stage, for Charles.

He's here—but how? Arranged by Hutton? Sent here to guide me home? My mind swirls with confusion, though a concurrent wave of serenity envelops me. I feel a grounding in the familiar, an unexpected comfort from home. A reassurance that in a way I'm not facing this all on my own.

"*Ausweis.*"

The guard's demand swings me back. He towers over me with hand extended.

I pass over the papers, and my sleeve retracts slightly. To conceal the marks as best I can, I keep my palm downward and fingers closed. My hands have gone relatively still. I plant them across my waist regardless.

This is the first test of Evelien's ID, a trial run with no room for error. Slowly he studies me and the girl. One of her braids partially obscures her face, and I wonder if he'll demand a better look.

He regards our documents again. Has he noticed something off? I await a peppering of questions...that don't come. He simply returns our paperwork and moves along.

We've passed, for now. Of course, I can't fully relax until Charles too is cleared.

So as not to prompt suspicion, I resist turning around. The train hurtles forward. The cityscape blurs by. Anxiously I listen, waiting for the MP to finish. When finally he moves on to the next coach, I dare again to twist back, seeking a view of Charles's face.

Only to discover that the man in the fedora, with a snub nose and prominent overbite, is merely a stranger.

He was never Charles at all.

CHAPTER 79

A short walk from Station Tilburg leads to the secondhand bookshop Boekhandel Lange. Scents of ink, leather, and dusty pages greet me and Evelien at the door, where the tinkling of a bell announces our entry. Past a wall of newspapers and magazines, a lean, bespectacled clerk with dark hair glances from behind the counter, then promptly refocuses on the female customer before him. They're discussing her purchase in an apparent local dialect. Their accents are different but comprehensible.

The sole other stranger in the room is a man reclined in a corner chair. A brimmed hat rests over half his face. He keeps his legs crossed at the ankles and arms over his chest, napping.

Or maybe just waiting. Listening.

Could this be my contact? Was he seated the same yesterday when I failed to show?

I encourage Evelien, "Go on and look around, and we'll figure out your breakfast after I finish."

She agrees easily, intrigued by the muted rainbow of book covers on display. A slew of empty slots makes me wonder how many publications have been lost to Hitler's bans on anything deemed not in line with National Socialism.

Assembling my scripted lines, I venture toward the counter.

"And here is your change." The clerk presents the woman with coins, which she transfers to her handbag along with a book. "I apologize I cannot wrap it for you today."

"Oh, no bother." She understands: practically everything these days suffers from a shortage.

When she steps away, the clerk calls over to Evelien, "No touching the books, now." His tone resembles more of a reminder than a chiding as she peruses the shelves with the doll dangling at her side. Then his blue eyes turn to me; the fogginess in one implies partial blindness. "Yes, miss?"

I edge forward and attempt to sound natural while projecting loud enough for my presumed contact. "Good morning, sir. I'm looking for a first edition—"

"Darling, wake up." The woman jostles the man in the chair. "We can go."

After a snort, he adjusts his hat, then stretches as he stands and trails her out. He was but a customer.

"Miss?"

The clerk.

Slowly I turn back with looming dread. Did I lose my only chance by arriving a day late? Or is this clerk in fact the right person?

"You were saying?" He switches to standard Dutch.

Acutely aware this could be for naught and unsure where that would leave me and Evelien, I push myself to restart. "I'm looking for a first edition of *People Without Space*—for my uncle."

A beat passes. "For a special occasion?"

The question strikes as the correct response.

I perk cautiously and submit, "His birthday. He much prefers its author to the likes of Hendrik Marsman." In contrast to the referenced book, one long revered by the Nazis, the Dutch poet Marsman was supposedly killed by a U-boat while fleeing to Great Britain. The sentiment, expressed in reverse for safety, is a deliberate choice for the code.

However, the clerk doesn't reply. He just tilts his head as befuddlement crosses his face.

I brace for disappointment.

"Are you...Ida?"

Such relief rushes through me that tears prick my eyes. I answer with certainty. "I am."

He looks again at Evelien. "But you have a child."

Reminded of the upending of our plans, our lives irrevocably changed, I clench my jaw to keep myself intact. I explain simply, "She's family, and we leave together or not at all."

After a pause, the man turns sharply and strides away. It seems a rejection until he reaches the door, where he peers out the window and flips the sign to declare the shop closed. Then moving toward me, he's about to speak but stops short, an internal debate.

What is he not saying?

Evelien scampers back to my side. "Can we eat now?"

The clerk offers a smile I'm unable to read. "Come upstairs," he says. "We have food and will discuss everything further."

On the upper floor, in the kitchen of his modest home, the clerk hastens to clear the table of battered books in various stages of repair. "Sit and rest, and my daughter will prepare you both a meal. Perhaps some *hutspot*. Mixed with even a bit of sausage."

The teenager, bearing a petite if solid form, plants a fist on the hip of her skirt. "Father, you know we scarcely have enough—"

"You will feed them."

With eyes weary beyond her years and limp brown hair framing a pretty face, she expels a huff. But she then marches toward the cupboards.

Evelien tightens her hold on my hand, registering the tension. To ease it, I assure the clerk, "Sir, we would be more than glad to pay you." Aside from being fair, it's only practical. "As soon as we cross the border, we'll no longer need guilders."

"True...yes, but..." He struggles to finish. "That could be a while yet."

It seems we've arrived at the underlying issue.

"How long is a while?"

"A week—I believe. Possibly more. I am uncertain."

I gape at him. Given the circumstances, anything beyond a few days is eternity. "Why so long?"

Before he can answer, his daughter sets a plate of sliced bread firmly on the table. "Because your assigned mountain guide is dead. As are the two airmen he was escorting."

The clerk *tsks* at her. "The child," he says. His daughter looks away, incensed. But moisture glimmers in her eyes, a suggestion of grief, before she retreats to the stove in the corner.

He angles back to me, applying a smile. "I must return to the shop. When an update comes through, we will know more. Until then, the other safe houses are full, but you will stay here for now."

His daughter jumps in. "No. They can't! We already—" She catches herself and goes silent. I sense her fuming as her father waves Evelien and me toward the chairs at the table.

"Enjoy the bread," he says with forced cheer, "and we will get you some milk." With that, he joins his daughter at the stove, where they argue in low tones.

I lift Evelien into her seat. Once she starts eating, I proceed into the kitchen and interject quietly, "Please, there *must* be a way out sooner for us." I need to convey it's not a matter of impatience, yet without including details that would endanger these people more. "The girl… they're searching for her. The longer we stay, the more treacherous it could be for anyone around."

The clerk and his daughter absorb this, trading heavy glances. Then she says to her father, "There *is* another option."

He shushes at her to stop.

"What is it?" I ask. "Tell me."

He frowns. "It is no trip for a woman, much less a child."

"At least let me hear it." I press when he hesitates. "Sir."

He's vacillating, even as he concedes: "There's a boat headed for England."

"England?" I'm half thinking I misheard him. "When?"

His daughter answers for him. "Tonight."

A thrill must show in my face because the clerk adds sternly, "There are patrols to navigate, and the waves and currents. To say nothing of the Germans' Atlantic Wall defenses."

I've heard vaguely of the coastline fortifications—bunkers and batteries, anti-aircraft guns and trenches—having no idea how extensive they've become with so many countries to cover.

The teenager pipes in again, still directed at me. "My father is right about this, generally speaking. But manpower has been limited, same for materials and fuel, so construction here has been slow."

I attempt to clarify. "In other words, this leaves narrow openings through the waterways."

She nods. "There are indeed risks, but the skipper has done this many times."

On this point, the clerk seems unable to argue.

I consider the factors, weighing them as I've always done. If a boat crew plans to leave, they must believe they can sneak through. And it's not as if hiking the Swiss Alps was going to be easy street, as the guide and airmen's deaths have only further proven. Every train ride and stop, every safe house and contact, increases our odds of capture. That's presuming I could even acquire new travel papers...

Still all that aside, is sailing in darkness through the middle of a war complete insanity?

I look at Evelien nibbling on her bread. She appears so tiny in her chair, wholly reliant on me for protection. Our continued survival is based on impossible choices. On a feeling in my gut, a tug in my heart. On my hope that prayers and luck will be enough.

Gathering my courage, I turn back to the clerk. "Where do we board the boat?"

CHAPTER 80

Just northwest of Tilburg, the Biesbosch area is a natural hideaway for evaders, I learn. A web of creeks, islands, and estuaries forms a labyrinth in the freshwater delta region that leads to the North Sea. On the map imprinted in my mind, the distance from here to the English shore appears a mere hop, but reality and the potential of lurking Germans will lengthen the crossing like no other.

When it's finally dark enough, shortly after eleven, the skipper of the barge we've boarded directs the other passengers—seven males from teens to middle-age—to quietly pole us away from the river's edge. Viewed as potential Engelandvaarders, literally "England paddlers," we risk being captured by patrollers and dragged off to camps, if they don't shoot us first. Only when we're well away from the wharf and small surrounding town do we dare turn on the engine.

Under a hazy sky faint with moonlight, except for subtle shimmers, the water is black as tar. Halfway to the river's mouth, the skipper drops anchor and uses a boom to hoist our boat from the barge's hold, a smuggling tactic as cleverly basic as Russian dolls. Again the other passengers assist, guiding the smaller vessel as needed into the water.

I restrain my compulsion to help. They have it handled, and I have Evelien.

"Have you ever been in a small boat?" I whisper to prepare her. I haven't ridden in one myself since my childhood in Michigan.

She shakes her head with a sense of intrigue, unafraid.

At least that's one of us.

As we wait, I glimpse my silhouetted hands. I washed them clean in the clerk's home before departing for the bus. I can still envision the reddish-brown water swirling down the drain. Now, same as then, I refuse to mull. Thankfully within minutes, it's time for all but the skipper to pile into the smaller craft.

At ten feet long, with at least a third of it occupied by a motor, the boat isn't exactly spacious. One more reason my and Evelien's presence hasn't been celebrated by all. Following our handoff by the clerk's daughter in a shed at the wharf, two in the group were gracious and welcoming. The rest showed indifference or glowered. The addition of a useless child and woman wasn't part of their plan.

But we're here and squeezed in among them, the bunch of us brave or foolish. I keep Evelien on my lap, wrapped in a blanket gifted generously by the clerk. If only he could have supplied a life preserver as well. At the dock, none could be spared for a single one of us. My basic swimming skills will have to do if the sea grows tumultuous enough to—

I wad up the thought, toss it away with any others that will do us no good.

A long night awaits.

The skipper attaches a towline and reawakens the barge engine. All is quiet save for its rumbling and the buzz of our collective nerves.

Slowly our boat is towed downstream, conserving our gasoline and delaying our motor's signature sound for as long as possible. Each of us scans the darkness—for patrols, for noises, for movement—until at last the skipper idles the barge, this time to detach the line.

"*Succes*," he whispers, then sends us off and heads upstream.

We're on our own.

Through what appears a wide stretch of river, we float on the outgoing tide. After a couple miles, we near the river's mouth and one of the men starts the engine. I grimace at the sound, even more so after the escalating rumble sputters and coughs, then dies. The man tries the engine again, to the same result, except the effort perishes with more of a belch.

Anxious gazes skitter throughout the boat.

Another fellow nudges the man aside, his younger brother based on appearance. When this one has no better fortune, the two softly bicker through their alternating attempts.

I notice we're drifting. Toward the open sea. Without a working engine, we'll be at the mercy of the currents. Surely this raises our changes of becoming lost in every way. Swallowed up by the water, we could disappear without a trace.

I hold Evelien closer.

Just then, the motor comes to life. When it maintains, there's a groupwide exchange of smiles and sighs, though once on our way, our scanning and nervousness resume.

We tread at low power to limit noise from the engine. Our default captain, the elder sibling, blames the speed for his struggle with steering. After nearly grounding us into a sandbank, he says there's no choice but to accelerate. The obvious consequence is a volume that could very well get us caught.

I aim to stay calm for Evelien, even as we rock from a slight swell. We're entering the sea. Her head remains in the curve of my neck, her stray hairs fluttering. The spray from a wave catches the wind. Easterly. An advantage if it continues.

The captain increases our speed, raising the vessel's nose to best handle the swells. Still we rise and fall, water splashing. His brother periodically checks a compass by flashlight, its glow kept brief and confined by his coat.

We charge on for a good ten minutes before a passenger points in a warning. "*Moffen.*"

We all look and discover the silhouette of a German patrol boat crossing our bow, traveling north at a fast clip.

Instinctively I duck with Evelien. "Shh," I tell her as our motor drops to a purr. The captain keeps us idling, letting us sway with the waves. The plan goes without saying: we'll all stay silent, play statues, hope not to be seen as the Nazis pass through and out of range.

The groan of their engine wanes. But is it from distance, or are they slowing?

It's harder to discern while the brothers again quarrel in undertones. They're debating strategy when suddenly our boat lurches and speeds away, southward, parallel to Holland's coastline. The younger brother has taken charge. And now there's no question if we've been heard. A searchlight beams from the patrollers, sweeping their surroundings.

We have no option but to try to outrun them.

The misty air whips across my face. An edge of the blanket flaps behind me. I clasp Evelien's hand—solely for her. Strangely I feel no rise of panic. Perhaps I'm too tired, in every sense. Besides, there's no control to be gained nor benefits from fear.

"They're looking toward the coast," someone says in Dutch over the roar of our engine. Indeed, the searchlight is directed away from us. It shrinks by the second. Then the beam shuts off, snuffed out like a flame.

Sustaining the light could make them sitting ducks, I realize. We're not the only ones being hunted.

Our boat slows a bit, giving way to a droning sound. We look to the skies. The noise grows from an unseen aircraft. It could be Allied or German. Is the pilot's view of us clearer than the reverse? A strafing run could be the end of us all.

More searchlights flash on, these ones ahead in the distance. Seemingly from land. Or are they from additional patrol boats? It occurs to me we're being boxed in. But then the lights arc upward and a series of fireballs burst through the darkness. The chug-chugging of anti-aircraft guns indicates that the plane, at least, is on our side.

Our captain turns us west, away from it all. He and his brother are still testy but relieved, as are the rest of us. For now.

"Pretty," Evelien coos, pointing toward our wake. Green luminescence leaves a glowing, almost mystical trail.

I can't help but smile a little, not only at the irony in the setting but at the innocence that her life somehow, incredibly, hasn't crushed.

"It's beautiful," I agree and gaze back at the water until it fades to black.

Later in the night, tension returns at the sighting of two boats traveling together. They move so quickly a passenger assesses them to be British motor torpedo boats, yet for the chance they could be German *Schnellbooten*, the group decides it's best not to draw attention.

Hence, with the older brother firmly reasserting his duties, he simply slows our pace, hoping not to be spotted. Once the speedboats vanish from sight, he increases our speed and continues on.

The air turns colder as the winds pick up. My stomach goes slightly queasy from the worsening swells. A couple passengers look terribly ill. One retches off the side.

I do my best to protect Evelien from the insistent splashing that causes us to shiver. Seawater swishing in the boat seeps into my shoes, curling my toes, numbing them. Occasional peeps from Evelien denote when chilled drops have snuck past her blanket. I attempt to soothe her by quietly humming tunes, nearly matching the rhythm of water being scooped out in unison by an adult with a bucket and a teenager with a mug.

One of the passengers volunteers to climb forward to cover the bow with a tarpaulin to reduce the boat's intake of water. The motor is slowed to assist him. He's just finished attaching the oiled cloth and is crawling back when the dip of a wave causes him to slip. I gasp, thinking we've lost him. But another man catches his forearm, and the volunteer hangs off the side. A second helper yanks him back in, and after the shock of the ordeal, all three of them share a light chuckle.

Gradually the wind dies down, and with it the waves. I nod off in spurts, alternately lulled and jostled by the motion of the boat. Evelien quite nearly sleeps straight through.

With the eventual arrival of dawn, a transition I typically relish, also comes the shedding of night that cloaks us from the enemy. My one consolation is that the longer we travel, the greater our distance from occupied territory.

Once Evelien wakens, we share food from a wrapped bundle in my pocket: some cubes of cheese and baked pieces of potato, courtesy of the clerk. The midmorning sun warms our blanket. No land to be seen in any direction. All the passengers are alert. We're keeping lookout for distant specks in the sky and water, seeking friendly crafts of course, when a tiny cluster appears on the horizon. I blink hard to clear my vision, but the dots remain. A trail of them. Like ants marching toward their nest.

"There." I gesture. "Are those ships?"

All eyes home in on what resembles a convoy. Traveling north in this area, it would have to be the Allies. Several whoops and hoots break out on the boat, a presumption of the best. Our captain zips us straight toward the ships. My prayers that we're right are soon answered.

British sailors flock to railings, making it evident we too have been spotted. Toward the rear of the convoy, a destroyer slows and angles toward us. Relief flows through me, if not the sheer joy expressed by every man in our boat, unabashedly celebrating with hugs and tears.

As we approach, crewmen on the destroyer throw us a line and lower a rope ladder. I pass off Evelien to one of our group's stronger fellows, just long enough for him to carry her up piggyback to the ship. From there, surrounded by armed sailors—because goodness knows who we might truly be—we're all escorted belowdecks. In a wardroom, we're given soft bread and real butter, and naturally a pot of warm English tea.

Hours later, we dock at Harwich harbor, where police guide us into an assembly hall. They separate us to compare our accounts for discrepancies through multiple rounds of interrogations. I'm prepared to fight to keep Evelien with me, but they permit it without a battle. When all our answers are deemed acceptable, we're delivered to a canteen for dinner before our train ride bound for London.

A British sailor serving our table welcomes us as we settle in. I thank him, and he smiles at Evelien. "Well, aren't you a darling? Would you fancy a biscuit after your meal, luv? I believe you Americans call it a 'cookie.' Or perhaps I could scrounge up a lolly."

I'm about to explain that the girl speaks Dutch, preparing to translate for them both, yet Evelien beats me to a reply in her small voice, "Cookie, please."

Perfect English.

I gawk at her.

"Cookie it is." The sailor trots off toward the kitchen.

Of all the things Evelien learned from her mother, I might have guessed Thea's native tongue would be among them. But I know so little about this girl. And what she needs. And what, with any amount of certainty, we're to do next.

CHAPTER 81

Although back at the George in the safety of my room, I'm unable to release a full breath. I'm stuck between worlds, adrift. Rudderless.

I can't help but think I was foolish to ever leave the States. Had I remained on tour, perhaps Arie and I would never again have crossed paths. I wouldn't have known of the suspicions he'd raised, which led me to follow him across the sea. I wouldn't have been there to wake beside his body, somehow robbed of even a murmured goodbye.

Of course, without me, Evelien too might have been lost forever. And knowing this is even more maddening, for it's impossible to regret saving her young, defenseless life.

She rarely utters much. It's among several ways we make quite the pair, as I've never felt less sociable. She asks for candlelight while we sleep, and I've assured her I prefer the same. We share my bed, naturally. This doesn't prevent her nightmares, but at least when she cries out for her parents—as she does, at times, even during the day—I'm there to hold her and rock her until her tears run out.

Mine too have returned. Not the tears, which have strangely dried up within me, but nightmares that leave me trembling and sweating and dreading to fall back asleep. I guess it's unsurprising after the harrowing events of the prior week.

My word, was it that recent? Time is nothing if not peculiar, how it can reduce years to a blink and stretch days—nights even more so—into eons. The latter of which bring an onslaught of memories, if you allow such a thing.

I don't.

I strive not to anyhow.

Some still sneak through like water through cracks—fuel, more aptly, inflaming my anger. In the four days since returning to Beaconsfield, that's what I feel most: a simmering fury. At Hitler. The Nazis. The world.

At Arie.

Plainly he was aware of the shot to his side. Sure, he might have underestimated the severity or wasn't thinking clearly. Maybe he glommed onto a sense of invincibility as too many men do. More likely, he was being stubborn and playing the usual protector, keeping me from venturing out to seek help.

Granted, I admit...I would have done precisely that, regardless of consequences to me or others, Evelien included. And yes, with a low likelihood of success.

But here and now, I have no interest in logic. Not after what he did—or, just as inexcusably, what I did. Abandoning my defenses, surrendering my heart, and for what?

How naive of me, for even a moment, to view true happiness as anything but what it is: the cruelest illusion of all.

A roll of thunder reverberates through the pub at the inn, portending a gray day of rain suitable for the task awaiting me in London. Evelien flinches in the seat beside me.

From across the table, Hutton pulls the cigarette from his lips and beats me to an assurance. "Nothing to fret over, my dear." His eyes gaze brightly through his glasses. "They say it's just the giants playing bowls. Or the gods venting a bit of their anger."

Discharged from the hospital a week ago, he's back in his standard tweed suit. It's our second lunch visit since my escape with Evelien, who looks to me now for a final say—as has become her habit. Only a child would fail to see the shattered heap of my life, a floundering jumble that ought to preclude me from giving guidance to anyone.

Nonetheless, I nod and smile to put her at ease.

As she returns to the last of her sandwich, the sole other patrons in the room—an older couple—shuffle out and a trio of young girls

bounds in, all gaiety and giggles. I'm reminded it's Saturday; it's difficult to keep track anymore.

On the floor near the hearth, the girls unload game pieces from
a box: Snakes and Ladders, one of the many types of products I've
rigged with gadgets I no longer design. Even if asked to stay on with
MI9, I have no interest. My lone focus lies in bringing Evelien to the
States, far removed from the realities of war. But I'm finding that once
again, her required papers are difficult to procure.

I'm about to resume the topic with Hutton when one of the girls,
the manager's daughter, approaches Evelien with ribbon-bound hair
and a lilting British tone.

"Would you like to play with us?"

Predictably, Evelien's eyes invite my response.

"You may if you'd like," I say. "We have a little time yet."

She assumes a pleasant expression though follows the girl timidly
toward the game. Her trust in me would be endearing if I didn't feel
like an imposter, inadequate and unprepared.

My face must broadcast the thought, given Hutton's compassionate
look toward me, similar if less grave than his reaction to my news of
Arie, which I outlined in the sparsest of terms.

"I daresay," he offers, "you are doing quite a wonderful job of
mothering the girl."

"But I'm not her mother." I mean that with no distaste, merely to
honor Thea. "I haven't the slightest inkling what I'm doing."

He chuckles a bit. "Spoken like a genuine parent. Even an army
general, for that matter." He jabs his cigarette in the air for emphasis.
"If two wars have taught me a thing, it is that an embarrassingly large
portion of military strategy is conjured as one goes along."

I smile only because it seems a natural response.

Then he sips from his teacup and takes another drag. Emitting his
typical restive energy, minus the franticness and paranoia that led to
his breaking point, he's again agreed to help. And I'm immensely
thankful. Particularly after he confirmed with deep sincerity what I
had hoped: that he knew nothing of the brass's duplicity involving my
assignment to lure Arie out.

This is presuming, mind you, that Lenora correctly assessed Crockatt's discussion. To learn the truth, I could broach the matter personally, but not without compromising Lenora's position. Besides, what response would I get other than a denial? And either way, what would any answer change?

"So at the embassy," I say, circling back to the subject of Evelien, "is there anyone else you might have luck with?"

Hutton sighs, releasing a puff of smoke. "Although naturally I would be delighted to try, I suspect we won't fare any better. At least for a time." Before I can prod further, he leans forward to continue, either covertly or eager. "I have, rather, been tickled by an alternative idea."

Children are the only others in the room. I incline toward him regardless, aware he isn't always one for abiding by rules. "Which is?"

"As a child, you were raised Catholic, were you not?"

The tidbit is one of many I shared during our sessions developing gadgets, yet I'm unsure how it relates. "In my early years. Why do you ask?"

"Perhaps a sponsorship through the church would be more attainable. I understand the priests are being quite helpful in this respect."

I sink back in my seat. I suppose I was hoping for a bolder tactic than letter writing and waiting and hoping for who knows how many months ahead.

He adds, "Is there a personal contact you might be able to call upon?"

A single name returns with little effort. "Father Lawrence. In Eden Springs. I haven't the faintest clue, however, if he's still there."

"What of the girl's grandparents? Could they not assist in locating him?"

I mentally repel the suggestion. Contacting the Jansens would require my informing them of Thea and—if a military telegram hasn't yet been issued—of Arie too, all while bound by the Official Secrets Act. Classified or not, what words could I possibly put on paper that wouldn't destroy me, let alone them? Though I know the couple to be strong, how do any parents bear such a loss?

"Maybe." A placation. "I'll give it some thought."

Hutton's brow pinches in doubt, just as soon falling away at a sight behind me. "Ah. There is Private Walsh for you."

I twist to find Lenora entering the pub, having volunteered as my driver today. It's our first encounter since my trip. Her head must be full of questions.

She smiles but with slight formality. "Good afternoon, Major. Miss Vos."

We greet her in kind, and Hutton crushes out his cigarette. "Righto. I should take my leave." As we rise, he extends me a rueful gaze. "Best of luck, my dear."

He knows I'll be asked yet again to regurgitate details I'd rather forget, except that this time, I have queries of my own.

Turning to leave, he stresses to Lenora, "Drive safely, now, Private."

"Indeed, sir, I will." Belying her geniality appears a desire to tack on *I always do* through clenched teeth.

A mere week ago, the exchange might have drawn my laughter. But that too has evaporated from my internal well.

Lenora waits until Hutton is out the door before shifting to a mode of friendship, one fortified by a secret. "Oh, I've been so relieved you're safe." She embraces me, a welcome gesture until she asks quietly, "Your friend… Did you find him? Is he all right?"

I edge out the same meager answer I gave to Hutton. "He's gone."

When I add nothing more, her expression drops. "Fenna, no. I'm ever so sorry."

While it shouldn't, her injection of sympathy stirs my seething. Pity changes nothing. I reply evenly, "Thank you," because if I say more, I just might erupt. Diverting, I angle away and call out, "Evelien, put your coat on. It's time to go."

And with that, we all head for the truck.

CHAPTER 82

Adjacent to Marylebone Station, the Great Central Hotel serves as a transit camp, with an entire floor dedicated to the escape subsection of MI9. As such, save for its marble columns, the lobby resembles a moving quilt of uniforms. Soldiers and airmen mingle about: mostly British, Americans, Canadians. For my final debriefing, an impassive female secretary escorts me through the bustle and up the grand staircase.

I glance back and locate Evelien holding Lenora's hand as they exit the main doors. Enticed by a peek at the famed city of London and by my vow to reunite straight after, the girl had agreed to the stroll. A far better option than waiting with Lenora in a smoky lobby or a crowded hallway. Now that I'm aware she understands English, in light of the topic, I would never subject her to the coming meeting.

Still, as I proceed down a long corridor, I'm acutely aware of the vacancy at my side. They're unlikely to venture more than a few blocks, but already I can't help but worry.

The secretary stops at a door, gives a cursory knock, and directs me to enter.

I rope in my thoughts, needing to remember why I'm here.

The moment I step inside, the door shuts behind me.

The hotel's large double room has been converted into an interrogation space. Parked behind a lineup of document-strewn trestle tables, an unfamiliar fellow in a suit has beady eyes and a walrus mustache. Alongside him are two men with whom I'm all too well acquainted.

"Welcome, Miss Vos." Bogart motions to the chair at the center.

His wavy black hair is still fittingly slicked, the cleft in his chin as pronounced as I recall. "We appreciate your joining us."

Crockatt, dressed in his hallmark Royal Scots uniform with his bonnet set aside, offers a smile that reaches his green eyes. "Why, it's certainly splendid to have you back safe and sound."

Were you hoping the same for Arie? The demand forms on my tongue but I let it dissolve, due to the woman seated in the corner. With horn-rimmed glasses low on her nose, she holds a pencil to her steno pad, ready to transcribe my every word in shorthand.

I square my temper and assume my place in the chair. Patiently I comply, biding my time.

Through my summary of events—my detachment increasing with every telling—the group's agreeable nods and references to previous reports indicate my accounts align. Finally, after Bogart's requests for clarification and his reminder of my work being classified indefinitely, he reclines in his chair, satisfied.

"I believe that will do for now. We shall contact you should we require anything further."

"Once more," Crockatt inserts, "we are very grateful for your service, Miss Vos." Then solemnly: "And may we add our condolences on the loss of your friend, Lieutenant Jansen."

There it is. While yet again I'm vexed by the offering, particularly from anyone who might have sought this very outcome, it at least serves as a segue. I open my mouth with the question I'm most intent on voicing, only to have it stall midroute. Amid the awkward pause, I nudge my other concerns to the forefront.

"Regarding Evelien, the lieutenant's niece… I'm greatly in need of assistance in relocating her to America."

Crockatt maintains his caring look. "Major Hutton has brought the issue to my attention. I placed a few calls. Alas, the backlog of cases is quite extensive. If there is any progress, I shall promptly make you aware."

I nod at the update, which Hutton in fact already relayed, and move on to one I've yet to uncover. "What of Gerda? Do you know if she's okay?"

"Forgive me," Crockatt says. "She is...?"

"The housekeeper. The woman who assisted at Ziegler's home." I attempt to conceal my frustration over how easily the names of such brave, vital people could be forgotten. "At each of my debriefings, I was told someone could look into what became of her. I'm confident that someday Evelien would like to know." As would I.

The stranger at the table, silent until now, projects past the hedge of his mustache, revealing a Dutch accent. "Your inquiry was indeed passed along. I believe she was held and interrogated for several days." I tense from what that could entail before he adds, "Our sources related that she was then freed and remains in good health."

I sigh. "I'm terribly relieved to hear that."

The stenographer's pencil has gone quiet. That her notepad rests on her lap tells me I'm on the verge of being excused. Yet my pressing question fails to budge.

And so my mind seizes on another figure integral to my escape, though not free of suspicion.

"If I may ask," I slip in quickly, "about communications that were compromised, do you know if it was..." In this moment, I find I can't bring myself to accuse Willem; without him, I likely would have let the Nazis come for me and Evelien. "Was it the work of the Abwehr?" I say instead, German intelligence being a common and general culprit.

The British stranger's reply is measured. "I cannot say that we have reason to believe otherwise. As you well know, we have since adjusted to protect those in our employment."

In essence, it's a faux answer: a mix of doublespeak and information I gave to *him*.

Bogart rises from his chair. "It appears our business for today is concluded." He gestures toward the door, an unsubtle directive. "A secretary will escort you back down."

But I can't go—not yet. Not before I ask. At the anticipation of being dragged away, I cast out my question in pieces.

"Arie's body. After the war."

All eyes in the room stare.

"Will you bring him home? For proper burial."

Right then, I realize why the words so fiercely resisted the path to my lips. Because once out in the world, heard and addressed, the matter solidifies the reality of his death.

The men exchange glances. At the trepidation I detect in them, as if seeking the unlucky soul to break the news, I bristle in my seat.

"He was a hero," I remind them. Relegated to the shadows, he'll be awarded no medals or public honors. But this they can do.

"Miss Vos..." The humoring note in Bogart's tone only inflates my tenacity. Despite my anger toward Arie, this is about what's just. For the sake of his parents, if no one else.

Not letting Bogart finish, I acknowledge what the panel is surely thinking. "Yes, *in part* he was driven by a personal cause—for which, frankly, I dare any man in this room to have acted differently. But in the end, as you well know, he was wounded securing Nel's freedom. No doubt, in turn she'll continue to save others, specifically including our Allied airmen."

Bogart laces his fingers on the table, suggesting a mulling of my points. "I cannot disagree," he replies, providing a speck of hope. "Nevertheless, while the decision of repatriation would fall to the United States government in this case, I believe it only fair to warn you that there are many service members whose remains will never be returned."

Unsurprised by his answer, I insist, "But some will be. And with Britain's connections and access being stronger, I'd wager your government could lend a hand if desired."

More glances, the dread in them thickening.

"There is the rare exception," he concedes, "but I must stress that a great number of servicemen actually prefer to be laid to rest where they sacrificed their life for their country."

He says this as if he could possibly know what Arie would have wanted. I counter through a clamped jaw, "America is his home. And he could've come back to it if he'd chosen to fend for just his own interests."

"Which is why," Crockatt asserts gently, "he is being permitted to retain his honorable standing and, as such, will be listed as KIA."

The acronym is appropriate. Hence, through the immeasurable moment that follows, its effect on me isn't logical—I know this even as it's happening—but the letters strike like daggers. They penetrate my will with the finality in their meaning: *Killed in Action*.

"Miss Vos, are you well?" Crockatt leans forward in his seat.

Am I?

Beyond care for pretense, I answer in truth.

"No," I say simply.

Nor, I fear, will I ever be again.

CHAPTER 83

Wading through the teeming hotel lobby, I'm desperate to flee, yearning to retreat to the cave of my room. But Lenora and Evelien are nowhere in sight. I told them I wouldn't be long.

How far did they go? *Why aren't they back?*

"Fenna."

I trace the voice through the surrounding chatter, only to find Wing Commander Moretti. He boasts his usual warm smile, a marked contrast to our run-in at the airfield.

"I was so pleased this morning to hear you've returned. In fact, I had planned to visit you shortly." As if remembering a key reason, he removes his service cap in a motion of paying respects, his expression leveling. "I was quite sorry, of course, to learn of——"

"Don't say it." The command is instinctive. A means of self-preservation. Given the secrecy of Arie's file, Moretti doubtfully knows enough to plunge into details. But even a blanket consolation will nudge me toward a cliff, of which already I'm teetering on the edge. I explain in bare terms, "I just want all of this behind me."

He nods thoughtfully. "And 'this' includes England, I presume?"

"Soon, I hope."

"Will I at least see you at HQ until then?"

I shake my head. "I'm done with that as well."

A beat passes. "I see."

I'm unsure if the disappointment in his face stems from our paths dividing or from a judgment over my quitting, prodding me to justify. "Honestly, I just can't imagine I'd provide any real worth to anyone here."

"Well, I for one would argue that." He issues a tight smile. "Look about."

Impatient, I merely wait for his point.

"I said to look." His fatherly nature, more overt than ever, makes my behavior seem that of a stubborn teenager. Yielding, I survey the lobby filled with servicemen of all stripes. Many bear the gauntness of POWs. Some lean on canes. Others wear bandages and slings. And yet the beaming smiles among those greeting one another are somehow their most prominent features.

Moretti adds, "Nearly every chap in this room managed to survive by evading the Jerries and escaping Nazi territory. Do you think they accomplished that on their bloody own?"

The scene should make me feel proud that even in a small way I might have contributed to bringing these sons and fathers and husbands home. Instead, an ugly selfishness takes hold. For in a blink, I'd trade the entire group of them for one specific soldier, and the impossibility of that makes me want to scream.

Struggling to keep my composure, I stammer, "I...should go." As much for Moretti's sake as mine. I scan the entry in search of Lenora.

"Before you do," he interjects, "you must know..." Hesitant, he seems to be crafting his statement carefully, leaving me fearful of what's coming. "On the eve of his mission, Jansen requested a favor. In the event of the worst, I was to pass along a message."

At the brief pause, sudden dread binds my chest.

I push myself to look at Moretti's hands, expecting him to produce an envelope. But he makes no such effort, explaining, "He said you would find his missive already in your possession."

I stare back at him, thoughts racing. "What—but where?"

Worry pulls at the wing commander's face. "He insisted you would understand."

I comb through my memories. When he came to see me at Wilton Park, he carried my briefcase. Did he slip a letter inside? If so, I would have found it by now.

Then I remember: the wooden train. It's certainly possible I missed a new note tucked beneath mine, particularly if made of, say, brown paper and fitted to line the compartment.

Though would I truly want to read it?

From the entry, Lenora is waving. Returned with Evelien, she's ready to chauffeur us back.

Now the drive that only minutes ago I longed to begin might amount to the most conflicted imaginable.

CHAPTER 84

Sprinkles of rain dot the passenger window. I gaze at them idly as the truck rumbles out of the city and ever closer to the countryside. Lenora busies Evelien, who sits wedged between us, with questions of favorite foods, colors, flowers, and more. Light and happy topics for a child who's faced too much darkness.

The answers from Evelien aren't zealous or lengthy, a mere few words each, but her willingness to share is a welcome surprise. It's one I would relish if not for the distraction of Arie's message that apparently awaits.

Much too soon, we disembark at the inn. I nearly forget to thank Lenora, who recognizes my preoccupied state. She simply extends a smile and says she'll call on us in the morning.

She's just pulled away when the manager's daughter skips out the front door with her two usual friends. "Evie, you're back!" she exclaims. "Would you fancy feeding the animals with us?"

This would effectively fulfill my promise to Evelien, having already taught her the button trick. She's also encountered all the inn's cats, dogs, and pigeons but not yet been privy to the thrill of feeding them. She looks to me for approval. Her desire to participate shimmers in her sapphire-blue eyes, though for once I'm tempted to refuse her. Having her up in the room with me, I'd have good reason to postpone my daunting task.

Then again, why delay the inevitable? The sooner I act, the sooner it's behind me.

"You go and have fun. I'll just be up in the room."

She nods with a faint smile that twitches as if she's battling a grin.

When she scurries away with the giggly pack, I set my shoulders and venture inside.

The train sits on my pillow, daring me.

Retrieved from my trunk, it's but an arm's length from where I'm planted on my bed and working up my nerve. *Oh, stop dragging this out and look already.*

I grab hold of the blasted train and disengage the cab. From the compartment, I pull out my tightly folded note to uncover Arie's.

But there isn't one. Just vacant space.

I gaze back at my own note, the very one he returned.

Did he write something inside? A penciled message I missed? To add his final goodbye to what I believed to be my own seems a crude choice. Unless...he figured it a natural link for me to correlate.

I gear up with a breath and unfold the page. By light streaming from the sky of gray clouds, I examine both sides. What I discover is...

Nothing.

Nothing past my own writing, anyway.

No scrawling in the margins. No additions to the blank side.

I search my mind for an explanation, an alternative, but can think of no other "missive" I already possess.

Might he have sent me a letter back in the States? If so, addressed to where? His parents' home? In which case, why have Moretti deliver the hint to me here—or ever?

Then a prospect forms, though a grim one.

Prior to our full amends in Utrecht, our emotional spat revealed the grudge Arie carried for years. Before his trip, did he leave me the unsolvable riddle as revenge? Would he really have been that vindictive?

Or am I simply reaching for reasons to further justify my resentment?

As I seek other options, my gaze lingers over my nightstand candle. A childhood memory drifts back: the notes Arie and I used to share, each elusive in another way. From the first magic book he gifted me, we learned to write messages using acidic ink. With a paintbrush dipped in lemon juice, we'd scribe words that vanished once dry and were meant to reappear when hovered over a flame.

While doing so, I'd often relate a tale of Houdini and his wife. How he promised that, if able, he'd send her a message from the grave, a secret code only they would understand. For ten years after his passing, his hopeful bride held annual séances to no avail.

He should've just sent a telegram, Arie would smirk, to which I'd groan, indignant.

Well, I think it's beautiful, I would say.

And now I question...if maybe...

I bring the page to my nose and take a sniff.

No trace of citrus. On either side.

How silly to even consider it. After all, the lemon juice never worked as well as promised, and more than a few of our attempts ended with the paper on fire and our stomping out the flames. It wasn't until years later that I taught Arie a far more reliable and safer method, compliments of Madame Esme. Best of all, with an ink mixture of baking soda and water, the letters were entirely undetectable until...

The thought trails off, leaving a revelation.

A possibility.

And only one way to confirm.

Within minutes, aided by the inn's housekeeper—though not without piquing her curiosity—I collect the few items needed. Before my desk, too anxious to sit, I concoct a reagent by stirring turmeric into a small cup of rubbing alcohol. Then, with a lightly dipped rag and only seconds of hesitation, I cover the full back of my note with moist yellow streaks.

Almost immediately they emerge: dark-orange words in Arie's familiar hand.

I force a breath around the lump in my throat. My legs going weak, I lower onto the bed, and through the tremble in my grip, I begin to read.

My dearest Fen,
    If you're reading this, it likely means my
mission failed and I'm not coming home. Even so,
I won't regret trying, because at last I've found
my purpose, a chance to do something truly
special and lasting. Whatever happens, my final
thought in life will be this: I love you, Fen,
with all my being. And I'll carry you in my
heart forever.

                                  −Arie

The words fade through my blurring vision, distorted by tears. They arrive in a flood and spill hot down my face. I hold the note to my chest, remembering the warmth of his arm around me on the night he took his last breath. The memory, like a key, unlocks a chamber inside me. With the swing of the door comes a torrent of emotion, not evaporated all this time but trapped. It racks my body with a deep-rooted sob from all the pain and loss I can no longer contain. From the what-ifs and what-could-have-beens. From all the years I wasted without him.

Starved for air, I take in big gulping breaths. A pang shoots through my chest, and I envision my heart splitting in two. I scramble to cling to the anger fraying inside. Without its threads to sustain me, forging even the semblance of a seam, I fear I'll come apart.

The fury slips away regardless.

Though I manage not to crumble, what's left at my core is an agonizing ache, a gaping hole that can never be filled.

How could he leave me behind? How will my world ever be right without him?

On the bed, I sink onto my side. Tears pour, soaking my pillow, until my whole head throbs and my mouth goes dry. Until all I can do is shut my eyes and breathe and miss him so much it hurts.

Through the quiet, a soft noise enters the air. Raindrops on the window.

Tap. Tap-tap. Tap.

The sounds form a gentle rhythm, almost hypnotic, drawing me back in time. I'm in the Jansens' home, curled up on my old bed, my cheeks barely dried of tears. It's on the night of my quarrel with Arie, and he's sending a message through the wall, his last coded taps I'll ever hear.

FORGIVE ME? he says.

And I realize, at this moment, my answer to him is the same as it will always be.

OF COURSE

CHAPTER 85

Securing a sponsorship for Evelien takes close to six months. Hutton's suggestions prove sage. In a letter to the Jansens, I brought myself to pen words that no parent should have to read, sharing what I was able, concluding with a request for help. The couple's letter in response included no outpouring of grief—handled privately, as expected—and focused outwardly on their assistance in locating Father Lawrence. Evidently, the priest spared not a day before using his church connections, persisting with the Jansens against any obstacle, of which there were many.

Now Evelien, at last, has been cleared to immigrate.

After my initial burst of joy, the news settles on me as bittersweet. Beyond the cherished friendships I've made, I've become part of a team, even in the shadows, to win an unquestionably worthy war. To leave before it's over, with the outcome still very much unknown, feels wrong. Still, Evelien's safety has to come first, making the choice irrefutable.

Over our months of waiting, though I was replaced at MI9 as requested, I couldn't sit idly by. With Crockatt's permission and Hutton's quiet input, I've continued to tinker with gadgets—and with a bit of added help. Evelien has revealed herself to be a wonderfully curious child, especially while testing my prototypes, her questions increasing as her comfort grows. She reminds me of Arie in that way: puzzling over details of why and how contraptions work. A few of her queries have even led me to solutions.

That being said, there's less and less work to be done. At Hitler's prison camps, expanded distribution of X-ray machines now frequently catch our escape tools upon arrival. Fortunately, most of our POWs have already accumulated a surplus of supplies. Some of the prisoners' coded messages have even asked for the halting of shipments, as finding new hiding places has become a challenge.

An ironic problem to have, no doubt.

In the evenings, Evelien and I listen to the BBC, gathering what we can from updates of the Netherlands. Just after our escape, the Nazis announced that all former Dutch soldiers who'd initially fought the Germans would be deported as forced labor. In protest, Dutch miners, dairy farmers, and manufacturing workers went on strike to hinder the German war machine. Hitler's reprisals for this weren't light. According to reports, the country's restrictions, roundups, and searches escalated, along with summary executions.

I have to think, if we'd made it to the farm as planned, odds seem high we would have been captured soon after. Not that I can say for sure. All I do know is we're going home.

———

At Euston Station, on the platform where our train awaits on a bright October morning, I'm not the only one emotional over a parting. Obviously, not all the passengers here are bound for the Port of Southampton; few would have a destination as distant as ours. But during these times, every goodbye might be one's last.

After releasing my hug, Lenora brushes a tear from her cheek. "You'll let us know you've arrived safely," she insists.

"Straightaway."

"And you'll write often."

"I will." I punctuate this with a squeeze of her hand, our indelible bond felt through my travel gloves. For this is how we survived once together, a grasp that defied the chaos of a crowd. "So long as you remember, I expect a *telegram* when a date is set for wedding bells."

"Oh blimey, I'm in no hurry for that." She smiles, again downplaying how smitten she's become with a rather fetching Canadian translator.

"Yes, yes," Hutton interjects from behind her. "You ladies

continue this hubbub, and the train will depart before you're aware. I will remind you: it took my pulling of several ruddy strings to acquire today's ship vouchers."

The discreet roll of Lenora's eyes nearly makes me laugh. Then moving aside, she bends to bid goodbye to Evelien, who stands bundled in her travel coat, doll in her arms, ready for our next bout of adventure.

"Well, then," I say to Hutton. "I suppose this is it."

"So it is."

Granted, he's sworn it's not the last I'll see of him. Prepared for a tussle with the bureaucratic "Whitehall warriors," after the war is over—oh, what a thought that is—he's determined to publish a book of his official feats with MI9. For this, he foresees a grand tour through America. Receiving clearance for those writings might be trickier now that he's relinquished his commission—mind you, working part-time as a civilian for the RAF, he's still in the fight. Yet Hutton of all people will find a way to slice through the red tape of classified limits and ultimately see it through.

"But first, Miss Vos"—he retrieves an object from his overcoat pocket—"this is for you."

My eyes widen at the unwrapped box. "A present?" I don't intend to sound so surprised, but this is Hutton after all. He's not exactly the syrupy type.

He flaps his hands to speed me along. "Go on and open it. As I said, there is no room to dally."

Considering we have several minutes yet, and with my trunk already checked, I now sense his impatience is actually over the reveal of his gift. I subdue a smile and remove the lid.

What I uncover bewilders me.

Not only is the watch styled for a man, but with light scratches on the glass face, it appears well worn.

He explains. "You did mention having left behind your father's pocket watch in Holland. While nothing could rightly take its place, I imagined this could do as next best."

I smile, genuinely, the sentiment being sweet. Nevertheless, I find it humorous that he just might be gifting me an abandoned watch from the "Left Luggage" counter at King's Cross.

"I appreciate that. It's very kind of you."

"This isn't just any token, I will have you know." He buzzes with excitement, and now I'm curious. "I trust you recall the tale of my second meeting with Houdini, whereupon he revealed his trickery pertaining to my crate. Yet the portion you have yet to hear is that, by way of consolation, he presented me with a souvenir, as he described it: 'a fine silver watch.'"

My jaw slackens. Reviewing the timepiece before me with a vastly altered perspective, I brush my thumb over its features with the care of handling delicate china. "But, sir…I can't take this. It's so valuable."

"Indeed, it is—and it's not. You see, only much later, upon close examination did I discover it isn't silver at all but white metal and practically worthless. The clever chap had fooled me again." Hutton grins broadly, a contradiction in pride, and I break into laughter, once more buoyed by a person who'd become quite the unexpected friend.

"Thank you," I tell him. "For everything."

He offers a handshake. Instead, I lean in and touch a kiss to his cheek, causing him to blush.

"Take good care of yourself, Clutty." I don't say this lightly, nor is his response any less meaningful.

"You as well, Miss Vos. You as well."

CHAPTER 86

The ten-day ship ride to New York requires more zigzagging through the Atlantic. Once again, my priority lies in assuaging Evelien's fears, and in doing so, I too find a modicum of comfort.

Besides, what would our fretting change? More productively, I pass the time by teaching her basic card tricks and, on a night when the rough seas become worrisome, I think to lend her the wooden train.

"Roll the wheels," I whisper. "It'll make the world calmer." Through the rough jostling of our berth, the lulling rhythm from her thumb—*forward, back, forward, back*—soothes her enough to doze back off.

On smoother days, among the passengers enjoying the fresh, salty breeze of the upper deck—the majority strolling, smoking, leaning on rails—I notice a smattering of black armbands on upper sleeves. I view the dressing differently now: not simply a declaration of mourning but a symbol of connection for the many who have lost so much. A wordless assurance that we're not alone.

Though the ocean voyage is blessedly uneventful, our subsequent train rides bring relief in comparison, along with eagerness over our destination.

Disembarking on the platform in Amesboro, I spot them immediately. My heart warms even more than I expected. The Jansens' searching gazes snag on me, and their morphing from anticipation to frozen shock indicates they recognize Evelien at my side. Her uncanny resemblance to Thea, particularly in person, has to be unnerving.

I guide Evelien over. "Evie, say hello to your grandparents."

She sidles closer to my leg as Mrs. Jansen just stares.

Slowly removing his hat, Mr. Jansen lowers onto a knee before Evelien. "It is very lovely to meet you. I am...your *opa*. Your grand-papa." His tone is slightly awkward, though his eyes shimmer with emotion. "And this is your *oma*." He gestures to his wife.

"Come." Her voice borders on gruff. "We go home for food."

The abruptness is a tad startling, even from her. I pause from following, only to gather our belongings with Mr. Jansen, and hope this wasn't a mistake.

Waves of memories rush over me as I enter the house, intensified by the familiar scent of rye bread. I proceed inside. The furnishings, all unchanged, feel comfortable yet slightly foreign.

Evelien and I settle into my old room, where we'll continue to share a bed. To help her adjust to our surroundings, I tell her, "Before I lived here, this bedroom belonged to your mother."

As she studies the space in wonder, thoughts of my last night here, spent with Arie, unleash a mix of longing and gratitude and sorrow.

I nudge them away and focus on the family.

Unfortunately, their interactions neglect to improve as the day plays out: Mr. Jansen is stiffly affable, Evelien shy and wary, Mrs. Jansen stoic and watchful.

The second day brings more of the same.

After supper that evening, another meal strained by the unspoken, I perch on the bottom corner of my bed and, as usual, brush out Evelien's damp tangles from her bath. Shifting on her bare feet, she fiddles with the sleeve of her nightgown. When she turns to the doorway, I find Mrs. Jansen there in her housedress, her apron hung up for the night.

"Sit," she tells Evelien, flicking her chin toward the bed. That's when I notice a thin but large book in her hands.

Evelien looks to me for confirmation, a habit that's become infre-quent as of late, but for this situation, I can't blame her.

"Listen, now, to your *oma*." I encourage her by patting the area on the coverlet next to me. Defying the woman will earn Evelien no points, but also my interest is piqued.

Mrs. Jansen takes her place on the other side of the girl and opens the book—a scrapbook—and points to the first photo.

"This baby... You see?" She doesn't wait for an answer. "This is your mama."

Though still cautious, Evelien leans in for a closer view.

"And this boy—your uncle. Arie."

There's a sharp pull in my heart, as I've never viewed these pictures before, had no idea they existed. Moreover, their neat arrangement and the lingering smell of rubber cement suggests they were assembled only recently and with care.

Moisture rims my eyes as she goes from page to page. School certificates and report cards, even some classroom art projects are adhered throughout. Although her narratives are sparse, she addresses each of Evelien's inquiries over the contents.

Halfway through, at the top of another report card, the name penned in cursive takes me by surprise.

"You included mine," I realize aloud.

Mrs. Jansen *tsks*, her brow pinched, as if the observation is idiotic. "Of course. This is book for family." Then she promptly resumes her presentation, but the meaning behind her reply causes a few tears to sneak down my face. A few more follow when we reach Arie's military portrait. In his Army dress uniform, he's so dashing the sight briefly steals my breath.

Averse to dampening the mood, however, I latch onto the diversion of Evelien perking up at the next photos. Clearly sent by her mother, they include the couple's wedding portrait and a snapshot of them posing by a canal. Bubbling with growing excitement, Evelien volunteers the names of her uncle and aunt and cousins. It saddens me to know they're all gone, but then I marvel at how, in this moment, that doesn't at all sink the girl's spirits. And when she spots herself at various ages, I can't help but smile at her giggles.

As soon as we reach the end, Mrs. Jansen shuts the cover. No fanfare. "You sleep now," she tells Evelien. "When you are older, we read letters from your mama." She's about to stand but instead pauses and peers at Evelien. The girl gazes back, unblinking. Without a word, Mrs. Jansen touches the top of her granddaughter's hair, a tender stroke that trails off at her little round cheek. Then the woman rises and leaves the room, but not before I catch the glimmer of wistful tears in her eyes.

The following days roll into weeks, then months, and we all settle into our new normal. Evelien attends school, where she's made a good friend—a Dutch girl whose parents immigrated just before the war—and at home, she's learning to sew from Mrs. Jansen. I do my best not to chime in, even while I sit nearby sewing garments I take in to earn money for the family. Then after her homework most evenings, Evelien sits with her grandpapa, trading his lessons in Gronings for the latest trick she's mastering.

Which is what I presume they're doing just now. As I finish with dishes, bursts of laughter draw me to peek into the sitting room. Sure enough, Evelien's and her grandpapa's hands are all tangled up in string. Their joyful sounds radiate through the home, stretching my lips into a smile. And suddenly I think of Dirk and Klara.

I recall the madness I found in their hopes to start a family amid this ghastly war, and finally I understand. Evelien's not just a light in the darkness; she's a light that makes the darkness endurable. Even, quite often, surmountable.

Late that night, when Evelien wakes from a frightening dream—as we still do at times—by her request, I spin a story of a brave princess who defeats a dragon that for too long reigned over a village. As she listens, her eyelids grow progressively heavy. Once she's fallen asleep, I slip out of bed for a glass of water.

In the hall, I close the door behind me, and a soft creak from the kitchen turns me. For an instant, the past takes hold, and I expect to see Arie at the table, studying by lamplight.

But the noise was just the house settling. And once more the reality of his absence pummels me in the chest.

It's a trade-off of living back in this home. How some days I feel I could round a corner and find Arie there. That any second he'll come through the door, ready to sweep me off to a film we'd seen dozens of times together. Or I'll turn from the kitchen sink and he'll be boasting a smirk, egging on a sudsy battle.

That's not to say triggers of grief are confined by these walls. Practically every shop and street in the vicinity holds a memory, never mind a stranger's whistling of a tune or the passing scent of butterscotch. Sometimes the angst is so smothering I fear I might suffocate.

Then it wanes and I push myself forward, because with Evelien to care for, I don't have the luxury of wallowing for long. And thank heavens for that.

Gradually, I suppose, she'll need me less than I need her. A time will come when she'll ask for her own bed, even her own room. As no doubt she'll want the one that belonged to her mother, this will mean my moving to Arie's.

Since my return, his room remains the sole place in the house I haven't dared visit.

Could it finally be time?

Reluctantly in the dimness, I venture into the sitting room. I stop at the door to what was formerly the porch. Like dreading a nurse's shot, I remind myself how anticipation can be worse than the act. I have doubts that the same applies here, but what awaits is just as inevitable.

And so with strength from a deep breath, I at last step inside.

Light through the window, cast by a moon that regularly lured Arie out on peaceful walks, illuminates furnishings that have scarcely changed since I last saw them. My emotions swirl as I scan the time capsule of his life: the tacked-up posters of legendary bridges, the wallboards with tiny nicks from our coded messages, the novel on his nightstand with a bookmark set partway through, never to be finished.

I lower to sit on the bed. Pulling his pillow to my chest, I brace for a surge of overwhelming anguish.

Still I wait...

Seconds more…

Incredibly, it doesn't come.

Instead, here in the dark, alone with the melody of my own breathing, I remember the warmth of Arie's hand, the comfort of his rasp. And I realize, just as I needn't go to the Netherlands to feel closer to Papa, Arie's support, like his love, will never be far.

It'll all work out, I promise, he told me on our last night together. It was his final vow, assuring me everything would be okay.

While not in the way I had hoped, with enough time and healing, I sense he might be right.

EPILOGUE

August 10, 1945

Dear Miss Vos,

I was delighted to recently happen across your name and photograph in an article following your show in Appleton. I hope you don't mind my reaching out to the theater and asking them to kindly forward this post to wherever it would best find you.

You may not remember me after all these years, but I had the great fortune of helping care for you as a child during your time in Little Chute. I was dreadfully sad to see you and your father go, as you both added such joy to my life, but I always knew grand adventures lay ahead for you, darling Fenna—or "schatje," as your father would say—and I have clearly been proven right.

A few years back, my eldest son insisted on helping me clean out the attic, which I admit was quite overdue. And what a blessing the task turned out to be! For I found several photographs in a box of old keepsakes that warmed my heart. I am enclosing just one of them, as I'm afraid the others were too blurry to share—if only I'd paid better mind to lessons from the friend who had lent me her camera. Oh, and I did save a good one for myself. I hope you won't fault me.

In closing, I pray this message finds you and yours

*in good health and spirits. I continue to think of you and
your father often and will cherish our memories together
always.*

Most sincerely,
Anne (Roosa) Corman

———————

In my dressing room at the Marquis Theater in Chicago, I should be
focused on tonight's impending show. I ought to be rechecking all the
pockets, pulls, and compartments I've built into my costume, a black
satiny ensemble of shorts and a tailored coat. Instead, seated at my
vanity, I'm hampered by distraction.

Passed along by the box office this afternoon, the photograph
from Miss Roosa sits with her letter, propped against my mirror. It's
a picture of me and Papa, an image I'd never seen. Having believed
the photo I'd lost while escaping the orphanage was the sole one of
us together, the sheer existence of the picture before me feels surreal,
additionally for this reason: I've no recollection of it being taken.
Thus, to be staring at proof I was there is fantastically strange.

In contrast to the portrait I'd treasured, this particular photo is an
informal snapshot. No prim outfits or poses, no proper studio lighting.
We're simply seated at a kitchen table, where I'm too busy gobbling
down what was surely Miss Roosa's Dutch butter cake to connect
with the camera. Papa, hovering a fork over his plate, maintains a flat
line with his lips. His eyes hold a twinkle, however, an internal smile
he couldn't hide from the lens.

It's all so imperfect. And real. And beautiful.

Like life.

I try to resist, but my mind implores I consider yet another
hypothetical: If I'd been more persistent, could I have convinced Papa
to stay in Little Chute and marry Miss Roosa? There would have been
no hunger from the strike, no tragedy of the stampede, no devastation
and heartache over losing the boy I loved more deeply than I could
ever describe.

But then I realize I would never have known Arie. And no matter where that leaves me today, I can't fathom anything worse.

Soon I'll write back to Miss Roosa—or Mrs. Corman now—once I sort out what to say. How do I properly construe on paper what it means to me to have a renewed connection to both Papa's history and my own? Perhaps during my next trip through Appleton, over tea and dessert, we'll regale each other with memories that will feel as if they happened yesterday.

A grunt of frustration pulls me from my musings.

On the floor by the costume rack, Evelien sits crossed-legged in her overalls. Scowling, she pitches a handful of matchsticks at her splayed magic book. She's been working on the same new trick since this morning, taking a break only for my matinee.

"Care for some help?"

"No," she grumbles. "I'll get it." She blows out a breath. Then she collects her props and begins again.

I smile to myself.

At age seven, she certainly has a stubborn streak. Like Arie and her *oma*. And yes, like me. "Mulish," Arie would quip. Eventually, I'll teach her the wisdom in accepting help from others, even in asking for it, yet for now, I'll leave her to flex her independence. That doesn't mean it's always easy for me to stand by as she stumbles. But Mrs. Jansen is quick with a bolstering reminder:: *That is a mother's job.*

And she's right.

Though I don't always tell her so.

I'm not a mother, mind you. I'd never dare to take Thea's place. Not in that way. In fact, I like to think she's been smiling down these past two years, watching her beloved daughter bloom. Goodness knows she must have observed wide-eyed when, at Evelien's urging, Mrs. Jansen helped light a menorah during the last Hanukkah—just before she whisked us all off to her usual church service, of course.

As for my role as Auntie Fen, many motherly duties fall to me and I strive to honor them with the responsibility they deserve. I suppose that's what first drew me back to the stage after almost a year of our being home: a desire to live by example for Evelien's sake. How would I teach her to overcome her fears if I refrained from doing the same?

One might assume that climbing into a crate onstage would feel easy as pie after my narrow escapes from the grips of menacing Nazis. But no. Omit the necessity for survival and the urgency of saving a child, and the old trepidation of confinement returns. And so I trained, day after day, week after week, developing a tolerance as Evelien kept time on my watch from Hutton. Ultimately, with the support of the Jansens and the theater managers who still thought well of me, I pieced together my very own show, including a fancy crate trick and even some of my gadgets never used by MI9.

All to say, while I feel profound purpose in caring for Evelien, I've also rediscovered my need to bring others joy. Something of which we could all use more. Is this why I was spared when so many others weren't? I'll never know for certain. But as Evelien likes to say: *Everything is better with magic.*

How simply yet perfectly put.

From her quiet magnetism to her inquisitive nature, she still reminds me of Poppy at times. And I find myself wondering how my old friend has fared, if she now enjoys a family of her own and most of all her place in life. Looking back, I wish the same even for Ingrid, the relentless bully who swiped my precious boots though let me escape. I've been thinking of her more lately, what with Evelien outgrowing her latest shoes, bringing her excitedly closer to fitting into those same birthday boots from Papa.

Ironic, isn't it? How she thrills over wearing something old and used versus new and shiny. It's a testament, really, to connections built through story. For each time she asks for another telling—about the cobbler and my jubilance and the blistering walk home—her eyes are so intent, it's as if she's stepping right into the memory, and I rather adore the idea of her holding Papa's hand while strolling through snowflakes that drift on the night air.

Such a lovely, peaceful thought.

On a related note—of peace, that is—with the Nazis righteously defeated, people say the Japanese are sure to surrender anytime.

Whereas shows like mine previously served as a distraction from wartime worries, now they're a precursor to the big celebration. You can feel it everywhere, and most definitely in the theater. Audiences hum with mounting fervor, preparing to release a breath held for years.

To no one does that apply more, I imagine, than to *onderduikers* throughout Europe. Out of hiding at last, they're free to live, to mourn, to rebuild. Hopefully to heal. Someday I'll take Evelien back to the Netherlands. We'll find the graves of our loved ones, Lord willing, upon which we'll lay flowers and shed some tears. We'll walk the cobblestone streets unafraid and, if we're able, properly thank the brave many who risked their lives to help virtual strangers. Like Willem, Gerda, and Mr. Brouwer. Mrs. van der Meer and Dirk and Klara. The bookshop clerk and his daughter. The unnamed skipper.

Evelien knows of them all.

Until then, we'll concentrate on the steps before us, the life around us.

Now with her school out for the summer, my shows can run through the weekdays and farther from home, allowing her to experience more of the country. The expanded ticket sales are rather nice too, of course. A female escape artist is quite the novelty, they say, and rumors explaining my wartime gap from the industry have upped the intrigue. Most commonly, word has it I served as a spy in Europe for Churchill himself. My code name? Fox.

Fitting if rather on the nose.

I've been tempted to put all the conjecture to rest. But inspired by Houdini and Hutton, both public-relations masters, I merely respond, "That's quite an interesting theory." And I smile coyly, spurring reporters to scribble on their pads.

After all, what would a proper illusionist be without a healthy dose of mystery?

A triplet of knocks reaches my ears. I twist toward the door. "Yes?"

The assistant stage manager peeks in with his mop of ginger hair. He speaks around the small bulge of chewing tobacco in his lower cheek. "Fifteen minutes, Madame Vos."

"Is my team in place?"

"They sure are, ma'am."

I envision my two assistants in the wings, finishing their assigned preparations with a stagehand. Long enamored with magic, the sprightly gals are identical twins—which crowds do love—and the daughters of wealthy socialites, so they ask only that their expenses are covered and costumes supplied, all of which I design to be practical and elegant and far from scanty. Same as mine.

The fellow adds, "Got close to another full house, by the way." He crosses the room toward me. "Also, an admirer just left this for you. He was real insistent you have it before the show."

I accept the white palm-size box with skepticism. It's not the first time a gentleman caller has boasted a token of affection to be swoon worthy.

A card protrudes from the ribbon. *FOR LUCK*, it reads. No signature.

"You ready to work?" the assistant manager asks.

I glance up to answer, only to find he's speaking to Evelien, who pops onto her feet as if loaded on springs.

"Ready as ever!"

I call over to remind her, "You pay keen attention, now. I'm counting on you."

She offers quick, assertive nods, then scuttles off in her overalls—her "work clothes," she calls them—and trails the man toward the stage.

Left alone, I open the box and remove the protective tissue. At the sight of the handkerchief, lilac-hued and made of silk, my gaze cuts back to the card. *FOR LUCK.*

I'd cited that very reason when gifting a similar kerchief to Charles. The revelation of his presence jolts me. I clutch the silky square and hustle out the door. I look left, opposite the path to the stage. But there's no one.

I rush down the lengthy hall, passing framed posters of previous shows. At the end, I turn right, toward the stage doors, and find the back of a man with a familiar build.

"Charles?" For a split second, I fear my mind is once again playing games. But then he pivots my way. Indeed it's him, dapper in a pin-striped suit, his black curls tamed with tonic and amber eyes deep set. "You're here," I say in partial disbelief.

The corners of his mouth slide upward. "Yeah, well. Been hearing about a snazzy Dutch dame who vanishes in a crate. Since she's earnin' all the raves, figured I'd best size up the competition."

I can't resist smiling with a hint of both satisfaction and pride.

Fedora in his grip, he gestures while edging closer. "You got my gift, I see."

I glance down. "Oh... Yes, thank you. It was so generous of you." Sparked by memories of his plum kerchief, I recall our last encounter and with it my cowardly departure. No longer one to hold much in, I add, "Especially after how I left. Dashing off a note, not even speaking with you first." Undeniably, it was a shameful habit of mine. "Really, Charles, I'm very sorry—"

"Nah." He advances a full step. "It's me who's sorry." He shakes his head, reflecting. "There were things I was dealing with back then, and not real well. What with my 4-F gnawing at me, leaving me feeling like—" He lowers his eyes, conveying a revived humility. "Crux of it is, I was a downright chump."

How absurd of me not to discern the true root of his behavior before. As confident as I'd been about reading people's tells, I should have seen that his inability to serve in the war was never a relief to him. Apparently I wasn't the only one keeping up walls.

"So..." I offer him my hand. "We have a truce?"

He grins thoughtfully before humoring me with a shake. Then after a brief lull, he says, "Ya know, I'm back on the road next week. Maybe we ought to combine efforts sometime. Give folks twice the bang for their buck."

I shrug, withholding a smile. "Why not? I could always use another assistant."

He lifts an eyebrow and purses his lips, a sign of touché, and we both laugh.

"Hey," he ventures, "how about a late supper tonight? We could celebrate your stardom with flair."

I barely contemplate it; I have Evelien to consider. At the boarding-house, she needs her sleep, or by morning she'll become—as her *oma* says—an "angry berry."

"I'm sorry, but I can't."

He appears disappointed but resigned. This, after all, is what I do.

Then an option comes to me. "But maybe brunch tomorrow? Before the matinee?"

He blinks, surprised. "I'll leave my details at the box office."

I nod before it dawns on me to add, "Oh…I'll also have a little one with me. I hope you won't mind."

His eyes go wide before he attempts to downplay his startle. "Yeah. I mean, no, of course not."

I rarely bother to explain to strangers, but Charles is far from that. "Her name's Evelien. She isn't mine. But she is. In a way."

Now he looks confounded, though not without amusement. "So you're saying…we got some catching up to do." While the warmth he exudes harkens to the height of our friendship, the added creases around his eyes indicate that he, too, has stories to tell.

Where will we begin? How much can I divulge? Shall I tell him of the train ride to Tilburg, how in a despairing moment, he saved my life, and Evelien's, without even knowing it? He might not under-stand. How could he really? But then, maybe what's most important is just the sharing.

The ring of a bell echoes through the hall. A ten-minute warning, prodding me.

"Mercy. If I don't get moving, I'll miss my own show."

"See now? You caught my strategy of takin' out the competition." He winks and dons his hat at an angle. "I'll be there in the shadows cheering ya on."

I smile gratefully, and we go our separate ways. For now. Only when I round the corner do I register the significance of his parting words. How so often it's those in the shadows we come to rely on most.

I shake my head, casting off thoughts that can wait, and charge toward the stage.

Time to focus.

Through my strides, I tie the lilac kerchief chicly around my neck and smooth my hair, styled to my shoulders. In the right wing of the stage, I find Evelien perched on a tall stool. As she readies to draw the red velvety curtains, over in the left wing, my assistants signal that all is ready.

I sneak a glance at the sea of faces, the audience settling in. A giggle here and there breaks through the murmurings of conversations.

A swarm of nerves buzzes within me. I run through my mental and physical checklists, including my costume's features.

Minutes later, music projects from the pit, quieting the crowd.

On cue, Evelien races to pull the ropes with such concentration, it's clear she believes at least half the job is being done by her. All the while, the burly stagehand behind her works doggedly to yank the weighted, cumbersome ropes with his gloved hands.

"Ladies and gentlemen, boys and girls," the house manager declares onstage, "welcome to the show!"

My pulse races and chest tightens. While the man rattles off the usual rules of the theater, I take a moment to close my eyes. With hands clutched to my chest, I steady, as always, from the memory of a voice.

Breathe, Fen. Just…breathe.

"And now, please welcome to the stage the Mistress of Magic and Queen of Illusion, escapologist extraordinaire…Madame Vos!"

At the eruption of applause, I open my eyes, and without hesitation, I step into the spotlight.

AUTHOR'S NOTE

The premise of this novel came to me over a simmering stretch of several years—and a sudden flash. Seeking inspiration for a new book, I pulled out an old file of interesting articles and photos I'd tucked away. Among them was a black-and-white photograph that once again stopped me cold. I'd saved it years earlier, taken from the very same webpage, in fact, where I'd discovered a shocking picture of children being offered for sale, inspiring my novel *Sold on a Monday*—and this photo was just as haunting. More so, actually.

What I'd initially interpreted as a snapshot of children peacefully sleeping was, instead, a documentation of young victims of the 1913 tragedy in Calumet, Michigan, commonly known as the Italian Hall Disaster. At a Christmas Eve party organized for striking miners and their families, seventy-three people—the vast majority of them children—died in a stairwell stampede resulting from a false cry of "fire." The mere notion remains equally infuriating and heartbreaking. My realization that so few people outside that region seem to have ever heard of this today fueled me with a desire to share the story. Yet I couldn't help but worry that centering a novel on an event so devastating would be far too sad to write, much less for others to read. Thus, reluctantly I plodded on through my folder.

That was when I paused to reread a *Deadspin* article from 2015. "How Monopoly Helped Win World War II" by Mary Pilon described how game boards had been used to smuggle escape aids to Allied prisoners of war. Reportedly, should the game ever need to reup its wartime role, the British government kept this tactic classified for many decades thereafter. I was captivated by these lesser-known facts, but save for a POW story (which I'd written about in a previous book), I couldn't imagine a related premise unique enough to warrant an entire novel.

Still, out of curiosity, I did an online search about the topic. An extensive Eurogamer article by Christian Donlan titled "Inside Monopoly's Secret War against the Third Reich" promptly introduced me to Christopher Clayton Hutton (a.k.a. "Clutty"), the man responsible for tricking out Monopoly games and designing countless other escape-and-evasion "toys" for MI9. (I'd venture to guess I wasn't alone in my surprise, despite it being perfectly logical, that many numbered sections exist beyond the widely famed MI5 and MI6.) The covert agency managed to help an estimated thirty-five thousand Allied airmen and soldiers return to friendly lines, though its achievements were long kept classified under the Official Secrets Act.

As I continued to read, my interest further piqued over Charles Fraser-Smith, who it is said—together with Hutton—inspired the gadget-supplying character known as "Q" in the James Bond film series. Equally intriguing was a description of professional magician Jasper Maskelyne, a British army officer who used his unique skills to not only craft such devices as map-rigged playing cards but also to lead the Camouflage Experimental Section in Cairo—albeit largely unsuccessfully, according to reports. (Only after I added RAF Tempsford to my story, by the way, did I learn Maskelyne was the person responsible for cleverly designing it to look like a disused airfield turned farm.)

Upon my finishing the article, the Monopoly tale suddenly merged in my mind with the Calumet tragedy, as a driving backstory, for the journey of a fictional illusionist with MI9. Like watching a movie at double speed, I envisioned a rush of scenes from what would become *The Ways We Hide*. In hindsight, the foundation of the novel (and oh my goodness, the research) was really only beginning. Armed with a dose of blissful ignorance, I dove right in.

My subsequent research showed Hutton to be an eccentric man who defied bureaucracy and military protocols to serve the war effort, even employing a woman he called Mrs. Bote as a "temporary civil servant" to discreetly assemble escape-and-evasion packs—that is, until (as conveyed in my story) her stout-induced boasting at a local pub ended her duty. Hence, despite Hutton's lackluster views on women's driving skills and the "undignified, unnatural, and unwomanly" act of ladies' saluting—the latter of which he spouted upon first meeting his driver, Private Jill Warwick (the inspiration for the fictional Lenora Walsh)—I imagined he might very well have found appeal in recruiting a character like Fenna Vos, specifically due to his long-time fascination with Houdini.

As with most of Hutton's true accounts that made their way into the fictionalized scenes of my book—including his proud defeat in a crate challenge against Houdini, the related letter he carried in his wallet that led Crockatt to assign him to MI9, his surreal cemetery-based bunker, and on and on—the more I researched, the more I uncovered pieces of history so extraordinary, they bordered on stranger than fiction. Certainly, the designation applies no less to an astounding claim by biographical authors William Kalush and Larry Sloman. In *The Secret Life of Houdini,* they make a fiercely compelling case that Harry Houdini—born Erik Weisz, son of a Hungarian rabbi—regularly used his European tours to serve as a spy against the Germans, reporting to Scotland Yard in the days leading up to World War I. Given that Fenna would undoubtedly idolize the legendary magician and escapologist, the theory felt destined to further bind my story.

The same, I must say, applies to the Bethnal Green Tube Disaster. With a portion of my novel taking place near London in early March 1943, I set out to verify the respective weather in an online almanac. Mentioned as a side note on March 3 of that year was another tragedy that stunned me. Considered the worst civilian-casualty event of the Second World War, the stairwell crush referred to as "vertical stacking" resulted in 173 deaths and more than 90 injured, all of which went largely unreported at the time for fear it would damage public morale and feed propaganda material to the enemy. The parallel of this unfathomable incident with that of the Italian Hall, including the trigger of what amounted to a false alarm from the firing of a new British anti-aircraft rocket, couldn't have been clearer.

I often liken historical fiction to "literary Advil" in that, ideally, readers enjoy the sugarcoating of a story while benefiting from the "good stuff" (i.e., history) along the way. To pass along knowledge of both tragedies, and perhaps even inspire others to research more about the men, women, and children whose lives were cut far too short, is an honor I haven't taken lightly. For this reason, I attempted whenever possible to remain true to history, and only with reluctance did I (at least knowingly) take creative liberties, having to remind myself that the beauty of fiction invites, even requires, such leeway for an imaginative adventure not meant to be a documentary.

On that note, I came to accept that the timeline of the Italian Hall Disaster and World War II were nearly impossible to reconcile in the path of Fenna's life. After much pondering and debate, I settled on inventing the town of Eden Springs, fashioned after Calumet, bearing a Christmas Eve stampede based on the actual event. Due to the shifted timeline, I made appropriate adjustments, such as transforming the Slavic woman known as "Big Annie" to "Big Vera" and reducing the party attendees by several hundred given the decline in copper mining compared to the booming years of the actual strike.

Other liberties throughout the book include details involving Fenna's various gadgets. Aside from the timing of their inception are my portrayals, of course, of her inventing them at all. Hutton, along with his team, were the true heroes in this regard. According to his autobiography *Official Secret*—in which his personality, speech, and exploits practically leap off the page—the Hutton Flying Boots were designed, at least primarily, by him; they did, unfortunately, suffer from the same flaws and fate woven into my story. The soup-can trick, its unconventional crate delivery, and subsequent explosion are all attributed to "Clutty" as well, though the specific air commodore involved has been fictionalized. Likewise, Hutton indeed received an amusingly cheap watch from Houdini, but if he ever in turn gave it away, it obviously wasn't to Fenna.

Additionally, the dates of his stress-related hospitalization differ slightly in my book, as his actual admittance was February 20, 1943, and his discharge June 2. Without specifics to draw from, my depiction of the inciting incident was solely my estimation. During his time at Woodside Officers' Hospital, aside from starting to compile a chronology of his MI9 gadgetry—presumably for the autobiographies he eventually published—he expressed in a letter feeling "broken spirited" and "confined in this prison" to Norman Watson at John Waddington Ltd. Sadly, I surmise the missive wasn't a facade to continue his duties behind the scenes, yet in light of his obsession with his war work and his alleged (if denied) application later to serve the SOE, I like to think he'd have gladly persisted if given the opportunity and the right partner. The codes used for maps, incidentally, did include one referred to as "Dutch girl," which for me was just too fitting not to include.

When needed for narrative drive, I admit to entirely ignoring lunar cycles and giving myself wiggle room on nighttime visibility—because, yes, blackouts can be very, very dark. Also, I took liberties with Utrecht's tram access and routes and occasionally condensed timelines for pacing, most notably in the grim fallout at Bethnal Green station, as well as with Fenna's insertion and night-drop training. Granted, to be fair about the latter, I've had the great pleasure of listening to enough anecdotes from World War II veterans through the years to know that despite what was standard, there were always remarkable and necessary exceptions. It was wartime, after all.

In other areas of the novel, *Houdini's Big Little Book of Magic* (minus "*& Stunts*") indeed exists, though it focuses on close-up magic, not escalating to the showier tricks and escapes featured in his other books. As for words of note: I often referenced the Netherlands by the more period-colloquial (versus technically geographical) name of "Holland"; since Engelandvaarders doesn't have an exact translation in English, I chose "England paddlers," though it is often defined as England *farers* or *sailors*; and while *cemetery* more accurately applies to the setting of the gadget bunker, I used *graveyard* interchangeably due to Hutton's consistent use of the descriptor. Plus, let's be honest—it's a cooler, creepier word.

Furthermore, Fenna's night drop near Voorthuizen has been fictionalized, though not its location as a drop zone nor its typical sabotage during that period. The Abwehr, or German military intelligence, successfully used captured Allied radio operators and their codes to infiltrate and communicate with the SOE. In the counterintelligence operation Englandspiel, German for *England game*, this led to the entrapment and execution of nearly all the agents sent to the Netherlands. Similarly, Arie's mission, while fictionalized, was based on failed efforts at the time to unite various Dutch underground groups that worked largely independent of each other. Serving as additional inspiration was the formation of the Binnenlandse Strijdkrachten, which united three major Dutch Resistance groups in 1944. While "Bogart's" specific organization is never confirmed in the story, I imagined his role to be part of a precursor to the Bureau of Special Assignments, the Dutch secret service established in London, which worked closely with the SOE to support Allied Resistance efforts.

I should also point out that the daylight bombing run on March 31, 1943, was based on recollections in a Dutch memoir, but I can only guess that the planes were visible in Utrecht, and to prevent confusion, at times I simplified German and Dutch military specifics, such as referencing Ziegler's rank strictly with the SS over that of the Gestapo. (Besides, *Kriminalrat* somehow doesn't sound quite as intimidating.) Speaking of which, although Ziegler is a made-up villain, his twisted sense of game playing derives from various historical accounts, same for a jail breakout to free Resistance members through bribes and donning police uniforms, much like with Arie's janitor disguise.

Many more incredible experiences are documented in the series The Dutch in Wartime, Survivors Remember, edited by Tom Bijvoet and Anne van Arragon Hutten. Without question, Tony Stroeve's "How We Escaped to England," in the volume *Resisting Nazi Occupation*, particularly helped inform Fenna's crossing of the North Sea, even aligning almost eerily with her timeline. Of the approximately 1,700 Engelandvaarders who successfully fled the Netherlands, some even made the harrowing voyage in canoes and kayaks. The fact that more than a hundred Dutch escapers then returned as secret agents—roughly half of whom were soon captured—represents a level of courage hard to fully comprehend.

In closing, I'd be remiss not to add a delightful note regarding

Fenna's surname. When selecting it, I loved that due to its translation, Vos is a frequent nickname for someone deemed crafty as a fox. What I didn't discover until many months later was that despite the fox's reputation for being a solitary creature, the vixen will go to great lengths to protect her pups. An article about one such mother who kept her ensnared pup alive by bringing it food every day for two weeks, risking her own life and freedom, only confirmed that, for Fenna, I couldn't have chosen a better name.

For more details, featured videos, and a book club guide with discussion questions, themed recipes, activities, and more, visit KristinaMcMorris.com.

RECIPES FROM FENNA

Boterkoek

A favorite childhood dessert of Fenna's, this classic Dutch "butter cake" resembles a cross between a dense cake and a shortbread cookie, pairing perfectly with coffee or tea.

- 2 sticks salted butter, room temperature
- ¾ cup sugar
- 1 egg
- 1 teaspoon almond extract (or 1 teaspoon vanilla with optional zest from one lemon)
- 2 cups flour
- 1 egg yolk for brushing the top
- sliced almonds (optional)

Preheat oven to 400 degrees. In the bowl of a stand mixer, blend butter and sugar until light and fluffy. Add one egg and almond extract (or vanilla with optional lemon zest). Beat well. Mix in flour until well incorporated. Press dough evenly (with wet hands if helpful) into a greased 9-inch round cake pan or pie form. Use fork tines to create a lattice pattern. Brush the top with the beaten egg yolk. Layer with sliced almonds if desired. Bake until the top and edges are lightly golden brown (20–25 minutes; to prevent dryness, do not overbake). Cool completely to help set, then slice into narrow wedges and enjoy!

Hutspot

Hutspot, loosely translated as *mash pot*, is a popular Dutch winter dish also enjoyed year-round. Served annually at a festival on October 3 to commemorate the Dutch victory in the Siege of Leiden, *hutspot* bears an orange tint, the Dutch national color and a nod to the royal House of Orange, symbolizing the nation's freedom from oppression.

- 2 pounds starchy potatoes, peeled and cut into chunks
- 1½ pounds carrots, cut into large pieces
- 1 pound white onions, thinly sliced
- 2 bay leaves
- ¼ cup unsalted butter
- ½ cup hot milk
- ½ teaspoon ground nutmeg
- salt and pepper

Combine prepared vegetables and bay leaves in a large pot. Cover with water and bring to a boil. Add lid and cook over medium heat for 25 minutes. Drain and remove bay leaves. Dry the rest on paper towel, then transfer to a large bowl and mash well. Mix in butter, milk, and nutmeg. Salt and pepper to taste. Serve alone or with such meat as smoked sausage and mustard, smoked bacon, or meatballs.

Genever Sour

By 1880, thanks to exports of genever to the large population of Dutch immigrants in the U.S., about one in four cocktails mixed in America included the gin-like liquor, a favorite of Fenna's papa.

- 2 ounces genever
- ¾ ounce honey syrup (2 parts honey dissolved in 1 part hot water)
- ¾ ounce lemon juice

In a cocktail shaker filled with ice, combine all ingredients. Shake well and strain into glass. Garnish with a lemon peel.

Invisible Ink & Reagent

Fenna's recipe list would be incomplete without this special one—not to be eaten, of course, but used for secret messages.

- ½ cup water
- 1 tablespoon baking soda
- ½ cup rubbing alcohol
- 1 teaspoon turmeric

In a small bowl, thoroughly mix water and baking soda to create the invisible ink. With a small paintbrush or cotton swab, write a note with the solution on a piece of white paper. Allow to dry, typically 15 minutes. In a cup, create the reagent by combining rubbing alcohol and turmeric. (Apron recommended, as the solution can stain.) Atop layered newspapers to prevent discoloration of the surface beneath, paint over the sheet of white paper with the reagent and watch your message boldly and magically appear.

READING GROUP GUIDE

1. Did your impression of the child on the cover change by the novel's end? What about the title? Describe the various meanings it holds throughout the story.
2. From the Italian Hall Disaster and its parallel tragedy at Bethnal Green Station to the efforts of MI9, Houdini, and the Dutch Resistance, plus those of the Engelandvaarders, *The Ways We Hide* highlights myriad stunning pieces of history. Which among them fascinated and/or surprised you most?
3. Love, loss, family, and sacrifice are major themes of the novel and the driving force behind many of Fenna's and Arie's actions. Did you largely agree or disagree with Fenna's decisions? What about Arie's?
4. Several objects throughout the story—including the toy train, buttons, and, most frequently, a ball of string—help forge lasting bonds between characters. Which item was your favorite? Likewise, which possessions in your own life carry deep sentimental value given their link to a person or relationship?
5. Were you familiar with MI9 prior to reading this book? Which gadgets did you enjoy learning about most?
6. From Fenna's childhood, the stampede on Christmas Eve contributed significantly to shaping her life, even decades later. What childhood experience(s) most altered your own life? Were there resulting obstacles you later learned to overcome?

IMAGES FROM
FENNA'S JOURNEY

Although Fenna Vos is a fictional character, many elements of her story were inspired by actual events, locations, people, and more. These chronological images from her life offer a visual glimpse of the many ups and downs of her journey.

**Miners in Calumet and Hecla Mine shaft No. 2
in Calumet, Houghton County, Michigan.**

Detroit Publishing Co. Collection, Library of Congress

**Inside the Italian Hall the morning after
the 1913 Christmas Eve tragedy.**

Michigan Tech University Archives and Copper Country Historical Collections

**Thousands line the road at a funeral procession for victims
of the Italian Hall Disaster in Calumet, Michigan.**

Michigan Tech University Archives and Copper Country Historical Collections

An original pocket-size edition of
Houdini's Big Little Book of Magic.

In 1908, Houdini prepares for his famed Milk Can
Escape, which later inspires many escapologists
(like Fenna and Charles) to attempt the same.

Photograph by Bill Orcutt, courtesy of HoudiniRevealed.com

On the Wilton Park estate, the mansion dubbed the "White House" served briefly as MI9 headquarters, then continued to host its highly classified work throughout the war.

The George Hotel on Wycombe End in Beaconsfield often boarded military visitors of nearby Wilton Park.

© *The Francis Frith Collection*

**Christopher Clayton Hutton with his
flying boots and other gadgets.**

Courtesy of P. M. Froom Collection

**A reproduction of a typical MI9 "map deck" card used
for smuggling to escapers and evaders during WWII.**

Courtesy of Zachary Womack

Memorial in London featuring names of the victims of the Bethnal Green Tube Disaster.

© *Stairway to Heaven Memorial Trust, London, 2018*

Londoners take shelter at Aldwych Tube Station during an air raid in 1940.

A WWII-era British Monopoly board with cardboard tokens
(due to wartime supplies) and Reichsmarks, an example
of currency often smuggled into POW camps by MI9.

A WWII Allied military-issue silk map of Western Europe.

SECRET

SECRET

Dear Mr. Watson,

Reference our conversation today. I am sending you, under separate cover, as many maps as I have in stock of the following:-

Norway and Sweden
Germany
Italy

I shall be glad if you will make me up games on the lines discussed today containing the maps as follows:-

One game must contain Norway, Sweden and Germany.
One game must contain N.France, Germany and frontiers.
One game must contain Italy.

I am also sending you a packet of small metal instruments. I should be glad if in each game you could manage to secrete one of these.

I want as varied an assortment containing these articles as possible. You had then better send to me 100/200 games on the straight.

In those that are faked, you must give me some distinguishing clue and also state what they contain.

In the above I also include, of course, packs of cards, calendars, photographs and any other ideas you have.

I will send you in the next post some packs of cards for you to pack in fancy boxes, etc. and insert in bridge sets.

/1

A memo sent by Christopher Hutton to Norman Watson at John Waddington Ltd., ordering Monopoly games that covertly include maps and other escape aids.

Barns, tractors, and even grazing cattle helped disguise RAF Tempsford, the secret WWII airfield used routinely for night-drop missions, as a farm to overflying enemy aircraft.

At the airfield that paraded as Gibraltar Farm, the barn in which agents were issued their kits and gear prior to their flights now serves as a memorial to honor their bravery.

483

Domtoren (Dom Tower) and a tram viewed from
Zadelstraat, the oldest paved shopping street in Utrecht.

Utrechts Archief, CC0

Oudegracht ("old canal"), the central
canal that runs through Utrecht.

Rijksdienst voor het Cultureel Erfgoed, CC BY-SA 4.0

**Engelandvaarders who escaped German-occupied
Netherlands are rescued by RAF High Speed
Rescue launch 185 on February 24, 1944.**

Film shot by Captain A.J. Hardy of the 8th USAAF Bomber Command, CC BY 2.5

**Liberated Dutch citizens wave to
passing Allied aircraft in 1945.**

Nationaal Archief

FURTHER READING

In addition to the books previously mentioned, here is a partial list of the many resources used for *The Ways We Hide* for readers interested in learning more about the story's various topics.

For information about MI9 and its array of gadgets: *MI9: Escape and Evasion 1939–1945* by M. R. D. Foot and J. M. Langley, *Evasion & Escape Devices* by Phil Froom, *MI9* by Helen Fry, and *Great Escapes* by Barbara A. Bond.

Reads featuring RAF Tempsford airfield and WWII operative night drops: *Tempsford Academy* by Bernard O'Connor and the online article "Major Herbert R. Brucker, SF Pioneer" by Charles H. Briscoe (*Veritas* magazine).

For more about the history of Monopoly and its World War II use: *The Game Makers* by Philip E. Orbanes and *The Monopolists* by Mary Pilon.

For books recounting the tragic Italian Hall Disaster and its related strike: *Death's Door* by Steve Lehto, *We Are Many* by Ella Reeve Bloor, and *False Alarm* by P. Germain.

For various Dutch accounts: *Behind the Fireplace: Memoirs of a Girl Working in the Dutch Resistance* by Andrew Scott and Grietje Okma Scott, *Dutch in Michigan* by Larry Ten Harmsel, and *This Faithful Book: A Diary from WWII in the Netherlands* by Madzy Brender à Brandis, translated by Marianne Brandis.

For more about Houdini's history and even the secrets to many of his tricks: *Houdini on Magic* by Harry Houdini, edited by Walter B. Gibson and Morris N. Young; *The Right Way to Do Wrong* by Harry Houdini; and *Harry Houdini for Kids* by Laurie Carlson.

ACKNOWLEDGMENTS

To say I'm grateful to the following people for their support and guidance as I endeavored to write what has easily been my most challenging and ambitious novel to date would be an understatement. First and foremost, I'm thankful to Aimee Long; while this book might have existed without her help through well over two years of brainstorming, prose obsessing, and invaluable marks from her brutal red pen, the story would have looked very, very different—and not in a good way. To Shelley McFarland for her brilliant wordsmithing and sage insights, and to Tracy Callan for her perpetual cheering and boundless faith. "Friends are the family we choose," people say, and I feel fortunate beyond measure for our Golden Girls family of four.

For their unending patience and encouragement, I'm indebted to my beloved agent, Elisabeth Weed at The Book Group, and to my exceptional editor, Shana Drehs at Sourcebooks. And of course to Dominique Raccah and the rest of the stellar Sourcebooks team, whose clear love of authors and the belief that books change lives is as inspiring as it is treasured.

I'm also deeply grateful to the KB National Library of the Netherlands, namely to its remarkable Historical Collections specialist, Dutch historian Huibert Crijns, whose thoughtful corrections, suggestions, and research assistance went above and beyond anything I could have hoped for. The same could be said of German historian, linguist, and former U.S. Army Captain Michael Bunch, who undoubtedly endured far more questions than he ever anticipated; ditto goes for Alan Cagle, former 1Lt, Infantry, USAR, who once more generously shared his extensive World War II and military knowledge.

Enormous thanks to Dutch Holocaust survivor Anneke Bloomfield, British WWII and MI9 historian Dr. Helen Fry, and Margaret Grace of the Beaconsfield Historical Society for all their input and support; to Amanda Latchmore, née Watson, and Christopher Hartney of the Army Air Forces Historical Association for details on Waddingtons' history and Monopoly usage; to fabulous author friend and former emergency-medicine doctor Kimmery Martin for accuracy on wounds, recuperations, and more; to Erika Robuck for her Catholic insights but mostly her immeasurable support and friendship; and to the curator of art and cultural history at Het Spoorwegmuseum (a.k.a. The Railway Museum in Utrecht), Evelien Pieterse, for wartime specifics on Dutch trains and stations.

For immense help with all things culturally and linguistically Dutch, my heartfelt gratitude goes to dear author friends Kimberly Belle and Jean Kwok—and, by default, Jean's poor husband, Erwin Kluwer—as well as to Janet Lee Berg. Similarly, I thank Stephanie Cale for her assistance with my Ukrainian phrases; Claire Organ (as always) with my Gaelic and Irish brogue; and Marina Kruckmeyer and Nick Burger for additional help with my German dialogue.

For their valuable input on the Bethnal Green Tube Disaster, I'm tremendously thankful to survivor of the tragedy Babette Clark and to Sandra Scotting, Hon. Secretary of the Stairway to Heaven Memorial Trust. For feedback on illusions and escapes, I thank professional magician Brent Allan and John Ragone, a member of the Society of American Magicians Assembly 77, Long Island Mystics. I'm also grateful to the FB page "You Know You're in Copper Country When…" and to Keweenaw historian Lynette Webber, who even enlightened me on panking, chooks, and choppers.

Then, of course, there are you, the readers. Thank you for allowing my words into your imaginations and hearts. And to the booksellers, book clubs, librarians, and other book champions who continue to support and spread word about my stories, please know it truly means the world to me. Finally, above all, to my family: for the daily hugs and laughs, for keeping me fed through countless writing marathons, and for your infinite love throughout this journey.

ABOUT THE AUTHOR

© Holland Studios

Kristina McMorris is a *New York Times* bestselling author of two novellas and six novels, including the runaway bestseller *Sold on a Monday*. Initially inspired by her grandparents' World War II courtship letters, her works of fiction have garnered more than twenty national literary awards. Prior to her writing career, she owned a wedding-and-event planning company until she had far surpassed her limit of "Y.M.C.A." and chicken dances. She also worked as a weekly TV-show host for Warner Bros. and an ABC affiliate, beginning at age nine with an Emmy Award-winning program. A graduate of Pepperdine University, she lives near Portland, Oregon, where she somehow manages to be fully deficient of a green thumb and not own a single umbrella.

SOLD ON A MONDAY

2 Children for Sale

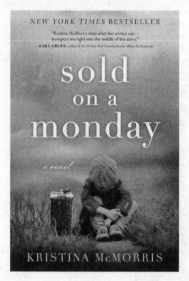

The sign is a last resort. It sits on a farmhouse porch in 1931 but could be found anywhere in an era of breadlines, bank runs, and broken dreams. It could have been written by any mother facing impossible choices.

For struggling reporter Ellis Reed, the gut-wrenching scene evokes memories of his family's dark past. He snaps a photograph of the children, not meant for publication. But when it leads to his big break, the consequences are more devastating than he ever imagined.

Inspired by an actual newspaper photograph that stunned the nation, *Sold on a Monday* is a powerful novel of love, redemption, and the unexpected paths that bring us home.

"A masterpiece that poignantly echoes universal themes of loss and redemption, *Sold on a Monday* is both heartfelt and heartbreaking."

—Pam Jenoff, *New York Times* bestselling author of *The Orphan's Tale*